BEYOND *the* MAPPED STARS

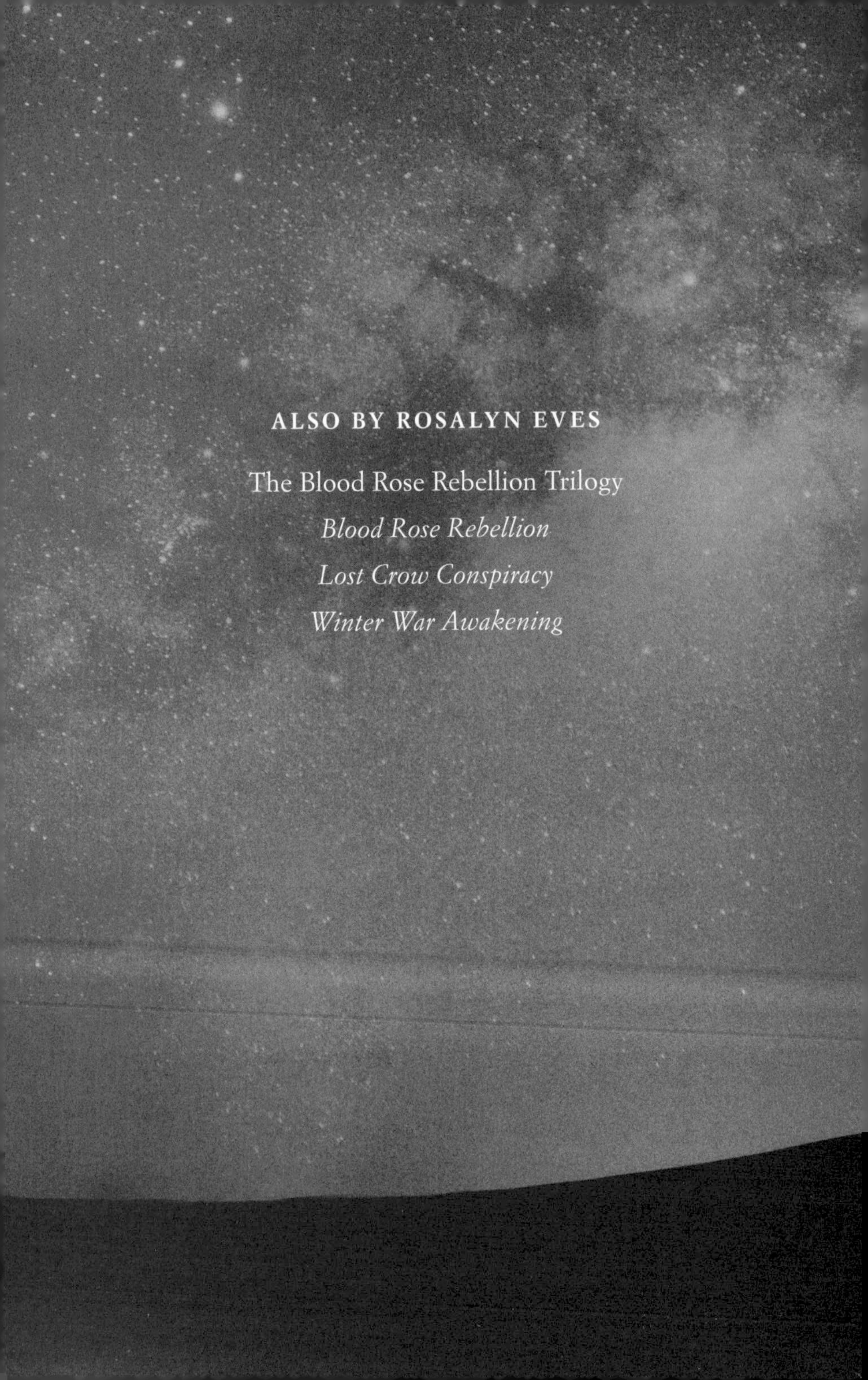

ALSO BY ROSALYN EVES

The Blood Rose Rebellion Trilogy

Blood Rose Rebellion

Lost Crow Conspiracy

Winter War Awakening

BEYOND

the

MAPPED

STARS

ROSALYN EVES

Alfred A. Knopf

New York

THIS IS A BORZOI BOOK PUBLISHED BY ALFRED A. KNOPF

All rights reserved. Published in the United States by Alfred A. Knopf, an imprint of Random House Children's Books, a division of Penguin Random House LLC, New York.

Knopf, Borzoi Books, and the colophon are registered trademarks of Penguin Random House LLC.

Visit us on the Web! GetUnderlined.com

Educators and librarians, for a variety of teaching tools, visit us at RHTeachersLibrarians.com

Library of Congress Cataloging-in-Publication Data is available upon request.
ISBN 978-1-9848-4955-7 (trade) — ISBN 978-1-9848-4956-4 (lib. bdg.) — ISBN 978-1-9848-4957-1 (ebook)

The text of this book is set in 11.25-point Simoncini Garamond.
Interior design by Andrea Lau

Printed in the United States of America
August 2021
10 9 8 7 6 5 4 3 2 1

First Edition

To Dan, for believing in me even when I doubt

✦

And to the skeptical believers and believing skeptics:
there is room for us too

✦.

Per aspera ad astra

CAST OF CHARACTERS

denotes real historical figure

MONROE, UTAH

Bertelsen family
    Anders: grist mill owner
    m. Elisa (1853, died 1865)
        Rebekka
        Four babies who died
    m. Hannah (1856)
        Hyrum
        Elizabeth
        Emily
        Mary
        David Charles
        John
        Henry
        Rachel
        Albert
    m. Olena Nilsson (1876)

Willard family
    Richard: farmer/carpenter
    m. Emma
        Older children living in Salt Lake City
        Samuel
        Christopher
        Lyman
        Vilate Ann
        Ellen
* Phoebe Wheeler: teacher at Presbyterian school

RAWLINS, WYOMING

* Thomas Alva Edison: inventor
* John "Texas Jack" Omohundro: performer
* Henry Morton: president of Stevens Institute of Technology
* Henry Draper: medical doctor and amateur astronomer, financed Edison's visit to Rawlins
* Anna Draper: Dr. Draper's wife and assistant
* Lillian Heath: would become Wyoming's first female doctor in 1893

DENVER, COLORADO

Lancelot Davis (owner of Trans-Oceana hotel)
Stevens family
    Ambrose: businessman
    m. Louisa Davis: manager of Trans-Oceana
        William Lancelot
        Alice
* Henry Wagoner: abolitionist, civil rights activist, clerk of the first Colorado State Legislature
Mrs. Segura: housekeeper at Trans-Oceana
Frances: maid at Trans-Oceana
* Alida Avery: medical doctor, former colleague of Maria Mitchell at Vassar College
* Maria Mitchell: astronomer, first professor of astronomy at Vassar College
* Emma Culbertson: former student of Miss Mitchell, aspiring physician
* Cora Harrison: former student of Miss Mitchell, graduate student in astronomy at Vassar College
* Elizabeth Owen Abbot: former student of Miss Mitchell, schoolteacher

COLORADO SPRINGS/PIKES PEAK, COLORADO

* Helen Hunt Jackson: writer, reformer
* Samuel Pierpont Langley: astronomer, first director of Allegheny Observatory, early aviation pioneer
* John Langley: medical doctor, professor of chemistry at the University of Michigan
* General Albert Myer: father of US Signal Corps
Daniela Navarro: guide

The world of learning is so broad and the human soul so limited in power! We reach forth and strain every nerve, but we seize only a bit of the curtain that holds the infinite from us.

—*Maria Mitchell: Life, Letters, and Journals*, p. 33

BEYOND
the
MAPPED
STARS

✦

chapter one

Friday, June 28, 1878
Monroe, Utah
Thirty-one days until eclipse

"Elizabeth!" Mama's voice floats up the valley toward my seat near the mouth of our narrow canyon, light as the cotton-wood seeds drifting in piles beside the creek.

Her call jars me from my book, and I blink at the long gold light of the summer evening lingering in the valley like a cup of honeyed tea. As the sound of my name settles, I close my eyes, blotting out the ink on the open pages before me, the faint stars beginning to emerge in the sky above. I wish it were so easy to block out my mother's voice.

I'm not supposed to be here, perched on a rocky outcropping overlooking the Little Green Valley like some fledgling about to launch from its nest.

I should be home, helping prepare the little ones for bed, bathing four-year-old Rachel and seven-year-old Henry, who gave themselves mud baths near the creek earlier.

But I'm not ready to leave. Not ready to abandon my perch or my view of the emerging stars. Not ready to face home, where I am surrounded by people I love but who are sometimes too much, their voices and bodies too big for the frame house Far built. Not ready to abandon my book, a gloriously ridiculous dime novel about a man named Texas Jack, army scout turned frontier hero.

Most everything about the book is unfamiliar, the pages full of blood-curdling deeds and high adventure, of betrayal and true love, and people who don't at all resemble the westerners I know. In Texas Jack's world, desperate thieves stage daring robberies. Tyrannical trail bosses misuse their cowboy employees. Fragile women faint at an oath, and cunning Indians plot against whites while mangling English. Worst of all are the Mormons, who are invariably dastardly or foolish dupes. I've never met an outlaw or known a woman to faint so easily. The Paiutes who live in our valley are mostly peaceful; Brother Timican, who attends our church meetings in a suit and collared shirt, speaks better English than many of the Danish and Swedish immigrants. And the Mormons . . . my sister Emily and I save the best passages to share, to laugh at how wrong these eastern writers get us.

"Elizabeth!" Mama's voice comes again.

Texas Jack never stands down from a challenge. I seldom stand up to my mother.

With a sigh, I snap my book shut, wiping fruitlessly at a smudge on the yellow cover. I relace my shoes and, tucking the book beneath the waist of my skirt, scramble down the incline of the hill toward an ill-defined trail beside the creek. As I walk, I watch for any sign of predators brought out by the dusk. We don't get many mountain lions in high summer, and any rattlers will be sluggish in the cooler air, but it's best to be wary. Flickering lights burn like stars in the grist mill below. Far must be working late again.

There's no moon tonight: this close to the new moon, I'll only catch a glimpse of the silver crescent at sunrise. I make my way by starlight instead. The North Star glitters down, and the stars of the Big Dipper. It's too early yet to see anything of the constellation Cygnus, though I can just make out Vega of the Lyre nearby.

I take mental notes of their positions, to record them in the notebook I use to track moon phases and planetary movements—a notebook I keep hidden beneath my bed with my dime novels. In less than a month, both the sun and moon will sit in the sky at the same time and place, a total solar eclipse that, for the first time in nearly a century, will cross the western territories of the United States.

And for all the celestial wonders I have seen, I won't get to see this. According to the newspaper reports, the path of totality will cross through Montana and Wyoming and Colorado and Texas—but not Utah.

Mama flaps her apron when she sees me, a white flag in the night. But the surrender she signals is all mine.

As soon as I come close, she begins. "Elizabeth Bertelsen, where have ye been? Moonin' after the stars again?" Mama's North British accent, worn soft by her years in Utah Territory, grows more pronounced when she's upset. "Ye should set your mind on higher things. God did not call us here to waste our lives dreaming."

What could be higher than the stars? I do not speak my thoughts. Mama is grumpy enough already.

She beckons me into the house. Baby Albert, red-faced, cries halfheartedly in fifteen-year-old Emily's arms as she rocks back and forth, back and forth, in the rocking chair. Her face is pinched with worry. Nearby, Mary, just a year younger than Emily, pushes a brush sullenly across the floorboards. From the attic, I hear one of the little boys calling after Mama.

Mama waves her apron at me again. "Take the baby from Emily so she can bring your da his supper."

Obediently, I start across the room, but Mama takes my arm and turns me to face her. "I can't have ye harin' off like this of nights. It's dangerous. And unseemly in a big lass of seventeen. I'd thought to take you with me to Richfield tomorrow, but perhaps it's best if ye stay here and mind the children. Your sisters can come in your place."

Mary perks up and drops the brush to tug on her strawberry-blond braid, now half undone. "You mean it, Mama?"

I take the baby from Emily and settle into her spot on the rocker. I should have liked the visit, though Richfield is no great city. Baby Albert looks up at me, his hazel eyes wide and wet, his chin still wobbling from his cries. He is warm and heavy in my lap, and though he smells sweet, like milk, his weight anchors me to this room, this house.

✦

The next morning, the birds are wild outside the three-walled shelter where we keep a cow and two horses. Both horses are missing and my heart sinks. Far didn't come home last night. I hope Far is back before Mama wants to leave for Richfield, or there'll be the devil to pay. I milk the cow and try not to think too much about what it means, that Far spent the night in town. I rest my head against the cow's warm flank and whisper a prayer. The familiar ritual calms me, lifting a burden from my heart.

Standing, my grip tight on the pail of warm milk I've just collected, I peer above the rim of the mountain, limned with gold. Venus, the morning star, glimmers down at me. I take another moment to find Jupiter, now in retrograde, so it appears to be moving backward in the sky.

Some people find the stars distant and cold. But I love them. According to the books I've read, the stars that look so tiny in the sky above are really enormous balls that radiate heat, like our sun. Some are even bigger than the sun. They're different colors too, if you look closely—some pinkish, some tinged blue, some yellow-hot. Some are red, like Antares in Scorpio. The lights I see have stretched across millions of miles and thousands of years to reach me, as though they have nothing to do but shine endlessly. We talk at church about eternity, how existence extends forever in both directions— our spirits lived with God before we came to earth and will again after we die. Sometimes the idea of eternity is hard to hold in my head, but when I look at the stars, I can almost grasp it.

I shake myself. I have much more to do, and I cannot dawdle.

There is always a chance, however slight, that Mama will change her mind and let me come to Richfield. Even if she does not, someone needs to be inside when Far gets home, to keep peace. That task used to be Rebekka's, but she is far away in Wyoming now, expecting her first baby.

I take a deep breath, glance up at the morning star once more, for courage, before going back to the house. I've learned a trick to watching the stars: if you look at the stars aslant, a little to one side instead of direct, they stand out more clearly. It's a trick I use at home too: things are brighter if I don't look at them directly.

Our house is big by local standards: a sitting room and a proper kitchen with a stove, two bedrooms on the main floor, and an attic for the boys. Mama reminds us to be grateful, as our first house here in Monroe was a dugout of sod and willow branches that always turned to mud in the midsummer rains.

But the house feels crowded when all of us are home: Far, Mama, and nine children. Only Rebekka no longer lives here.

Our ghosts crowd us too—Far's first wife, Aunt Elisa, who

died when I was five, and the four of her five babies who did not live past their first year, all of us sealed together for time and eternity. Far married Aunt Elisa in Denmark, where they met the Mormon missionaries, and they crossed the Atlantic and the plains together. He made Mama his second wife in Salt Lake City, after she'd worked her own way to Utah from England. I miss Aunt Elisa: she was sweet and soft, romantic where Mama is practical, and she told me fairy stories at bedtime to help me sleep. Sometimes I still sense her in tricks of light, in the smell of sugar caramelizing on the stove.

There is no sugar smell in the air now, as I wander into the main room. In fact, there are no smells at all. The stove is empty, the younger children crying for breakfast, their clamor drowning out the birdcalls outside the kitchen window.

I freeze. A weight separate from that of the bucket I carry settles over me. Mama must have had a bad night, to not have started breakfast already. My sisters Emily and Mary are at the table, slicing bread for Henry and Rachel, who are the youngest, save baby Albert. I stifle a sigh: Mama won't like it if all the bread goes to breakfast. She'll be wanting it for sandwiches on the road.

"Here, wait," I say. "I'll make some oats." I set the pail down on the table and find a battered pan, filling it with water to heat. It's not long before the oats are ready, and I dish them into bowls that Emily sets out for me—having the wit to be helpful, if not the wit to start breakfast on her own. I spoon fresh milk over the oats and drizzle a bit of sorghum on them before Mary hands the bowls around.

The boys tear through theirs as though they fear some-one might steal the food from them before they've eaten their fill. I smile a little: I don't think they remember being truly hungry. I do—there were lean years when we first came to the valley, both before and after the Black Hawk War. We have plenty now: it shows in the children's round cheeks, in Albert's baby rolls, even in me. Mama had to let out my seams again this spring, though I've not grown taller in three years.

Rachel stares at her bowl, her arms crossed and lips quiver-ing. I slip into place beside her on the bench.

"Aren't you hungry, darling?"

"I don't want oats."

I pick up her spoon and scoop up a bite soaked in sor-ghum. "But these aren't regular oats."

The lip quiver stops. "They aren't?" Her brown eyes fix on mine.

"They're oats made special for the fairy courts," I say, rais-ing the spoon to my own mouth. "Fairies eat them at every meal."

Rachel snatches the spoon away from me and stuffs it in her mouth.

"You shouldn't tell her stories," Mary says, watching us from the end of the table. "What if she thinks they're true?"

I exchange a glance with Emily, sitting on Rachel's other side, and we both smile. Mary doesn't know about our stash of dime novels either.

After three bites, Rachel puts her spoon down. She pats

the side of her head, leaving fragments of oats in her honey-brown curls. "What's in here, 'Lizbeth?"

"Your brain, with all your thoughts," I tell her.

Rachel mulls this over, chewing slowly. Then, "I want to see it."

Startled, I share another glance with Emily, who is holding in a laugh with both hands over her mouth.

"Whatever for?" I ask.

"So I can see how smart I am."

This time we all laugh, even Mary.

Footsteps sound outside the kitchen and I look up, expecting to see Mama with Albert, or even my older brother, Hyrum, before he goes down to the mill.

But instead it's my father, his cheeks rosy above a neatly trimmed ruff of a beard.

"Far!" John and Henry erupt from the table. Henry's half-empty bowl falls facedown on the floor, another mess waiting for me to clean. My brothers throw their arms around his waist.

Far pretends surprise. "But hold there—who are these young rascals attacking me in my own home?"

John giggles, but Henry protests, "I'm not a rascal, Far. I'm your Henry!"

Far peers down at Henry's face and lifts his eyebrows. "Why, so you are! I hardly recognized you, so big you've grown." He returns their hug, his glance flickering over their heads to meet mine. "Where's your mama?"

"I don't—" I begin, but then Mama appears behind Far. He steps aside, and she glides into the room, head high, her gray-brown hair immaculately pinned up beneath her Sunday hat. She doesn't look at Far.

"I've brought the horses for you," Far says.

Mama wipes out one of the boys' bowls, fills it with oats, and takes a seat at the table, regal as any queen.

Far tries again. "The wagon is hitched and ready."

Mama adds a pinch of salt and sorghum to her oats, then pours milk over the mixture. Beside me, Rachel slips down from the bench and wriggles past Far, escaping into the sitting room. Turning to Mary, Mama says, "Can you pack up the bread and some cheese for our lunch?"

"Damn it, Hannah," Far explodes. "I was talking to you!"

Emily, who has sat frozen at the table, springs up with a tiny *eep* and hustles the remaining children from the room. Sometimes she reminds me of a fawn, all big eyes and nerves, starting at a sound. She doesn't like it when Mama and Far argue, so it's left to me to make the rough edges in our family smooth.

"Have you eaten yet, Far?" I interrupt, my voice too high and too bright.

Far ignores me and marches to the table, planting himself across from Mama, his palms thudding against the wood. Mama chews calmly and swallows, then finally looks up at her husband. "I'd thank ye to mind your language before the children."

Far lets out a frustrated breath. "Did you hear nothing else I said?" My father, who speaks eight languages with varying degrees of fluency, cannot find the words to reach my mother.

"I heard ye," Mama says, still unruffled. "But I imagine ye have work at the mill. Hyrum can drive us. And how did ye find Olena this morning?" she asks sweetly.

I catch my breath. Olena Nilsson is Far's wife of three years, but Mama seldom mentions her.

Contrary to what the eastern newspapers write, not every Mormon man has a harem of a dozen wives. Most of the men I know have one wife, sometimes two, maybe three. Mama loved Aunt Elisa like her own sister and mothered Elisa's daughter Rebekka after her death. But Aunt Olena—Aunt Olena is Mama's own age, perhaps older. Far scrupulously divides his time between our two homes, and yet Mama cannot bring herself to speak of Aunt Olena—as if silence might deny Far's folly in falling in love again, at his age. When Far told Mama he meant to marry Aunt Olena, Mama threatened to walk all night to Richfield, to procure a divorce the next morning. Far wheedled her round, and she stayed. She must have forgiven him somewhat, else we wouldn't have the baby.

"My work can keep," Far says, not answering Mama's question. "I don't trust Hyrum to drive you so far and back again. I'll be outside when you're ready." Far nods, shortly, and marches from the room.

I sag with relief, and my stomach growls, reminding me I've not yet eaten. Grabbing a bowl from the table, I reach for the pan on the stove and discover that what little was left of the oats has burned while my parents—what? I could not call that a conversation, nor properly an argument.

I settle instead for Rachel's leftover oats and sit at the table beside Mama.

"Now, Elizabeth," Mama says, drawing my attention. "When we leave, ye'll be minding the boys and Rachel. I'll take Albert with me. Don't be losing yourself in your books. It's not right, the way they absorb ye."

I smother a sigh. Going to Richfield was always a slim chance, no matter how many things I did right. "There's nothing evil in my books, Mama." I close my mouth around my other words: that I'll need such knowledge if I ever make it to college. But Mama won't approve of such notions. And besides, I don't rightly know how one gets to college, or what one does afterward. How one gets from college to being an astronomer, for instance. The gap between what I know and what I want spans away from me, impossibly vast.

Mama's lips are tight, pinched. "Fancy ideas will only unfit ye for the life you're meant to lead."

"The glory of God is intelligence," I murmur, a quiet defiance. The only kind I'm capable of. "Emmeline Wells wrote in the *Woman's Exponent* that the better educated a woman is, the better wife and mother she can be."

Mama's expression turns sour like old milk. "Then ye best use that intelligence to do what I ask. I've no quarrel with suitable education—but ye want too much. Ye should follow God's will, not your own."

As though my own will were a drumbeat inside me that I could still if I wanted. As though God never planted yearnings in our hearts to drive us to bigger things.

Sometimes I feel as though there's an Elizabeth-shaped hole in my life that I'm supposed to fill neatly. But parts of me—ideas, desires—keep spilling out like tentacles of some sea creature. I'm forever stuffing them back in, smashing down ideas I'm not meant to have, shutting my lips on words I'm not meant to say.

"Yes, Mama."

✦

After lunch, I read a story to Rachel, and she falls asleep against my arm. I carry her to our room, marveling at the way her sturdy legs dangle over my arms, remembering the much smaller child I used to rock to sleep. After settling her into bed, I stand and stretch. The boys are outside, splashing and hollering in the creek. I long to join them: the house is warm in the late-June sun, even with the doors open. The breeze barely stirs Mama's muslin curtains.

My fingers itch for a book. I could take Maria Edgeworth's *Moral Tales* from the single shelf of books in the sitting room—Mama does not object to Miss Edgeworth's stories, so long as I do not steal away to read when there are children to be watched, food to be cooked. Issues of the *Woman's Exponent,* newspapers written by and for Mormon women, lay carefully folded on the shelf. I've read these issues over and over, trying to find myself in the pages of news and advice, trying to mimic the speaking and writing of women more educated than I am. Or I could fetch another of my dime novels from beneath my straw tick mattress.

In truth, I should begin on the bread for dinner.

But I don't want any of these things.

I want ideas, something to launch me heavenward instead of binding me on earth. I tried to explain this to Mama once, the wanting that was like a steady, low hunger constantly gnawing at my soul. She thought, at first, that I had dyspepsia and tried to press some Brigham's tea on me, made from the dried branches of a spiky plant that grows around here, but I cannot abide the bitter stuff.

"Ye should spend more time with your Bible, and less time in your books. Turn your thoughts to heaven, put your longing in God," she told me.

Mama doesn't get that wanting to understand the stars does not take away my wanting to understand God. But it does rather spoil my tolerance for domestic chores.

I stand. Rachel will sleep for an hour or more, most like, and I can be down to town and back in that time. Miss Phoebe Wheeler, who teaches at the Presbyterian school, has a small stash of books she's willing to lend out. As today is Saturday, I won't be interrupting her class. Mama won't ever know I wasn't strictly obedient.

Some folks were scandalized when the Presbyterians moved in, building a log cabin for worship services on Sundays and school during the week. They feared the Presbyterians would try to convert us all (they haven't, yet). But I was thrilled—a real school, with real books. Then Mama wouldn't let me attend, saying I was too old—never mind that my only schooling was the few years we lived in Fountain Green, and the rest whatever Mama could teach me. Maybe Mama was afraid too. Outsiders haven't always been kind to Mormons. Though Mama wasn't present for the massacre at Haun's mill, where Missouri militiamen killed seventeen Mormons during a time of truce, or the murder of our prophet Joseph Smith and his brother Hyrum before the Saints were driven out of Missouri, she's heard the stories. We all have.

But it's hard for me to feel stories of the past as a present danger, and so sometimes, when I haven't chores and Miss Wheeler hasn't pupils, Miss Wheeler will sit with me and help me with mathematics. I admit there's times neither of us can puzzle out the equations, but I love the excitement of successfully working out a formula. Maybe there's no call for higher math in a farming town—but didn't God devise math as surely as music? Isn't He as pleased with a well-wrought formula as a well-sung hymn?

Before I leave, I convince David Charles to come back to the house to be with Rachel—he is reluctant to leave the water, but I promise him a nickel and so he agrees.

I rattle down the dirt road that winds between our house and town, my booted toes kicking up dust, the sun hot on my head. Mama will surely scold me for my uncovered head—

I am already too brown, with freckles like constellations all over my arms and cheeks, a red-brown nearly of a hue with my hair—but she isn't here to catch me at it.

Monroe is quiet in the early afternoon: the men and boys minding the fields or the cows and sheep, the women indoors already at work on supper or canning or mending. A few children are out of doors playing, their happy shouts hanging in the warm air.

"And where are you off to, Miss Bertelsen?" Samuel Willard's mellow tenor voice catches me off guard. Samuel's a few years older than me, with a broad forehead beneath unruly brown hair and a trim beard. He's whittling a piece of wood in the shade of a big tree before the Willard cabin.

My cheeks burn, and not just from the sun. I do not know how to talk to Samuel Willard, whose voice teases the hairs upright on my arms, and who makes me feel as though my hands are disconnected appendages that I don't know where to place.

"The Presbyterian school," I say shortly. The minutes of Rachel's nap tick away in my head.

"Looking for some schooling, are you? Aren't you a bit old for that?"

"I'd rather be too old than too ignorant," I fire back. "Which are you?"

Samuel chokes, and without waiting to hear his response, I fairly flee down the road.

The Presbyterian building is just off the main street, toward the north end of town. Miss Wheeler is not in the schoolroom when I check: the four neat rows of chairs are empty and her desk clear. But I find her in her room at the boardinghouse a block away, reading.

She looks up at my knock on my open door, her face creasing in mild irritation at the interruption. As she recognizes me, her expression clears and a smile blooms. Miss Wheeler is a woman of what Mama would call "uncertain age," her blond hair fading but neat, her blue eyes hidden behind spectacles.

"Miss Elizabeth Bertelsen!" she says. "To what do I owe the pleasure?"

Most teachers wouldn't greet a pupil so formally, but this is what I like about Miss Wheeler. She treats me as an equal, someone whose ideas deserve respect.

I clasp my hands behind me. "I've come to borrow a book."

She laughs. "Of course." Setting her own book down atop a stack of newspapers, she turns to survey me. "Now, what are you in the mood for? A novel? The account of a world traveler? A history?"

My cheeks warm. "I'd like a science book, if you please." I pause a beat, wondering if I am imposing too much, and add, "Do you have any I haven't read yet?"

"As it happens, I just got a shipment of books from a cousin, who thought I might be able to use them." She rummages through a box near her dresser and produces a volume with a maroon cloth cover. Gold lettering embossed across the front reads: *On the Connexion of the Physical Sciences, by Mary Somerville.*

I feel a curious lifting inside my chest, wiping away my last lingering annoyance from my encounter with the Willard boy. "A science book by a woman?"

Miss Wheeler smiles. "I thought you'd like it. It was written twenty years ago, but is widely respected. Mrs. Somerville is a scientist in her own right."

Scientist. The word dissolves on my tongue, all hard and sharp edges together. It's a foreign word here, in the dry heat and arid fields and pine mountains around me. It belongs to worlds I've only read of in books, to cities and laboratories and libraries.

How can I want something so much, when I don't have any real experience of it?

How can I want something so much, when it might be all wrong for me?

I wrap my new treasure in a cloth, exchange a few more words with Miss Wheeler, and set off for home, my heart humming, my fingers trembling with eagerness to open the book, to burrow into the new ideas offered there.

I'm nearly home when I catch sight of a figure racing down the dirt road toward me, arms waving above his head. I recognize the shape before I can see his features. It's David Charles, and he shouts something at me. A long moment passes before I can disentangle his words.

"It's Rachel!" he cries. "She's gone missing."

chapter two

Saturday, June 29, 1878

Monroe, Utah

Thirty days until eclipse

Though the sun is sweltering overhead, at once I am cold everywhere. Gooseflesh pricks on my arms and legs, and ice leaks through my stomach.

"Gone?" I picture Rachel, her golden-brown hair in soft ringlets, her warm brown eyes. "Have you checked the barn?"

David Charles nods. John comes running up behind him and skids to a stop, looking like David Charles's slightly shorter twin, his cheeks red and eyes wide.

"The orchard?"

Another nod.

God forbid. "The creek?"

His face clears. "Not yet."

"Then go!" I turn to John. "Go fetch Hyrum from the mill."

As both boys turn and race back up the road, I pick up my skirts and run after them, all the while whispering a prayer under my breath.

I reach the shadowed shallows of the creek just behind David Charles. Rachel is not at the spot where the boys were splashing earlier. I send David Charles to follow the creek up toward our canyon while I trail the stream back toward town.

Darting between cottonwood trees, I scan the black ripple of water between the stones. The cold inside me seems to deepen. The sun bores down in incongruous yellow beams between the branches.

A flash of pink catches my eye, and I scramble forward. A jam of leaves and twigs has slowed the creek's flow, creating a kind of pool. A limp figure rests near the bottom, dress tangled about her legs.

Rachel.

The cold inside me turns solid, ice in my veins that makes me sluggish, pins me to the spot. *Move,* I tell myself.

Rough hands push me aside, and I stumble, falling to my knees. But I don't mind the stinging pain, because it's my older brother, Hyrum, splashing into the stream and catching Rachel up to him, water plastering his white shirt to his arms. He carries her out of the water and crouches, resting Rachel facedown across his knee so that her wet curls dangle past her cheeks. He thumps her back: once, twice, three times. He flips her over and puts his mouth on hers, breathing air into her lungs.

Paralysis broken, I crawl toward him, tears stinging salt against my tongue.

My sister's face is white, some waxen doll with a smudged cheek and gnarled hair. *Thump, thump, thump.* Hyrum turns Rachel over again.

John catches up with us, and I take his hand as I stand. He squeezes tight.

This time, Rachel coughs weakly, and I release my held breath on a grateful sigh. Then Rachel gags, and a torrent of river water washes out of her, over Hyrum's ruined shoes, over mine. Her eyes flutter briefly, but do not open.

Hyrum stands and carries Rachel back to the house. I follow, accusation keeping time with my footsteps. *Selfish, selfish. If I hadn't left Rachel* . . . Mama will have my hide for sure, but I would brave all Mama's anger if only Rachel might live.

Hyrum sets Rachel in the bed I share with Emily, rather than pulling out her own trundle bed. He looks at me, brown eyes wide and helpless, and I step in, stripping off her wet clothes and tucking the blankets in tight around her. Her fingertips and lips are blue.

The front door bangs, and I jump. A wild hope fills me— Mama is back early. But the footsteps running toward my room are light and eager. My hope dissolves into guilt. It's only little Henry. I forgot all about him. Suppose something had happened to him too?

Another bang, and my door opens. Henry never could move quietly. "What's going on? I saw everyone running." He inches around John, standing unusually still in the middle of the room, and peers at Rachel. "Is she dead?"

"No," I say, more sharply than I mean to. *Please, no.* I look over my shoulder at John. "Take Henry into the other room and keep him there."

"Where's David Charles?" Hyrum asks as the boys leave, looking around the room as though the oldest of the trio of younger boys might materialize from the walls.

I nearly forgot him too, in my single-minded concern for Rachel. Perhaps Mama was right to doubt me. "He's still looking for Rachel, alongside the creek."

Hyrum walks toward the door, shoes squelching. "I'll fetch him back."

"Wait," I say. It's Rachel that worries me, Rachel that needs our attention. *Rachel that needs a miracle.* "Should we ask the elders to administer to her?"

In our faith, only men are formally ordained to hold God's power. Unlike in many Christian faiths, where priests have to study to lead their congregation, any worthy man can be given the priesthood and use it for healing. As a girl, I won't ever hold a priesthood office or be ordained to such power. I have never minded before—but I have never stood helpless in front of my little sister, pale as a corpse on my bed.

"Far won't like it," Hyrum warns, not moving.

Far would hate it. I nod, though I do not let the idea go

entirely. If Rachel worsens . . . "Will you pray with me, then?" Maybe our faith will be enough.

Hyrum ducks his head, not looking at me. "I—I don't know as I can."

I stare at him in dismay. Why should my shy, kind brother feel he cannot pray?

"I'll fetch Sister Larsen," Hyrum offers instead, naming the midwife who delivered Albert, the closest thing we have to a doctor in town. He disappears out the front door.

Dropping to my knees beside Rachel, I whisper a prayer. The words stick to my tongue and teeth, heavy and earthbound. No familiar warmth surrounds me, and a deep, churning cold settles in my gut.

Maybe Mama is right. Maybe my obsession with the stars is blocking my view of heaven.

I go to the kitchen and stoke the fire, putting a kettle on to heat. Then I return to Rachel and put my hand on her head. She's no longer ice-cold, but her skin is clammy beneath mine. I lie down on the bed beside her, curling around her, trying to will my warmth into her.

David Charles comes in later—I don't know how much later, since time has gone strange on me. It feels like hours since Rachel went missing, and like no time at all.

"I found your book," he says, holding up the precious copy that I borrowed from Miss Wheeler. The cover is a little dusty, a few pages crumpled. He sets the book on the pillow beside Rachel's head. I don't touch it: the words feel poisoned, each curl of ink reminding me that I put them before my duty, and my sister might be dying.

"Thank you," I manage, because David Charles is still standing by the bed, stricken.

"What can I do?" he asks.

"Mind your brothers," I say, and he nods but doesn't move.

I force a smile. "It will be all right." If I'm lying, and Rachel dies, then I deserve to be damned for my actions and my lie.

Some of the tension leaves his thin shoulders, and he scampers out. I rouse myself to fix some tea for Rachel.

"Rachel," I say, gently shaking her shoulder. *Wake up.* "I've brought tea to warm you." I test the temperature in the cup with my finger, and then bring the cup to her lips. When I tip it, the liquid only runs down her cheek.

I swallow against the tightness in my throat. I don't know what else to do. I leave the tea to cool on the floor and curl back around her. The slight lift and fall of her chest is her only movement.

Hyrum comes back into the house. "Sister Larsen wasn't there—she's gone out to the Zabriskies' to help with a baby. Her daughter said she'd tell her, soon as she's back."

After that, there's nothing to do but wait and try to pray.

As the light fades, I fix a cold supper for the boys. I watch as they devour the food, but I cannot bring myself to eat anything, not even when Hyrum tells me I should.

Leaving David Charles to wash up the dishes, I go back

to Rachel, hoping to get her to take some milk, at least. But Rachel's arms are flung wide, and a bluish pallor clings to her lips. Her breath is low and rattling, and when she inhales, her chest does not lift but draws in.

I rush into the sitting room, where the boys are wrestling. Hyrum is on the floor, the three smaller boys piled onto his back like pancakes, giggling. At my entrance, they fall silent. Hyrum sees my face and shakes the others off. Henry, still giddy with his earlier success, tries to tackle him again.

"Rachel's getting worse," I tell Hyrum. "Can you go out to the Zabriskies' and ask Sister Larsen what we should do?"

Hyrum stands swiftly, dumping Henry to the floor. Henry starts to cry and David Charles scoops him up, trying to distract him with promises of a story.

I follow Hyrum to the door and watch as he disappears down the road. Mars, the evening star, burns a baleful hole in the darkening sky. Where are Mama and Far?

I put John and Henry to bed, though both complain at the early hour. I gather up Rachel, blankets and all, and settle in the rocking chair in the sitting room. Her slow, rattling gasps make my own lungs ache in sympathy, and I time my breaths with hers as though somehow I can breathe for her.

David Charles watches me, his narrow face worried. "Is she going to be all right?"

At twelve, he is too old to believe an easy lie. "I don't know. I hope so."

He curls up on the nearby sofa, a book in his hands. I think he means to keep vigil with me, but before long, his head is nodding, and soon after that he's snoring gently, a discordant counterpart to Rachel's rough breaths.

Finally, hooves sound on the road outside, accompanied by the creaking of wagon wheels. Hope pricks painfully at my heart that it's Hyrum, returning with Sister Larsen, but Far's merry voice rings out in the night.

A pang of disappointment that it's not the midwife is washed away by relief. My parents are back, they're not fighting anymore, and Mama will know how to help Rachel.

I carry Rachel to the door, watching as Far helps Mama and the baby from the wagon. My sisters Emily and Mary climb down from the back.

Mama's face pales when she sees me. "What's happened?"

She hands baby Albert to Emily and takes Rachel from me.

Surely it's cowardly to hesitate for fear of Mama's anger, when Rachel might be dying? I tell her about Rachel and the creek.

Mama looks at me sharply. "How did Rachel come to be playin' alone by the creek?"

I tug at a hangnail on my left thumb. The prick of pain feels right: I deserve this. A spot of blood appears in its wake. "I left her with David Charles and went to the school for a book."

Mama only looks at me, her mouth tight. Far shakes his head. "You're better than this, Elizabeth."

I wish they would shout at me. I say, "Hyrum's gone for Sister Larsen."

Mary, perpetually emotional at fourteen, starts crying, and Far sends her to bed. Emily follows, bouncing Albert gently in her arms and fretting her lower lip with her teeth.

Mama settles Rachel on the sofa and sends Far into the kitchen to heat water again for tea. I start to follow him, but he waves me back. Mama acts as though I am not in the room at all. She sets two candles on the floor, one at either end of the sofa, at Rachel's head and feet, and lights them. The twin flames flicker in an invisible breeze, the thin shadows of their smoke rising like ghosts against the wall.

A short time later, Hyrum arrives with Sister Larsen and a couple of women from the ward. Far peers into the room but turns away upon seeing the newcomers, heading to his own room. Hyrum, after pressing a quick kiss on Mama's cheek, ducks into the kitchen.

The four women gather around Rachel. I press my finger against the still-bleeding hangnail. Sister Larsen glances at me where I stand, awkwardly in a corner, with something like compassion. If I could swallow my questions, if I could fit myself more surely to the role Mama offers, would they ask me to join them?

One of the women drops a bit of oil on Rachel's head; another sister murmurs a prayer. This is not a formal priesthood affair, but a blessing of faith. The women set their hands on Rachel—on her arm, her legs. Mama brushes a bit of hair from Rachel's cheeks and puts her hand on her forehead. Then Mama prays, a short earnest plea that pierces me. *Heal her, Lord. Let her take no injury.*

Silently, I echo Mama: *Only heal her, Heavenly Father, and I'll try to be better. I'll put my family first and be obedient at home. I won't ask for more than I'm given, not even for the stars. Just let her live.*

If He hears me, He doesn't answer. I want to pray to my heavenly mother too. She surely understands the hurt of a sick child, but I've never been taught how to address her. Though we believe in a divine partner for our father in heaven, we don't talk about her much. I add, tentatively, *Please, Heavenly Mother.*

After the prayer, Sister Larsen takes the hot water and brews tea with thyme and sage, waving the cup beneath Rachel's nose. The other women wrap their arms around Mama. Though Mama has not attended church much in the three years since Far stopped going, she remains a part of their sisterhood.

Sister Larsen puts the teacup in Mama's hands. "She'll be well, Hannah. I feel it is God's will that she live." These women move through a world where the sacred mixes daily with the ordinary: to them, miracles are as expected as the sun rising after a long night.

Yearning for their certainty makes my stomach cramp.

Mama begins to weep. The women hold her, murmuring into Mama's hair. When her sobs grow soft, Sister Larsen says, "You should rest, Hannah."

Upon Mama's protest that she should be with Rachel, Sister Larsen says, "Let Elizabeth stay with her."

" 'Twas Elizabeth's negligence brought Rachel to this."
Mama will not look at me.

"I swear I will watch closely." My voice emerges raspy, as
though scraped from me. Mama does not move.

"Elizabeth is a good girl," Sister Larsen says, watching
Mama, "and you've had a shock. Sleep will do you good."

The midwife's kindness pinches more than Mama's cold-
ness, because I do not deserve it. At Sister Larsen's words,
Mama allows one of the sisters to lead her gently down the
hallway, putting her to bed like she would a child.

When the woman returns, Sister Larsen turns to me.
"Should Rachel worsen, send Hyrum to fetch me again."

As though his name were a charm, Hyrum emerges from
the kitchen again, to drive the women home. I take a blanket
and settle on the floor beside Rachel. I'm still awake when
Hyrum returns sometime later, though I pretend to sleep
when he passes me. I cannot bear to talk now.

Today has been all wrong. *I've* been all wrong, my desires
and will selfish and wicked. I think of my silent prayer, whis-
pered alongside the words of women of greater faith. *I'll do
anything,* I promise again. *Never quarrel with Mama. Give up
the stars. Only let Rachel live.*

Let her live.

chapter three

Sunday, June 30, 1878
Monroe, Utah
Twenty-nine days until eclipse

I startle awake, pulled from a dream of drowning to find the blanket tangled about my legs. At once, memory pours over me and I jerk upright, searching for Rachel. I didn't mean to sleep. In the dim predawn light, I can just see that she's still breathing, her little chest rising and falling. Her rest is still the dull, unmoving rest of the night before. Her face is slack, her lips parted.

Rising, my back stiff from the night on the floor, I settle myself on the sofa beside Rachel. The house is dark and hushed. Footsteps pad across the wood floor toward me, and I look up to find Emily, her dark hair falling loose from the braid she's worn to bed.

"Is she better?" Emily whispers. When I shake my head, she asks, "What can I do?"

"Can you sit with her?" I can't heal Rachel, but I can make the day less painful for Mama and the others. I'm resolved to do everything right today, as if I can atone for yesterday's catastrophe through work. I'll stay home from church to care for everyone. I'm supposed to teach a children's class, but if I don't go, the other teachers will manage somehow.

Emily hesitates. "What if she gets worse? What if I make things worse?"

You can't make things worse than I have. Drawing a deep breath, I gather my patience. It's not Emily's fault that she's timid, any more than it's Mama's fault that she gets her moods. "Then come fetch me or Mama."

Emily takes my place beside Rachel, and I slip outside. I look up instinctively, but a hazy veil of clouds covers the sky. There are no stars for solace, not even the rising sun.

I milk the cow, give the horses their feed, then head to the kitchen to make a hasty pudding from ground corn for breakfast. Far is already settled at the table, reading the *Salt Lake Tribune,* now more than a week old. Folded neatly on the table before him is the *Rocky Mountain News,* out of Colorado. His Sabbath practice these days involves studying the news instead of the Bible. I wonder if there's anything in the paper about the eclipse, but I don't ask.

Far hasn't said anything more to me about Rachel, but his silence feels like a slap.

While I wait for the water to boil, Mama stumbles into the room, Albert clutched in her arms, her graying hair hanging loose about her shoulders. Mama's eyes are heavy-lidded, with a dead look in them that I've come to dread. She's having another of her bad spells. I'd rather Mama cried or railed than suffered this emptiness. Sometimes her moods come for no reason, but sometimes they're triggered. Is it Rachel's condition that's brought this on? One more fault to add to my tally.

Mama settles at the table beside Far and unbuttons her nightdress to feed Albert, with slow movements like one sleepwalking.

I want to say something to her, to apologize, but her eyes are fixed on something far away. I turn back to the stove, staring unseeing at the boiling water for a long moment before I scoop the ground corn into the pan.

"Why are ye not dressed for church?" Mama asks abruptly.

"I'm not going," I say, turning to face her. "I mean to stay here and help you with the children, with Rachel—"

"Ye should go. Rachel needs your repentance more than your minding."

"Let her stay, Hannah," Far says. "She's better off here than filling her head with foolishness."

"So she can fill her head with your kind of foolishness, thinking herself smarter than God? Better a righteous fool than a godless one. It's you and your papers and books that tempted Elizabeth from her duty in the first place."

"So now I am responsible for Rachel? Don't be ridiculous, Hannah." Far snatches a newspaper up from the table, stalks toward the door. There he pauses to catch my eye. "Elizabeth, I wish you'd stay." Then, before Mama or I can respond, he ducks out of the room.

Mama's grip on Albert tightens, and the baby breaks off nursing with a startled cry.

I release a long, slow breath. My chest aches from holding it.

I love my father, who is generally sunny and good-humored and tells better jokes than anyone. But I don't like being tugged between his will and Mama's, especially not when I think Mama is right. I've seen what Far lost in leaving the church—a faith, a community, a way of life. I don't want to lose that too.

It began four years ago with the United Order, a call from President Brigham Young to share all things in common. We were asked to turn all our possessions and profit over to the church, and then the bishop would dole them out as needed. Far had been one of the first to join, proud of his faithfulness.

Then the bishop asked Far for the use of the mill horses. It'd be one thing if he wanted them for church business, but he didn't. He wanted them for his own use. Far refused. The bishop threatened to turn him and Mama from the faith, strike their names from the church records. To be treated so after all his sacrifices stung Far to his very heart. He'd leave the church rather than be forced out by a man pretending to speak for God.

He never went back. It was pride that kept him away at

first, but the longer he stayed away, the more faults he began to see with the church. The Order did not long outlast my father. If it had been meant as our crucible, we had all cracked in the firing.

The pudding begins to boil, drawing me from old memories.

Mama says, "Brother Yergensen has been asking about ye."

I nearly drop the spoon I'm using to stir. "Brother Yergensen already has a wife."

Mama says, "I was a second wife. A husband would steady ye, give ye better things to think about than books."

Words clot in my throat, and it is a moment before I can breathe.

I do not believe this is just about my waywardness. Mama wants to be rid of me. I can't blame her, after Rachel.

But I cannot do what she wants.

I don't know how to fit my beliefs together so they lie smoothly. I believe God calls prophets—imperfect though they be—and the prophets say God has instituted polygamy. I am myself a product of it. But I do not want it to be *my* choice, or my future. Yet how do I proceed when what I feel is right goes against what the prophets say? Am I right, and the prophets wrong? Are they right, and I am a heretic? Or could it be that God only announces general principles and leaves it up to us to work out the wrinkles as they apply to our lives?

Is it prideful to even ask such questions?

Mama is still waiting for me to answer. And because Rachel is sick and Mama has asked it of me, I say, "All right, Mama. I'll go to church."

I hold on to this small rebellion, though: I don't promise anything about Brother Yergensen.

✦

Hyrum and I walk the mile or more to church, the late-June sun hot on our backs. My sisters have stayed home to help Mama, and the boys are too unruly. The air is still and stagnant, curdled in the heat. We've had no rain in more than a month, and the dry air shimmers against the horizon. I try not to think of Rachel, chilled and limp back at the house, or my heart will fail me.

Hyrum doesn't say much as we walk. He never does, weighing his words as carefully as gold.

"Are you all right?" I ask him. We haven't talked since he went for Sister Larsen last night. His quiet refusal to pray hangs in the air between us.

"I'm well enough," he says.

"But—?" I prompt.

His booted feet scuff the dust. They're his old boots, split at the toe, as his good boots were ruined fetching Rachel from the creek. I shall have to save all the money I get from selling eggs to buy him new ones.

"Do you think—" Hyrum starts, then stops. He clears

his throat. "Do you think God loves some of us better than others?"

"Of course not," I say fiercely. I peer at him, but he won't meet my eyes. "Has someone said something to you?" I've got some choice words for anyone who has dared.

"No. Only I've been thinking. Maybe if I were different, better, I could have helped Rachel more. I could have prayed with you." He sighs. "Shouldn't I be wanting a home of my own, a wife, more responsibilities in the church? I'm not an elder yet. And I like things as they are."

I shrug a little helplessly. "How should I know? I don't want a husband either."

"But you might, someday? I'm not sure I'll ever want a wife. I don't feel about girls as I should, to marry one."

"Feeling different from how other folks think you should doesn't make you unworthy," I say.

Hyrum spreads his hands wide. "At church we're told the highest level of heaven is for husband and wife, sealed together. Will God still want me if I don't want that?"

I don't know the answers to everything he's asking, spoken and unspoken, but something hot boils up inside me. "I don't believe God loves you any less for being who He made you to be. Just like He loves Mama with her moods, and Emily with her fears, and Far with all his pride."

Hyrum squeezes my hand tight. "And you."

I smile back, but my heart aches. Maybe God loves us for what we cannot help, but surely my unruliness, my disobedience, are choices I have made. But if I can't quite believe that acceptance extends to me, I have no doubt of Hyrum.

We don't say anything more until we reach the rock-walled church house. Hyrum stays at the building for the morning meetings, while I walk on to the school, which the Presbyterians let us use for our Sunday school for the children. Because the day is fine, I gather my small class outside, beneath a cottonwood tree. We've just begun a story from the Book of Mormon, about a woman named Abish, when a man and a young girl approach us.

When they draw nearer, I see that it's Brother Timican, one of the local Paiutes who was baptized into our church some years back. I don't recognize the girl with him, who looks to be about ten, her black hair braided in a thick plait, her skin a warm, rich brown.

Brother Timican stops before me. "This is my daughter, Sarah." He's wearing a cotton shirt and trousers, instead of buckskin, and his daughter wears a blouse and skirt much like mine. She tugs at the skirt and pulls at the cuffs of her sleeves, as though they chafe.

I have never spoken with Brother Timican before, despite seeing him at church many times. He makes me nervous, though I don't know why. The Indians who drove us out of the Little Green Valley during the Black Hawk War were mostly Utes, not Paiutes. Far says the Indians were angry because the cattle that the pioneers brought west destroyed the grasses and seeds they relied on for food and clothes, and the settlers took over the good land on the riverbanks where the tribes used to farm.

I'd be angry too if someone did that to my home.

Brother Timican says, "I want my daughter to learn to live among you, to learn your stories as well as our own." *Your stories,* he says, as though the stories of scripture are not his.

Sarah ducks her head, and the quick, shy movement reminds me of Emily. I hold my hand out to the girl and smile at her. "If I tell you one of my stories, will you tell me one of yours?"

She nods, returning my smile.

The other children watch her curiously. Brother Timican whispers something to her, and Sarah relinquishes his hand. Dappled sunshine filters through the cottonwood to speckle us with light. Her fingers settle, gentle as a bird, in mine. My heart squeezes tight as I remember all the times Rachel has done the same. For a moment, I forget where I am, what I am doing. *Please, God, let her live.*

I show Sarah a place to sit beside the youngest of the Willard children, a round, friendly girl of twelve. Then I go back to my story, but I stumble over it. Abish was a Lamanite, the only one of her people to believe in our God. With Sarah's dark eyes fixed on me, I wonder for the first time what it cost Abish to be different. What it costs Brother Timican and Sarah to be here. What it might cost me, someday, if I cannot conform as I ought.

✦

Between Sunday school and the sacrament meeting, most folks head back to their homes for dinner. I want to go home, to check on Rachel, but Mama told me in no uncertain terms I was not to come back until after the second meeting. I don't know if she is punishing me, or if she hopes church will cure me of my faults. Either way, it seems rather a lot to ask from one Sunday.

Hyrum joins me beside the cottonwood tree, to share the sandwiches I've prepared. Just as I've taken the first bite of my sandwich, the Willard family passes us: parents and five children behind them like ducklings—though they make strange ducklings, as only the youngest is still shorter than her mama.

Samuel catches my eye, smirking a little, and I choke on the dry bread, remembering that I insulted him the last time we met. Was that only yesterday?

Sister Willard, a round middle-aged woman with laugh lines creasing her cheeks, stops walking to look at me with sympathy. "I was that sorry to hear about your sister. We've been praying for her, for your family. I do hope she'll make a full recovery." Like Mama's, Sister Willard's English accent has been worn soft by her time in Utah.

"Thank you, Sister Willard," I say, warmed by her concern.

The line between her eyebrows deepens. "You're not planning to sit out in this sun, are you? Come along home with us. Least I can do to help your mama is feed you."

There's no graceful way to refuse an offer like that. I stow our sandwiches back in my bag and stand. Hyrum falls in between Samuel and his next youngest brother and says something to make them both laugh. I smile at them, pleased by their easy acceptance of Hyrum, whose soft-spoken gentleness doesn't always draw people to him.

Vilate Ann, two years younger than me at fifteen, catches my smile and sidles up beside me. Her curly blond hair wages a mostly successful war to be free of the braids down her back. "Handsome boys, aren't they?" She doesn't wait for an answer before continuing. "Mama likes you, you know. You could marry any of my brothers with her blessing."

Better Samuel than Brother Yergensen. The thought flits across my mind before I can remind myself that I am not interested in marriage. I grit my teeth, then say, perhaps louder than necessary, "I don't mean to marry any of your brothers."

Samuel turns, his teeth flashing white in a grin that pulls up the corners of his beard, his brown eyes crinkling at the corners. "I believe it's customary to wait until you're asked before refusing, Miss Elizabeth."

I freeze for a moment, my face burning hot as a stove. Perhaps the earth will open beneath me and swallow me up. There have been tremors in the valley before. It's not an impossible wish.

Thankfully, we soon reach the house Samuel's father built—one of the first log houses in the valley, with planed square planks instead of the more usual round ones. Word is, when Sister Willard arrived in the valley, she refused to live in a sod house, saying she wouldn't go into the ground until she was buried there. The interior is dark and cool, thanks to the thick walls, and Sister Willard and Vilate Ann bustle into activity, setting out fruit and bread on the table, ladling stew from a pot simmering on the corner stove. A heavy wood table dominates the center of the room, and a pull-down ladder in another corner indicates sleeping quarters in an attic upstairs.

The boys tease their sisters, who respond smartly and then laugh. The very ordinariness of the scene makes my throat tighten. This could have been any meal at my house, before yesterday.

After a prayer, the food is passed around the table. Hyrum tucks into the crispy bread and tart cider, but I can't bring myself to eat much, thinking about Rachel. Sister Willard, sitting beside me, presses my hand instead of telling me to eat, and that motherly kindness nearly undoes me. I sniff, blinking back tears, and raise my eyes to find Samuel watching me from across the table. He makes a horrific face at me and I choke on a startled laugh. Oddly enough, it makes me feel better, though I would never give Samuel the satisfaction of knowing that.

After we eat, we return to the church house. The Willard family fills an entire pew and spills into the next. I miss the days when my family did the same. Now, mostly, it's just me, sometimes Hyrum. Occasionally Mama comes with Emily and Mary or sends the littler boys to Sunday school.

I spy Brother Yergensen seated across the chapel with his family, and I pull Hyrum into a pew behind the Willards. Samuel swivels around in his seat to wink at me, and I pretend I do not see him.

Closing my eyes, I let the murmured voices swirl around me. Ours is no fine chapel, of carved stone and colored glass windows, that invites awe and reverence. But with my back against the cool wood, a hushed sensation rises in me, a stillness I sometimes name as the Holy Spirit. It's the same sense I get lying on the ground beneath a star-studded sky, of being part of something much bigger than me. Here, in the curious anonymity one gets in a group, there's a blessed pause where I don't have to be anything other than who I am.

Sometimes going to church is like trying to study astronomy and stumbling up against gaps too big to fill with what I know. But other times the sky clears, and I catch glimpses of the infinite.

The bishop starts the meeting by talking of Rachel, asking the congregation to pray with him. As he begins, I peek at the bowed heads around me. Sister Larsen, who delivered Albert and blessed Rachel just last night. Brother Collings, who helped Mama run the mill the summer Far was struck with fever. Sister Aditi Tait, who married a Mormon missionary in India against her mother's wishes and followed him to Utah, and who gave Mama a length of patterned silk the color of the sky at sunset, because she heard Mama was sad and thought the fabric would cheer her. Brother Hunt, who carried David

Charles two miles home the time he broke his leg stealing apples from the Hunts' orchard. All of them praying now for Rachel. For my family.

This is what my faith looks like in practice. The homely wonder of it makes my eyes prickle, and I close them in time to echo *Amen.*

✦

After the meeting, folks cluster around us as we leave the building, asking about Rachel, offering to help. Sister Larsen agrees to go by the house to check on her, two other sisters promise to bring by food, and Brother Willard offers to take a shift at the mill to help Far. Beside me, Hyrum blinks and ducks his head, shy in the face of all this attention. But the tips of his ears are pink, so I know he doesn't entirely dislike it.

I thank everyone as warmly as I can, trying not to notice Brother Yergensen hovering behind the crowd like an ill-omened bird.

At last the press disperses, and Brother Yergensen stands in front of me, twisting his hat in his hands. The sun glints off his scalp, visible beneath the thinning hair of his head. He is not an unkind man, but I scarcely know him. He is closer to my father's age than mine.

"Sister Bertelsen, may I speak with you?" He glances uncomfortably at Hyrum.

Sister Yergensen stands some distance away, watching us

with a toddler on her hip. She gives me a thin-lipped smile. What does she think of this strange courtship? I wish I dared ask her.

"I must get home," I say, trying to put him off. "My sister—"

"We've been praying for her," he says. "Perhaps I can come visit you, to see how she gets on? Maybe Tuesday night, after the Mutual Improvement Association meeting? I could walk you home."

If I say no, Mama will never let me hear the end of it. And I promised God I would try harder to do as Mama asked. But if I say yes—

I remind myself this is not a marriage proposal. "All right," I say, and the twisting of the hat stops as Brother Yergensen returns it to his head.

Someone brushes past me, jostling my shoulder, and I look up to see Samuel, his sister Vilate Ann just behind him. Samuel says nothing, not even an apology, though his eyes meet mine with a flattened expression that makes my heart pinch.

"Thank you," Brother Yergensen says, nodding to me and turning back to his wife.

✦

I watch the house warily as Hyrum and I approach. When no one rushes out to greet us with bad news, my shoulders relax a fraction.

I hesitate only a moment before following Hyrum inside, my desire to see Rachel outweighing my fear that Mama won't want to see *me*.

Mama is beside Rachel, stroking her unmoving hand. Mary sits darning in the rocking chair, and Emily reads to Henry and John in the far corner. Sister Larsen is already there, examining Rachel.

"Her color's better, and her breathing. It may be a bit before she wakes, but you'll have your girl back, Hannah."

Mama presses her hand to her lips. "God will it be so."

I stoop to kneel beside Rachel, and Mama doesn't stop me. I pluck up the small, pudgy hand and kiss it.

Rachel lets out a long breath like a sigh, and her eyes flicker open. " 'Lizbeth," she says, her voice dry and cracked.

Beside us, Mama sucks in a sharp breath.

"I'm here, my darling." Relief makes my voice waver.

Rachel's lips slide into a satisfied smile. Then, apparently exhausted by this exchange, she shuts her eyes again.

The others all crowd around us, talking at once: Hyrum and Mary and Emily and John and Henry. Sister Larsen says something about warming some broth to feed Rachel. But it's Mama I watch: Mama, who kneels beside me to cup Rachel's face in her hands; Mama, who turns, at last, to see me, her eyes wet with tears.

chapter four

Tuesday, July 2, 1878

Monroe, Utah

Twenty-seven days until eclipse

Tuesday morning dawns unfairly clear and bright. If Brother Yergensen truly intends to call upon me this evening, by rights the skies should be lowering and gray. I rival even Mary for snappishness, and Mama sends me out to gather the laundry from the line.

Sunlight beats against my head in an unrelenting assault. Unpinning clothes hanging limp in the heat, I resist the urge to run Henry's clean shirt against the sweat dripping from my cheeks. I spy Hyrum coming up the road from the mill, waving a slip of paper. "Telegram for Mama!"

A telegram means something urgent.

Hyrum ducks into the house and I follow. The house is

near as warm as the outside, but the dimmer light is not so brutal.

As I cross the sitting room, I check compulsively for Rachel. Her voice floats in from the bedroom, a singsong conversation with her dolly. My stiff shoulders relax a fraction. Though she still spends much of her day resting, each day marks new improvements.

Mama is in the kitchen, running a flat iron across the clothes I've already brought in from yesterday's wash, using the kitchen table instead of a board. Mary and Emily sit darning nearby.

Setting the iron back on the stove to heat, Mama takes the telegram from Hyrum and reads it swiftly. She looks up, lips pursed. "Go fetch your father," she tells Hyrum, and then refuses to say anything more until, one skirt and half a dress later, Far appears in the doorway. His eyes are wide in alarm, his chest heaving after his run. "Hyrum says there's a telegram."

Mama nods. "It's Rebekka." My half sister, Far and Aunt Elisa's oldest daughter, gone east to Wyoming these three years or more. "It's nearin' her time and the doctor is worried for her—telegram doesn't say why, but perhaps they're worried it will be like the other babes Rebekka lost before her time. Ammon wants her to have family with her at the birth."

Far rubs at his forehead. "'Tis only natural that a girl should want her mama at such a time. With Elisa gone, you're the closest she has."

Mama's hands go still on the iron. I don't think Far sees that. "Rebekka's a good lass, and Lord knows I love her like my own daughter." She hesitates, and I pick at a hangnail on my smallest finger. I think Mama loves Rebekka more than some of her own daughters: she's the standard against which I fail Mama, time and again. Mama continues, "But how am I supposed to leave now? Albert still suckles, and I can't be leavin' Rachel so soon after her near drownin'."

Neither of them say a word about Mama's dark spells, though surely they must be thinking of them. If one of her moods hits while she's helping Rebekka, who would help Mama?

Both Mama and Far stare, dismayed, at the telegram lying crumpled on the table. Mary drops her darning and has to scramble after it. I think of Rebekka, saving scraps of yarn to make a colorful cap for my doll, when my six-year-old self worried she'd get cold in winter.

"I'll go." The words escape me in a rush.

Mama and Far both turn to gape at me. Far responds first, his eyes brightening. "That's kind of you, Elizabeth."

Kindness is only part of this. I imagine riding the train, the mountains and plains spinning past as I'm carried east. Away from questions about my future, away from the immediate press of family duties, away from the constant guilt. Away from Brother Yergensen and his unwanted courtship.

Far continues, "You'll have to leave soon to be there before the birth. Today, if I can find someone heading north to Salt Lake City, where you can catch the train to Wyoming."

"I don't know," Mama says doubtfully. "Can we afford it? Can we trust Elizabeth to go so far on her own? Is it safe?" She doesn't look at me as she adds, "She's not the most responsible lass."

"I've got a bit saved up," Far says. "And it's not so far. Elizabeth'll have company to Salt Lake, and then there will be porters and others on the train. It's but two days to reach Cheyenne from Ogden, and Ammon can meet her at the station."

He does not add, *Even she can manage so much,* but I know both he and Mama are thinking it.

"I'll be safe, Mama. I'll do everything you wish me to. And think how much more comfortable you will be, to have someone you know with Rebekka." I catch my breath. Have I said too much?

"It's what Elisa would want," Far says, and I could kiss him. The line between Mama's eyebrows smooths out. She's weakening.

"But who will help around the house, with the little ones?"

Far waves his hand. "It's time Emily and Mary helped more anyhow. Elizabeth won't be here forever."

"It's not fair," Mary mutters. "I want to see Rebekka too. And ride on a train."

"And ye will mind your stops and not miss them? And find yourself a nice family to sit beside, so the strange gentlemen don't bother ye?" Mama pins me with her eyes.

My hands are trembling. I clasp them together on my lap. "My word on it, Mama."

Mama lets out a long breath. "All right. I do not like it—but ye may go."

I escape outside before the bubble of joy in me bursts out in unseemly noise. Hiding my face in the laundry still on the line, I let loose something between a laugh and a howl. Heaven has dropped an adventure in my lap. The warm sunlight falling on my uncovered head, my exposed hands, no longer feels like an assault, but a caress.

I mean to keep my promise, but if I can be obedient *and* see something of the world, I shall not repine.

✦

Far returns home a couple hours later to tell me he has found passage for me to Salt Lake City, leaving within the hour, if I can be ready. "One of the Willard boys is taking some furniture up to his brother, just as soon as they can get the piece finished. They're nearly done."

"Which brother?" I ask. *Not Samuel.* Samuel Willard is a nuisance and a tease, and I can't think about Vilate Ann's hint at Sunday dinner without a flush of mortification.

Far shrugs. "One of the middling ones? There are so many children in that house. Besides, what does it matter? His sister goes with him."

"There are many children in this house," I point out. "Yet you manage to remember each of us."

Far squints at me. "Which one are you? Mary?"

I laugh, though it's bittersweet. I shall miss Far.

"Ye'd best hurry," Mama says. "If ye mean to join them."

I've already packed my trunk while waiting for Far, so there is not much that remains. Mama gives me a small velvet satchel with a mixture of herbs and spices to brew a tea to soothe Rebekka as she labors. She tucks the satchel and a small vial of oil into the bottom of my trunk, in case it is needed to bless Rebekka before the baby comes. Besides the trunk, I have an old carpetbag to hold a few things for the train. It can be unfolded to serve as a blanket, though I can't imagine needing it in the July heat.

Mama tilts her head at me. "Your hair's come undone." She leads me to her room and sits me at the small vanity. She pulls the remaining pins from my hair and runs a comb through my reddish-brown curls. As a child I loved the feel of Mama's fingers against my scalp, her touch tender where her words were not. It has been many months since Mama has brushed my hair, and I close my eyes to savor this. Despite her stern words, her fingers say she has begun to forgive me for what happened to Rachel.

"Be sure that any ties on Rebekka's clothes are untied, that the doors and windows are unlocked, so the baby can find its way into the world. And cover the mirrors and open the bottles," Mama says, revealing the Old World beliefs that have snuck into her New World faith.

"Yes, Mama." Now that the time has come to leave, I'm suddenly unsure. Is it right of me to leave Mama and Rachel?

Am I making the same mistake again, indulging myself at the expense of my family?

"It's a good thing ye're doing," Mama says gruffly. "I begin to have hope for ye."

I smile a little. I *think* Mama means this as a compliment.

"Be good and helpful, and mind Rebekka. Put your family before yourself and put God before all, and ye shall be well."

"And happy?" I ask.

Mama's fingers still, so briefly I wonder if I imagine it. "Happy is the girl who does what she ought." With deft hands, she sweeps my hair up and pins it so I can settle a bonnet over it. She does not kiss me goodbye, as Mary and Emily do, or hug me as the little boys do, but she rests her palm against my cheek, her gaze steady.

When I go to the bedroom to see Rachel, still tucked in her bed, my sister tries to give me her dolly. "So you will not be lonely," she says, and I swallow against a sudden tightness in my throat and kiss both her round cheeks.

Far presses a few dollars into my hand, for expenses, and then Hyrum helps me load my battered trunk into the wagon and we set off.

We do not speak for a while, rattling along the dirt road. I can tell Hyrum wants to say something, though, from the way he keeps pursing his lips together and glancing sidelong at me. I wait. I've learned there's no hurrying him.

At last, he says, "Are you scared, to be heading out alone?"

I don't think this is what he meant to say, but I shake my

head. "No, not scared. Excited to see Rebekka, guilty at leaving Mama and Rachel and the others. Sorry to leave you."

"I wish you weren't going."

Even with my guilt at leaving Mama, I can't wish that. "I wish you could come with me."

Now Hyrum shakes his head. He waves his hand around at the valley, the fields hazy in the afternoon sun. "I don't want to leave. This valley is home. These rocks and canyons, they get into your blood somehow. But you—you've always been different. Always wanting something new, something unexpected, where I like what's known and familiar."

I laugh. "You never have liked surprises." The fall Hyrum turned sixteen, I planned with some of his friends in town to surprise him with a party. I told Hyrum that one of his friends needed help with some carpentry work, and so Hyrum had turned up, dressed in old clothes and carrying his tools, to find half the young people in town, all arrayed in Sunday best. He had opened the door to the light and noise and happy cries and backed right out of the house. It had taken all my persuasive skills to get him to return inside.

Then I sober. This visit to Rebekka's must have come as an unpleasant surprise too—nothing like this had been planned this morning. "I'm sorry this has come on so sudden. But Mama couldn't go and Rebekka needs help."

Hyrum doesn't look at me but fixes his gaze on the road in front of us. "Will you come back?"

My heart pinches tight. I used to think I'd leave this valley for college, to study the stars. But of course that was only fool-ish dreaming. How could I leave Hyrum? Mama needs me too—I can't leave her to Emily and Mary's casual care. And Rachel—if I left, I would miss seeing her grow. "I'll always come back."

Hyrum shoots me a small, sideways smile, and I do my best to return it, though my lips feel stiff.

When we reach the Willard cabin, Vilate Ann is already outside, sitting on the spring seat of the wagon, a straw bon-net tied neatly over her blond curls. She waves when she sees us, a smile splitting her rosy cheeks.

Hyrum helps me down and fetches my trunk from the back of our wagon. As he lifts it to the Willard wagon and pushes it underneath the seat, Vilate Ann leans toward him.

"What a gentleman you are, Brother Bertelsen. They say a man who's kind to his sisters will be kind to his wife too."

Hyrum casts a quick, almost frightened look at Vilate Ann and ducks his head in response. I smother a giggle. Vilate Ann would be hard-pressed to find a less willing recipient of her mild flirtation.

Luckily for Hyrum, before Vilate Ann can say anything else, Samuel and another of his brothers emerge from the house, carrying a heavy wooden table. A third brother ap-pears with a pair of chairs. Hyrum helps them load the fur-niture.

I wait beside the wagon, wishing the heat did not make me so inclined to perspire. There's nothing elegant about dampness.

When everything is secure, Vilate calls to me, encouraging me to take my seat beside her.

I give Hyrum one last hug and promise to write. Hyrum nods at the Willard boys, avoids Vilate Ann, and turns our wagon back toward home.

As I'm about to take the outside seat, Vilate Ann stands and ushers me into the middle seat. She curls her arm through mine. "I'm so glad you're coming with us. I do love my brother, but he does not appreciate my need to *talk*."

At that I laugh, though a part of my heart is following Hyrum back up the road. Some of my excitement is fading before the reality of our departure, and I still don't know which Willard brother is to drive us.

Lyman, just younger than me, disappears around the side of the house and reappears a moment later leading two horses, which Samuel helps him hitch to the wagon. Lyman would be all right as a driver. I don't have any embarrassing memories involving *him*.

The three Willard brothers confer briefly; then Samuel slaps his nearest brother on the back and climbs into the driver's seat.

Thanks to Vilate Ann's maneuvering, I am right next to him, his thigh brushing mine, our elbows jostling as he picks up the reins and flicks them, clicking to the horses to start.

I dart a glance at Vilate Ann, but she only smiles back at me, her face suspiciously innocent.

I press my lips together in annoyance. Already, my cheeks are warming beyond what is warranted by the heat of the day, and my mind is scrambling for something, anything, innocuous to say. Worse still is my intense awareness of him, of the heat of his body, of the cheerful humming that inexplicably sets my heart jumping, of his smell—like wood dust and juniper.

Lord, help me.

chapter five

Tuesday, July 2, 1878

Between Monroe and Salt Lake City, Utah

Twenty-six days until eclipse

"Everything in order?" Samuel asks me as we pull away from the cabin.

"What?" I say. Because of course just when I most want to avoid embarrassment, all my wits desert me.

"You all ready for the journey?" Samuel doesn't look up from the road, but there's a slight curl to his lips that suggests amusement.

"I'm here, aren't I?"

Samuel only hums a little to himself in answer.

Vilate Ann asks, "How's your sister faring?"

"Much better, thank you." The image of Rachel offering her dolly rises in my mind, and I swallow. "She'll be up and about soon."

Samuel doesn't say much after that, but Vilate Ann chatters enough to cover our silences, with opinions on everything from the weather (unbearably hot) to the new dress pattern her mother is cutting for her (unbearably fine) to her hopes that we reach Salt Lake City before July fourth and get to see some fireworks.

"I doubt it," Samuel says. "Unless you can somehow fly us over the mountains or induce a new rail line to appear, I don't expect to reach Salt Lake City before next week."

We spend the first night in Richfield, with friends of the Willards'. The family feeds us stew and biscuits until our stomachs groan, and we sing songs around their battered piano until we cannot keep our eyes open. When darkness and quiet finally descend on the house, I whisper my prayers beside Vilate Ann, before climbing into the trundle bed we are to share.

All the next day, we continue traveling north through Sevier County, in countryside that still looks so much like home that I'm given no chance to miss it: red rock, cottonwoods along the riverbeds, scrub pine and juniper on the mountains. On the third day, the road we're following starts to climb toward Manti, and in early evening we pass by a lake, low and glittering in the fading light. Our destination is a homestead a little farther on, someone else the Willards know.

It's Independence Day. I wonder if Mama and the others went to Richfield to celebrate, if Rachel was well enough to go with them.

Vilate Ann hasn't repeated her wish for fireworks, but as the stars start to appear, I point out familiar constellations for her: the Big Dipper, Cassiopeia's crown, the cross of Cygnus directly overhead. Then, so faint I think at first I have imagined it, a falling star above the eastern horizon.

Samuel asks, "Do you know any stories of the constellations?"

He's on the far side of Vilate Ann tonight, and I have to strain a bit to hear him.

"Are you sure you want me to tell stories of the stars?" I ask. "I might not be able to stop."

"Oh, I'll stop listening if I have to. Vilate Ann has given me lots of practice."

Vilate Ann pokes him, indignant, and Samuel only laughs. I like his laugh—it rises from somewhere deep inside him, booming and infectious. I'm not sure I like noticing his laugh, though, so I switch my attention to the star-studded sky. I tell Samuel and Vilate Ann about Phaethon, the son of Helios, who begs to drive his father's chariot for a day. His drive ends in disaster, as he cannot control the chariot, and Zeus destroys it—and him—with a thunderbolt. Phaethon's dear friend Cycnus grieves by the river where Phaethon's body falls, diving repeatedly into the water to try to rescue his friend's charred body. The gods, moved by this devotion, turn him into a swan and put him among the stars.

When my words fade away, there's silence as all of us stare upward. Then Vilate Ann says, "If you crash *this* chariot because you're staring at the sky, Samuel Willard, don't expect me to collect your charred bones. I don't want some old gods to stick me in the sky."

"If they did, you wouldn't be a swan," Samuel says. "You'd be a hummingbird—small, brightly colored, and always buzzing around."

Vilate Ann says, "I do *not* buzz. And if you were a constellation, you'd be a cat. A lazy, vexing creature that likes to sleep all day."

"You forgot good-tempered," Samuel says.

"Yes, so long as no one tries to touch it, scratch its ears, or take its dinner," I say tartly, annoyed that Samuel remains so irritatingly calm while riling up his sister.

"Meow," Samuel says. I can't help it. A surprised laugh bubbles out of me, warm and loose.

"What about you? What constellation would you choose?" he asks me. "Wait—let me guess. An owl."

I flush in the growing darkness, trying to figure out how he means to tease me with this. "Because I can rotate my head unusually far? Or because I cough up the bones of my prey?"

"Can you?" Samuel asks, leaning forward to see me around Vilate Ann, his eyes bright with interest. When I don't answer, he continues, "No, only because you have a kind of quiet grace and you're always so focused. And smart. Owls were associated with Athena, weren't they? The goddess of wisdom?"

They were, but I'm surprised Samuel knows this—and that he thinks anything so nice about me. To cover my confusion, I say, "I'd rather be a comet than a constellation. A light burning through the sky, a mystery people write about centuries later."

"But what good is a comet, if it doesn't last?" Vilate Ann asks.

"Some do," I say. "Halley's comet reappears about every seventy-five years." Then I think: *Perhaps my life already is like a comet, following a predetermined path.*

"You love the stars," Samuel says. It's an observation, not a question.

"I used to dream of going to Vassar College and studying with Maria Mitchell, the greatest female astronomer in America," I say. Then I clamp my mouth shut, because it's a ridiculous dream for someone like me, and anyway I've promised to forget it.

Vilate Ann says, "Why would you want to go to school if you did not have to?"

"Used to?" Samuel asks, and there's nothing mocking in his voice, only a gentle curiosity.

To Vilate Ann, I say, "I like to learn new things. I'd have gone to school in Monroe, if Mama had let me."

I don't answer Samuel.

We drive on a ways in silence. Just when I think Samuel has forgotten my words, he says, "I think you'd make a fine astronomer, Elizabeth Bertelsen."

And though the breeze blowing through the desert night is cool, suddenly I'm flushed with warmth.

Late morning on the fourth day of travel, we pass through Manti. Workers swarm a hill above us, hauling masses of white stone and laying the foundation for what will be the third temple in Utah (though only the one in the south, in St. George, is finished). I can't see anything of the building yet, but four large terrace walls rise one above another, wrapping perhaps a quarter of a mile around the hill like the walls of a castle. Someday, I'll come here for my endowment, the promise I'll make to God that can only be made inside a temple.

Vilate Ann perks up in her seat. "Oh, may we stop?"

Obligingly, Samuel pulls the wagon over to the side, and Vilate Ann all but climbs over me getting out of the wagon. She dances lightly up the hillside, toward the workers, and Samuel and I follow at a more sedate pace.

There's something about this place that moves me, though I've never seen a temple before. A stillness, despite the busyness of the workers, a sense of roots that go deeper than the foundation walls. Or maybe it's what the building represents: the sacrifices of people who, like me, don't have much to offer but their faith and their labor.

By the time we reach Vilate Ann, she has cornered a young worker and is asking a million questions as the boy's cheeks grow pinker. When she sees us approach, she waves us on, so Samuel and I continue our walk. It's a warm day, and I'm grateful for the meager shade of my bonnet. It must be hot work, assembling the rock foundation above us, even if it's holy.

Samuel surveys the building going on above us with a considering eye. "I wonder where they'll get the wood for the inside of the temple."

His father is a carpenter, the craftsman of the furniture we're hauling to Salt Lake City. "Are you a carpenter, like your father?"

"Something like. Pa wouldn't call my inexpert efforts carpentry, though." A wry smile twists his mouth.

I think of Samuel's understanding words from the night before and realize that for all his good humor and seeming openness, I don't really know much about him. "And what do you do, when you're not woodworking?"

"Besides tease my sisters?" He shrugs. "I read some, write some. I'm actually very ordinary—if you know my family, you know the best part of me."

I frown. This is the second time in as many minutes that he's dismissed himself. "Isn't there anything else you want? Something bigger? Something just for you?"

"Like the dream you used to have, of studying astronomy?" Samuel sends me a sideways look.

I flush. Is he teasing me? I turn away, running my hand along the rough stone of the wall.

"You never said why you gave it up," he continues.

Irritation goads me, and I swirl back to face him. "How could I hold on to a dream like that? There's not much call for an educated farmer's wife. Already some people think I talk too fine." I've spent hours poring over newspapers and books and journals, writing out sentences that imitate the cadences of what I've read, trying to sound smarter, more educated—and all I've achieved is a reputation for snobbishness, and, if Mama is to be believed, heresy.

Samuel spreads his hands wide, palms up. "I'm not trying to upset you. I'm just looking to understand why you would give up something you want just because other people don't think you should do it."

"Just because I want something doesn't make it the right thing." I don't like this conversation. It makes me feel prickly and defensive, like a porcupine, though what I have to defend I don't rightly know.

"Doesn't make it wrong, necessarily, either. If your fancy words fret folks, it's their problem, not yours." Samuel glances behind us. I follow his glance back to Vilate Ann, but she's still determinedly chatting to the young workman. The boy doesn't seem to mind the distraction.

"You never answered my question, about what you want." I've revealed more about myself in this conversation than he has.

There's a long moment where he looks at me, and I look back, and my heart begins to pound an oddly uneven rhythm. I break the gaze first, dropping my eyes to the worn toes of my shoes and fighting back a blush.

"I don't know," he says finally. "I suppose I don't think about it much. I like my life just fine—and, well." He stops walking, and I stop with him. He looks around, as if searching for the right words. "My parents crossed the plains with the Martin handcart company—you know, the pioneers who got caught in early winter snows. My family was lucky. They all made it through. It was before I was born, but my oldest sister talks about how she used to wake up with her braids frozen to the ground, it was so cold. And then my family got to the valley, and things were so unsettled. When I got old enough to see how my ma fretted over all of us, I guess I aimed to be someone she didn't have to worry over."

My insides jolt with recognition. Maybe I'm not the only one who puts aside the things they want because their family needs them.

But Samuel is still talking—slowly, as if he's puzzling something out. "I suppose I'd like to travel some. Meet new people and see new places. I'll be going on to Denver after I drop off our load in Salt Lake, to talk to a furniture maker there about some new tools and techniques coming from back east, like machine joinery and wood graining. Pa says I can go so long as the furniture we sell in Salt Lake fetches enough."

As we angle past the wall, hot light refracts against it, nearly blinding me. I blink. I didn't know Samuel was going on to Denver. "Will you see the eclipse?"

He shrugs. "If I'm still there. It'd be something to see, wouldn't it? Will you see it, where you're going?"

Something to see? The shimmering heat around us feels heavy, as though I might swim through it. After a moment,

I manage, "Only part. Cheyenne will miss totality." I remind myself of my promise to fit myself more neatly to the mold Mama expects of me. But the bitter taste in my mouth lingers.

He does have the grace to look chagrined. "I'm sorry for that. I know it means more to you than me."

I nod a terse acknowledgment. Then something occurs to me. "Wait—if you're going to Denver, are you going by way of the railroad?"

"I plan to."

"Then why are we only going as far as Salt Lake City together?"

"Why, Miss Bertelsen, I didn't know you cared so much for my company!"

I resist the urge to smack him.

Maybe he reads my irritation in my face, because he adds, "I've got some work to do for my brother first, and your pa said that it was important you get to Wyoming as soon as possible."

My fingers clench at my sides. He's right. *Rebekka.* In the pleasure of seeing this new place, in talking, I've lost sight of the urgency behind this journey. I can't let myself forget again. "We should go," I say, and Samuel turns us back toward Vilate Ann.

We reach the town of Moroni late Friday afternoon and Nephi on Saturday: all these small towns scattered across

Utah with names drawn from the Book of Mormon. I wonder what names these places bore before the Mormons came.

We spend our Sabbath in Nephi, attending the local ward services in the morning with the widow who lent us beds the night before. The sky is overcast as we walk toward the ward building, a welcome coolness after the heat of the preceding days. Thunder rumbles in the distance.

Someone has planted lavender in a field near the town, and the tips bleed purple across the horizon. I stand for a moment, moved by the juxtaposition of color against the dark band of the sky and mountains. So often I go through the world without seeing, but then suddenly I am caught, transfixed and wordless, by some trick of light or nature or God. It's this sense, of the world being so much bigger, of it revealing its secrets in bits and spurts, that keeps pulling me back to church, when there is so much I still do not know or understand. So much I question.

There is some confusion when we arrive at church and are taken for a family—a young man with two plural wives.

"This is my brother," Vilate Ann says, laughing, but after a sly look at me she does not clarify that I am not Samuel's wife. In the rush to find seats before the service starts, there's no chance to correct the misunderstanding.

Periodically through the sermon, I catch myself imagining what it might be like to marry someone like Samuel instead of Brother Yergensen, to settle fully into the life Mama wants for me, the life Rebekka chose. Then I refold my arms, irritated at letting my mind wander—and because the idea does not distress me as much as it might have a week ago.

It begins to sprinkle on our way back to the widow's home. Samuel holds out his hand, catching the raindrops on his palm. "I hope the rain doesn't turn the roads to mud."

My stomach tightens. Muddy roads mean waiting for dry weather—and delaying my arrival at Rebekka's. "It's only sprinkling," I say, trying to speak evenly. "Surely that won't affect the roads much, as dry as it has been."

Vilate Ann huffs, "I'd rather not travel in the wet. I don't want to take cold just before we get to Salt Lake City. It's my first time to see the city!"

"Oh, but Elizabeth makes a habit of swimming fully dressed. She might enjoy the experience of traveling in wet clothing." Samuel darts a quick glance at me, his eyes shining.

A wave of residual embarrassment washes over me. "I do not," I say crossly, memory following quickly on the heels of my mortification.

Last summer, Mama was feeling poorly, some aching in her joints, and Sister Larsen thought the local hot springs might do her good. We waited until evening, when the sun overhead was not so unbearable. That close to solstice, the evenings were long and full of light. We wore our oldest dresses, as we did not have proper bathing suits, then drove to Mr. Cooper's homestead. Mr. Cooper had built a wooden box to house the spring, and charged a small fee for its use, open alternating days for men and women. We paid the fee, then climbed the steps to the pool and settled into the warm water. The only other woman there was Sister Willard, Samuel's ma.

I thought the water was marvelous, like a full-body hug, but Mama was not so keen on it. After only a couple of minutes, she complained that the water drew the mosquitoes and the heat made her aches flare instead of subside.

I helped Mama out and followed her to the small hut Mr. Cooper had built for changing, thinking to help her out of her wet things. But once I'd unbuttoned the back of her dress, she shooed me out.

Still dripping, I began walking up the road, rubbing my arms and hoping the exercise would warm me. And that, of course, was when I encountered Samuel, who had come to fetch his mother.

I looked like a drowned rat.

Samuel, dry and comfortable, couldn't quite hold back his laughter when he saw me. But rather than let me retreat in humiliation, as any gentleman would have done, he tried to make conversation.

"Good evening, Miss Bertelsen. Are you here for the springs?" Samuel asked. "My mother finds the waters soothing."

A bead of water rolled from my hairline and dripped off my nose. "No," I said. "I always walk about in soaking clothes."

"Naturally," he said, grinning. Clearly, he did not believe me. He reached out to gently flick water from the tip of my nose. "The waterlogged look suits you. You should do it more often."

I don't remember what I said, only that my whole body burned with shame as I hurried up the road to find Mama.

I come back to the present with a jolt, to find Vilate Ann staring at me with wide eyes, and Samuel's eyes narrowed at me in amusement. "Are you never serious?" I ask, lingering mortification making my voice sharper than I mean it to be.

"I was born to speak all mirth and no matter," Samuel says, his lips twitching again.

I didn't expect Samuel to know Shakespeare, and surprise robs me of some of my annoyance. I respond with a twist on Benedict's line to Beatrice. "Should I call you my dear *Lord Disdain*, then?"

Samuel catches my hand and kisses my knuckles like some old-fashioned courtier. "You may call me what you please." He pauses, and I mistrust the twinkle in his eye. "Only don't call me late for dinner."

A drop of rain splashes on my nose. Vilate Ann groans. *"Samuel."*

Lightning flashes near the western mountains. A few moments later, thunder rolls through the valley. Samuel picks up his pace. "If we hurry, we might be able to get out in front of the storm. I'd rather not get stuck here."

I hasten after him, ignoring Vilate Ann's plaintive "Must we?"

Within only a few minutes, we've packed up our trunks

and settled everything under an oiled fabric, to keep the water off the furniture. I open my carpetbag, spreading it across my lap and Vilate Ann's.

We rattle along the road for some time. The wind picks up, sending the rain sideways into our faces. I tip my head down, so the brim of my bonnet catches some of the water, and Vilate Ann pulls the carpet up against her chest. "I knew this was a bad idea," she mutters, but neither Samuel nor I respond, and she subsides into silence. So much for getting ahead of the storm.

Despite the rain, we make decent progress. Somewhere just past Mona, as the road angles east around the mountain, we hit trouble. Rainwater gullies across the road: a fast-moving, churning brown ribbon.

Samuel urges the horses slowly through the water. It doesn't appear to be deep, but the horses are nervous and Samuel murmurs soothingly to them. Vilate Ann clutches my arm. A sudden surge of water shifts the entire wagon, and one of the horses bucks against his harness. I catch my breath.

Samuel climbs down to lead the horses through, and after a few tense minutes, we're past the water. I release my breath slowly, but don't relax until Samuel has climbed back into the wagon. His trousers are soaked nearly to the knee.

We drive on in silence for a few moments more, and then, with a sickening lurch, the wagon stops. Samuel clucks at the horses, but all their pulling against the harness doesn't budge us.

Once again, Samuel climbs down. He inspects the side of the wagon and, unexpectedly, begins to laugh. "We are well and truly stuck."

"Can you get us out?" I ask, dismayed, starting to calculate how long this will set us back.

"Not without help," he says. "Are you offering?"

I don't relish sliding through the mud when I'm already damp, but I don't want to be stuck either. I clamber down from the wagon seat and sidle around the wagon to Samuel, the wet ground slurping at my boots as I go. It's bad—the left wheel has sunk nearly to the axle.

Samuel calls up to Vilate Ann to take the reins and lead the horses forward. Then the two of us settle behind the wagon. "One, two, three, push!" Samuel says.

We both push, throwing our weight against the backboard. The wagon rocks forward a fraction, but the wheel doesn't move.

We try again.

And again.

I'm beginning to sweat beneath my damp clothes. I set my shoulder against the board and we push a fourth time. The wagon budges a few inches. After our earlier failures, the movement catches me off guard, and my feet slide out from beneath me. I land on my hands and knees in the mud.

Samuel surveys me. "Elizabeth Bertelsen—a stick-in-the-mud if ever I saw one." Then he holds out his hand.

I ignore Samuel's proffered hand and pull myself up using the wagon to brace myself. My left foot slips sideways, but though my stomach falls, this time I do not fall with it. "Is everything a joke with you?"

He pulls his hand back. There's a smear of mud across his knuckles. "I thought some humor would help—you're so serious about everything."

"At least I care," I say, stung.

"What's that supposed to mean?" he asks, putting his shoulder against the back of the wagon and pushing.

Vilate Ann hollers, "Is everything all right?"

Neither of us answer her.

To Samuel, I say, "Better to care about something than nothing, as you do."

"Is that what you think? That I don't care about anything?"

Arguing with Samuel is like trying to catch rainwater in a sieve. For some reason, his refusal to get upset only makes me more so. "I'll bet your family was happy to send you away for this journey—such a care-for-nobody ass who likes to think he's funny." I'm not even sure if what I'm saying is true.

The tips of Samuel's ears turn pink. He shoves fruitlessly against the wagon. "And you think you're so much better than me? A girl who wants the stars but is too afraid to do anything about it?"

"At least I *have* dreams. At least I don't just drift through my life in order to keep the peace."

Samuel steps away from the wagon. Without looking at me, he says, "I'm going to need to take one of the horses back to Mona to get help."

Then he leaves me, standing ankle-deep in the mud, with

dirt crusting over my fingers and the hem of my dress, not nearly as triumphant as I thought to be at finally nettling Samuel Willard.

✦

It takes perhaps an hour or more of waiting with Vilate Ann, huddled together beneath a nearby tree, before rescuers come with Samuel from Mona. After that, though Samuel does not outright ignore me—he is exquisitely polite when he has to talk to me—he's distant. He still cracks jokes with Vilate Ann, but I might as well be invisible. More than once, I've begun to apologize but caught the words back. Samuel does not seem to mind our new distance. If he does not, why should I?

The rain passes and we manage to reach Santaquin that night, and, in cleaner clothes and on drier roads the following two days, we make good time, reaching the Salt Lake valley just as Tuesday afternoon edges into evening.

Samuel drives directly to the Union Pacific station.

Vilate Ann says, "Are you sure you don't want to stay at my brother's house tonight? You would be welcome."

My eyes flick to Samuel, but he is busy unloading my trunk from the back of the wagon.

"I've been a week on the road already. I should go—the baby may already be here." I send up a tiny prayer, asking for Rebekka to be all right. And there's no need to delay— I stocked up my bag with provisions the day before, when we stopped by a market.

"But you haven't seen anything of Salt Lake City," Vilate Ann says.

"I'm not here to enjoy myself," I say. It sounds like something Mama would say, and for a moment the sting of missing her pricks at my throat.

After a rather teary goodbye from Vilate Ann, who promises to write every day (but will likely forget), and a polite but distant farewell from Samuel, I grip my carpetbag in one hand and the handle of my trunk in the other and march to the ticket window outside the small station.

"To Ogden," I tell the man at the ticket counter, pleased that my voice does not waver. I carefully count out the bills for the fare from my purse. In Ogden, I will purchase a second ticket to carry me east all the way to Cheyenne.

"Last train is at nine twenty-five p.m.," he says, and I nod. I hand over my money, and he stamps a paper ticket with the date and gives it to me with my change. Though it's still two hours from departure, a dozen or so people are already waiting, sitting on long wooden benches beside the track behind the station.

Samuel and Vilate Ann are gone. I can just see the back of their wagon at the end of the street. I drag my trunk to a bench and sit, arranging my skirts around me and settling my carpetbag on my lap.

I take a deep breath, then two.

I have never been so far from people and places I know.

I remind myself: *There is nothing so scary about this. I know where I am.*

If I were to look out from the front of the station, I could see the building site where the walls of the Salt Lake City temple are rising, only a few blocks away. If the worst happens, if the train fails to appear, I could stop anyone in the street and ask them to direct me to a Mormon bishop, who could help me find a place to stay—perhaps even find Samuel's brother's house.

I will not be afraid.

I can do this.

The train comes rushing into the station a few minutes after nine, belching steam and squealing on its iron rails. I've never seen a real train before, much less been on one.

I am not sure what to do, so I watch the other passengers. I see how they ask porters or male family members to carry their trunks aboard, and they follow with their bags.

A uniformed porter stops beside me, seeing my puzzled face. "Need help, miss?"

"Thank you," I say gratefully, and he lifts my trunk with practiced hands.

"Where to?"

"The train?" I say, rather stupidly, then blush. I dislike feeling ignorant, and everything about this moment has me out of my depth.

"May I see your ticket? I need to know which car."

I pull out my ticket to see that "second class" is printed across it. The porter glances at it and nods. "First time on the railroad?"

"Yes, sir," I say.

"You can sit in any of the passenger coaches." He gestures to a couple of cars tucked behind the baggage car. "The last coach is first-class, and your ticket doesn't cover that. I'll be taking your trunk to the storage car; another porter will fetch it out for you when you arrive."

With a cheerful salute, he walks off with my trunk. I watch him lift the trunk into the car behind the engine and exhale.

I think back to my dime novels: Was Texas Jack ever scared to board a train? He'd scorn the thought.

Squaring my shoulders, I climb the metal stairs into a second-class car.

chapter six

Tuesday, July 9, 1878
Salt Lake City, Utah
Twenty days until eclipse

Though several windows are open in the train car, the air inside is, if possible, even warmer than the outside air. The sun has just set, but enough light remains to illuminate the cabin with a gray glow. The seats are arranged in rows, some facing forward, some back. Most of the rows are occupied by at least one person, most of them men. An older black woman sits by herself in a row facing north, her curling gray hair drawn back in a neat bun.

I hesitate. I promised Mama I wouldn't sit by any strange men, but the only other empty seat is by the woman, and I've never spoken to a black person in my life. There aren't any in Monroe. As though she feels my eyes upon her, the woman looks up at me. Her glance shifts away quickly, but her eyes are kind.

Someone outside blows a whistle, and the train lurches forward. Unprepared, I stumble, grabbing a nearby seat for balance.

I make my way toward the woman. "May I sit here?"

"Suit yourself," she says, but she smiles, so I do.

As the train leaves the station, the gas-lit streets of Salt Lake City pass by slowly, as though from a wagon, and then pick up speed as the train does, swirling past until the muted colors blur together. The jerkiness that nearly knocked me down eases with the increased speed.

I study my seatmate from the corner of my eyes. Her skin is a lovely smooth brown, deep and rich, so different from my pale, freckled flesh. I'm not sure what train etiquette is. Should I speak to her? Are white folks supposed to speak to black folks? Surely it can't hurt to be polite.

I turn to her. "Thanks for letting me join you. I'm Elizabeth Bertelsen."

"Evening, Miss Bertelsen," she says. "Jane James. Where you heading?"

"To Ogden, and then east to Cheyenne. And you?"

"Just to Ogden, visiting some friends. You from around here?"

I shake my head. "I was born in Salt Lake City, but I don't remember much of it. My parents moved to Sevier County when I was still little."

"Salt Lake's a fine place," she says. "It's been my home for over thirty years."

I do some rapid calculation: she must have arrived with the first wave of Mormon pioneers in 1847. I look at her in some surprise. "You're a Mormon?"

She chuckles a little. "Have been since before your mama was born, most like. Almost forty years now. I traveled from Connecticut to Nauvoo, Illinois, walked most of the way, even lived with the prophet Joseph."

A hot wash of shame makes my cheeks burn. Why did I assume—? Did I think all Mormons should look like me, like my family?

If Sister James notices me blushing, she kindly ignores it. Turning the conversation away from my gaffe, I ask, "What was the prophet Joseph like?"

Her eyes take on a faraway look. "He took me and my family in when we showed up with nothing, our shoes worn out from walking so far across frozen ground. Gave me a job. He wasn't a perfect man, but he was the finest man I ever saw."

"Did your family come with you to Utah?" I ask.

She shakes her head. "Only my husband and oldest son, Sylvester. Another son was born on the trail. But my mama and sisters and brothers stayed behind."

I want to ask Sister James why she came west when her family stayed behind, but Mama would say such questions are none of my business.

Maybe Sister James sees the question in my face, or maybe her reminiscences carry her, because she says, "I came anyway, because I wanted to be with the Saints. It hasn't always been easy. Sometimes I miss my mama, though she's gone now. And the Saints are only human, no better nor worse than most folks. But what they say and think of me doesn't matter so much as what God thinks, and I'm right where God wants me to be."

I shift in my seat, trying to find a better position on the uneven cushion of my chair. It doesn't sit right with me, the idea that maybe Sister James hasn't always been treated well by other Saints. I wonder if it's because of her color, or something else.

But mostly, I envy her certainty. "How do you know? Where God wants you to be?"

She looks at me sharply. "I can't tell you where God wants you. It's not my job, and you wouldn't want my advice anyway. You've got to figure that out yourself. One thing I am sure of: God wants you. He wants all of us, in our own ways."

A man in uniform stops by our seat, breaking off our conversation. I'm relieved. I don't want to think about which version of me God wants: the dutiful daughter who cares for her family, or the unruly girl who wants to study the stars. I'm afraid I already know.

The conductor inspects my ticket closely, checking the stamp on the back, and runs it through a tiny punch that leaves a crescent-shaped hole. He tears off part of the ticket, then returns it to me. He does the same for Sister James.

After he leaves, Sister James turns to the window, watching the darkened landscape flash past. She begins to hum, a low, warm rumble. After a minute, I catch the tune. It's a familiar hymn, and I begin to hum along with her.

Gird up your loins, fresh courage take
Our God will never us forsake.

We don't speak again until lights start appearing, like tiny earthbound stars. But the silence, like the car we ride in, feels warm. I sit up, tightening my grip on my carpetbag. The train pulls into the station with a screaming cry, and I resist the urge to clap my hands over my ears.

Everyone around me stands, making their way toward the door at the rear of the car. I do the same thing, with Sister James following close behind. I step carefully down the metal steps onto the wooden platform.

I drift behind others as they walk to the front of the train, where the porters, many of them black like Sister James, are handing down trunks. I spy mine and drag it toward the wooden frame building of the station.

All around me people are hugging on the platform, exchanging greetings and then going off with friends and family for the evening. I spy Sister James embracing a tall black woman somewhat younger than her. I stand for a moment, letting the wash of bodies ebb and flow around me, trying to get my bearings in this new space.

I've never been in Ogden before. How strange, to climb into a metal car and emerge in a new world. At least the nearly full moon overhead is familiar.

Samuel and Vilate Ann feel very far away in Salt Lake—Monroe farther away still. Everyone at home will likely be asleep by now, unless Albert has woken for a night feeding, or Rachel is restless.

A fierce, unexpected surge of homesickness sweeps over me, and I swallow. Squaring my shoulders, I walk into the small box of the station and see the ticket booth in one corner, shuttered for the night. A second pang hits me, this one of smoke-dark dread.

I assumed, somehow, that when I arrived in Ogden there would be another train waiting to take me east to Wyoming. But if the ticket counter is dark, there can be no trains for hours yet.

For a moment, everything swims around me, and I bang my shins against my trunk as I stumble. What am I to do? On the platform, I spy a few individuals tucked up on their trunks, blankets tight about them, prepared to sleep the night through beside the station.

I have slept beneath the stars before, on fine summer nights—but that was always with family sleeping beside me. I think of sharing this open space with strangers—with strange men—and something cold twists inside me. But what is the alternative? I know no one in Ogden, and though I might find a hotel near the station, I do not have the money for it.

The sense of possibility that filled me when Far mentioned traveling to Wyoming has utterly vanished. How could I think I might handle college away from home, if an empty train station undoes me?

I grip the handle of my carpetbag with both hands and stare fixedly at my fingers, blinking hard so I will not cry.

"You all right, miss?"

I look up to find a porter beside me, brown skin a few shades lighter than Sister James's.

"Yes, I'm fine," I say. "Only I thought I could purchase a ticket for the train to Cheyenne."

"Next train doesn't leave till morning," he says, nodding at a time board on the wall. It reads: OMAHA, 8 A.M. Next to it, in smaller print, are some of the intermediary stops: LARAMIE, CHEYENNE, KEARNEY.

Eight a.m. Nearly nine hours away. I suppose I can sit up all night. I've done it before, when one of the children was sick. But the thought of those long hours stretching out in this unfamiliar station is almost more than I can bear. "Thank you," I choke.

The porter tips his cap. "My pleasure." He strides off across the platform, to more important (and likely paying) business.

The strains of the hymn Sister James was humming come back to me: *Fresh courage take.*

Mama left England alone, without any of her family, to sail on a strange ship to a strange new place because she believed it was right. Samuel's family crossed the plains with only hand-carts to carry their goods, often sleeping on frosty ground, or in snow. Sister James walked to Nauvoo from Connecticut in worn-out shoes. I could weather an evening alone on a warm summer night.

I pull my luggage up to the wall of the station, stow the few

items in my carpetbag in my trunk, and then curl atop it, rolling up the carpetbag under my head for a pillow. The night is full of sound: insects, the gentle and not-so-gentle snores of my fellow passengers, the rattle of carriages on the street beyond the station, a faraway owl. The stars waltz across the sky in orchestrated figures.

✦

When morning comes, reaching gray fingers across the sky, I sit up and stretch. I don't feel as if I've slept at all, but I must have. Relief swirls through me, making my limbs weak: I made it through the night.

I swig some water from my canteen as I repack my carpetbag, and then splash some on my face. My mouth feels stuffed with cotton, and I have an urgent need for a bathroom. I find an outhouse not far from the station, then purchase some fruit from a stall for breakfast. Last of all, I buy the ticket for the train that will carry me to Cheyenne.

The train arrives only a few minutes late, and before long, we're speeding across the valley, toward the Wasatch mountains towering along the eastern rim. We plunge into the canyon, rocky ridges rising up around us, stone monoliths punctuating the landscape. The canyon levels out to brief flatness, and then the rocks close in. While we cross through a tunnel, the light vanishes, reappearing once we're out again.

Everything is new, and I cannot look away.

A water boy comes through the cabin, and I refill my canteen. Eventually I rise to walk about the car. I want to explore further, to see the finery of the first-class carriages that I only glimpsed before boarding, but when I open the door at the rear of the car, I see the wheels rushing across the rails beneath me, and there is a painted sign asking passengers not to stand on the small platform. To cross to another car, as the water boy and conductor do, I'd have to brave a two-foot gap—impossible with my long skirts. I take a deep breath and return to my seat.

There are all sorts of people in my car, as though the railroad is a little slice of America: White farmers in plain homespun clothes like me. Some white men in suits far nicer than any I've seen before, with silk cravats and embroidered waistcoats. An Indian couple, colorful woven blankets about their shoulders. A handful of black men, who, from their conversation, are tired of the gold mines in California and determined to try the silver mines in Colorado. I picture our paths as bright lines on a map, drawn from all over, converging briefly on the train, then diverging again once we reach our destinations.

It is just past one in the afternoon when we pull into Evanston, our first stop in Wyoming. The preceding stops, some nine of them, were all brief: only long enough for a few passengers to disembark and others to board. We are to have a half-hour's break here to eat, and I join the crowds waiting to leave the train.

Near the station is the Mountain Trout Hotel, which, true

to its name, serves up fried mountain trout. The rich smell fills the air as soon as we enter the dining room, and my mouth waters. I have a few remaining dollars in my purse, but I cannot squander them all now. Instead, I order a biscuit and some tea and am seated at a table with a few other ladies. Many of the waiters bustling through the crowded room are Chinese. I wonder how they came to be here, if they like it so far from home. Or maybe Wyoming is home now.

My tea has scarcely begun to cool when I see people already rushing back toward the train. I gulp down the rest of it, though it scalds my tongue and throat and makes my eyes water. My second-class ticket does not give me stopover privileges. If I miss this train, I shall have to purchase an entirely new ticket, and I haven't the money for that.

As I pass through the restaurant, I scoop up a discarded Colorado newspaper on one of the seats, then dash for the train.

The train begins to move just as I've finished climbing to the car, and I'm forced to grab the side of the door to maintain my balance. I walk down the rocking aisles to my seat— only to find it occupied in my absence by an elderly couple.

I look around for an open seat, and spot one by a prim middle-aged woman, whose erectness of carriage suggests she might be a schoolteacher. I make my way toward her. "Is this seat taken?"

The woman turns her head to look at me. Her eyes travel slowly from my handmade straw hat to my home-sewn clothes and dusty shoes. Her nose pinches slightly.

"Are you from Utah?" she asks at last.

"Yes, ma'am."

"Are you a Mormon?"

Some imp prompts me to respond, "I belong to the Church of Jesus Christ of Latter-day Saints." That's the official name of the church, though it mostly only gets used in sermons.

She continues to stare at me, eyebrow raised.

Deflated, I add, "Some folks know us as Mormons, ma'am."

She looks away from me, out the window, drawing her skirts toward her as though she fears my very presence will pollute her. "Find somewhere else to sit."

I stand frozen for a moment, heat rising from my neck to suffuse my face until even my forehead burns. Everyone near us is staring at me. The elderly couple who have my original seat whisper to one another. A few of their words float back to me: "deluded," "brazen," "dirty."

Shame tastes sharp and bitter in my throat.

Tightening my grip on my bag, I turn around, marching toward the rear of the car.

Finding a pair of empty seats, I take the seat by the window so I can turn my face outward and only the glass can see the tears stinging my eyes. I unfold the paper, breathing deeply the smell of wood pulp and ink, and let the pages obscure my face. I forgot I was no longer in Utah, that the opinions of outsiders aren't just ink on pulp, but living in real, breathing folks.

I search the pages, looking for more news of the upcoming

eclipse to distract myself. At last I see it, squirreled away in a small box on the penultimate page.

> **Miss Maria Mitchell, Professor of Astronomy at Vassar College, is planning an expedition to Denver to view the eclipse in the company of several current and former students. Though we assume such an outing will be good for airing of the old girls (who do not otherwise get taken out much), we question whether they will be able to add much to the luminaries already gathering for the historic event: Thomas Edison, Henry Draper, Dr. Charles Young, James Watson, and many more. Undoubtedly a case of "girls can too," we shall see if the girls can, indeed, contribute anything other than ornament to the study of science.**

My own shame forgotten, I let the paper fall with a gasp, torn between outrage at the ridiculous tone and a thrill of pleasure. Miss Mitchell—my scientific hero—will be in Denver? Denver is not far from Cheyenne, less than a day's ride by train.

I indulge in a few minutes of spectacular daydreams, of offering my services to Professor Mitchell. Of somehow contributing something that would transform our understanding of eclipses. Perhaps I would glimpse Vulcan, the planet some astronomers believe exists in orbit between Mercury and the sun. Perhaps I would notice some new feature of the corona.

In my daydream, Professor Mitchell is so moved by my work that she offers me a spot at Vassar at once.

But the daydream cannot survive the rude interruption of reality. Even supposing Rebekka does not need my help (and what new mother, with a weeks-old baby, is fully healed and restored?), how am I to afford the train to Denver? As it is, I shall have to wire Far to send me more money when I am ready to return. And why should Professor Mitchell offer a valuable spot among her crew to a girl who is essentially untrained?

I sigh and fold the paper up and try to let the gentle rocking of the train across the Wyoming plains lull me to sleep.

✦

The train lurches to a stop. Startled, I flail awake and peer out the darkened windows. Around me, people are sleeping, though a few have been awakened by the stop as I have.

I can see no lights outside, except the stars, the wash of moonlight across empty plains. Has there been an accident?

A door bangs in a carriage farther up the line and I hear shouting.

Then a single gunshot, loud in the still night.

Around me, others rouse, their voices raised in anxiety. All down the rail car, the word whispers like a wave: *Robbery.*

chapter seven

Thursday, July 11, 1878
Somewhere Near Rawlins, Wyoming
Eighteen days until eclipse

A man in a white mask bursts through the forward door of the carriage and several women scream. One, near the door, faints and her startled partner waves smelling salts beneath her nose to revive her, the acrid scent filling the car. I slide some of my thin stack of bills and loose coins into my boot, my heart beating wildly, and start to pray.

The man tells us to stand, waving a gun carelessly. He herds us toward the back of the compartment, where a single lamp burns beside the door and where we cannot gang up behind him.

"Right, then." He gestures with his gun again and moves down our ragged line, relieving women of jewelry and men of pocket watches and dollar bills and stuffing them into a bag.

When he reaches me, I swallow at the narrow mouth of the gun pointed at my head.

No wonder the heroines in all those dime novels faint when confronted by train robbers. Fainting seems infinitely more pleasant than this cold knot of fear lurching through my belly. I could die here. How did I ever think stories like this were exciting?

I hold out the remainder of my money. The man takes it, feels how flimsy the stack is, and snorts. My hidden money burns like a brand against my leg.

"Open the bag."

My carpetbag is looped over my arm: I grabbed it out of habit, not any logical thought. I wrench it open, exposing my book, some bread and apples, and a change of undergarments. The robber paws through, dirty fingers brushing against my most intimate things.

He shoves my bag back at me, and I stumble against the man behind me. I fall to my knees, but the man I've bumped into manages to catch himself, his fingers digging into my shoulder.

The robber's gun swivels between us. "Here, now, nothing funny."

I remain still, my knees pressed painfully against the hard floor of the rail car. The man behind me releases my shoulder and lifts both hands in a sign of surrender. I watch him from the corner of my eye.

"The girl fell," he says. "Nothing more." He has the light,

cultured voice of an eastern businessman and dark, shining hair. He reaches into his coat pocket, and the robber fires, the bullet whizzing past the dark-haired man's head and cracking through one of the glass windows of the train.

A wave of dizziness passes through me, my bent knees cutting off the flow of blood to my head. I need to stand, but I don't dare.

The man behind me holds out a thick wad of bills. His arm trembles. "Sorry. I was just reaching for this."

The robber takes the money, eyes glittering behind his mask, and while he quickly flicks through the stack, the dark-haired man helps me stand.

A single coin, knocked loose from my boot by my fall, drops to the ground with a faint clink.

I freeze.

The dark mouth of the gun swings back to me.

"You holdin' out on me?" The robber stuffs the dark-haired man's money into his bag and stalks toward me. He presses the cold muzzle of the gun right up to my temple.

The man leans toward me, his breath hot against my ear. "I've a mind to shoot you right here, show these folks what happens when they try to cheat me."

My own breath halts.

There are faint protesting murmurs in the car around me, but nobody tries to stop the man.

✦

This is it.

I'll not see Mama nor Far nor Hyrum nor Rachel nor any of the other children again in this life. I close my eyes, my whole body braced for the loud retort, the explosion of pain.

That hot breath comes again. "Lucky for you, I'm feeling generous. Take off your boots."

I bend slowly, my fingers fumbling almost blindly for the laces at the tops of my boots. The gun follows my movements, still fixed to my head. I have to hitch up my skirts to get at my boots, and on top of the fear pulsing through me, there's a dark thread of humiliation that I have to expose my legs, my stockinged feet, to the staring eyes of strangers.

Now is no time for modesty. I tug at the laces, nearly weeping when they won't come. Impatient with my slowness, the robber says, "You keep at that. I'mma collect money from the rest of these folks and be back for what you owe me."

The gun leaves my head, and I draw a long, shaky breath.

The robber makes his way down to the end of our line. Everyone obeys this time, handing him their money and valuables in silence. I keep working at my laces. I pull one shoe free, then the other. There's no money in the second shoe, but the robber won't know that, and I don't want to risk his wrath again.

The robber returns just as I remove the second shoe. "Dump them in," he says, gesturing with his gun at the bag he holds.

I shake out the first boot, and all the money I have in the

94

world tumbles into the bag. My ankles and feet feel exposed—the metal floor of the carriage is cool beneath my skin. I shake the second, and nothing falls but a bit of lint.

The man's gaze flicks up to mine, assessing. The eyes behind his mask are blue like ice.

He lifts the gun again, and I flinch.

From somewhere down the line, a whistle sounds, piercing and sharp.

The gun lowers.

The masked man backs away toward the door, his gun still fixed on the carriage, on me. He reaches behind him for the handle, and the door swings open with a bang. He whirls, jumps from the car, and disappears into the night.

A woman starts sobbing.

I grasp the back of the seat nearest me, not sure my legs will hold me. The dark-haired man scoops up my carpetbag and dusts off the bottom before handing it back to me.

"Are you all right?" he asks.

I nod, not trusting myself to speak without crying.

Around me, others start drifting back to their seats, stumbling a little in shock. The dark-haired man returns my nod and then heads back up the carriage.

Collapsing onto the seat I've been gripping, I set my bag beside me and hug my boots to my chest. Then I start shaking and can't seem to stop.

I stare out the window into the Wyoming darkness. The landscape is washed silver by the nearly full moon. If I crane my head, I can just make out Jupiter and the Lyra constellation.

We're alive.

It's all right.

It's all right.

It's all right.

The words keep time in my head with my ragged breathing. I try to offer a prayer of gratitude, but I can't find the right words.

I'm still shaking when the conductor comes through the car several long minutes later.

"Tracks have been sabotaged," he says. "We won't be able to move on till they're fixed."

"But what are we to do?" a woman asks.

"You can shelter in the car for tonight. We've wired ahead to Rawlins—they should be sending along wagons and aid in an hour or two."

At the growing murmurs, the conductor lifts a hand. "Or you can walk. Rawlins is just a few miles down the road—you can be there in an hour or two yourself."

"And our baggage?" an older man asks, his skin ruddy against his white hair.

"A wagon will fetch it. You can wait for another train in Rawlins."

"And what of the robbery? Will the sheriff get our money back?"

The conductor shakes his head. "You'll have to ask the

sheriff." He waves off further questions, making his way to the next car down the line.

I stay motionless for a moment, letting his words sink in. The train car still bears the acrid scent of smelling salts and fear. It no longer feels safe.

All at once, I can't bear being inside this iron car with its sloping walls, waiting for help to arrive. Better to be doing something. Better to be moving under the stars and the moon. I stop hugging my boots, slipping them on my feet instead.

I stand and go to the door of the carriage, my carpetbag clutched in my fist. Opening it, I peer out to find a handful of people—mostly single men—already disembarking to walk along the rail line toward Rawlins. The moon casts an eerie glow across an unfamiliar landscape. The phantom memory of the gun still presses against my head. I'm not sure I can make the trek alone, or with a strange man.

Especially not with a strange man. The glittering ice eyes of the robber rise in my mind.

I nearly go back to my seat.

Wait.

At the end of the train, the first-class compartment disgorges a couple. Young, from the energy in their steps. She wears some well-cut traveling dress in a pale color, and his collar and waistcoat gleam in the moonlit darkness. Her curly hair is done up underneath a hat covered in some gauzy stuff, and he wears a derby.

Releasing a slow breath of relief, I climb down the metal

stairs and approach them. "Excuse me! Are you walking to Rawlins?"

The young woman looks up at me: she's pretty, with wide, dark eyes and full lips. Though the moon leaches color from everything, I think her skin is a few shades darker than mine. "Yes, I believe so. By the time help arrives and transports this lot to Rawlins, there will be no place to be had in town for love or money."

Not that I have any money. I push the thought aside. I'll work for my lodging, if I have to. "May I walk with you?"

Her companion shrugs. "It's a free country, isn't it?"

The young woman pokes him and whispers, "Will! Be nice. She's just been through an ordeal. We all have."

The young man—Will—whips his derby off, revealing tight dark curls beneath, and gives me a very formal bow. "I beg your pardon, madame. My name is William Lancelot Stevens, and like my namesake knight, I am at your service."

His gesture is so extravagant that I find myself smiling, some of the chill that has lingered since the robbery lifting from my body. He grins at me, his teeth flashing white in the moonlight. I dip a rough curtsy. "Elizabeth Bertelsen."

Will nods at the young lady beside him, whose folded arms and fissured brow suggest she doesn't find him as amusing as I do. "My sister, Alice."

"How do you do, Miss Stevens?"

"As well as can be expected, considering I have to walk to the next stop, instead of sleeping cozily in my compartment." But she smiles, to take the sting from her complaint.

As the pair starts walking again, I scramble to catch up with them. Only a handful of travelers are moving, strung alongside the rails like beads on a cord. Most of the passengers have opted to wait for help.

Some hundred feet or so in front of the train we see the sabotage—someone has wrenched up the iron tracks, rolled aside the wooden supports that hold the track in place. No trains will be coming this way tonight. I wonder how many trains will back up behind ours before the tracks are fixed.

We pass the time at first with introductions. The Stevens siblings are from Denver—a fact I learn with a sharp stab of envy. They have no other siblings, and their grandfather, Alice tells me proudly, owns one of the finest hotels in Denver.

"The Trans-Oceana," she says. "Our grandfather escaped from slavery as a boy, and made his way to Chicago, where he worked for an abolitionist magazine. A friend of his convinced him to come west, to make his fortune, and he did."

In the last couple of days, I've had more conversations with black folks than I have in the whole of my life. They haven't been anything like I expected: Sister James was a Mormon like me, and the Stevens siblings have more money and education than anyone I know in Monroe, judging from their clothes and speech. My assumptions have been born of newspaper articles and conversations I've overheard, but I should have known better. Goodness knows people have enough faulty notions about Mormons. What else have I gotten wrong?

A good scientist should always examine her assumptions.

"Your grandpa sounds pretty remarkable," I say, and Alice smiles at me. "I never knew my grandparents. My parents came to America from England and Denmark and left their parents behind."

Alice asks me about my family, and I tell her about my nine siblings. Her eyes grow wide.

Will says, "I suppose you never lack for company."

"No," I agree. "But sometimes I wish I did."

I don't tell them my family is Mormon. I'm not entirely sure why, except that I think of the woman on the train who refused to let me sit by her. I don't want to see the open expression in the siblings' faces grow cold and closed.

We walk on, following the tracks in the moonlight. Will and Alice tell me some of the sights they saw in California, where they went to visit their father's sister: orange groves and the ocean, old Catholic missions. I have no similar stories to share, but I enjoy listening to their easy banter, though it brings with it an unexpected pang of homesickness. Sometimes my sisters and I would tease each other so. Hyrum was never one to tease, but I miss him too. I wonder how Rachel is doing, and shiver.

Alice notices. "Are you cold?"

"A little," I say. Even July nights can be cool in this arid region. But our movement helps, and at least the cool air means any rattlesnakes will be sluggish.

Most of the other walkers, men with long strides, have outpaced us. My flat-bottomed boots handle the uneven terrain just fine, but Alice's fine boots, with their pretty little heels, struggle occasionally. Alice is game, though, and doesn't complain.

Some distance into our trek—perhaps an hour?—a motley collection of a carriage and a pair of wagons appears, on a narrow track scarcely visible in the dim light. Each vehicle has a lantern hanging by the driver, as yet unlit because the moon renders them unnecessary.

I eye them as they approach. The first carriage is mostly filled already, with men in hats and sober expressions who are no doubt officials of some sort—perhaps the sheriff and his men, with a doctor along for support. The two wagons between them won't carry all the passengers remaining on the train. I suspect it will be a long wait for some of them.

"You comin' from the train?" The driver of the carriage hails us.

Will murmurs, "What train? We are but hardy souls who delight in taking a midnight pleasure stroll in the middle of nowhere."

I smother a grin. Will's irrepressible humor reminds me of Samuel's.

"Yes, sir," Alice calls back, sending a sideways look at her brother.

"Very good. The sheriff may be wantin' to speak with you after we've finished with the train, if you could please make yourselves available at the hotel. Rawlins is about four miles that way." The driver gestures behind him. "Can't miss it if you follow the tracks."

Four miles? The conductor said Rawlins was only an hour

or two away, but four miles, in the dark, will likely take us nearly two more hours. The conductor's measure of distances must be affected by the speed of the train. Will and Alice exchange a look.

The men on the wagon don't offer us a ride, which is just as well. I doubt they'd have room for us and the waiting passengers, and at their speed—only scarcely faster than ours—we'll reach Rawlins well before they can reach the train and return.

My optimism only lasts another quarter of an hour, at which point clouds draw across the moon, blotting out the landscape. I step on an uneven pocket of ground and stumble, dropping my carpetbag again and catching myself on my hands. They sting, but close inspection shows they're only scratched.

"Are you all right?" Alice asks.

"I'm fine." I get to my feet and brush my hands against my skirts, then pluck up my bag.

There's a little light, as the moon peeps intermittently through the clouds, but it's not consistent. We've still another hour or two until dawn, and it's almost impossible to see when the moon vanishes. At least we can still make out the tracks, stretching out before us, and the way is mostly clear. No dense thickets or wooded areas for us to fight through, though the sagebrush and other low-lying shrubs snag at our skirts as we pass.

We trudge on.

When I set out, a stroll beneath the moon had seemed

preferable to remaining in a stuffy passenger car full of the memory and smell of the brief terror of the robbery. Now I'm not so sure.

Something shuffles through nearby grasses. Something large.

Alice freezes, grasps Will's arm. Will fishes in his jacket and comes out with something small and gleaming. A pistol. I feel again the cool echo of the gun against my head and step away.

"What was that?" Alice asks. "There aren't wolves this close to the rail line, are there?"

I don't tell her that wolves generally know better than to make themselves known to their prey through their noise. My own heart is beating harder and faster than is comfortable.

"We'd have heard them howling," Will says, reassuringly, though he doesn't put his gun back.

Could be a bear, I think.

The clouds break just then. A shaft of light illuminates the landscape around us, and the grasses rustle again.

A tawny furred creature emerges from behind a bush, spindly-legged and the size of a large dog, with white spots sprinkled along its back.

"Oh," says Alice, laughing a little in relief. "It's just a deer."

The creature blinks at us.

"I don't think it's a deer," I say. "Look at the coat—it's just a baby." Maybe elk? I've seen elk a few times, but seldom this young.

Alice takes a step toward it.

Then, even through my exhaustion, alarm sings through me. "Don't touch it!" I say, more sharply than I intended.

Alice blinks at me. "But it's just a baby."

Will, who must have had more experience with nature than his city-bred sister, catches on quickly. "I doubt it's a—"

Before he's finished speaking, there's an unearthly noise, something between a scream and a growl. A much larger shape erupts through the shrubs, and the three of us emit various shrieks.

A cow elk faces us. She's tall—much taller than I am, probably taller even than Will. It's early in the day for her to be abroad. Maybe we passed her nest and woke her. She stares at us a moment, her large dark eyes unblinking, her nostrils quivering. Her ears lie back. She stomps her front feet—then charges.

The ground beneath us seems to rumble. A roaring sound fills my head.

And as I always seem to do in times of crisis, I freeze.

There's a strand of trees not far from us. I know—*I know*—that the trees offer our best protection. But I can't seem to get my brain to stop spinning and my feet to start moving.

Alice grabs my hand and starts to run, shocking me from my stupor. But she's running parallel to the tracks, not toward the grove.

"The trees!" I manage, pulling Alice to the left.

Will, possibly with some misguided notion of chivalry, darts across our path, toward the tracks, and waves his arms in the air. The cow ignores him—perhaps because his waving arms make him appear a threat, perhaps because our fluttering skirts draw her attention.

She's coming straight at us.

I knew a man that died, accidentally trampled by a bull. Shoving Alice ahead of me, I duck behind a tree. Alice sucks in air beside me, her back flat against a trunk.

The cow elk, satisfied that she's defended some invisible territorial line, shies away from the trees and drops her head. She barks once at her calf, and then the two trot off.

Alice and I look at each other.

"Glory be," Alice breathes. "Was that a moose?"

"No," I say, still fighting to breathe properly. "An elk."

Then we both laugh, relief and hysteria mixing together until we are both crying. Will lopes over to us, carrying Alice's hat, which fell off in our mad dash. The elk put her foot square through the gauzy thing, leaving a gaping hole.

"Whoo," Will says, grinning fit to burst. "That was some rush, wasn't it?"

Alice catches her breath, spies the hat, and sets off laughing again. My sides ache from laughing, but it feels good too—a release of all the tension and fear and anxiety of this night, the past two nights, really, since I left Salt Lake City alone.

And then the skies open up.

chapter eight

Thursday, July 11, 1878
Somewhere Near Rawlins, Wyoming
Eighteen days until eclipse

For a moment we just stand under the rain, laughing, because the alternative would be to cry. Nothing about this night—morning?—has gone as I planned. My only hope now is that neither dawn nor Rawlins is too far off. Within the span of the last half hour, I have been by turns terrified, tired, cold—and now wet, with blisters starting on both feet, thanks to my damp stockings.

Will starts walking again, and, grumbling only a little, Alice and I follow. My stomach growls, though it's impossible to hear over the distant rumble of thunder. My skirts, growing slowly heavier with the water, tangle about my legs and I have to step carefully to avoid tumbling over. Walking through the downpour is like trying to swim fully clothed.

That look suits you. I shake my head, trying to clear the echo of Samuel's words from my head. No doubt he would find all this funny. For a brief second, I find myself wanting to tell him, if only to hear his laugh. I push the feeling away. We were never really friends, and after the way we left things in Salt Lake City, not even that.

In the absence of her hat, Alice's finely coiffed hair is falling down about her cheeks in messy curls. A great hunk of hair slips over her eyes just as her boot slides along the muddy ground, and she lets out a decidedly unladylike word. Or two. Will catches her before she falls.

She looks back at me swiftly, one hand over her mouth. Does she think I would judge her for her words?

I grin at her. "I couldn't have said it better myself."

She laughs and presses forward.

My wet dress begins to chafe. A gust of wind whips sodden hair into my eyes, and I blink at the sting. I'd give every dollar I don't have just to be dry.

Will begins singing. "Then meet me at twilight before the bright waters . . ."

Alice sighs. "Bright waters, Will, really? Isn't the rain enough for you?"

He flashes her an unrepentant grin over his shoulder and continues to sing the love ballad. Am I imagining things, or is the landscape growing brighter? No—a thin gray line edges the horizon ahead of us. And beneath that—

"Are those lights?" I ask.

Alice lifts her hand to block the rain from her eyes and

squints into the dimness. "I do believe they are. Hallelujah—Rawlins at last!"

Sighting the town gives us renewed energy, and we stumble toward the lights. But hope also makes me incautious: I haven't gone a dozen steps before I put my foot on a mud slick and go down. But there's no Samuel to laugh at me here.

Alice exclaims, and she and Will help me to my feet. I'd attempt to brush the dirt off my backside, but I'm afraid clean clothes are a lost cause and the mud will only spread. I'll simply have to hope that my trunk arrives with the train before too long. At least there will be hot food at the hotel, and it will be dry.

There isn't much to the town as we stumble into it, but it looks plenty fine, and a good sight nicer than the bleary darkness we've traveled through. A simple wooden station lit by a few lanterns stands alongside the tracks. Beside it rests the hotel, the front ablaze with lights. Scattered before it lie a handful of houses and other buildings, most everything coated in the same rust-red paint.

We head directly for the hotel. In the lobby, Will pauses. "Why don't you ladies take a seat in the dining room, get some tea or something warm in you? I'll take care of the rooms."

I bite my lip. I haven't any money to my name, let alone a sum sufficient to cover the cost of a room—but I can't simply hole up in the dining room until the train arrives, which might take another day or two. Perhaps the clerk will let me work in exchange for lodging—I could wash dishes or clean rooms.

"Thanks all the same," I say, "but I can arrange for my own room."

Will shrugs. "Suit yourself, Miss Bertelsen."

"Oh, please call me Elizabeth. After the night we've had, it seems silly to be so formal."

Will only nods. In the dim glow of the lamplight, his light brown skin looks chalky with exhaustion. His fine hat is matted and droopy. Alice, too, looks ready to drop. There's a smudge of dirt across one cheek, and her hair is all undone. I probably look even worse—my skirt torn and muddy where I fell.

Alice and I follow Will to the front desk. A skinny young man with a prominent Adam's apple looks up as Will approaches. After a quick survey, his gaze goes back to some papers before him, and he pretends to be engrossed.

"Excuse me," Will says. "We've come from the train—no doubt you've heard now about the damage to the track and the robbery. I'll need two rooms for the night, for me and for my sister."

The young man lifts his head again, his blue eyes disdainful. "I can't give you two rooms. We've already got a group here for that eclipse, and we're expecting a load from the train. I can put you in with another man, and your sister will have to share. Unless you're wanting to share yourselves."

Will sighs. "That will be fine."

The young man's eyes skip past Will to me, and his tone brightens a bit. "And you, miss, are you needing a room?"

"Maybe," I say. "That is, yes, I hope so, but how much are the rooms?"

"Six dollars," he says, after a pause that makes me think that is not their typical rate. Alice's gasp behind me confirms that. My heart sinks.

"Six dollars!" Alice says. "Why, that's extortion. My grand-father doesn't charge more than five dollars for the finest rooms in his Denver hotel, and it's ten times nicer than this one."

"There's no other hotels here and there's going to be lots of folks looking for rooms." The young man shrugs. "Take it or leave it."

"We'll take it," Will says, waving at Alice to be quiet.

"I'm afraid I haven't so much," I say. "All my money was stolen on the train. But I can work for you—cleaning, wash-ing, whatever you need. Surely you'll need extra hands with the crowd coming. And I don't need my own room."

"Lady," he says, in a tone that suggests he thinks I am any-thing but, "nobody is getting their own room tonight. And if you can't pay up front, you can't have a bed."

Everything in me aches. I am cold, I am wet, and the thought of sitting up for hours, even in the dry dining room, makes me want to cry. I wish I was home, warm in my own bed, listening to my sisters snore.

Will reaches in his pocket, then freezes. He looks up at the clerk, eyes wide. "I—the robbery. I can wire for money from my father, but it might take some time to arrive."

The clerk sighs, and repeats, as though to a slow child, "If you can't pay up front, you can't have a room."

"My grandfather owns the Trans-Oceana in Denver," Will says. "I promise you my family is good for the money."

Alice lifts her chin and sails past Will and me, coming to a stop at the desk and setting her palms atop it. "Mr. . . ."

"Colburn," he supplies with obvious reluctance.

"Mr. Colburn. Tonight I have survived a train robbery, an elk attack, and a thunderstorm. I do not intend to be routed by a small-minded clerk who is likely pocketing the excess of his extortionate rates. I suppose your manager might be quite surprised to find out about your new charges—you see, I do understand how hotels work." Her eyes glow, and despite her bedraggled state, there's an elegance to her I wish I could imitate.

The man's eyes grow wide, and he steps back a pace, even though there's a desk separating him from Alice.

Alice reaches up, unfastening a choker that was hidden beneath the high collar of her shirt, a cameo hung on three strands of pearls. "These pearls are genuine. They should more than cover our stay, however long we choose to stay, and whatever attentions we might demand."

"Yes, ma'am," the man manages.

Alice looks back at me. "Elizabeth, why don't you stay with me? Your thinking of the trees saved me from death by elk trampling tonight, so it seems only fair. And you'll spare me from listening to Will snore—or rooming with a total stranger."

"I—" My nose prickles with imminent tears at her kindness. She's the one that saved me, by getting me moving when I stood frozen.

"You should say thank you," Will advises. "It's faster."

"Thank you," I say, thanksgiving welling up inside me along with actual tears. I blink rapidly and brush them from my cheeks.

Alice turns back to the clerk. "You'll find my brother a room with a gentleman, if you please, and have someone bring some tea and toast up to our rooms as soon as can be managed. We'll want some warm water too."

"Yes, ma'am." The clerk fetches two keys from somewhere beneath the desk, and hands them both to Alice. Then he leads us, personally, up to the second floor, showing Alice and me to an empty room at the end of the corridor and Will to one a few doors down.

We help each other out of our wet and muddy dresses, a difficult task with cold fingers and sodden fabric. The room has two narrow beds, one against each wall, and I wrap myself in the blanket, already feeling more cheerful now that I am no longer freezing and face the prospect of a real bed. While Alice fusses over her bed arrangement, I whisper a prayer of genuine gratitude.

I mean to stay awake for the arrival of hot water and food, but I don't make it more than a minute before I collapse onto the bed and sleep.

chapter nine

Thursday, July 11, 1878

Rawlins, Wyoming

Eighteen days until eclipse

There's still no sign of our trunks later that morning when we awake, so Alice and I do our best to brush the dirt from the dresses we wore the night before and put them on again. I inspect the contents of my carpetbag in some dismay. My canteen suffered no harm, and the small wooden comb is still intact, but my two books are soaked through, their pages buckled and smeared. I take them out with a small cry.

Alice whirls from her spot at the small vanity. "What is it? Are you hurt?"

"No," I say, though I wish it were only that I'd hurt myself. The books belong to Miss Wheeler, and how I shall replace them I don't know.

Alice's eyes fall to the books clutched against my chest.

She walks briskly across the room and opens the window, letting a sweet-smelling breeze into the room. The summer day is rich with the scent of wet earth. Alice takes one of the books from me, and sets it on my bed, near the window— open so a few pages flutter in the wind.

"Maybe some air will dry them out," she says.

I hurry to add the second book to the first. I shouldn't hurt so for a book—but it's not just the physical damage, it's the thought of letting down Miss Wheeler, of losing the words myself. "Thank you."

After we've repaired our hair as best we can, we head downstairs. The small dining hall is full to overflowing— clearly, the passengers from the train have all been rescued, and they've been joined now by the passengers on the westbound train, forced to wait in Rawlins until the track is repaired. There's no sign of Will.

A new clerk, a middle-aged man with a drooping mustache, suggests that we try the Union Pacific restaurant, as it's likely to be less crowded.

My boots still squelch a bit as we walk down the street, and I notice Alice wincing as she steps. We're both recovering from the long trek last night.

If the Union Pacific restaurant—a square, boxy sort of place with round tables shoved close together—is any less crowded, I can't see the difference. But we do spot Will, sitting with a pair of strangers at a table near the back, and he waves us over.

We weave through the crowd to the table. There are not quite enough chairs for all of us. Alice offers to share one with me, but I worry that my wide hips won't allow her enough space to sit and so I refuse. One of the gentlemen with Will, a tallish man with a bushy mustache, stands and offers me his seat. My face burns—I didn't mean to displace anyone—but I sit down.

Will's eyes are bright. "Alice, may I introduce you to my roommate from the hotel?" He gestures to the man beside him, a handsome young man of about thirty, with a clean jawline. "This is Mr. Thomas Edison!"

I nearly fall off my seat. Now that Will has named him, I recognize him from his photos in the paper, though of course people look so much more vivid in real life. How has he come to be in Rawlins? I answer my own question—for the eclipse, of course. Rawlins must be in the path of totality. If the eclipse were not still more than two weeks distant, I'd think our train accident was providential. But surely the trains will be up before then, and duty will carry me on to Cheyenne and out of the eclipse's path.

Will introduces the second gentleman, the one whom I displaced, as Dr. Henry Morton, who is the president of Stevens Institute of Technology. Knowing his importance, I feel all the more wretched at having forced him from his seat.

I try to apologize, but Dr. Morton says, "Nonsense! You must allow me to be of service to a lady."

I watch Alice dip her head gracefully in acknowledgment

and try to do the same, wishing furiously that I had something nicer to wear than my torn, stained dress, with my hair pulled back in a severe braid. Dr. Morton's "lady" is generous, and I like him for it.

Alice and Will make light conversation with our new acquaintances as Mr. Edison finishes up his breakfast. From the empty plate before me, I deduce that Dr. Morton was already finished. I'm too overawed to do much but listen, but as Mr. Edison pushes his plate away and prepares to stand, I manage to speak.

"Are you here for the eclipse, Mr. Edison?"

He smiles a bit wryly at me, one side of his mouth dipping up more than the other. "Yes, though more in the capacity of a student and observer than a true researcher. I told reporters before I left New York that I know no more of an eclipse than a pig does of learning Latin. Dr. Morton and Dr. Draper are the true scientists of our group."

Dr. Morton shakes his head. "Edison knows more than he's letting on. But it's true that I've had some experience with eclipses—I helped photograph the 1869 eclipse in Iowa, and a rare experience that was."

Edison claps his hands on his trousers and stands. "We really must be going—we've got work to do, setting up our observation site, but we hope to have at least a rough frame up by evening. You're welcome to stop by to see Dr. Draper's telescope, if you'd like. It's quite extraordinary."

Dr. Morton shakes his head in mock displeasure. At least, I think he's not truly upset, because a smile flickers around his mouth. "Edison, if it were up to you, the whole town would turn out for our telescopes."

"And why not? Isn't science meant to be shared?" Edison smiles at me. "What do you say, Miss Bertelsen?"

"I'd be honored, sir!" I no longer care that I'm hungry and dirty—I've an invitation from *Thomas Edison* to see a real telescope.

The two men depart, and Will leaves us to flag down a waiter. Alice turns to me, a slight smile tugging at her lips. "First those science books in your bag, now the eclipse. I admit, I'd not even thought of the eclipse in connection with these men and couldn't for the life of me figure out why someone as renowned as Thomas Edison was staying in a rotten hotel in the middle of nowhere. You've been holding out on me, Elizabeth. Are you a scientist too?"

"Not really," I say quickly, lest Alice give me more credit than I deserve. "Only interested, is all. I'd like to study astronomy, but there's not much call for that in the small town where I live, and my family needs me."

"Hmm," Alice says. "I'm not sure need is the only worthwhile reason for doing something. Look at me. Do you know what I'd like to do more than anything?"

I shake my head. I don't remember Alice saying anything the night before about great dreams, but surely a girl with money is capable of bigger dreams than a poor frontier girl like me. But then, being a woman always seems to limit some dreams, and probably being colored affects the kinds of dreams she lets herself have, like being Mormon affects mine.

Sometimes the things we are, whether we choose them or not, shape the things we can be. Sure doesn't seem fair, though.

Alice hesitates. "Promise you won't laugh?"

"I promise."

Alice's eyes go starry, and she stares up at the ceiling, blotchy with smoke stains, as though seeing something I can't. "I want to study art. I've nearly persuaded my parents to let me go to the Pennsylvania Academy of Fine Arts, in Philadelphia. After that, I want to go to Paris. The École des Beaux-Arts does not admit women students, but Mary Cassatt went to Paris anyway and studied with the masters privately."

"Why would you think I'd laugh at that?" I ask. "I think it's wonderful."

Her gaze comes back to me and she smiles, a genuine smile tinged with gratitude. "Thank you. My papa is a doting father who sees my going to school as a gift one gives to delight a child. My mama accepts my study as polish that will make me a brighter ornament for a husband someday. And Will—he takes nothing seriously, especially not his baby sister's hobby."

It makes my heart ache that she should be grateful for so little. Perhaps we are not so different as I supposed. "My mama believes astronomy is not a suitable study for a woman. She wants me to marry and settle down to the real work of life."

Alice laughs. "Your mama should meet mine."

I grin back at her.

"Anyway," Alice says briskly, "some would say that paint-

118

ing is not a necessity, particularly not for women, who do not need to earn their living as men do, to support their families. But I say that is foolishness. Doesn't a woman have a need to support herself, if others cannot or will not? And anyway, art sustains my soul."

"I'd like to see your work sometime," I say. "Do you draw, or paint, or sculpt?"

"A bit of everything," she says. "Only drawing when I travel, mostly painting at home. I'd like to try sculpture, but I've not found a good teacher for that."

Will comes back then with some boiled eggs and biscuits. The eggs are cold by the time he reaches us, but we are both starving, and no one complains as we eat.

We spend the rest of the day wandering around the town (after carefully wrapping our blistered feet) and sending letters home. The circuit of town takes rather less than an hour, the letters, somewhat more. Alice sends a long wire to her mother in Denver. I beg a coin from Alice, promising to repay it as soon as I can, and send a much shorter telegram to Rebekka, telling her my arrival will be delayed. I wish I felt more guilty—Rebekka needs me, the baby may already have arrived—but I'm too happy at having met the scientists, at the promise of the telescopes tonight.

Surely this is more evidence of my wickedness.

After a supper of some rather gamey meat and indifferent boiled potatoes, we meet up with Mr. Edison and his party in the lobby of the hotel. As Dr. Morton predicted, we are not the only ones Mr. Edison has invited to see the telescopes. In addition to us, there are half a dozen others gathered in the lobby, and we acquire two or three more on the walk from the hotel to the backyard of a residence, where a rough shed is being assembled to house the telescopes.

We meet the rest of Mr. Edison's party—Mr. and Mrs. Draper, who have financed the expedition; Professor George Barker; and Dr. Morton, whom we've already met. I watch Mrs. Draper, a pretty redhead with a kind smile, rather enviously. From her easy conversation with the others, it's obvious that she knows a great deal about science, enough that she's regarded as Mr. Draper's assistant and not merely his wife. I cannot imagine such a life, such a marriage. In Monroe, marriages are partnerships of necessity—everyone has to work hard, and men and women rely upon one another for their labor. But a partnership of the mind? A mutual joy and interest in scholarship? I have never seen such a thing before.

One of the people we acquire on the way to the telescopes is a young girl, about twelve years old, with a round face and twin dark braids framing her rosy cheeks. She reminds me a bit of Mary, but that may be a trick of her size, because she's got nothing of Mary's moodiness, and she talks more than enough for three of Mary. She latches on to me, perhaps because, as the shortest (and, barring some of the older men, the roundest) of our group, I am the least frightening.

Her name, I discover, is Lillian Heath, and she means to become a doctor. "Sometimes my pa lets me attend him when he assists Dr. Maghee. I've even helped cut open dead bodies," she adds with rather ghoulish relish. I hope she doesn't mean to tell me of them. My interest in constellations and astral bodies doesn't extend to corpses.

Luckily, Lillian quickly seizes on to Dr. Morton, asking him questions about chemistry with unselfconscious eagerness. And now I'm jealous of a child, because even at twelve, she has no doubts about who she is going to be, what her life is going to look like. She does not ask questions hedged in by what others think she ought to be, to do.

As we gather around the larger of two assembled telescopes, the sun sinks below the western horizon, shafting light across and through the houses, turning everything in its path to gold. The torn clouds drifting across the sky light like fire. It stops my breath. What curious combination of atmosphere and light and chemicals turns the sky twice daily into such a glory? Dr. Morton might know, were I brave enough to ask him.

The telescope is a long, glorious thing, half again as tall as a man on its three-legged mount. It's of some shiny metal, wider at the upper end and narrow at the bottom, where we take turns peering through the eyepiece. Dr. Morton explains that two rounded glass lenses inside the telescope magnify the light from the stars.

I wait my turn as others inspect the telescope and exclaim as the stars burst into their vision. Overhead, more and more stars appear as the light fades. The moon isn't up yet, giving a clearer view of the constellations. I pick out familiar ones, following the cup of the Big Dipper to the North Star, then rotating to see Cygnus, and then the Dog Star, Sirius, in the middle of Canis Major. It's the brightest star in the sky, easy to see even without a telescope. The distant reddish light winks at me.

All across the dark arc overhead, stars twinkle, brighter and brighter as the night deepens. And though Rawlins is a place I didn't know existed a week ago, the sky is as familiar as my own hands. I don't think I could ever tire of this.

Then it's my turn. My hands shake a little, so I tuck them under my armpits. Dr. Morton peers into the telescope first, making sure it's still aligned. He points to a nebulous cloud of light in the Sagittarius constellation. "Messier 8," he says, referring to Charles Messier, the astronomer who extensively cataloged stars and nebulae in his quest to find comets.

When I peer through the narrow lens of the telescope, I find that the nebula isn't just a faint cloud of light, but dozens of distant stars in an oval shape, all clustered around a central bright patch. I've seen that nebula all my life, but never before have I seen the stars within it.

What other things do I miss because I haven't the apparatus to see them with?

"Do you see that brightness in the center?" Dr. Morton asks.

"Yes," I say. "What is it?"

"John Herschel—son of William Herschel, the famous astronomer—named it the Hourglass Nebula. I'm not sure I see the hourglass shape, myself, but it is rather pretty, isn't it?"

Rather pretty? That's like calling the sun a dim light. "It's magnificent," I say, my eye fixed to the telescope. Everything in me—mind, body, heart—concentrates on this moment.

"The stars do have a way of giving us perspective," Dr. Morton says. "*Per aspera ad astra.* Through hardship to the stars. It's the motto of the Stevens family, you know, who founded my university."

I pull away from the telescope to look at Dr. Morton. His gray hair gleams silver in the moonlight, and he looks to be everything a scientist should be. Dignified, wise, kind. "What does it mean?" I ask.

His mustache twitches. "You might also translate it as 'To the stars in spite of hardships.' I always think that one must persevere, to win the greatest rewards. The stars shine brightest, after all, that are the hardest sought for."

"Through hardship to the stars. *Per aspera ad astra.*" Whispering the words to myself to remember them, I peer through the telescope again, marveling that a bit of glass and wood and brass can make the sky come alive.

I don't ever want to leave.

chapter ten

Friday, July 12, 1878
Rawlins, Wyoming
Seventeen days until eclipse

A loud banging pulls me from a sound sleep. For a moment, I'm lost, the strange room all plain walls and angles in the brilliant moonlight. Ah—the hotel. Rawlins.

The banging persists. Our trunks still have not arrived, and I'm in my underclothes, but I creep to the door and open it cautiously, peeking down the hallway.

A man dressed in fringed buckskin with a wide-brimmed hat stands pounding at a door only a few down from ours. A long nose terminates above a dark mustache and narrow, frowning lips. Dark hair waves about his shoulders. In any other situation, I might think him handsome, like something out of one of my dime novels. But just now, fear stabs through me. I know the door. Will's door. The man wears a gun holstered at his hips—the handle gleams in the faint light of the hallway.

Heart pounding dully in my throat, I shut the door. What if this man intends harm, to either Will or Mr. Edison? I don't know why anyone would want to hurt Mr. Edison. But Will—sometimes folks don't take kindly to black people for no other reason than the color of their skin.

"Alice," I whisper. When she doesn't stir, I repeat her name louder. "Alice!"

She blinks at me and sits up. She's wrapped a length of cloth around her head to keep her curls fresh, and she tucks a bit that's come loose back in place. "What is it?"

"There's a man in the hallway, banging on Will's door. He's got a gun."

Now Alice is on her feet. She darts past me to the door, peering out. She shuts the door, leans against the wall as though thinking. Then she grabs the blanket off her bed, wrapping it around her shoulders like some night-robe, and dashes into the hallway.

I snatch my own blanket and follow her.

By the time we're both in the hallway, Will—or Edison—has already opened the door and the man has pushed his way into the room. At the sound of loud, unhappy male voices, we rush down the hall, crowding into the doorway.

The stranger is standing between the two beds, the gun now free of its holster and glinting in his hand. Mr. Edison is on his feet, a robe slung hastily around him. Will is still in bed, sitting up with his back against the wall. He doesn't look frightened yet, just alert, his eyes oddly bright.

"I'm looking for Mr. Edison!" the man roars. The edges of his words fray a little. I think he might be drunk.

Beside me, Alice lets out a long sigh but doesn't ease her tense posture. The man might not be looking for Will, but he's drunk and armed, so he's still dangerous.

"I'm Thomas Edison," Mr. Edison says in a calming voice, his hands out, palms up. "What do you want?"

"Want to meet the inventor. He's a great man, they say." The man waves the gun toward himself. "I'm a great man too. Name of Texas Jack."

When no one in the room responds, he says, louder, "Jack Omohundro! In these parts, folks know me as Texas Jack."

Something about the name tickles my memory. Why do I know it? I'm certain I've never seen the man before.

"I'm sorry," Mr. Edison says, his brow wrinkling. "I'm afraid I don't recognize—"

Texas Jack cuts him off. "Buffalo Bill Cody, know him? Wild Bill Hickok? Great men, good friends of mine. I'm a scout, like them. A showman."

I blink. Texas Jack, a scout . . .

Oh.

I know now where I've read his name—he was the hero of one of the dime novels Emily smuggled home, his name and face emblazoned across the cover. I didn't realize the books had been written about the exploits of a *real* person.

Or maybe the person is real and the stories fictional? But now hardly seems the time to ask.

A weird sort of thrill runs through me. Just wait until I tell Emily.

Texas Jack was rather handsomer in the cover sketch than now, red-nosed and ruddy-cheeked, with dark circles under his eyes. He seems to be deflating a little. His gun hand drifts down to his side.

Mr. Edison edges closer and puts out his hand. "Pleased to meet you, Mr. Omo—Texas Jack."

There's a commotion behind me, and then someone shoves Alice and me aside. "Out of the way, out of the way." It's an older, balding gentleman with a pink nose and pink ears. I think he might be the hotel manager.

Once past Alice and me, the manager stops and surveys the scene, hands on hips. Then he shakes his head and approaches Texas Jack. "Come now, Mr. Jack, put your gun away. You're waking my guests. I'm sure Mr. Edison would be pleased to see you again tomorrow. You can even take tea in my own parlor, how's that?"

Texas Jack allows himself to be led from the room. Beside me, Alice sags against the wall in relief, and Will makes his way toward her. I leave the siblings to themselves and follow Mr. Edison and Texas Jack from the room.

Now that the immediate danger is gone, the scene begins to feel rather ridiculous. I wish Samuel was here to appreciate—*no*. I'm not going to think about Samuel.

"I'm afraid you don't look well, Mr. Jack," the manager

says. "Would you like a bit of whiskey in my office before you head, er, back to your camp?"

Texas Jack shakes the manager's arm free. "I feel fine. I've been out with a party hunting and heard that Mr. Edison was here when we got back." He turns to Edison again. "I'm the boss pistol-shot of the West, you know. It was me who taught Dr. Carver how to shoot."

There's a proud, boastful note in his voice, and, unexpectedly, Texas Jack whips his revolver back out of the holster. The manager and Mr. Edison both recoil, as do I and the handful of guests who have been drawn by the noise.

"See that weathervane?" Texas Jack asks, pointing with the barrel of the gun to a vane atop the train depot, just visible through a wide window open at the end of the hall. He pulls the trigger. There's a loud *bang,* and the sharp smell of gunpowder and smoke.

The weathervane pops off the top of the depot.

Screams erupt up from some of the gathered guests, and all down the hallway doors fly open.

"Who's been killed?" someone demands.

Texas Jack smirks and replaces his gun.

"Damned fool," mutters Mr. Edison, but I don't think anyone but me hears it.

"No one's killed," calls the manager. "It's an accident. Go back to bed!" He turns to the gunman. "Mr. Jack, I really must ask you to leave." He waves at a clerk that appears at the top of the stairs, drawn by the noise. "Here, take Mr. Jack outside."

The clerk scurries toward us, a terrified expression on his face. But Texas Jack, having apparently satisfied us—and himself—of his prowess with a gun, puts up no resistance this time.

As he's led away, the manager turns back to Mr. Edison. "He's not a bad sort, really, not like some of the gunmen we get around here. The sort that robbed the train the other day. Truly bad and dangerous, those. Mr. Jack is just . . . Well, between you and me, Mr. Jack's down on his luck. It's hard to be held up as a hero in all those books, and not have your life match the reality. His shows don't draw crowds the way the others do, and now the West is more settled, there's not so much call for hunting guides. A body, especially one like Mr. Jack, needs some meaning in his life."

Alice and Will have joined us in the doorway by this time. Will frowns thoughtfully at the open window, at the line of the depot roof. "He's a performer, you say?"

The manager shrugs. "Is. Was. It's hard to say now."

Will doesn't answer, but his eyes narrow. Alice pokes him. "I know that look. What trouble are you brewing up?"

"Nothing," Will says, but spoils the effect by adding, with a wide grin, "yet."

chapter eleven

Saturday, July 13, 1878

Rawlins, Wyoming

Sixteen days until eclipse

Just after breakfast on Saturday, the first train in two days leaves the station: a westbound train that's been sitting at the station since Thursday morning.

"Line must be fixed at last," our waiter says, bringing us word along with our bill. "Eastbound train'll be here soon."

Soon. My heart leaps a little. "How soon?" Do we have time to fetch our things from upstairs? I have to assume my luggage is still on the train, as it never showed up here. I catch myself wondering if Samuel is on a train toward Denver yet, but I squash the thought before it can flower. I've no business thinking of Samuel. He made it very clear he didn't think much of me.

The waiter shrugs. "Train'll be at the station for a good while loading up folks."

We've already lost so much time here. In some ways, it's been idyllic—seeing the stars through the telescope, getting to know Alice and Will, even having that wild adventure with Texas Jack. But with the real world pressing on me, all my anxiety over Rebekka floods back. Is she all right? Has the baby come yet?

Alice and I rush upstairs to gather our things. I stow mine into my carpetbag and refill my canteen, wishing that the descent of so many passengers had not cleared out the town like grasshoppers eating the first crop of wheat in the Salt Lake valley. There's little remaining food to be had, and certainly not at prices I can afford, even with the dollar Alice pressed on me after she and Will received a wire of funds the day before. I'll have to find something at the next stop.

We make our way to the hotel lobby. On the way down, I spy Dr. Morton in the hotel dining room, and I hesitate.

I was hoping to say goodbye to Mr. Edison, even though he would never remember some nobody he met so briefly. But it would feel like *I* mattered, to have someone like him know my name, if only for a little while.

Dr. Morton isn't Mr. Edison, but he's a scientist and chemistry professor and he was kind to me at the telescope. I turn to Alice. "I'll see you at the station."

I hail Dr. Morton, and he turns to me, surprise visible in his raised eyebrows. "Can I help you, miss?"

He doesn't appear to remember me, though we've spoken twice now, and he gave me his seat at breakfast that first morning. I take a deep breath. "I wanted to thank you for helping us with the telescope the other night. It was glorious—it made our forced stop at Rawlins more than worthwhile."

"Oh?" he says politely, glancing at his watch.

I rush on, compelled by something I hardly understand. "I'd like to be an astronomer myself, someday."

Now I have his full attention. He peers at me, his eyebrows drawing together. "A young lady like yourself? Whatever for?"

I falter. I thought a scientist like Dr. Morton would understand. "To study the stars? To understand the orbits of comets? *Per aspera ad astra.* You taught me that."

"You'd do much better to leave that work to real scientists."

"But Mrs. Draper—"

"Assists her husband. Oh, I don't deny astronomy is well enough as a hobby, and Mrs. Draper has been useful to her husband, as Miss Herschel was to her brother. But astronomy—as a mathematically based science—is much more suited to the masculine mind than the feminine. As a point of fact, Dr. Clark has argued that such strenuous study in women can coarsen their features and inhibit their ability to bear children. I do not think it coincidental that the only female astronomers one finds are spinsters. The exclusive study rather unfits women for other, more seemly duties. You cannot wish to stunt your life before you've scarce begun it."

I catch my breath. I've carried the blissful glow from that telescope view with me for more than thirty hours, and Dr. Morton has snuffed it with one comment. I try once more. "And Mrs. Mary Somerville?"

"She is more a generalist than an astronomer, but I daresay her existence is the exception that rather proves the rule. Name me one such other woman who successfully balances domestic life with her studies."

I have no answer for him.

Rather smugly, Dr. Morton plucks up his hat from the table and settles it on his head. "If you want my advice, I suggest you study something more conducive to your own happiness, like domestic sciences."

He rises, then walks away without looking back. Mouth dry, I hitch my carpetbag higher on my arm. I walk out of the hotel into blazing sunshine. The heat hits me like a wall.

Will and Alice are already on the platform beside the tracks when I reach the station, but I don't join them at once. They've been extraordinarily kind, but they owe me nothing, and I can't help but feel that my presence has been an inconvenience. And after Dr. Morton's words, all my pleasure at the prospect of our journey has been shaken up.

But Alice is made of sterner stuff than I am, and when she sees me, she waves me over to them. "There you are." As if my being with them is a matter of fact.

The relief that washes over me is short-lived.

Alice drags me after Will, toward the first-class car. I stop, loosing my arm from hers. "Alice, I don't have a first-class ticket."

Will must hear me, because he stops too. He and Alice exchange a look, and then, without a word, Will swerves toward the second-class car just in front of the first-class cabin. Unlike the car I rode in before, the rows of seats are divided up into compartments.

By the time we reach the car, most of the compartments we pass are full. Will finds a compartment occupied only by a couple and opens the door. "Good afternoon, friends. May we join you?"

The wife sniffs and looks out the window. Her husband rubs at a bristly mustache and asks, "Haven't you seats somewhere else?"

"Alas, the occupants took umbrage at my two wives and asked us to leave. But I am sure you will not be so narrow-minded," Will says, leaning toward them with an engaging smile.

Two wives.

Alice's quiet gasp is covered by the woman's cry of outrage. "I never! The affront of some people. Be gone! Or I'll call the porter and have you ejected."

My head has gone weirdly floaty.

We move on. Will is shaking, trying not to laugh, and Alice nudges him with her elbow. "You're incorrigible."

Will shrugs. "They were going to send us away as soon as

they saw our skin color—you saw the woman's reaction. Might as well give them something truly objectionable. Though it's even odds whether they were more offended by my having two wives, or having one of them be white." He makes a face at Alice.

I say nothing.

At the front end of the car we find a compartment with only one gentleman sitting beside the door, and as soon as the door opens, I understand why the seats have remained empty: the gentleman has been smoking heavily. The entire compartment reeks of it, and the haze still hanging in the air makes me cough and blink back tears.

But the man doesn't do more than glance at us when we enter and doesn't protest when Alice walks across the car to open the window. I sink into the bench by the window and stare out, pressing my forehead against the warm glass. Alice takes a seat beside me, and Will sits across from us. They begin talking, but their words touch me without making an impression. The floating feeling has vanished, and now I only feel hurt, and embarrassed at feeling hurt. What Will said was no more than most people believed about polygamists. He didn't know I was Mormon—how could he? I'd said nothing to them.

Alice notices my silence first. "Elizabeth? Are you all right?"

"My father has two wives," I blurt, and then press my lips together to keep any other foolish words from escaping.

Both siblings stare at me.

"Has?" Alice asks. "Or had?"

In for a penny, in for a pound. "Both," I say. "He was married when he met Mama, but his first wife died. He married again a few years ago."

"And your mama?" Alice asks, staring at me with a slightly glazed expression, as though I am some beast she's never encountered, and she's not certain how dangerous I am.

"They're still married." I add, perhaps unnecessarily, "I'm Mormon."

Will and Alice exchange a carefully neutral look, and my heart falls. No doubt they'll remember a reason why they need their first-class seats, and I'll never see them again.

"Hmm," Alice says, digesting. "I suppose if you were raised to it, it would not seem so strange."

Now it's my turn to stare at her. "You're not . . . offended?" I think the man in our carriage might be—he's drawn up a newspaper to hide himself and hunches away from us, as though my religion is catching.

"I—" Alice starts, catches herself, and squares her shoulders. "I admit it's not what I am used to."

"There's polygamy in the Bible," I say. "And no one says the prophets were wrong."

"I know. But somehow it's easier to accept things that are done long ago or far away. Well," Alice says briskly, as if coming to a decision, "if your mama doesn't mind your papa having more than one wife, why should I?"

I laugh a little. Mama most certainly *does* mind Aunt

Olena, but she is only offended in her particular case, not about polygamy in general. She loved Aunt Elisa like a sister. "You're very generous. Most people think we're heathens."

The train lurches forward, pulling away from the station.

Alice grins at me. "Most people think Will's a heathen too."

"What's wrong with being a heathen, anyway?" Will asks. "Seems like just a label some people stick on someone else when they want to feel superior, as though they chose to be born into their religion and corner of the world. If they'd been born in a different place, they might well be heathen themselves. People waste far too much time judging others when they could simply look into a mirror."

Touched—and a little amused—by Will's expression of sympathy, I settle into my seat, watching the last of Rawlins vanish behind us.

✦

We have a quick lunch in Como, and then the afternoon stretches long and hot before we reach Laramie. Will takes a nap, his derby tipped over his face; Alice and I take short walks up and down the corridor outside our compartment and talk.

Alice tells me about the series of domestic paintings she is working on: intimate scenes, of the sort the Impressionist Mary Cassatt paints, only more rustic. "I think easterners have a very set idea of the West," Alice says.

"Yes," I laugh, thinking of my dime novels and the weird encounter with Texas Jack. "We are all dressed in fringed leather and wear gun holsters."

Alice smiles at me. "Even the women."

There is nothing of that rustic impression in Alice, whose gray-and-lavender travel suit bears fine lace at the hem and along the neck, though now a little torn after our muddy walk from the train. Sometime during our stop in Rawlins, she acquired a new hat—a beautifully shaped straw confection dyed gray like her dress.

"I am working on a collection to show that there are all sorts of people in the West: Fine men and ladies, farmers, barbers and butchers and teachers and actors. Even some vaqueros from Texas."

"Some what?" I've never heard the word before.

"Cowboys," she says, smiling again.

"Do you only paint people?" I ask. "Or if you mean to paint the West, do you paint landscapes as well?"

Some indecipherable emotion flickers across her face. "No. Or, not really. I have tried a few, but it is difficult for a lady to paint a landscape without venturing *into* the landscape, and I don't have much opportunity for that."

"It's hard for women to go out alone at night to view the stars too." Mama certainly doesn't think it appropriate. Nor does Dr. Morton, whose opinion stings more than Mama's.

Alice stops by a window to look at softly contoured plains rushing past. There's a curious austere beauty in them, very different from the striated rock mountains of my valley. "Will you get to see the eclipse, where you are going?"

I shake my head. "Not fully. The path of totality doesn't run through Cheyenne."

She turns back to me. "Then you should come to Denver."

A surge of longing passes through me and leaves me trembling. "I wish I could. But I need to care for my sister, and anyway, I haven't money."

Alice waves her hand, as though all these things, these tiny, thin strands that comprise my life, are only insubstantial objections. "Then come only for the eclipse, for a day or so. Surely your sister can spare you so long. And you can stay with me, so the cost will be minimal."

There is still the cost of the railway tickets, and as sick as Rebekka has been, I don't know if she can spare me, but Alice's expression is so kind and hopeful I say only, "I'll think about it."

+

As Laramie comes into sight, Alice and I press up against the window. First, there's a vast, sprawling building belching smoke, then a tall windmill, spinning in the summer breeze. Or maybe just the wind of the train's passing. Behind the windmill, a round reservoir holds water for the train engines.

We pull into the station—the largest I've seen yet, a long

two-story building with pointed roofs, depot and hotel combined.

As we wait for the hallway outside our compartment to clear of passengers, Alice says, "You wouldn't think it now, but Laramie used to be one of the roughest of the frontier towns. Some of the first founders were self-appointed lawmen who were lynched for corruption and violence in the very halls they helped build."

But there's no sign of that rough town in the clean, white-washed station, or in the neat streets beyond it. Will and Alice find seats in the dining room, but I don't want to borrow more funds than I already have, so I find market stalls outside the station and purchase purple-red serviceberries along with some bread and cheese for my supper.

We climb back on the train and retake our seats without incident, though the smoking gentleman doesn't rejoin us. Perhaps an hour out of Laramie the train slows to a near crawl. My heart picks up speed as the train slows. "Is something wrong?" I remember the robbery, how the train slowed, then stopped unexpectedly, miles from a station. Outside, the landscape stretches brown and dry and rocky.

"Nah," Will says. "We're approaching the Dale Creek trestle is all. The train can't go above four miles per hour across it." He grins. "Best part of the journey."

Alice presses her lips together. "You might like it, William Stevens, but I don't. That trestle bridge is a sight too long and too high, and I don't care what masterpiece of engineering it is, it looks like a child stuck twigs together with glue. I'm not sure it won't all come apart at a high wind."

"Well, at high winds they won't let you cross," Will says reasonably. "So if they let you cross, you're safe enough."

I press my forehead to the window, but all I can see is a guard posted outside by a sign that warns us of the four-mile-an-hour speed limit, and piles of rocks on either side of the track. I grimace. That sounds a miserable job, to spend the day beside the railway track to stop the train if the winds are too high. All that heat and emptiness for only a few minutes of actual work each day.

The train eases onto the trestle. Is it only my imagining, or can I hear the bridge creaking below us? As soon as we clear the guard, I see why Alice dislikes it so. The trestle stretches perhaps a hundred feet above a steep ravine, its inclines strewn with boulders, a few windblown trees clinging to the dirt as though they've given up hope of anything better.

I don't mind heights: I've climbed the walls of our canyon often enough. But the ground is always solid beneath me. This—I can only catch glimpses of the thin iron rods of the trestle out ahead of the train. Where we are looks as though the train is floating in midair, an uncertain miracle of engineering. The early-evening sun shafts through the gorge, making everything waver in the heat.

Shivering, I pull back. "Has the trestle ever collapsed?"

"See?" Alice demands, just as Will says, "No. Couple

trains a day pass this way, have for more than a decade, and nothing's ever gone wrong. You're safe as houses."

Will jiggles his leg for a bit, then stands and leaves the compartment.

"Will!" Alice hisses after him, but he's already out of sight.

She doesn't look well. Sweat beads along her hairline, and her hands are gripped tight on the seat. Her eyes meet mine.

"I'll go," I say, and follow Will into the hall. The windows alongside the narrow corridor all give an expansive view of the gorge beneath us. I swallow and put one hand against the wall to steady myself.

I find Will at the end of the car, standing in the open doorway leading onto the narrow metal platform. The wind pulls at his curls, and he grins at me. Through the doorway, I can make out the gap between cars, and the flicking rails as the train crawls along the bridge. Far below, water glints from a stream at the base of the ravine.

It's terrifying.

"It's marvelous, isn't it?" Will asks. "It feels as though I'm on top of the world, as though I'm flying."

Has anyone ever fallen from a train platform and down through the gaps in the trestle? I swallow again. "Will, come back to the compartment, please. Alice isn't well."

"Scared of heights is all," Will says. "She'll be all right when we're across."

But he follows me back to the seat anyway.

At Alice's request, I try to read her novel out loud to her, to distract her. Her eyes are shut, her complexion clammy. I don't think the distraction is working. I keep looking out the window, at the emptiness beneath us. My words trip over themselves.

Will doesn't appear to hear us. He looks out the window, a tiny smile curling his lips. I mistrust that look. It's the look David Charles had a couple springs back when he decided to go out hunting the bear cub someone had seen near our canyon. Luckily Hyrum got word before David Charles'd gone too far and dragged him back before he could get himself killed by the cub's mama.

The rock wall of the far side of the bridge appears, and the front of the train edges onto solid ground again. Alice opens her eyes. "Are we across?"

"Nearly," I say, and she releases a long breath.

Will says, "I want to walk the trestle."

We both stare at him. "What?" Alice asks.

Will repeats himself. My stomach sinks. I was right: he was planning something stupid.

"No," Alice says flatly. "You'll kill yourself."

He shakes his head. "The rail ties are plenty wide. I was watching them. It won't take but fifteen, twenty minutes to walk back across the tracks—I'll be across before the next train comes, and I'll catch the next eastbound train and meet you in Cheyenne in a few hours."

"Will, don't," Alice begs as Will stands again.

He looks down at her, his usually smiling face still for once. "You know what Papa's like, and Grandpa. I want to remind myself I'm alive before I go back to all"—he waves his hand vaguely—*"that."*

"And wasn't a train robbery exciting enough? Or a man waving a gun in your room at midnight?"

Will's eyes brighten. "Oh, they were exciting. But they weren't for *me*. They weren't my choice." He evades Alice's grasp for him and slips down the hallway.

We've passed the rock piles marking the end of the trestle, and a solitary guard watches the train pass. Maybe he'll have sense enough to stop Will.

Alice and I scurry after Will, calling his name. Some of the passengers in surrounding compartments look up at us, but most seem largely uninterested. I bet that would change if they knew what Will was planning.

Throwing open the door to the platform, Will steps onto the metal floor. The train moves slowly, at a walking pace, and wildlife scuttles away from the tracks. A hare bounds away, a lizard slithers into the crevice of a rock.

"Will!"

But Will doesn't turn at his sister's voice. Easily, gracefully, as though he's done this a dozen times or more, he jumps from the train. He stumbles a little on landing, his arms pinwheeling, then regains his balance. He doesn't even lose his hat, which he doffs to us.

Alice steps out onto the platform and I crowd after her, watching Will. If we bend over the metal railing, we can just see him, sauntering toward the wooden planks where the rails meet the trestle.

The dark shape of the guard moves to intercept Will, and I pray hard, for Will, for Alice, that he stops him. But Will bends down to him and says something, and the guard shrugs and steps aside.

Fingers pressed tight on the railing, Alice whispers, "I'm going to kill him." I'm not sure if she means Will or the guard.

The last thing we see, before the train slides around a curve, cutting off our view, is Will's tall, trim figure, dancing out onto the trestle.

chapter twelve

Saturday, July 13, 1878

Approaching Cheyenne, Wyoming

Sixteen days until eclipse

Alice and I don't speak much the rest of the way to Cheyenne. We stay out on the platform well past the point where we can no longer see Will, until the conductor comes through the car and tells us, rather sharply, that it's dangerous to ride on the platform and would we kindly return to our seats.

We sit stiffly for some time in silence. I calculate in my head how long it might take to walk across the trestle. It didn't take long for the train to cross—perhaps ten minutes to get all the cars back onto solid ground. A person could surely cross the trestle in about that time, or a little more. Whether Will succeeded—or failed—he must have done so by now. I try not to think about what will happen if he's failed.

The aching tension reminds me of the long night I spent

waiting to see if Rachel survived. It was unbearable then; it must be unbearable now for Alice. I reach out, and Alice grips my hand as though it's a lifeline pulling her to safety.

By the time we reach Cheyenne, Alice seems to have come to some decision. She releases my numb fingers, sits up straight, pats her hair, and adjusts her hat. She pins a smile to her lips.

We wait our turn to disembark from the train, then approach the luggage car, where porters are setting down the trunks marked for Cheyenne. Alice gives one of the porters an address where her luggage is to be delivered.

"It's my favorite of the Cheyenne hotels," she tells me. "If W— If people want to find me, they'll know where to look. And luckily, I am known there, as I'm down to my last few dollars."

I wonder if Alice knows how telling this detail is: that she has sufficient wealth and leisure to travel out of Colorado often enough that the owners of a hotel in Wyoming know her by name. No one but Rebekka knows me in this part of the world.

"You're staying the night? Couldn't you just go on ahead without Will?"

She flinches at her brother's name. "My parents are a little . . . traditional . . . when it comes to my brother and me. My mother wouldn't like me to be traveling alone, especially at night, even if the circumstances behind it were not of my making."

In other words, I suspect, she might find herself in more trouble than Will if she shows up at home without him.

Where is Will, right at this moment? I hope he's on a train (or waiting for one) and not shattered at the bottom of the ravine. *Please, God.*

Some of the buildings around the station are fine brick stores, and others are squared-off wooden buildings with signs painted across the front: BILLIARD SALOON, MEALS FOR FIFTY CENTS. Children stand in front of several, ringing bells furiously and hollering to attract customers from the train.

I consult with a carriage driver outside the station and a clerk at the Western Union office and discover that it costs nearly the same to hire a carriage driver as it does to send a telegram to Ammon informing him and Rebekka of my arrival. Hiring a carriage would spare Ammon the long drive into town from their farm out near the fort, but neither is within my slim means. Alice would loan me more money, if I asked her, but I can't bear to do so. Our friendship already feels unbalanced as it is; she's given me so much. I'll walk if I must.

Alice looks over at me as we leave the Western Union building. "I suppose you'll want to be going. It will be getting dark soon."

She's right: I don't want to wake Rebekka and Ammon with a late arrival. And Alice has a hotel waiting for her, where Will can find her when he arrives. (I do not let myself think about the other alternative.) She does not really need my company any longer.

But even as I think this, my heart contracts. I do not want to go to Rebekka's and wait for the baby to arrive, to fill my days and hours with small talk and housework to spare Rebekka during her lying-in. I don't want to be reminded, by contrast with Rebekka, of all the ways I fail to be an ideal Mormon woman. Even if such charity is supposed to be my highest aspiration. Even if I love Rebekka.

I want a bigger world than that.

I want to stay here, and make sure Will is all right. That Alice will be all right.

I want Denver, with the coming eclipse and its accompanying talk of ideas. I want the entire universe, the stars in the sky. If the glory of God is intelligence, if God is both wise *and* good, can't I serve God as well by learning as by serving others?

But *want* isn't the same as *should.* And maybe Dr. Morton is right, that women are best fitted for domestic life. As a professor, he would know.

Enough, I tell myself. *You have enough.* I force myself to think of Rachel, of the promise I made in exchange for her healing.

Perhaps Alice sees some of this in my face, because she says abruptly, "Let me show you something before you go. My treat."

She leads me to a restaurant by one of the whitewashed hotels near the station. She doesn't tell me what we are doing, but when the waiter comes to take our order, she asks for lemon ices.

The waiter returns with two shallow bowls, each bearing a pale yellow ice molded into the shape of a rose. Alice digs into hers at once, but I prod mine with my spoon, loath to break the pretty confection. At last, I spoon off a narrow sliver and set it in my mouth.

The cold feels delicious on a hot summer evening, like a bit of unexpected winter snow. And it's sweet, so sweet that it makes my teeth hurt, but I like it. I take a heaping spoonful, but it is too much at once, and the cold goes direct from my tongue to my brain, making my whole head ache. Sometimes in the winter Mama makes us a treat by pouring sugar syrup over snow, but that is nothing to this explosion of sweetness.

I finish the treat, wishing I had some way of sending it back to my brothers and sisters. To Rachel, especially, who loves anything sweet. Alice tells me that in fine confectioners' shops back east—and soon, in Denver too—they serve ices made with cream and eggs, even richer and sweeter than the ice I have just finished. I can't imagine such a thing.

Though I scrape the bottom of the bowl with my spoon, making Alice laugh, soon there is nothing left of the ice, and nothing to keep me from going. Alice walks back to the station with me and, before I can stop her, negotiates a ride with a carriage driver she deems safe.

"Are you sure you won't come to Denver for the eclipse?" she asks again. "You would be welcome."

"I know," I say. "You've been so kind to me. But I don't think I can accept."

She doesn't press me, but reaches into her purse and hands me a small card. *Alice Stevens* it reads, in flowing script. On the back, in tiny print, is her address. "If you change your mind, you can reach me here. And even if you don't, perhaps you can write to me? I've enjoyed our short time together."

I take the card and slide it into my carpetbag. "Meeting you and Will was the best thing that happened to me." I intend to write her more faithfully than Vilate Ann will likely write to me—which is not at all.

Alice laughs. "Between the downpour and the robbery and the elk and the midnight visit of a crazy man, I'm not sure there was much to choose from." She sobers, and I know we are both thinking of Will.

"Are you going to be all right?"

"I'll be fine. Will's like a cat, with nine lives waiting to be abused. He always lands on his feet. When he was fifteen, he tried to get into Miss Mattie Silk's establishment, though Papa had forbade him from setting foot on Holladay Street."

From the mildly scandalized expression on Alice's face, I can guess what kind of establishment Miss Silk runs, and my face heats.

"Will stole one of my dresses and one of Mama's hats with a little veil and presented himself at Miss Mattie's, as a new girl in town. He made it all the way to speak with Miss Mattie too, before she realized he was not a girl. Instead of having him whipped, Miss Mattie just laughed at his cheek and sent him home in her own carriage. My parents were out, and Will sweet-talked all the servants into staying quiet, so they never did hear of it. That's just how he is—he does the wildest things and never gets caught."

Despite her light words, her face is tight. "No doubt he'll

come banging in just as I've gone to sleep and wake the whole floor."

I wonder how often Alice has borne the brunt of Will's actions, smoothing things over for Will as I smooth things over for Far. For Mama. I want to hug her, but I'm afraid she might find me impertinent, to presume at such intimacy. I content myself with pressing her hand.

Turning back to the carriage, I find the driver has finished lashing my trunk to the back. Since Alice is watching, I climb inside. The interior is some dark fabric that smells of dust and grease, and I hold myself apart from the cushions as the vehicle lurches forward.

I wave to Alice, who waves back.

As soon as the carriage swings us around the corner, out of sight of the station and Alice's too-kind eyes, I bang on the roof. The carriage sways, then stops.

I stick my head out the window. "Can I be let down here? I can walk the rest of the way."

The driver, a rotund man in his middle age with a large family of daughters (Alice asked), sighs heavily. "What's the trouble?"

"I don't have enough money to pay for the full journey, but I didn't want to distress my friend."

He sighs again. "Are you sure? It's a bit of a trek with your trunk and all."

I don't need charity. "I'm sure," I say, with more firmness than I feel.

Obligingly, he climbs down from the driver's seat, helps

me out of the carriage, and unloads my trunk. I give him a quarter I can hardly spare for his effort, then ask him the way to Rebekka's, as he seems to know it.

He shakes his head at me. "Girl, you oughta know it's not nice asking a man a favor when you've cheated him out of a good fare. You're as green as you can stare, aren't you?" He flips my quarter, which glints in the dim light, into the air and catches it. But he gives me the directions anyway. I repeat them to him, making sure the details are right.

Still grumbling, the driver mounts his seat and drives off, the wheels rattling over the rough road.

I draw a deep breath, orienting myself to this strange street, this strange city.

My journey is almost over. Another hour or two, and I'll see my sister. My thoughts flash to the unexpectedly long, wet walk from the train to Rawlins, and I'm torn between laughing and crying. Hopefully there are no elk this time.

Trunk thumping behind me, I start moving. Wind whistles up the street, filling my ears and blocking out the bustle from the train station a couple of blocks behind me. Overhead, a cloud scuttles across the sky, blotting the stars and the three-quarters moon. Lamplight flickers behind drawn curtains in the buildings I pass. Occasionally laughter breaks out across the street.

The buildings give way to houses, the houses to farms.

I walk into the rising dark.

chapter thirteen

Sunday, July 14, 1878
Outside of Cheyenne, Wyoming
Fifteen days until eclipse

It's late when I arrive outside Rebekka's home, a small frame house some distance from a tiny community I trudged through. My arms both ache from dragging my trunk, one side at a time. The moon has come out again, lining the road with silver, but there are no lights on in the house before me. Have I come to the right place?

Silence greets my knock.

A cool wind whistles around the house, making the planks of the house groan and the willow trees along the nearby creek shake their shaggy limbs.

I've just about settled to sleeping atop my trunk underneath those willows when the door creaks open.

A round face with tousled blond hair and a shaggy red beard peers around the edge of the door. "Who's there?"

I mentally compare this face to the one I remember meeting at Rebekka's wedding—Ammon Walton was thinner then, and beardless, but I remember the rosy cheeks and clear eyes. I let out a breath of relief. At least I've got the right house. "Ammon? It's Elizabeth Bertelsen, Rebekka's sister. I'm sorry the train was so late."

"Elizabeth!" Ammon flings open the door and scoops me up in a bear hug before I've time to do more than squeak in alarm. Ammon's impulse to embrace the world would terrify me if he weren't so good-natured.

"Come in, come in! Rebekka's asleep and I don't want to wake her, she sleeps so poorly of late." He shoos me into the house, then plucks up my trunk from the yard.

I look around, my eyes adjusting slowly to the gloom. Moonlight filters through some pretty white cambric curtains to show a living area, a pair of chairs facing a table, coals glowing low in the corner stove.

"You hungry?" Ammon asks, a little doubtfully. "There's some bread in the cupboard, I think."

"I've eaten. I'm just tired."

Ammon looks relieved, then his eyebrows draw down again. I forgot how transparent he is: every emotion flashing clearly across his face. "We don't have a bed made up for you. We wasn't sure when you were coming."

"A blanket and a pillow is all I need." I indicate the rug, a pretty, round thing that looks like Rebekka's handwork. "This spot will do just fine."

All the same, I feel off balance as I accept a blanket and pillow from Ammon. I've come all this way and there's no place for me. If I don't fit in at home or abroad, where do I fit in?

✦

My vague despair of the night gives way the next morning, lifted by rest and sunlight. After a breakfast of burned oats and cream (I make a quiet resolution not to let Ammon cook for me again), Ammon leaves to tend their livestock, and I go to see Rebekka in the bedroom.

It will be the first time I've seen my sister in three years.

Memories tumble through me. Rebekka, sitting beside me in the guttering light of a lamp, painstakingly teaching me to read, sounding out each letter over and over again until the sense of it burst in my mind like sunrise. Rebekka, laughing when my stitches in the darning Mama had set for me came out crazed, and then redoing them for me so I could slip outside to catch the moonrise. Rebekka, talking Mama down when Far was out late again, courting Aunt Olena.

Mama's voice: *Why can't ye be more like Rebekka?*

And then Rebekka left, and all her tasks fell to me.

I draw a deep breath, knock softly, and push the door open.

Rebekka's on her side in a bed set against one wall, piled

up with blankets. The curtains are drawn, but morning sun picks out a pattern on a cheerful rug, and a vase of fading pink roses sits beside the bed. If there's a faint smell of medical ointments in the air, I ignore it and make my way to my sister.

She blinks awake at my approach, her pale cheek curving in a smile. Her lips have scarcely any color, but her red-gold hair, braided down her back, is just as vivid as I remember. I bend down to brush a kiss across her temple, and she reaches out a fragile hand to take mine.

Blue veins stand out against her white skin, and I swallow my alarm. She's so thin. Surely a woman near term should be fat and rosy?

"You look well," Rebekka says, patting the coverlet beside her for me to sit. "I'm glad you've made it. We were worried when we got your telegram. But tell me of your travel, of everyone back home. It's so lovely to have you here—like a bit of home with me."

Her warmth melts my diffidence. I tell Rebekka of all our siblings back home, of Far and Mama, of baby Albert, whom she's never met. I describe the journey by rail. She laughs at our midnight encounter with the elk and gasps at the right places when I tell her about Texas Jack.

I don't tell her about the robbery or the memory of cool metal kissing my temple.

I don't tell her about Rachel's near drowning.

I don't tell her about Samuel Willard either.

While we're talking, Ammon comes back in. "How're you feeling today? Do you need me to stay home from church?"

Rebekka shakes her head. "Elizabeth is here. You should go to the meeting—you can tell me all about it afterward. It'll do us both good."

Ammon exchanges his work hat for a nicer derby and shrugs into a coat. "I'll have Sister McPherson call after church, to see how you're getting on."

"There's been no spotting today," Rebekka says. "But bring her, if it will soothe you."

"The baby is moving?" Ammon has made no motion toward the door.

"Sleeping now, I'd say, but moved a bit earlier." Rebekka smiles up at her husband. "I am well, truly."

Ammon turns his hat around in his hands a few times, watching Rebekka as though the entire world turns in her face. I wonder what it would be like to have someone watch me like that—if it would feel like sanctuary or suffocation. I do *not* wonder what it would be like to have Samuel look at me like that.

Finally, he stuffs the hat onto his head, kisses his wife, and leaves.

A long sigh leaks from my sister. "Ammon is a good man," she says. "He'll be a good father."

I'm not sure how to answer her, but it turns out it doesn't matter. Rebekka is already asleep, exhausted by two short conversations. Unease pricks my gut as silence shrouds the small house.

I tiptoe out of the bedroom and survey the kitchen and

sitting room. The place is a mess: papers stacked randomly across the table, dishes drying crusted in a tub, clothes (I cannot tell if they are clean or not) piled in a corner, dust drifting from every flat surface.

When Rebekka lived at home, our house was always spotless, even when Mama had her spells. If the house has gotten like this, then Rebekka has been sicker than I supposed.

No spotting today. Mama said Rebekka has lost babies before. Will she lose this one?

And what if the baby comes today, while Ammon and the others are at church? I have no idea where to go for help. I've been at Mama's births, for Henry and Rachel and Albert, but I only fetched and carried. That knowledge seems a fragile net to hold the weight of Rebekka and her baby's health.

I should have asked Ammon before he left.

Pushing aside my misgiving, I tidy up the little house as best I can and inspect the cupboard shelves near the stove for ideas of food, should Rebekka wake hungry. Rebekka has a new issue of the *Woman's Exponent* on a round table in the sitting room, but I only pick it up to swipe a dust rag beneath it. Rachel's near drowning hangs in my thoughts like a ghost—I'm afraid to fail at any duty now, as if Rebekka's life and that of her baby depend on my obedience.

Sister McPherson, the midwife, follows Ammon home from church. A middle-aged woman with a stout waist and large, squarish hands, she looks just like the sort of woman a heavenly mother would call as a midwife. She tuts over

Rebekka but announces there's been no real change. After she leaves, Rebekka rouses herself to come to the table for dinner—soup and cold bread—but even such little effort tires her and she goes to bed without eating much. Ammon and I eat the rest of our meal in silence. His unusual quiet unnerves me almost as much as Rebekka's exhaustion.

If Rebekka is so weak already, how will she survive childbirth?

Just before dark, a single rider comes up the road, bearing a message from Alice on pretty, scented paper.

Dear Elizabeth,

As predicted, Will turned up about midnight, none the worse for his adventure. In fact, he recommended that I try walking the trestle at the soonest opportunity. No, thank you! I admit I'm of two minds about his return. Obviously, I'm glad he's safe, and glad he's come so that we can return home. But I would not have minded if something small had happened to punish him—maybe he turned his ankle on reboarding the train—something to remind himself that he is not, *in fact, a cat with nine lives, and that his hare-brained decisions affect people other than himself. Alas, no such salutary lesson has occurred. I'm penning this just before we're to head to the station. When next I write, I shall be home.*

I hope you and your sister are well.

Your friend,
Alice Stevens

I look up from the letter, smiling, to find Ammon watching me. "Who's the letter from? I didn't know you knew anyone around here." Ammon isn't a fool—this letter wasn't delivered by the US mail or a telegram.

I fold the letter up and stick it in the pocket of my apron. "An acquaintance I met on the train. A lady and her brother. They were kind to me." That adventure has begun to feel like something that happened to a different girl, in a different lifetime.

Ammon only grunts in response.

✦

We retire early that night. Outside, the summer evening is still full of light. At least my bed is a trifle better: Ammon borrowed a feather mattress from someone at church, so I don't have to sleep on the floor.

It's a long time before I fall asleep.

✦

Monday, I tackle the wash.

At home, Mama takes care to always have our wash done on Monday—even on her bad days. The waving flags of clean laundry on the line signal a careful housekeeper, and whatever might happen privately at our home, our public face is always clean and tidy.

I suspect Rebekka feels the same.

I wash everything: the baby's small clothes, the bedsheets, my own clothes, dusty from weeks of travel. I heat the water for the laundry in a big tub on a fire before the house, coughing at the smoke that billows up when I prod the logs too vigorously. After adding the soap and a bit of lye to the water, I scrub the fabric against the washboard before rinsing in a separate bucket and wringing out. When the clothes are clean, I hang them on a wash line stretched between two willows.

The sun scorches my face and arms.

By the time I am finished, my hands are red and raw and my back aches. I don't feel Mama's satisfaction at a job well done, but I'm glad to have spared Rebekka this. I set some of Sunday's soup on the stove to heat, then go back outside.

A couple of rosebushes wilt alongside the wall of the house. I fetch some water from the nearby well and drizzle it over the bushes, watching the water spill across the shriveled leaves, soaking instantly into the cracked ground. Roses are rare in Monroe—the first rosebushes had to be carried as seedlings across the plains, and subsequent bushes were grown from carefully transplanted cuts. Ammon likely fetched these at a pretty price for Rebekka, who always loved them.

A sharp cry from the house startles me, and I drop the knife I brought from the kitchen, intending to cut a few blooms for Rebekka to replace the dying flowers by her bedside. My left hand grazes a thorn, and I stick my finger in my mouth as I hurry into the house. The blood is sharp and salty against my tongue.

Rebekka writhes on her bed, the sheets tangled around her.

"Rebekka?"

"I think the baby's coming," she says, then clutches her stomach, groaning.

"Are the pains coming regular?"

She nods, lips pressed tight. "Regular enough. Tell Ammon . . ." For a long moment she can't speak. "Fetch Sister . . . McPherson." She ends on a gasp.

Tell Ammon. I start to run from the room, then wheel back around. "Where is he?"

"North field."

I race outside. The fields simmer in the July heat. Sweat drips into my eyes, and I swipe it away. It takes longer than I like to find Ammon. "The baby's coming," I say. He drops the hoe he's been using, takes half a dozen strides to the horse grazing in nearby shade, and mounts.

He doesn't even look at me as he rides away.

I run back to the house.

Rebekka's room is dark after the brilliance outside. I blink, then sit by Rebekka. Her fingers lock around my wrist.

"I'm scared," she whispers.

My mouth dries out. Growing up, it was always Rebekka who comforted us when we were scared, Rebekka who always knew what to say. I don't know how to play that role for her.

But I put my other hand over hers, and maybe that's enough, because her grip relaxes.

She stares up at the ceiling. "I get lonely here, sometimes." A pain grips her—her whole body seems to tighten—and she doesn't speak till it's past. "I know I shouldn't. I'm where

God wants me to be. But it's hard. I miss you. I miss everybody back home."

"We miss you too," I say, though the words feel horribly inadequate. I want to say: *I don't know how to do what God wants me to do either.*

I hold Rebekka's hand through another pain. Then she says, "When I started spotting, I thought this baby had died, like all the others. And for a moment I was glad—glad!—that I would not have to go through a full birth, that I wouldn't have someone so small and helpless depending on me when I am still so weak." She pauses, and I think maybe it's another pain, but her face is smooth, a single tear streaking down her cheek. "Does that make me wicked?"

I grip her hand. "No." I don't think Rebekka could be wicked if she tried.

"I want this baby now," she whispers. "But maybe I don't deserve her. Or him."

"If God only doled out babies to folks who were deserving, there'd be a sight less babies in the world," I say tartly, letting Mama's cadences fall into my voice.

Rebekka smiles weakly.

"You'll be a good mama," I say firmly. I add, my voice wobbling a little, "You were always a good mama to me."

We don't talk much after that. Rebekka grips my hand when her pains come, and I try to count them. Five minutes or so between most, sometimes less.

I'm mighty glad to see Ammon return with the midwife.

She's brought a couple of other women with her from the ward.

Sister McPherson looks at Ammon. "Where do you keep your oil?"

"Mama sent some with me for a blessing," I say, then run to fetch the oil from my carpetbag, the glass smooth and cool to my touch, and bring it to Sister McPherson.

The midwife then sends Ammon from the room, telling him this is women's business. She and the other women settle around Rebekka's bed, preparing to bless her, as is common in childbirth.

Sister McPherson turns to me. "Will you say the blessing?"

Surprise and pleasure jolt through me. I've never done this before—it's always been the task of older women. More faithful women.

I remember my failed prayers over Rachel and hesitate.

But Sister McPherson smiles at me. "There's nothing to be afraid of. I'll show you how, if you'd like."

"Please, Elizabeth," Rebekka says. "It'll be a bit like having Mama here, since you carry her name." Elisa. Elizabeth.

We help Rebekka into a loose-fitting shift, and I let the midwife show me everything: we wash her belly first, then drop a bit of oil on it, smoothing it across the hot, tight flesh. Sister McPherson shows me how to bless her.

My voice unsteady, I echo, "We bless your stomach, that it might hold your babe securely, and release the child safely when the time comes." The women circled around me set their hands on Rebekka and murmur, *Amen.*

Repeating each action in turn—wash, anoint, pray—we bless her head and neck, her breasts, her legs, asking that each part of her body perform its appointed function in the safe delivery of her baby.

When we are finished, Rebekka grips my hand tight and cries, but she is smiling too, so I know I've done the right thing. What Mama would have done. What Aunt Elisa would have. I think of the chain of women I've suddenly become part of, all of us linked by faith and hope on the cusp of life (and sometimes death), and a dormant sense of wonder stirs in me. I thought I'd mastered the trick of looking at my life aslant, like the starlit sky, to make the lights seem brighter. But maybe I haven't been looking at it right at all, because all I've seen of my mother's life—of my future life—is the hard work. I've missed entirely this sense of being part of something bigger than yourself.

After the blessing, Sister McPherson makes Rebekka get out of bed and move. I support Rebekka as she walks around the room. One of the women goes to the kitchen to heat some water; I hear her talking to Ammon. The midwife strips the sheet from the mattress, spreads some newspapers across the bed, and replaces the sheet.

Rebekka sags against me as another of her pains hits her. Her grip on my hand is hard and tight.

"I want to lie down," Rebekka says, but Sister McPherson says no—it's better to keep moving till the baby gets closer.

Time begins to blur as the hours pass. The other women and I take turns helping Rebekka walk tight circuits of the room, and when she groans, the midwife encourages us to keep moving. Sometimes she checks Rebekka, feeling up beneath her shift in a way that makes me turn away in embarrassment.

Ammon paces in the kitchen and sitting room outside.

When night falls, we light a lamp in the bedroom, and I remember the herbs Mama sent for just this moment. The midwife insists on sniffing them first, as though she does not trust the judgment of some unfamiliar mother, then says, "Well, I do not know as they will help, but they aren't likely to hurt."

Another of the sisters brews the herbs into tea, and I hold it to Rebekka's lips for her to drink. The tea smells of cinnamon and cloves and something I can't quite place. A smell like caramelized sugar wafts back from the kitchen, the scent I always associate with Rebekka's mother. Maybe her mother is here in spirit.

Rebekka walks some more. Her pains are closer together now, but nothing seems to be happening. The midwife checks her again, frowns.

Rebekka catches the expression. "What is it? What's wrong?"

Sister McPherson clears her face. "Nothing's wrong. The babe is slow in coming, but that's not uncommon for first babies."

Sometime after midnight, we help Rebekka back into her bed. While the midwife and one of the sisters fuss over her,

I go around the room and unfasten the ties to the curtains, the strings that bind my apron together. I thought it was only Mama's superstition, to untie all binds during birth, but something is not right.

I slip outside. Dawn threads gray fingers into the sky, where the moon hangs, a flattened, washed-out circle.

I go back in. Rebekka's pains have slackened, and she twitches in a kind of half-sleep. The midwife paces the room, gnawing the knuckle of one finger. I sit by Rebekka, holding her hand, and pray.

"Is it false labor?" I ask the midwife. Mama had spells like that, with Rachel.

She shakes her head. "No. The signs are all in place for the baby to come—he's just taking his sweet time."

Morning comes along with Ammon, checking on the progress of the birth. He eyes his wife's pale face with concern, and the midwife says nothing to comfort him. The two sisters who came with Sister McPherson leave—they have their own families to mind, now day is come.

Ammon tends the animals, returns.

I make breakfast—boiled eggs and toast—but only Sister McPherson eats.

The day passes with agonizing slowness. The sun burns high overhead, then begins its steady descent. Insects hum and grate outside the window. Inside, it's stuffy and quiet. Rebekka has mostly gone silent, even when her now infrequent pains strike. Periodically, I help her sit so she can drink some of the warmed-over tea that Mama sent.

Midafternoon, the midwife sends Ammon to a neighbor for some beef broth.

"I don't like Rebekka's color," she tells him quietly.

I sit beside Rebekka and stroke her hand. I'm not sure she's aware of me at all—she seems far away, sealed in her own little world of pain, her eyes glassy.

As the afternoon edges toward dusk, the midwife checks Rebekka again. When she looks up, her face is grim. "Brother Walton, I think you'd best call for a doctor."

chapter fourteen

Tuesday, July 16, 1878
Outside of Cheyenne, Wyoming
Thirteen days until eclipse

The nearest doctor, Sister McPherson tells me after Ammon has run out the door, is in Cheyenne. It will be some time yet before he finds the doctor and returns. Doctors are expensive, usually called only as a last resort in childbirth.

I make a sandwich for the midwife, press some more tea on an unresisting Rebekka. It dribbles along her chin, and I wipe it away.

The faint scent of burned sugar intensifies—I check the stove to make sure that nobody spilled something there. It's clean, but the smell surrounds me.

Is Rebekka dying? I want to ask the midwife, but fear of her answer keeps me silent. I try to pray, but the words stick to my tongue. I sit by Rebekka and pick at a hangnail.

It's dark by the time Ammon arrives with the doctor. The doctor washes his hands, using some of the soap I used for the laundry, and then examines Rebekka. Ammon hovers awkwardly over his shoulder. The doctor asks questions about the time of labor.

"It's certainly well that you called me. When a laboring woman's pains slack off, as Mrs. Walton's have, it can be serious. My estimation is that the baby may be locked—I shall see what I can do to adjust its position and stimulate the return of labor."

The doctor mixes a few grains of dark powder in some water, and tips it down Rebekka's throat. Some of it spills down her cheeks, and she coughs. The midwife takes Rebekka's hand, and there's nothing for me to do but stand back and watch my sister.

A memory surfaces from my childhood. Hyrum and I had been playing with a pair of dolls that Aunt Elisa had sewn for Rebekka from empty grain sacks. A neighbor boy had swooped in and turned our domestic scene (two friends having tea) into a dueling battle. An arm popped off one of the dolls. Rebekka came in to find me and Hyrum crying in unison. She gave Hyrum the rest of a peppermint stick she had saved from Christmas and showed me how to stitch the arm back on the doll. A few days later, she presented me with a third doll, smaller and more misshapen than the others, but that I loved better because it had been made for me.

I don't want her to die.

Is this somehow my fault too? I cannot see any way that

I've neglected Rebekka as I did Rachel, but maybe my faith failed her. Maybe the blessing didn't take because of some fault in me. Because I haven't kept my promise as I should, because I keep wanting a life bigger than the one laid out for me.

I add a silent prayer: *Mother, Father, let her live.*

Rebekka groans and turns on her side, and the midwife snatches up an empty bowl from the top of a dresser and presents it to Rebekka just as she vomits.

"It burns," Rebekka says weakly.

"The pain is part of the blessing," the doctor says. "As Eve did, so all women must do."

Sister McPherson shoots him a frowning look. She leans close to Rebekka to whisper, "Never you mind him. You just do what your body is made to do."

Whatever the powder was, it seems to work. Rebekka's pains start up again, and she grips my hand so hard my fingers turn white.

Finally, the baby comes.

"Praise be!" the midwife says.

The doctor eases the baby free, and there's a moment of dizzying relief—the baby is here!—before fear sets in again. The baby isn't right. She—it seems to be a girl—is limp in the doctor's hands, her skin a kind of pale purple. She's not crying. Albert came out red and shrieking.

The doctor passes the baby to the midwife, who rubs a soft cloth across her face, her belly. The baby doesn't move. Beside the bed, Ammon asks, "What is it? What's wrong?" No one answers him.

Rebekka slumps back across the bed, a sudden, appalling gush of blood washing from her. The midwife shoves the baby into my hands, as both she and the doctor turn to Rebekka. Ammon drops to his knees beside the bed, his prayer so fast and harsh it might be an incantation.

I'm left alone, holding a baby that might be dead.

A familiar freezing creeps over me, my mind spinning helplessly.

No, I think. I can't freeze here. Not now. Not when Rebekka needs me to help her baby.

I force myself to think, to act. Anything. The umbilical cord is still attached to Rebekka, so I cannot move far. I take the soft cloth the midwife was using and rub the baby's face again. She's so lovely and still and warm and my heart is breaking with each brush. A tiny shadow moves in her throat. A pulse? Only my desperate wish?

I hold the baby closer to me, remembering how Hyrum breathed for Rachel beside the pool until she could breathe for herself. I pinch the miniature nose closed, and put my mouth over the tiny rosebud one, and breathe. One, two, three. Each breath becomes a prayer: *Please.* I pull back. Nothing. I press her chest gently, as though that might remind her to breathe. Then I breathe for her again.

I don't know how long I repeat this, trying to focus on the infant so I don't see the whirl of activity around Rebekka, the bright flash of red that keeps spreading.

Pink creeps slowly back into the baby's face, so slowly I almost miss it until the tiny chest rises. Once, then twice, and then the baby is breathing steadily, making small noises in her throat. I start to cry. Fetching one of the baby blankets Rebekka made before illness forced her to her bed, I wrap the infant up tightly. "The baby—" I try to speak, but choke.

The baby whimpers.

At the sound, the others, who have been arguing about something, fall silent.

Ammon turns to me in astonishment. "Is the baby—"

The little girl lets out another cry, louder this time, and his face crumples in relief. In the bed, Rebekka is white-faced and still. For a heartbeat, I think I've saved Rebekka's baby only to lose Rebekka. But no—her chest lifts and falls.

The midwife takes the baby from me, gently.

After that, things blur together. Eventually, it seems Rebekka will live, at least through the night, and the doctor takes his leave. The midwife tucks the baby into a cradle, and I stumble into the sitting room to my bed.

We've made it through.

I waver on my feet, my missing night of sleep finally catching up with me. I'm asleep before I hit the ground.

✦

Rebekka is still alive, but weak, when I check on her the next morning. The infant girl is tucked into the bed beside her, suckling. Rebekka's eyes are fixed on the baby. She strokes the downy fuzz on the baby's head and croons softly.

I know that look on her face. It's the way I felt when I first realized what stars are: the light of a thousand distant suns.

The midwife bustles around the room, collecting up her things. "You did a good thing last night, Elizabeth. You kept your head during a crisis and saved that baby. I'd say you have a knack for midwifing."

I should be pleased at her praise, pleased at her confirmation that I have a clear and right place in this domestic world I've chosen. That Mama and Dr. Morton are right.

And part of me is pleased—glad to have done something right, for a change. Grateful to have been able to help Rebekka and her baby. Another part of me is conscious of a slow, creeping chill that settles in my chest, wrapping around my heart.

Sister McPherson is still waiting for a reply.

I say, "I'm here to serve."

✦

The next few days pass in an exhausted blur. Sister McPherson comes back daily to check on Rebekka, who grows slowly stronger. I write a quick letter to Alice, to let her know the baby has come safely, and a longer letter to Far and Mama, with fuller details of the birth. Rebekka insists I bring the letter to her bedside, where she adds a postscript in wobbling handwriting, telling them I saved baby Ida's life.

I even start a letter to Samuel, but throw it into the stove fire when I catch myself. Clearly, I must be tired.

A bevy of sisters from church show up each morning to stock Ammon and Rebekka's larder with food and to wash out the baby things, which seem to collect at an astonishing rate. I forgot this paradox of babies, that something so small can make such tremendous messes.

The midwife continues to come daily to check on mother and baby. Ida's color is back and she is starting to regain the weight she lost at birth. When I look at her, at the honey-blond fuzz on her head, I see Rachel. I see redemption.

Rebekka looks at me as though someone has made me a saint. When she thanks me—about thirty times a day—I try to laugh and shrug it off. I'm no saint. If *I* truly saved Ida, I was only making up for past failures. And if I was the conduit for a miracle, I was only the tool, not the hands that wielded it.

I come in from hanging yet another batch of baby linens on the line to find Rebekka sitting up in bed, watching Ammon, who holds the tiny bundle of his daughter to his chest and spins in a slow circle. He sings, "Rockaby, lullaby, dear little rover, into the stilly world, into the lily world, go, oh, go—"

Rebecca's laugh peals out. "Into the stilly world? What on earth does that mean?"

Ammon stops singing. "Heck if I know. I don't know what a lily world is either!" His booming laughter makes the baby jerk awake. Her thin cry only makes her parents laugh harder.

Something squeezes tight around my heart.

I turn away quietly and creep back out of the house, letting the warmth of the sun wash over me like a benediction.

Busy as the days are, the nights are harder. Sister McPherson tells Ammon and me that Rebekka is to sleep as much as possible. Ammon has his own chores to do during the day and tends to sleep right through the baby wailing. That leaves me to walk the floors at night when baby Ida stares, entirely too bright-eyed, at the new world around her. I have yet to convince her that nights are meant for sleeping.

On the third night of baby Ida's life, I take her outside into the warm darkness. The waning moon reflects in her wide, blinking eyes. I make note of the moon's position, but it seems a pointless thing to do. I've left my notebook back in Monroe, and anyway, I'll be too tired in the morning to care.

Ida weighs almost nothing in my arms, her lightness a reminder of her uncertain beginning. One tiny fist emerges from the blanket I've swaddled her in, her wrist only a little bigger around than my thumb. The movement catches my heart, snags. The prophets tell us that there are untold numbers of souls in heaven, waiting for bodies. Waiting for mothers to carry them. I study Ida's little old-man face and think: *Maybe.* Maybe I could be one of them.

Light catches in Ida's eyes, and I look up.

Beneath the Perseus constellation, sparks of light fall like rain. The Perseid meteor shower. I snuck out last summer once to see the meteors—it was worth all the extra chores Mama set me when she caught me coming back in—but in the rush of the last few weeks I forgot about them.

I snuggle Ida to me and sit on the stoop to watch. She's warm and slight, and she nuzzles my neck, rooting for food. I'll have to take her in to Rebekka soon.

This is what Mama wants for me—this domestic life, with a husband, and a child, and only occasional glimpses of fire in the sky. I think of Rebekka and Ammon laughing with Ida. The way Ida searches my face like I search the sky.

This is enough, I tell myself.

I lean back on the stoop and watch the stars fall.

✦

By Friday, Rebekka is well enough to totter into the kitchen as I'm making breakfast, leaving Ida sleeping in the bedroom.

"Should you be up?" I ask, alarmed.

She waves her hand dismissively. "I have to get up sometime. I won't be long." She seats herself gingerly on a wooden chair at the table and accepts a bowl of oatmeal from me. She inhales. "It's nice to be alive. To taste food again. To kiss my daughter."

"I was worried you wouldn't be," I admit, taking a seat across from her.

She smiles a little ruefully. "I was worried I wouldn't be too. At first. Then I was too weak to care. Worse, I might have welcomed dying because it would mean I wouldn't hurt anymore." She lifts her shoulders, not quite a shrug. "All mothers walk through death. It's the price we pay for children."

I lift a spoonful of oatmeal, turn it over above the bowl, watch the oats fall back to be reabsorbed by their fellows.

Rebekka chews thoughtfully a moment, then swallows. "I thought I saw my mother, you know. Before Ida came."

I remember the caramel smell in the kitchen. "I'm sure she would have wanted to be here."

Rebekka's clear blue eyes rest on me. "Are you all right, Elizabeth?"

"I'm fine. A little tired."

"Do you know what I remember of you as a child?" my sister asks.

I shake my head, startled by her change of subject.

"You were always so full of questions and ideas, I thought Aunt Hannah would explode listening to you. Everything interested you, and you walked around like you had a lantern glowing inside you. But I've been watching you this week. You're quiet. You don't ask questions. It's like someone took that lantern and snuffed it. What happened to you, Elizabeth?"

There's an unaccountable prickling in my eyes. I must be more tired than I thought. I stare at my bowl, blinking so I won't burst into tears and alarm Rebekka. "Nothing happened. I'm trying to do the right thing, is all."

"Yes, but *whose* right thing?"

My head snaps up. "Isn't there just one right thing? As women, we grow up, we have families, we serve, we die."

Rebekka's lips tip up at the corners. It might be a smile. "You forgot the part where we're happy."

"It never seemed to me that God cared much if we were happy, as long as we do what we ought to."

"That sounds like something your mama would say," Rebekka says, sighing. "Your mama is a good woman, but she's wrong about some things. The Book of Mormon says, 'Men are, that they might have joy.' What does that mean, except God cares about our happiness? Don't confuse what your mama wants with what God wants."

I try to swallow, but the oats stick in my throat.

"If you could do anything you wanted," Rebekka says, "what would you do?"

I don't even have to think. "Go to Denver and see the solar eclipse happening later this month. Find a way to study astronomy."

Her pale eyebrows lift. "How would you support yourself in Denver?"

"I have a friend. I think she'd let me stay with her until I found work, long enough to see the eclipse." I didn't realize I planned so much of this out already.

"Then why don't you go?"

"What?" I stare at her. "But you—the baby—"

"You gave my baby back to me. I can't ask for more than that. And anyway, Ammon has a cousin that can come help, or the sisters from the ward. There are always babies going to be born and needing care. You can't make yourself responsible for all of them. And how will you know which path is right for you—what your mama wants for you, what you want—unless you try it?"

"I promised God," I blurt out. "I nearly killed Rachel—she almost drowned because I was distracted when I should have been watching her. She lived, and I promised I'd be more obedient."

Rebekka stirs her spoon around her bowl. "A promise is serious business. But I don't think God works on a barter system. And how do you know who you are meant to be? Perhaps you're meant to study the stars."

Her words sear through me like fire. Have I gotten this whole thing wrong? Have I confused God's will with Mama's? "You think I should go?"

"What does your heart tell you?"

My heart pounds in my throat. *Go, go, go.*

I think of the telescope, back in Rawlins, how a smudge sprang into clusters of light under the right focus. Maybe my own conflict is like that smudge—the effect of asking the wrong question, of choosing the wrong focus. Maybe I'm not meant to be a wife and mother, to be *my* mother. Maybe I am meant to study the stars instead.

Per aspera ad astra.

I spring from my seat, my bowl of oatmeal mostly untouched, and kiss Rebekka's cheek. "How are you so wise? You're going to be a wonderful mama."

Rebekka flushes with pleasure and returns the kiss. "I had lots of practice with you and the other children. Now, what are you going to do?"

"I'm going to Denver."

chapter fifteen

Friday, July 19, 1878
Outside of Cheyenne, Wyoming
Ten days until eclipse

Announcing that I am going to Denver proves to be far easier than accomplishing that fact. First, there are expenses. I use my last three quarters (all right, Alice's quarters) to send a telegram to Alice, to see if she's still willing to host me for a day or two and to ask if her grandfather might have need of a worker in his hotel. Rebekka has a few dollars saved from her housekeeping accounts, but it is not enough to cover the full cost of the train ticket—and I can't take all of her savings.

Ammon returns to the house at lunch and finds Rebekka and me sitting at the table, three crumpled dollars and some loose change spread out before us. He's got a brace of rabbits slung over his shoulder.

"What's all this?" he asks.

Rebekka explains that I'm going to Denver, an announcement that causes only a tiny ripple of surprise on Ammon's face. Few things upset him for long. "But we're short the money we need," Rebekka finishes. "Most of our savings went to the doctor."

Ammon scratches his red beard. "I can take these rabbits down to the general store. That'll bring a bit more."

The store. My heart starts pounding. "Do they sell anything at the store aside from foodstuff and general goods?"

"A few toys and books and other specialty items, like jewelry and mirrors," Rebekka says.

I go to my bag and fish out Mary Somerville's book. Of the two books I borrowed from Miss Wheeler, it has fared the best. The other dried all wavy and water-damaged, but this one is nearly intact, only a little discoloration on the edges and a few curled pages. I hand it to Ammon with a pang. I hope Miss Wheeler will understand what I'm about to do with her book.

"See if this fetches something too."

✦

By late afternoon the following day, I'm going through a now familiar routine: climbing down the metal stairs onto a wooden platform, retrieving my luggage from a porter. I marvel that only a few weeks ago I had never done any of these things.

I arrive with my sister's words still echoing in my ears:

How do you know who you are meant to be? Perhaps you're meant to study the stars.

Now that I'm in Denver, I intend to find out what I'm capable of. I mean to see the eclipse, to seek out the scientists in the city, to learn as much as I can about the eclipse and figure out how someone like me can get to college to study astronomy.

Setting a goal like this—a goal just for me, a goal that flies in the face of what others expect of me—is both exhilarating and terrifying. Maybe this is how Will felt, when he stepped out onto the trestle.

It's a feeling I could get used to.

I skirt the station and emerge into the cross streets before the Denver and Rio Grande building. Though it is early evening, the street is ablaze: gas lamps lining the streets, lights from the hotel adjoining the station, and long gold streams from the brick-front businesses facing me, their doors thrown open late to catch the traffic from the incoming train.

Streets splinter away at right angles from the tracks, opening up before me like some darkening maze, and as I peer down them, they appear endless, crammed with three- and four-story buildings, church spires soaring above them in the distance. I have never seen a city so big—bigger even than Salt Lake City.

But before the city has time to completely overawe me, Alice is calling my name and waving to me. Will saunters behind her.

"Well, what do you think?" she demands, gesturing at the city around her.

"It's so . . . big," I manage.

"The crown jewel of the plains," she says proudly. "When the Union Pacific Railroad snubbed us and ran through Cheyenne instead of Denver, everyone thought Denver would shrivel away. Instead, we raised nearly three hundred thousand dollars in just a few days to run our own railroad, the Denver and Rio Grande, up to Cheyenne, and now we are the fastest-growing city in the West."

If I mean to make a study of entire universes, I can't let one city daunt me. I lift my chin. "It's lovely."

Will tips his hat. "Good to see you again, Elizabeth."

"And you, Will. I'm happy to see you're all in one piece."

Will glances uneasily at Alice, who has folded her arms across her chest. "Ah, about that . . . My parents don't know, and I'd take it as a favor if you don't mention it to them."

I nod understanding, and follow the Stevens siblings to the curb, where a carriage waits. It's big and dark and gleaming and nicer than anything I've ever ridden in, including the trains. Their driver loads up my trunk, and Will helps me into the vehicle.

We drive down Sixteenth Street, where they point out the enormous four-story, white-brick hotel that belongs to their grandfather.

"The Trans-Oceana," Alice tells me.

"It's magnificent," I say, and they both grin at me.

Buildings flow past the window of our carriage: hotels and churches, bakeries and groceries, blacksmiths' forges, dressmakers' shops, saloons, laundries, and so many more. The overwhelming feeling from the station begins to creep up me again, and I take a deep breath.

The buildings begin to spread farther apart, interspersed with occasional houses with neat yards and picket fences. We turn left, passing before a large building with a clock tower, which Alice tells me is the local high school. I crane my neck to watch it as we pass: A whole building, devoted just to upper students? I can almost feel the electricity of ideas gathering about the place.

We come at last to a street of grand houses, and stop before a gabled home, painted gray with white trim. Will helps Alice and me climb down from the carriage. A dark-haired woman in an elegant blue dress waits in the doorway.

Alice leads me toward the woman and introduces us. "Elizabeth, this is my mama, Louisa Stevens, the finest woman on either side of the Mississippi."

Alice must get her high cheekbones and wide, dark eyes from her mama. I take Mrs. Stevens's offered hand and shake it.

Mrs. Stevens says, "You'd best all come in. I've got Cook laying out a cold supper for you."

My stomach gurgles, and I clap my hands across the offending organ. Will smothers a laugh. But if Mrs. Stevens hears, she politely pretends not to. A manservant goes out to the carriage to unload my trunk, and then the driver takes the carriage away.

Louisa Stevens leads us down a wide hallway to a dining room, where a maid is laying the table for three, setting out slices of cold meat alongside porcelain bowls with strawberries and cream. Pretty little pink roses dance across the rim of the bowls, around the perimeter of the plates.

We all settle down to eat. Before I've even finished the berries—so ripe, they burst in my mouth—the maid has returned, bearing slabs of a thick, fruity cake. A tall white man with light brown hair and a bemused expression follows in her wake.

"Papa!" Alice says as he seats himself at the table beside his wife. "I didn't think you'd be coming tonight."

A lick of surprise jolts through me. Alice didn't mention that her father was white—but then, why should she? Interracial marriages are not common in the West, especially now that many places have laws against them, but they are not unheard of either. It's my own fault for making assumptions again.

"Just in time for dessert, I see," Mrs. Stevens says, a trifle drily.

Mr. Stevens leans over to kiss her cheek. "Best part of the meal." He smiles around at his children, but his expression hitches a little when he reaches me.

"Papa, this is Elizabeth Bertelsen. We met . . . in Rawlins," Alice says. "After the accident."

His expression clears. "Ah, yes. You mentioned she was coming." He reaches a hand across the table and shakes mine firmly. "It's lovely to meet you."

"And you, sir."

"Alice says you are here to see the eclipse," he says. "You must take a keen interest, to come all this way alone."

"Yes, sir," I say. "I've had an interest in astronomy since before I was old enough to spell the word."

Mrs. Stevens smiles at me. "It's good for young ladies to have hobbies to keep their interests balanced. You should ask Alice to show you her paintings."

"I hope to." I pick up my fork. But despite my hunger, I can't touch the cake. There's something I need to make clear. I turn to Mrs. Stevens. "You've been so kind to me, letting me stay on almost no notice, feeding me this splendid meal. But I don't mean to impose. If you know of work, at your father's hotel or elsewhere, I'd like to support myself while I'm here."

Apparently Alice didn't convey that part of my message to her mama, because Mrs. Louisa Stevens raises her eyebrows. "Nonsense. You're Alice's guest, and it would be our pleasure to let you stay. We don't require guests to work for their board."

"I appreciate that, ma'am. But my mama always taught me that as a guest or part of the family, it's my job to contribute something. I'm used to hard work. I'd be glad to help out if I can," I say.

Mr. Stevens says, "Nice to see that not all young people have lost sight of the value of hard work."

Will lets his fork and knife fall to the table with a clatter. Alice stares fixedly at her lap. Mrs. Stevens says, "Ambrose, perhaps this can wait?"

"Wait for what? I'm only expressing approval of a good work ethic."

Will flexes his hands. "And disapproval of your only son? I'm sorry I'm such a disappointment to you, Papa."

"I didn't say that," his father says. "But since you've brought it up: Why won't you show an interest in the business you were raised to? Your mama and I both work to help your grandfather run the hotel, but you've not turned up for a day of work since your vacation in California. If a young lady with only a glancing connection to our family is willing to work for us, why won't my son?" He looks at Will, who sits stone-faced. "It's time you settled to something. Air dreaming and charming the ladies do not constitute work."

Without a word, Will stands and leaves the room.

The sweetness of the cake has gone clammy in my mouth. "I'm sorry. I didn't mean to make trouble."

Mr. Stevens sighs. "No, it's my fault for bringing it up at supper. It's only that I worry for the boy." He turns a rueful smile on me, and despite my discomfort, I'm not immune to the charm of it. "A father does, you know."

We pick at our cake in silence for a moment.

Then Mrs. Stevens says, "If you're serious about the work,

I'm sure Father could use the extra hands, what with all the people coming for the eclipse."

"I am." I take a deep breath. "Thank you."

Alice adds, "Elizabeth is Mormon, Mama." Maybe she thinks this will account for any odd behavior, or maybe she means to distract from the awkwardness about Will, but I feel myself blushing. I didn't mean to reveal that quite so abruptly.

Mrs. Stevens freezes, her cup halfway to her lips. She sets it down carefully, with a tiny *clink*. Even that small noise sounds refined. My fingers go cold, despite the warm evening, and I brace myself for what's coming. *Please go.*

"Are you all right?" Mrs. Stevens asks me, studying my face. "Not hurt? Is anyone . . . looking for you?" She doesn't wait for me to respond but answers her own question. "It doesn't matter. You can stay here as long as you need. We won't let them take you back."

I stare at her, utterly lost. What is she talking about?

When I don't say anything, she continues. "I read Mrs. Stenhouse's book. I know what it must have been like, poor darling. Did your husband . . . hurt you?"

Ah. Fanny Stenhouse's exposé of polygamy. Of course she read it. Seems almost everyone has—it was in all the newspapers when it came out six years ago. The mean things outsiders say about Mormons I can mostly brush aside, because they come from a place of ignorance. But Fanny Stenhouse— she was one of us. She talked with the prophets. Worshipped in our temples. And then decided she didn't believe any of it and wrote up all our secrets, all our sacred beliefs—mixed with a fair bit of nonsense—for outsiders to pick through and scorn.

"I'm not running away from a plural marriage, ma'am." I think of Mama encouraging me to become a second wife and sigh. Well, it's mostly true. "But I *am* Mormon. That's how I was raised, what I believe. If it troubles you to have me in your home, I understand."

Mrs. Stevens continues to watch me, a slight frown marring her smooth forehead. Then her face clears. "Well, I assume you need food and shelter same as anyone, and I can see that your manners are nice. I don't suppose you can help what you're raised to."

"Mama!" Alice says.

I smile a little—Mrs. Stevens has only said what Alice said, on the train, but more gently. I've heard worse.

Mr. Stevens changes the subject. "Alice, you should take Miss Bertelsen to that dance you're all going to tonight."

"Does your religion allow dancing?" Mrs. Stevens asks.

"Yes, indeed. Brigham Young was a great fan of dancing; he believed it was important for the body to be exercised, and for people to have a break from work."

Mrs. Stevens says, "I was a great fan of dancing, in my youth."

"I'm still a great fan of your dancing, my dear," Mr. Stevens says, smiling at his wife, who only shakes her head at him.

"Do come. It promises to be grand. And don't you dare

say you've nothing to wear," Alice says, just as I say, "But I've nothing to wear to a dance."

Everyone laughs—partly, I think, in relief at finally moving past the earlier uncomfortable conversations.

Mrs. Stevens clears her throat. "I'm sure I can find something in my closet that will fit you well enough." Alice's mama is a little taller than me, but we are both rather round. I'd never be able to squeeze into one of Alice's dresses.

"You should come," Alice says again, so I agree.

Even on this short acquaintance, I've learned better than to argue with Alice. Trying to resist her is like trying to stand up to the wind that scours through Monroe canyon. It's easier to let her have her way, even if part of me would rather stay in this lovely house and sleep.

While Mrs. Stevens sails off to find a dress, Alice shows me upstairs.

I'm given a room on the second story, with a big window that faces toward the buildings of downtown Denver. The coverlet is white and lacy, to match the curtains stirring at the window, and a painting of a mother and child in a rose garden hangs on one wall. The woman looks like Mrs. Stevens.

"Is this yours?" I ask Alice.

"One of my early ones," Alice says, making a face at it, but I like it. It's warm and full of light.

A maid turns up a short time later with a gold dress spilling over her arms, and Alice leaves to change. The maid helps me undress, then fastens a bustle about my hips before buttoning me into the gown. The gold color complements my skin and hair, but the wide neckline exposes more of my shoulders (and the freckles across them) than I'm used to. The padded bustle adds depth to the folded swirls of skirt, but it makes me feel off balance and wider than usual. I'm not quite sure how to walk in such a thing. Mama would say the dress was a worldly extravagance—but I watch myself in the mirror as the maid does my hair, and I look like a different person. Like someone brave. Like someone who could study the stars.

In all, I feel both pretty and wicked.

There isn't room for all of us to fit into the carriage, thanks to the full skirts the ladies wear. So Will, Alice, and I pile into the carriage, with Mr. and Mrs. Stevens promising to follow shortly. Will is in high spirits, having either forgotten or chosen to ignore the conversation at dinner.

Alice wears the most stunning dress I have seen yet: a deep blue silk with long, flowing lines, a seamless cut from shoulder to hem. It's the latest European style, she says, fitted through the waist to the hips, with the heavy layers of the skirt drawn up artfully behind her with only a very small bustle. It makes her already slender figure elegant and regal, and the color makes her skin glow. I do not know how to sit in the carriage without squashing both my bustle and my gown, and so I spend the distance to the hotel uncomfortable and rigid, holding most of my weight off the seat.

By the time we reach the hotel, the whole of Sixteenth Street is crowded with carriages of people arriving for the dance. The Trans-Oceana is a beautiful structure: four stories, with a roof that doesn't come to a point all at once, but has two slants to each side. Inside, a half-circle desk of dark walnut fronts a wall with matching key racks. An ornate wooden box hangs on the wall near the desk, with a series of numbers on the face and small arrows beneath each number. As we walk across the marbled flooring of the entryway toward the desk, a small bell jangles and one of the porters rushes out of the lobby into the hallway beyond it.

"Grandpa has the best of everything in his hotel," Alice tells me. "That's an annunciator—if guests want anything, they have only to push a button in their room and it rings a bell at the desk. The arrows tell the porter which room rang the bell."

I marvel at the technology, which seems almost akin to magic. If I'm given a chance to work here, I shall inspect how the buttons in the rooms communicate with the bell.

We don't go immediately to the ballroom; instead I follow Alice and Will a short distance down the hallway to an office, where a man with nearly white hair and brown skin sits behind a desk, working through a ledger. Alice introduces me to her grandfather.

Mr. Lancelot Davis greets me gravely and kindly before teasing Will for his fine clothes and giving Alice a kiss on her cheek, telling her she looks lovely. I wonder if he always works so late, or if he is also here for the dance.

Alice explains to him that I am looking for work, and we settle that I will come in mornings through the week of the eclipse. He doesn't seem to mind that tonight I'm a guest and

Monday I will be an employee, and I like him all the better for it.

"I don't think I could employ you full-time, but I own another pair of hands will be helpful," Mr. Davis says, shaking my hand to seal our deal.

Finding work in Denver has proved easy enough, but I fear the next task will be more daunting: to get through a dance with strangers in an unfamiliar city with my dignity intact.

chapter sixteen

Saturday, July 20, 1878
Denver, Colorado
Nine days until eclipse

The Trans-Oceana doesn't have a formal ballroom, but the dining room has been cleared of tables and chairs, and gas lamps burn brightly around the room. The aroma of roses surrounds us the instant we step inside, drawn from garlands strewn liberally about the walls and blooms placed in vases at tables around the edges of the room. Food and drink weigh down the tables, and chairs line the walls for those not inclined to dance.

Butterflies jitter in my stomach. At home, a dance like this would be a pure pleasure, but I am not sure the energetic jigs and reels I know are the same kind danced among such fancy folk.

I tie a dance card around my wrist with a crimson ribbon,

and run my finger down the list of dances: Plain Quadrille, Nine Pin, Polka Redowa, Gladiator, Pop Goes the Weasel, Gallopade, Varsovienne. . . . Most of these I do not recognize. What if someone signs my card for one of those unknown dances? What if no one does? What if I knock someone over with this bustle?

Drawing three deep breaths, I quell the rising surge of panic. I'm here at Alice's request; I do not have to dance. And who knows? Perhaps one of the visiting scientists will be present tonight.

Alice leads me around the room, introducing me to her friends. The crowd here is mixed: mostly white folks, some black, but nearly all seem to be well-off, and everyone likes Alice. I wonder if this mix is normal for Denver, or just reflective of the Stevens family.

I step carefully behind Alice, conscious of the bustle swinging with my steps and the train dragging behind me. Among the guests, I meet Henry Wagoner, an older black man, with chin-length white hair and a full white beard. Alice tells me that he is a friend of her grandfather who now works as a clerk for the Colorado legislature, and that they met in Chicago, where Mr. Wagoner worked on setting type for an abolitionist magazine. "If it weren't for Mr. Wagoner," Alice says, "Grandpa would never have come to Denver to make his fortune."

Mr. Wagoner winks at us. "All Lance's best ideas came from me. Well, excepting your fine grandmother, God rest her soul. Marrying her was all his doing."

A couple of Alice's friends sign their names on my dance card, which relieves my fear of not being asked but raises a new fear. I peek at my card after they have gone, praying I do not make a fool of myself.

Eventually, the music starts up, from a four-piece orchestra in a corner of the room. A caller stands near them, announcing the name of the first dance, a quadrille. And just like that, the dance begins. At home, we open with a prayer and a grand march, with the community heads promenading around the room in time to music. Here, there is no such warning.

I could have used the warning, as Alice and I take our places on the floor with our partners, in a square made of four couples. I am not ready for this dance, not sure of my steps, or the bustle that weighs me down. At least my gloves hide my sweating palms. My partner, a tall boy with sandy blond hair, bows to me and I curtsy back, then curtsy to the partner at my right. The caller, bless him, calls out the steps as we go, and though this quadrille is not quite the sort I am used to, I find I do know several of the steps and if I am not especially graceful, I am not *dis*graceful either.

We dance a Nine Pin next, which Alice tells me is a newly fashionable import from the East and works well in Colorado, where there are more men than women, since it requires an extra gentleman, who takes his position inside the circle of dancers and then turns each lady in succession. Whenever the music stops, whichever gentleman is without a partner must take his position inside the center of the circle. There is some confusion in our group when the music stops, and much laughing, and another layer of my anxiety flakes away. I am not the only one who doesn't know all the steps.

During a break in the dancing, Mrs. Stevens joins me, a glass of wine in one hand. "I hope you're having a pleasant time," she says. "Have my children been taking care of you?"

"It's a lovely party. Alice has introduced me to so many kind people. She seems very popular."

"Good," she says, though she frowns a little. Her eyes skim the crowd until they settle on Alice, dancing with a young black man. "I do worry that she sets people at a distance sometimes. A girl her age should be thinking of settling down, not talking of studying art in distant schools. Her grandfather and I have worked hard to build this hotel, hoping that Alice might enjoy a social position that we never did. But she seems determined to have none of it."

I don't know why Mrs. Stevens is telling me this. Perhaps the wine is more potent than she realizes. I'm relieved of having to answer when Alice waves at me after the dance ends, beckoning for me to join her. I excuse myself and cross the floor toward Alice.

Alice gestures to her father, who stands a few feet away talking to a slim, dark-haired woman, and says to me, "There's someone I think you should meet."

"Ah! Dr. Avery, you remember my daughter, Alice?" Mr. Stevens smiles at us as we approach.

I wonder if I have heard him right—*Doctor* Avery? I study the woman doctor with new interest. She is a little above my height, with intelligent eyes and lines about her mouth that suggest she smiles a great deal.

"Of course I remember Alice," Dr. Avery says. "I sat for one of her paintings only a few months ago. She's very talented." Her voice is cultured, smooth—the voice of an eastern transplant, not someone who's grown up in these mountains.

"She's a fine little artist," Mr. Stevens says. Does he notice how the glow in Alice's face dims at his diminishing words?

Alice says, "Dr. Avery, may I introduce my friend Elizabeth Bertelsen? She's come to Denver from Utah for the eclipse."

Dr. Avery turns to me. "Have you?" A smile tugs at her lips. "What a curious coincidence. As it happens, I have a group of women astronomers who are coming to stay at my house for the eclipse. Miss Maria Mitchell is an old friend of mine. Do you know of her work?"

Maria Mitchell? Truly? For a moment I can only gape at her, until Alice squeezes my hand encouragingly. "How could I not? She's the finest astronomer in America."

Dr. Avery's smile deepens. "Would you like to meet her? She arrives tomorrow, but I should think by Monday afternoon she'll be sufficiently rested for company. I know she's always keen to encourage girls in the study of science."

I give my enthusiastic assent, and our little party breaks up. I turn to Alice. "Did you know? About Miss Mitchell?"

"I might have heard something," Alice admits, grinning.

"I don't know how I can thank you enough."

"You can sit for me," Alice says, so promptly that she must

have been planning this already. "For my portraits of the West series? I haven't got a Mormon yet."

Something about how she phrases that, as though all Mormons are interchangeable, chafes at me. But for her kindnesses—introducing me to Dr. Avery, giving me a place to stay—I could forgive Alice anything. Still—I look at her doubtfully. "Are you sure your viewers won't be shocked?"

"What if they are? Besides, that red of your hair is lovely. I'm itching to catch it."

I flush, pleased. "I'd be happy to. Only say when."

Still glowing from his most recent turn around the floor, Will saunters up to us. He's not sat out a single dance, and from his partners' expressions, I gather they enjoy the exercise nearly as much as he does.

"Having a good time?" Will asks me.

"Very much so!" I say, thinking of Dr. Avery's invitation to meet Miss Mitchell.

"But you haven't danced with me yet," Will says. "How can you say you're enjoying yourself? We must fix that at once." He demands to see my dance card and scrawls his name beside the Varsovienne. I look up in dismay.

"I can't dance that with you, Will. I don't know the steps. I'll tread all over your feet, I'm sure of it."

Will only grins at me. "Then I will wear those bruises as a badge of honor."

"You can't wish me to make a fool of you in front of all your friends." What I mean is, you can't wish me to make a fool of *myself* in front of your friends.

But Will doesn't seem to understand my subtle plea, and his charm is impossible to resist, so when the next set forms and Will extends one white-gloved hand to me, I follow him to the middle of the floor. His smile is wide and sparkling as he takes in the energy in the room. He's a born leader, this boy, with more charm than is good for him.

Turns out, the Varsovienne is a kind of waltz that opens with a polka step. I'm distracted by Will's nearness, by the sharp piney smell of his soap, and the warm, firm touch of his hand to my back. Alice whirls past on the arm of a dark-haired boy.

I look around the room, the couples swirling past us. "It feels as though we might be at the center of the universe."

"Here?" Will laughs. "Denver is well enough, but it's a veritable backwater compared to some of the big cities in the world. New York; Washington, D.C.; Paris."

"You've been to Europe?" It might as well be the moon.

"Once," Will says. "It's a little staid for my tastes. I'd rather go west—see the islands of the Pacific, or China, or India. Where's the sense in traveling somewhere you already know about? I want to travel to places I don't know."

The dance shifts, speeding up, adding a series of quick, graceful steps that I struggle to follow. As we pass by the door into the hall, I catch a flash of movement in the doorway, a face and silhouette so familiar my heart seizes for a moment. *Samuel.*

Surely I'm only imagining him. I crane my head to see better, but as my attention lapses from my steps, my feet tangle in the full skirts of my gown. There's a brief flip of terror, and then I am falling, pulling Will down with me.

Will turns his body, so that he hits the floor first and I land atop him.

Will is laughing, his face so close to mine that I could count the freckles on his cheeks if I wanted. So close I can see the flecks of gold in his eyes, smell the lemon and sugar on his breath.

Face burning, I try to scramble to my feet, but the bustle makes it nearly impossible to move. I have to wait, humiliatingly, for Will to stand, to pull me to my feet. My dress may be pretty, but it makes me helpless as an infant. Maybe that's the point.

Alice rushes toward us, unsuccessfully trying to suppress the amusement that twists her lips. But I can hardly attend to her, or to Will, who is trying to ask if I'm hurt.

I'm still looking around the room for a brown-haired boy with a wide forehead and kind eyes. Samuel said he had business in Denver—but why should the thought that Samuel might still be in Denver make my heart pound so hard and fast? We scarcely parted as friends.

Even so, when I can't see anyone like Samuel in the room, I brush aside Will and Alice's questions and surge through the crowd toward the door. The hallway is empty when I reach it, and I dash—well, waddle, my bustle swinging behind me— toward the lobby.

A cheerful melody floats behind me from the ballroom. The lobby is nearly empty. I'm about to turn back to the ballroom, when I spot a young man standing at the desk, talking to the clerk.

"Samuel!"

The man looks up, just as Alice slides to a halt beside me. "Is everything all right?" she asks.

It *is* Samuel. He's wearing the suit he usually wears to church, with a curly-brimmed derby I've never seen on his head.

"Yes," I say. "It's all right. Just a friend from home." The conflicting emotions surging through me at the moment might give the lie to my statement, but Alice doesn't need to know that.

Samuel leaves the desk to join us. His eyes flicker over my borrowed finery, but his mild smile doesn't change. "Good to see you, Miss Bertelsen. I didn't recognize you."

I'm not sure how to read this. Is it a good thing, that I don't look like myself? His formality suggests perhaps it is not.

Alice nudges me, and I flush. I'm forgetting my manners. "Alice, this is my friend Samuel Willard. Samuel, Alice Stevens. Her grandfather owns this hotel."

"Pleased to meet you," Samuel says, doffing his hat. "It's a fine hotel. I've been staying here the last couple of days while I'm in Denver on business."

"And how do you find Denver?" Alice asks.

"The crown jewel of the plains, or so I'm told," Samuel says, a familiar grin curling his lips. "The city's pretty, the women"—he tips his head toward Alice—"even prettier."

Alice laughs. "Very *prettily* said, Mr. Willard."

"I do try," Samuel says with false modesty. He casts a swift, glinting look at me as if to say, *See? Some people appreciate my wit.*

Alice smiles. "Excuse me, I must go—I'm engaged for the next dance. But you are welcome to join us, Mr. Willard."

"Only if you'll dance with me," Samuel says, quick as that.

Alice laughs again. "It would be my pleasure."

Samuel watches as Alice walks down the hall, a tall elegant figure in a softly swishing dress. I fight down a strong desire to poke him. When Alice disappears into the ballroom, he turns back to me.

His eyes drop from my face to my chest and then flash up, his cheeks flushing red. I wish I had a shawl or something to cover my shoulders. A gown like this didn't stand out in the ballroom, but under Samuel's scrutiny, I'm reminded that no one at home owns a dress like this. No one at home would expose so much of her shoulders or bosom in public.

I brace myself for judgment.

"You look beautiful," Samuel says. "Like you're wrapped in sunlight."

Maybe it's not all bad that I don't look like myself.

"How did you come to be in Denver?" he asks. "I thought you were in Wyoming with your sister."

"I was. I helped Rebekka at the delivery, and then she decided I looked unhappy and helped me get to Denver for the eclipse. I'm staying with the Stevenses—Alice's family."

"I'm glad you'll get to see the eclipse. I know it's what you wanted."

I listen for a note of irony, but there's none. He means it.

We both stand there for a moment. Finally, Samuel sets the derby hat on his head. "It's been good to see you, Elizabeth. I hope you have a fine time at your party, and that the eclipse is everything you hope it will be."

He turns away. I don't know if he's heading back to his room, claiming his dance with Alice, or exiting the building, but he's leaving me.

My heart thuds against my breastbone. If I say nothing, if I let him walk away now, we'll go back to that casual neighborliness we shared before we left Monroe. He will tease me sometimes, and I will ignore him most times.

Do I want that?

Or I could say something. I could apologize and bring him back and open the door to something bigger: a real friendship. Maybe more. Somehow, that scares me more than saying nothing.

But Samuel said I looked like wrapped sunlight, wearing a dress that makes me brave and maybe a little wicked.

"Wait," I say.

It's not the most eloquent start to an apology. But Samuel stops and looks at me.

I swallow and run my tongue across my lips. Samuel's

eyes follow that movement and fix on my mouth. I blush. "I owe you an apology. I didn't mean those terrible things I said about you back by Mona."

A familiar, teasing gleam comes back into Samuel's eyes, and my body loosens in relief. Then he says, "Are you expecting me to eat my words too? I should tell you, I don't eat crow. Or humble pie."

This time I do poke him.

Samuel falls back a step, laughing. "But words? I suppose words go down easy enough. I'm sorry too." He holds out his hand to me. "Truce?"

I take it, shaking firmly.

"I suppose I'd better accompany you to this dance of yours. I promised your friend I'd dance with her." He holds out his arm, and I take it.

As we walk, I tell Samuel about the robbery, about meeting Alice and Will.

He looks startled. "I heard about the robbery. I didn't know it was your train! By the time I came through from Salt Lake, everything was back to its regular order. Are you all right?"

"I'm fine. And now I shall have a story for the children when I get home." *When I get home.* For a moment, it's hard to breathe—I feel the close expectations of home gathering around me, disapproving of where I am, what I am wearing.

When we reach the ballroom, another dance has already started. Alice stands near the head of the room with a partner. Beside me, Samuel heaves a mock sigh.

"I've been jilted. You'll have to save me from disgrace and dance with me."

I peek at my dance card. The spot for the current dance is conspicuously empty. Satisfying as it would have been to show Samuel I was already claimed, I suppose I should take pity on him. He is a neighbor, after all.

No one but Alice seems to mark our entrance, and she grins at us. We find an unoccupied bit of floor in one corner. Unfamiliar music wafts through the room, and my heart sinks a little, but it turns out it's some kind of waltz.

Samuel takes me in his arms.

His hand is warm at the small of my back, his grip firm but not hard. It takes us a minute to find our footing—I step on his shoes and he treads on the hem of my skirt. But eventually we figure it out and relax into the movement. Samuel tells me about the furniture seller he visited that morning to learn about a new inlay technique, and I tell him about Rebekka, the tense birth, and baby Ida.

I try not to notice how well our two bodies move together.

Maybe it's just that seeing someone from home in a new place makes all their angles seem softened, their annoyances seem friendly just because they're familiar.

But maybe—

I glance up at Samuel and find him watching me. When our eyes catch, a blush like sunburn spreads across his cheeks.

Maybe it's something else entirely.

chapter seventeen

Sunday, July 21, 1878
Denver, Colorado
Eight days until eclipse

The next morning, a Sunday, the Stevens family invites me to attend their Methodist worship services with them, in a brick church on Stout Street. I don't realize until we walk into the chapel that it's a black Methodist church, with a black minister leading the congregation. Mr. Stevens and I are among only a handful of white faces spread through the crowd. I feel uncomfortably exposed, more aware of myself and my round body, my pale skin, than I normally am. I wonder if this is how Will and Alice feel all the time, in a mostly white city like Denver.

The opening hymn pulls me out of my thoughts, grounding me in the pew. I've never been to another church's service, and at first everything seems strange, from the songs I do not know to the energetic way the congregation responds to the preacher's sermon. "Amen! Hallelujah!"

The sermon touches on the upcoming eclipse and the wonder of God's creation. Crimson and gold light streams through the stained-glass window at the front of the church, spreading glowing pools across the wooden pews.

I think about Sister James, whom I met on the train. She could have worshipped in a congregation like this, served by a minister who shares her race. Instead she chose my same religion, even though she has faced prejudice there, even though, like many churches in America, we do not ordain black men to the priesthood. Sitting beside Alice, I'm embarrassed that I haven't thought about this much, because it didn't affect me. But I should think about it. I should care. The Bible teaches that we are all one body in Christ—that which touches one of us should touch all of us.

I can't hold God accountable for the foolish things people do in His name, but maybe I can set a higher standard for people. For myself.

At church we talk about how *we* have God's truth. Sister James's path to God led her to the Mormons. But Alice's led her here, to the Methodists. Maybe there are lots of places where people can find God, and lots of paths to Him. Where will I find mine?

The sermon winds down, and the strains of the final hymn ring out. This time, I recognize it, though the music is a little different. "O God, Our Help in Ages Past."

I sing with gusto, my voice mingling with Alice's in a subtle harmony.

✦

After a lunch of cold meat and fruit and cheese, Alice shows me her paintings, all kept in a room on the upper floor with a south-facing window that lets in lots of light. Some are done in watercolors, some in oil paints, but all are breathtaking in their realism, in their attention to light and shadow and blend of color. There are men and women and children, of all sorts of skin tones, from umber to ivory. Some of them wear rich velvets and silks, some wear linens and leathers.

Alice watches me anxiously. "What do you think?"

I turn to face her fully. "I've never seen anything like them. You have a true gift—I hope you make it to Paris to study. Your artwork should be in museums, for everyone to enjoy them."

"Thank you." Alice flushes with pleasure. "You don't think it silly for a young lady to spend so much time dabbling with paint?"

The way she articulates the words, in a cadence not quite her own, makes me think someone has said as much to her. "No. Of course not. Just because someone else can't see the importance of your work doesn't make it silly. If it's important to you, it matters."

"My parents do not really understand it. Even Mama, who

has worked so hard on the hotel, does not see her work as a career, but a way to give Will and me a better life."

"But art isn't just a career for you, is it? It's a vocation. Maybe art is what God means for you to do." I give her the words Rebekka gave to me.

Alice stares at me for a good minute, so long that I think either I've offended her, or I have something on my face from lunch. Surreptitiously, I brush at my upper lip.

Finally, she says, "I have never— No one has ever said something like that to me. Even my drawing masters treated my work as though it were an expensive hobby. Sometimes I have felt that maybe my gift was God-given, but that seemed too like blasphemy." Her voice cracks a little.

"Before I came to Denver, my sister told me, 'Maybe you are meant to study the stars.'" My voice cracks a little too. "It's the reason I was able to come."

Alice holds out her hand. "We should make a pact—I will do what I can to help you study the stars while you are here, and you will do what you can to help me with my art." She grins. "Starting with your sitting."

"Deal." I take her hand and shake it, a delicious thrill of defiance running through me.

Following Alice to the door of the studio, I glimpse a painting set on an easel by one wall, partly covered by a cloth. I move toward it. "What's this?"

Alice intercepts me. "It's nothing, really. Just a sketch I'm playing at. It's not finished at any rate."

"Could I see it?" When Alice hesitates, I add, "You could sketch something blindfolded and it would still be better than anything I can do. If it makes you uncomfortable, I won't press. But I'd like to see your new idea."

With a deep breath, Alice lifts the cloth aside. It's a forest scene, with just the hint of snow-capped mountains towering in the distance. Right now the shapes are still rough, not the fine-edged things of her portraits, but there's something about the scene that tugs at me. Some quality of light, filtering between the massive trunks. It feels like being in the Methodist church, watching light stream through stained glass above the altar.

"Alice," I breathe, turning back to her. "This is— Is this the kind of landscape you were talking about?"

She nods.

"It's amazing." Her portraits are careful, detailed works of art. But if the domestic scenes hum, this sings.

Alice shrugs diffidently. "It helps to get it out, anyway. Maybe if I can get the scene on paper it will stop haunting me."

"Will you do more like this?"

"The landscape? No. No one wants landscapes by a woman—I'll have better luck getting into school with the domestic portraits."

"But—"

Alice cuts me off. "It's not your decision. It's mine. Besides, domestic scenes are important too. We like to praise nature as this immense, sublime thing—but really, most of our lives are made up of small, domestic moments. Those moments matter too. That's what I'm showing in my paintings."

She's right, of course. It's not my business to tell her what to paint.

And she's right about the importance of her scenes too. Lots of people would dismiss Mama's life—Rebekka's life—as one of no importance, as not being worthy to record in history books. But there are hundreds, thousands, of lives just like theirs—lives that are no less worthy because they are recorded privately instead of publicly.

But when Alice turns back to the painting and lowers the cloth again, she lowers it with the care one would take in handling fine, fragile china. Everything she told me might be true, but it's clear that this painting matters more to her than she's willing to say.

✦

At dinner that night, Mr. and Mrs. Stevens pick apart the sermon as they cut apart their meat. I listen closely, fascinated by their friendly banter.

"I don't know that God Himself had a hand in all created things," Mr. Stevens says. "I think maybe He set things down and let them sort themselves out."

Mrs. Stevens says, "The scriptures say that not one sparrow falls but God knows about it. How could He do so if He's not actively involved in creation?"

Mr. Stevens looks at me. "What do you think, Miss Bertelsen?"

I think about what he's saying. There's not much thoughtful challenging of doctrine at home—Papa tends to dismiss things outright, and Mama treats everything said at church as God's own truth—but I like their approach, the idea that you can have different interpretations and still find meaning inside your faith. "I don't know that God governs the shape of every living thing. A tree that grows twisted in the wind is shaped by its environment."

Mr. Stevens lifts his eyebrows at his wife, who only shakes her head at him.

Flushing a little, I add, "But that doesn't mean He's not mindful."

"Spoken like a true diplomat," Will says, laughing at me.

Mrs. Stevens changes tack. "What are your plans tomorrow?"

"I'm hoping to see a man about a new carriage horse," Mr. Stevens says.

"I'm starting my shift at the hotel," I say.

"I mean to take Elizabeth to lunch after her shift," Alice says, smiling at me. "And paint."

"And you, Will?" Mr. Stevens's tone is light, but I see the way the others tense slightly. "Do you intend to be at the hotel tomorrow? Your grandfather could use help with the ledgers."

Will grimaces. "I've made other plans, Papa. Me and some of the fellows—"

"You can't keep doing this, William. If you'd like to go to university, we'd gladly fund your way. But if you won't, at least make an honest living for yourself."

I stare down at the cloth napkin covering my lap and run a finger over the nails of my left hand.

The chair legs shush against the carpet as Will pushes his chair away. "To make an honest living as you have, all I need to do is find a rich wife."

Mrs. Stevens's shocked "William!" follows the sound of Will's footsteps from the room. Mr. Stevens stalks from the room as well, and a moment later the front door opens and closes. Beside me, Alice tears her roll into smaller and smaller pieces. Mrs. Stevens watches the empty doorway, a troubled expression on her face.

✦

Monday morning, the Stevenses' driver takes me into town to the Trans-Oceana hotel. It's so early that only the stars are out to see me off, but the familiar constellations overhead quiet some of the anxiety stirring in my gut. I watch the route carefully—I don't want to inconvenience the driver more than necessary, and perhaps tomorrow I can walk. It is not far, maybe a mile or so.

We pass Champa Street and a thrill shoots through me. Dr. Avery said I might call on Miss Mitchell today. This afternoon, after my shift is over. After lunch with Alice.

The desk clerk has a porter take me to the head housekeeper, Mrs. Segura, a middle-aged woman with white-streaked dark hair and the faintest of Spanish accents. Mr. Davis must have apprised her of my coming, because she only looks me over once and asks me if I know how to clean and tidy beds. When I assure her that I do, she sets me to work with Frances, a blond girl about five years older than me.

Frances shows me the linen room, where they store the clean bedsheets, and both of us load our arms with fresh linens and carry them up the stairs. I marvel at the details of the second floor: the rich russet-and-yellow-patterned carpets, the bronze chandeliers at intervals along the corridor. Frances knocks at the first door, and when no one responds, she tugs a key from her waistband and opens the door. Inside, the room is covered with a yellow-and-white-striped wallpaper, with lush velvet drapes trimmed with satin and yellow and black braid around a small balcony. I spy the button for the annunciator by the bed, but resist the temptation to push it and summon the desk clerk upstairs to us.

The room is only a little untidy and we make quick work of it, beating the rugs at the window, setting the lace curtains straight, and replacing the linens on the bed. My task is to carry the soiled linens downstairs, where they will await pickup by a local laundry.

Frances talks as we go, almost incessantly, of the famous local guests they've had; of the upcoming eclipse and the reams of tourists, whom she hopes will tip well; of her beau, who has been courting her for nearly two years but can't yet afford to marry her; even of the Davis family themselves.

"They have an awful lot of money, for a colored family," Frances says. "I suppose that's why Mr. Stevens married into it."

"I think Mr. Stevens married Mrs. Stevens because he likes her," I say, thinking of how he looked at her over dinner, before Will upset everything.

Frances looks at me scornfully. "Where'd you say you were from again? Utah? I don't suppose folks have much by way of standards where you're from."

Words crowd along my tongue, filling my mouth, but I swallow them down. If I want to keep this job, making trouble with another employee won't help me. But when Frances tries to draw me out in gossiping about the Davis-Stevens family again, I ignore her. Eventually she stops talking.

But I notice that afterward Frances leaves the worst of the messes in the rooms for me to clean. Over a stretch of carpet smeared with grease and tobacco stains, she meets my eyes, as though daring me to complain.

✦

My shift ends in the early afternoon. Frances watches me narrowly as we walk downstairs to report to Mrs. Segura. She seems disappointed at something—perhaps that I don't seem more exhausted by the unrelenting work? It's no different from what I'm used to at home, caring for seven younger siblings.

Frances ties on a bonnet and marches down the hall

toward the back entrance. I draw on my own hat, but then hesitate. Alice won't be here for a few minutes yet.

Before I can let myself think too closely about my actions, I go back to the desk clerk and ask for Samuel's room number. I haven't seen him since the dance on Saturday.

I brace myself for the possibility that he's out for the day, but at my soft knock, Samuel calls, "Come in!"

The room looks much like those I've spent the morning cleaning, the windows open to let in a warm breeze. Samuel has been reading scriptures: the familiar book lies open on the bedside table.

"Elizabeth!" he says, standing up. "What are you doing here?"

Is he displeased to see me? My cheeks warm. I didn't think beyond a vague desire to see his face again, to hear his voice. "I—I've a shift cleaning rooms here. I'm on my way back to the Stevenses', but I wanted to see you."

Samuel's eyebrows lift, and his lips curl up with amusement. "Ah. You wanted to see *me*." He holds his arms out theatrically and does a little pirouette. "Now that you've seen me, how do you find me?"

Is it possible for my face to burn off entirely? "A tease, as always."

His voice softens. "Does it distress you? At my house it's a mark of honor—we only tease those we like. My sisters are very well liked."

I can't help laughing at that, picturing Vilate Ann's indignant expression. "Are you saying you like me or that you view

219

me as a sister?" The words are out before I can call them back. There's no way Samuel can answer that question without embarrassing at least one of us.

Samuel's eyes flicker from my face to my boots, just visible beneath my skirt, and back up again. "Well, I certainly do not see you as a sister," he says. As I begin to blush again, he adds, "You're too short, for one thing."

This surprises another laugh out of me.

"Come, where are you going? Have you eaten?" Samuel says. "I'd like to buy you lunch."

"Alice is taking me to lunch," I say. A sudden pang of disappointment prompts me to add, "Perhaps she'd be willing to let you join us?"

Samuel nods agreeably, and we head downstairs to find Alice pacing, periodically checking a handsome pocket watch. She looks up as we approach, her face clearing. "There you are!"

Her gaze darts to Samuel and her expression sharpens. "And suddenly I understand why you were late."

"My apologies," I say, blushing again.

"Your beau should certainly accompany us to lunch," Alice says. "I know just the place."

"He's not my—" I break off, flustered.

Alice leads us outside to where the family carriage waits. Her driver takes us to a swanky new restaurant that serves oysters, which are delivered direct to the restaurant packed in ice from the railcar. Samuel opens the paper menu and his eyebrows twitch. I peer over his shoulder, and my eyes go round at the prices. Perhaps we should not have let Alice pick the place.

But Alice plucks the menu from our hands when the waiter comes and smiles sunnily at us. "My treat," she insists, and proceeds to rattle off several different kinds of oysters I've never heard of.

We have oysters raw—served still in their shell and nestled on a bed of rapidly melting ice squares—and fried into little cakes. We squeeze lemon slices over the raw oysters and slip them whole into our mouths. I don't really like the cold, slippery feel of the thing, but it tastes the way I imagine an ocean might. The fried ones are much more familiar, like the fish cakes I've had at home, mixed in buttery crackers. We have scalloped tomatoes and blackberry pie. The tomatoes are delicious, but Mama's pie is better.

I'm beginning to understand why Alice loves Denver so. What I do not understand is how she is not as stout as me.

As we finish eating, Alice turns to Samuel. "Have you ever sat for a painting?"

"No, ma'am," Samuel says. "Why do you ask?"

"I'm working on a series of paintings about people in the West. Elizabeth has already agreed to sit for me, but I think I'd like to paint you together." Alice taps her chin thoughtfully. "I can call it my Mormon marriage."

Samuel and I exchange a look.

Alice intercepts the look. Her eyebrows lift. "Does that make you uncomfortable? You know a painting can be as much a fiction as a work of literature."

221

I think of my pact with Alice. "Please, Samuel? I know you are busy, but it would mean a great deal to me."

Samuel shrugs. "I don't mind, if you don't."

"I don't."

"Good!" Alice says. "Then it's settled." But she cannot refrain from adding, with a sly look that makes us both pink, "Then again, sometimes even fiction gets at the truth."

chapter eighteen

Monday, July 22, 1878
Denver, Colorado
One week until eclipse

Alice wants to begin our portrait right away, but I remind her
Dr. Avery suggested I call on Miss Mitchell this afternoon. I
have wanted to meet Miss Mitchell since I was nine years old
and first read of her discovering a comet.

"Tomorrow, then," Alice says, signaling her driver to stop
outside the Trans-Oceana to return Samuel to his room. "Will
four o'clock suit you both?"

Samuel agrees, then presses my hand and waves at Alice
before climbing down from the carriage. "I'll see you tomorrow," he says, before disappearing into the hotel.

Alice turns back to me. "Shall I come with you to
Dr. Avery's? Or I can drop you there as easily."

Dr. Avery is much less likely to forget having met me with Alice along. "Are you sure you don't mind? I'd like that. Thank you."

At the corner of Champa and Twentieth Street, Alice's driver lets us down. Dr. Avery's house is pretty, with two stories and big glass windows and French doors opening onto prim little balconies on the upper floor. Around the house spreads an expanse of green grass with a profusion of flowers in neatly kept beds. I take a deep breath beside the wrought iron fence, then march up the walk to the door and knock, Alice close behind me.

I hear women's voices inside, laughing, then a pause as someone gets up and heels click against the floor. Dr. Avery opens the door herself, wearing a loose, ruffled tea gown the color of fresh cream.

Suddenly, I cannot remember how to talk.

Dr. Avery smiles at Alice, "Good afternoon, Miss Stevens. And Miss—?"

She's already forgotten my name. "Bertelsen," I say quickly. "We met at the dance on Saturday."

Her face clears. "Oh, of course. You were the young lady who hoped to meet Miss Mitchell. Please come in. Miss Mitchell is in the parlor, though I'm afraid not all her party is here. There's been some terrible mix-up with their luggage. One of the prized telescopes has gone astray, something to do with the rail war between the Kansas Pacific and Denver and Rio Grande railroads."

We follow the doctor down a hallway with bright floral

paper on the walls, to a large sitting room with flowered chintz sofas and white curtains. Several women of varying ages look up with inquiring eyes as we enter.

Dr. Avery introduces us around the room. Miss Mitchell's sister, Phebe Kendall, an artist. (Alice perks up at that.) One of Miss Mitchell's students, a dark-haired Miss Culbertson, who means to be a doctor, like Dr. Avery. A writer friend of Dr. Avery's from Colorado Springs—"Mrs. Jackson, the writer," Dr. Avery says, as if I have heard of her.

And Miss Maria Mitchell.

Though it's July, and hot, even in this airy room, Miss Mitchell wears a black dress with a white shawl about her shoulders. Her hair is gray, verging on white, and her round face is lined with wrinkles. She looks like someone's grand-mother, not one of the most preeminent scientists in North America.

But what *do* I think a scientist should look like? A dis-tinguished gentleman, like Mr. Edison? Or Dr. Morton in Rawlins? Surely part of becoming a scientist is being able to imagine myself—or another girl or woman—in that role.

Miss Culbertson offers me her place on the sofa beside Miss Mitchell, and Alice goes at once to sit beside Mrs. Ken-dall, the artist. The doctor brings us both tea and a plate of pound cake. I curl my fingers around the cup, absorbing its warmth, but don't drink it. I'm warm and uncomfortable enough without the tea's added heat. Maybe it was a mistake to come. These women with their education and careers and goals exist far outside my orbit.

The conversation—checked briefly as we entered—picks up with energy.

From her new perch near the wall, Miss Culbertson says, "But that's just what Mr. John Draper argues in his book, that as scientific discovery continues to progress, it will grow more and more estranged from organized religion. Ultimately the two are not compatible."

Dr. Avery nods thoughtfully. "Certainly I see that in my own life. I was born a Methodist, and today, well, I'm not sure what I would call myself."

Miss Mitchell says, "We cannot have science held back by religious tradition. If we are to do this work, we must believe that the natural and spiritual worlds are full of mysteries and wonders and be ready and willing to question socially acceptable truths." Sunlight makes the muslin curtains behind her head glow like a halo.

I take a gulp of my tea, and it scalds all the way down. I try not to choke. Is this true? Is Mama right, that my interest in science will ultimately take me away from God? I don't want to believe it, but surely these women know much more than I do.

Alice says, quietly, "Religious faith can also be a beautiful thing, informing the work we do, whether that is an experiment, a surgery, or a painting."

"Yes, of course," Dr. Avery says agreeably. To the others, she adds, "Miss Stevens is a very talented painter." Dr. Avery describes the painting Alice did of her, and Miss Mitchell's sister leans forward to ask Alice a question about her technique.

The writer—Mrs. Jackson?—turns toward me and asks, "And where are you from, Miss Bertelsen? Are you also from Denver?" Beneath her gray hair, her eyes are bright with interest. She reminds me of a bird, all eager inquisitiveness. "Or are you a western transplant, like me?"

"Utah born and bred, ma'am," I say, "though my mama is British and my far—that is, my father—is Danish."

"Utah?" Mrs. Jackson echoes. "Are you Mormon, then? I visited Salt Lake a few years ago, with a dear friend. Such a fascinating city and people. I've written all about it, you know, in my newest book, *Bits of Travel at Home.*"

I drop my eyes down to my teacup, my body rigid. I never know how folks will react to my being Mormon—if they'll try to be kind, like the Stevens family, or openly rude, like the woman on the train. I want these women to like me, to respect me, even. And though Mrs. Jackson does not seem disgusted at the idea of Mormons, only interested, I don't know about the others, except that they don't think religion is compatible with being a scientist—and I very much want them to see me as a scientist.

Who am I, outside my family, my faith? I take a deep breath, don't let myself think of Mama, or God, and say, "My father was a Mormon convert, but he no longer practices the faith."

It's not a lie. But Mrs. Jackson accepts the misdirection

with relief, the shape of her shoulders softening. Alice narrows her eyes at me, and I look away, blushing.

"I met with many polygamists when I was in Utah," Mrs. Jackson continues to the room at large. "I own I was pleasantly surprised: the women and children are not the malnourished, deformed creatures you might expect on reading the medical reports, but rather frank and bright and hardworking. The men are another matter. I saw their so-called prophet, you know, and a rougher, more sensuous man I have never seen. I did not speak with a single woman who favors polygamy, though of course they cannot say so publicly. And who can blame them? I should not want to share my husband."

My stomach coils in on itself like a live snake. I do not like the reflection I catch in her words, as though I am looking in a mirror and someone else is telling me what I see. I don't see my father in Mrs. Jackson's words, or Mama, or Aunt Elisa. There is an itching across my skin I cannot get at. But I have only myself to blame: She would not be so blunt if she knew who I am. What I am.

"Indeed, it seems a degradation to women," Dr. Avery says.

I swallow, wondering how to answer—if I should answer. Polygamy is hard and complicated and not something I want for myself. Yet for some, it's a holy practice. I don't say anything.

Unexpectedly, Alice says, "Without full knowledge of their circumstances, I am not sure how we can judge them fairly."

There's a taut beat of silence.

Miss Culbertson says, "One mustn't let sentiment inter-fere with rationality. That would be bad science—one has only to look at the results of scientific studies to see the bad effects of such customs."

Then Dr. Avery sighs. "Perhaps. And yet we should be generous in our judgments. God alone knows how often I've been judged for my choices, as a childless, single woman who has put career before all else."

Miss Mitchell clears her throat and turns to me. "I be-lieve Dr. Avery said you were interested in astronomy, Miss Bertelsen. Are you here for the eclipse, as we are?" Like Dr. Avery's, her voice is that of an eastern transplant, her words more brisk than mine.

"Yes, ma'am," I say, grateful for the change in topic. "I've never seen anything like it before. I've always wanted to."

"We're very hopeful about this eclipse. I took a group of students to see the Iowa eclipse in 1869, and such a splendid string of radiations we saw, streamers extending across the sky like pearl beads."

"What do you hope to see this time?" I ask.

"We are hoping to better establish coordinates for the sun and moon, and to study the corona—and perhaps to catch a glimpse of Vulcan." Miss Mitchell studies me curiously. "Have you much formal training in astronomy?"

The others have largely moved on to their own conversa-tions: Miss Culbertson and Dr. Avery talking to Mrs. Jackson, Alice speaking quietly with Mrs. Kendall. Miss Mitchell and I seem cocooned in our own little sphere. I wish I had an actual place in this circle, not the illusory one that our conversation gives me.

And so when I answer, once again I am not completely truthful. "Some. I don't have college training, but I've studied all I can from books. And I know how to use a telescope." That is, I've handled the telescope Mr. Edison showed us. I don't tell her that I barely grasp the complicated math required for astronomy, that I have less than two years of formal schooling.

"How are you at sketching?" Miss Mitchell asks.

"Fair enough." I am surely going to hell for lying, but Alice and I made a pact to do what we can to forward one another's careers (and our own), and I can't see any other way to get this experience.

"Elias Colbert, from the Chicago Observatory, is offering a class at the high school Thursday night, for those who wish to learn to sketch the corona during the eclipse. We could use another set of trained hands on Monday, if you'd be interested in helping."

Miss Mitchell has handed me a gift I didn't dare ask for. "Thank you," I manage. "I should like that very much." I resolve to ask Alice to take me to the library for more astronomy books, to supplement my deficient knowledge. A city this large must have one.

There's a commotion in the hall: the two young women who've been at the station looking for the telescope. Miss Mitchell stands as they come in. "Any luck?"

One, a pretty, freckled girl with brown hair, shakes her head. "Not for lack of trying! And there's not a spare telescope in the city to beg, borrow, or steal. It would be such a pity to miss even part of the eclipse after coming all this way."

Miss Mitchell rises and pats her hand. "Have faith, Miss Abbott. It won't come to that."

Alice catches my eye, making a motion toward the door. This disruption is a good time to take our leave. We stand and thank Dr. Avery for the tea.

As I pass by her, Miss Mitchell catches at my sleeve. "Come again, Miss Bertelsen, and we'll see if we can put you to work."

"I will," I promise.

We slip out of the house, and I pause for a moment on the front step, letting the hot sun burn across my cheeks.

Alice says, "You lied to those women."

"I didn't lie." Though I may have stretched the truth nearly to breaking point.

"Then you let them believe a lie."

Shame makes my words sharp. "My being Mormon has nothing to do with my potential as a scientist. It would only prejudice them against me, if they knew."

"You don't know that." Alice steps gracefully down the steps to the walkway.

I shake my head. I can't risk it. Not when I'm so close to everything I hoped for.

"Does being a woman prejudice others against your art?" I ask.

"Yes," Alice says reluctantly. "As does my color. But I can't believe these women are so judgmental as you think. And isn't science about the pursuit of truth? How can you base that study on a lie?"

"Who I am has nothing to do with what I study," I say, nettled. "And I could ask you the same."

Alice stops walking. "My art isn't based on a lie."

"But you lie to yourself, about what you want to paint."

I know as soon as I've said the words that I've gone too far.

Alice's eyes flash. She whirls away, stalks down the walk-way, and throws open the door to the carriage. It bangs shut behind her.

It would serve me right if Alice drove away this instant and never wanted to speak to me again.

But Alice is a better person than I am. The door opens again.

"Are you coming?"

I hurry toward the carriage, stumbling only a little as I reach the wrought iron gate. Before I get in, I say, "I'm sorry. I had no right to say what I did about your art. But if I can trust you to know what is best for you and your art, can you trust me to know what is best for my study as well?"

Alice sighs and makes room for me on the seat beside her. "I only hope you know what you're doing."

chapter nineteen

Tuesday, July 23, 1878
Denver, Colorado
Six days until eclipse

The next morning, Frances continues her tactic of giving the worst of the messes to me during our shift, and as the hotel is full to bursting with people drawn to town by the impending eclipse, I have a lot to do.

We come to Samuel's floor. I'm carting an armful of linens from the room next door when Samuel's door opens.

"Elizabeth!" he says, pleasure lighting his face. The tips of his eyelashes look gold in the morning light. I never noticed before.

Frances, coming out of the room behind me, casts me a sharp look.

"Go on ahead," I tell her. "I'll be there in a moment."

Frances mutters something under her breath as she passes. I set the linens on the floor, stretching.

"How was your visit to Miss Mitchell?" Samuel asks.

"Miss Mitchell invited me to come back. She says she may have work for me." In my enthusiasm, I grasp one of his hands in both of mine. My thumb slides across the rough calluses of his palm, sending a prickling all the way up my arm. I try to ignore the sensation.

His fingers tighten around mine. "That's wonderful! Though no more than you deserve." He peers at me closely. "What is it? Why don't you seem more pleased?"

Samuel is too damn perceptive sometimes. I pull my hand free and fold my arms across my chest. After the high of yesterday's meeting, I spent the night thinking about all the ways I fall short of the women in Miss Mitchell's circle. And my discomfort is not helped by the way I exaggerated my own experience. "Miss Mitchell and her students are all so educated, and I lack their training. There's this chasm between what I want and what I know, and I don't know how to cross it."

"Why not?" Samuel asks, ever practical. "You're the smartest person I know, and there are schools everywhere, if that's what you want. You could start somewhere like the Brigham Young Academy in Provo, and then apply for schools back east. You'd not be the first Mormon woman to go to college. You just take one step at a time."

Not the first Mormon woman. He's right, but he says this

so casually, as though it's an easy thing to be a different kind of Mormon woman than the only kind I've ever known.

One step, I think, breathing slowly. I'm not afraid of hard work; it's only unfamiliar work I quail from. But I can do this. After my shift is over, I can stop by the train station to see if there's any word of the missing telescope, then perhaps find a library. And tomorrow . . .

"Elizabeth?" Samuel says. "I've got to go. But I will see you this afternoon."

I blink at him. "This afternoon?"

"At Miss Stevens's? We promised to sit for her painting. Will you walk over with me?"

"I'll meet you there," I say. "I've got errands to run after my shift."

Samuel nods, unruffled. "See you then."

I take my load downstairs, then return to find Frances beating a rug rather savagely.

"Took you long enough," she says.

"Samuel's an old friend."

"Old friend or no, you shouldn't be fraternizing with the guests. Mrs. Segura keeps a strict house and don't hold with nonsense between staff and guests. I've seen women fired for as much."

Frances hands me the rug and stalks off.

She means to threaten me, but her threat holds no teeth. So long as Alice and her family support me, there's not much Frances can do to harm me.

The Denver and Rio Grande station is quieter than it was last time I was here. A few passengers wait for the next train, but I have no trouble staying out of their way as I enter the station and flag down a porter.

"Excuse me, where would I seek for lost luggage?"

He waves me toward a door in the far wall. I'm not quite to the office, when I pause. Two of Miss Mitchell's students—the dark-haired Miss Culbertson and one of the young women who came in as we were leaving—are standing in a shadowed corner nearby. The second woman looks distressed, color high in her fair cheeks. Miss Culbertson presses her hand, then brushes a honey-colored curl away from the other girl's face. Something about the moment seems rather intimate, and I look away.

I pretend to study a rail map on the wall near the office, trying to decide what to do. If the students are here, they must have just asked about the telescope, and so there's not much purpose in my doing the same.

Footsteps sound behind me, and a gentle touch lands on my shoulder. I turn to find the second young woman smiling rather shyly at me. "I beg your pardon, but I do believe you were at Miss Mitchell's yesterday? In all the fuss, we weren't introduced. I'm Cora Harrison, graduate student in astronomy."

"Elizabeth Bertelsen," I say, holding out my hand.

She shakes my hand and smiles, betraying a dimple in her lower right cheek. "What brings you to this sorry corner of the city?"

My cheeks heat. "Same as you, I expect. I thought I might check on Miss Mitchell's telescope, perhaps save you a journey if it was here."

Miss Culbertson strolls up beside her friend, eyeing me coolly. "You don't need to trouble yourself, Miss Bertelsen. We are perfectly capable of addressing the problem ourselves."

Miss Harrison's cheeks flush a delicate pink. "I'm sure Miss Bertelsen only meant to be kind, Emma."

"I think Miss Bertelsen means to ingratiate herself with Miss Mitchell," Miss Culbertson says. "And our party is just fine as it is."

The blonde smiles at her, dimples flashing. "Well, and is that a crime? You can hardly blame her, when you did the same when you first met Miss Mitchell."

"I did not ingratiate myself," Miss Culbertson says.

Miss Harrison laughs. "No, you were merely your usual brilliant, blunt self, and Miss Mitchell, seeing your merit at once, requisitioned your aid."

"If you mean that I begged shamelessly," Miss Culbertson says, grinning at her friend, "you might be closer to the truth."

I don't mean to interrupt their banter, but the words burst out of me. "You're lucky, you know."

Both women look at me.

"To have studied with Miss Mitchell, to have families that can afford to send you to a school like Vassar. I haven't had your opportunities—the nearest college is days away, and my folks can't afford it. But I want to be an astronomer, and these few days before the eclipse might be my one chance to learn from someone like Miss Mitchell."

Miss Harrison says, "I'm from Denver. Vassar is a sacrifice for me too. But I understand what you mean."

I really need to stop making assumptions about people. I turn to Miss Culbertson. "Yes, I am trying to make myself useful—to ingratiate myself, as you said. But can you blame me?"

"No," Miss Culbertson says. Something flashes in her hazel eyes. "I can't blame you for that."

Is it only my guilty imagination that hears a slight emphasis on "that"?

Miss Culbertson and Miss Harrison exchange glances. Miss Harrison smiles, and Miss Culbertson throws her hands up in defeat. "Fine. Since Miss Mitchell does not seem to object to you and Cora likes you, you can help us."

"I can check for the telescope again tomorrow, at this same time," I offer, hoping I do not sound too eager.

"Thank you," Miss Harrison says.

Miss Culbertson says, "I hope you have better luck tomorrow than we have had today."

After they leave, I pursue my second errand. A few questions to a porter tells me that the library, lacking funds for independent operation, has recently been relocated to a wing of the public high school on Arapahoe Street, some six blocks away.

The summer day is windy, clouds tearing across the sky, but I make the walk in good time. I've a nagging feeling that I'm forgetting something, but it's likely only anxious excitement over the prospect of helping Miss Mitchell's group.

And for that, I need more resources.

The high school is a magnificent brick building: three tall stories with a small clock tower at the top. It dwarfs its neighbors, mostly houses and other residences. Daunted by the imposing front doors, I nearly turn away. But I think of Miss Mitchell, gather my courage, and march up the stone stairs.

The library is a single room in the south wing, but the whole room is devoted to books. Shelves upon shelves, filled with perhaps a thousand or more volumes. I've read about marvels like the burned library at Alexandria, but I've never seen so many books in one place before. The room smells, intoxicatingly, of musty paper and ink and ideas.

A prim older woman with silver hair coiled neatly about her head directs me to the astronomy section, where I run my finger across dozens of spines. I could read for weeks—years—and never run out of material. Here, there's no need to hide volumes beneath my bed or squirrel them outside to peruse on a sun-warmed rock. Here, I may study in a sunny nook overlooking the street and watch the high school students as they pour from the school, talking excitedly to one another.

I pull a volume from the shelves, William Chauvenet's

A Manual of Spherical and Practical Astronomy, and flip to the table of contents. Finding that there's an entire section on eclipses, I pull up a chair at a table, and dive in. His explanation of the different kinds of eclipses—solar, lunar, and occultation of planets by our moon—is easy enough to follow.

But then he presents this:

NS. Let S', M', be the centres of the sun and moon when at their least true distance, and put

β = the moon's latitude at conjunction = SM,

I = the inclination of the moon's orbit to the ecliptic,

λ = the quotient of the moon's motion in longitude divided by the sun's,

Σ = the least true distance = $S'M'$,

γ = the angle SMS'.

We may regard *NMS* as a plane triangle; and, drawing $M'P$ perpendicular to *NS*, we find

$$SS' = \beta \tan \gamma \qquad\qquad SP = \lambda\, \beta \tan \gamma$$

and hence

$$S'P = \beta\,(\lambda - 1) \tan \gamma \qquad M'P = \beta - \lambda\beta \tan \gamma \tan I$$

$$\Sigma^2 = \beta^2\,[(\lambda - 1)^2 \tan^2 \gamma + (1 - \lambda \tan I \tan \gamma)^2]$$

I do not know what half of the notations represent. I read and reread it, but it might as well be a foreign language. Miss Mitchell sets great store by her students' knowledge of mathematics—this seems just one more sign of the ways I am wrong for this work. With a long sigh, I shut up this book and pull down another. This second book, happily, is less mathematical, and I lose myself in explanations and diagrams, and it's not until the clock atop the high school chimes the hour—five distinct chimes—that I remember.

Alice.

The sitting.

At four o'clock.

I hurry to replace the book and dash along the hallway, down the stone steps. The high school is closer to the Stevenses' home than the Trans-Oceana, but it is still not close.

I begin to run.

Folk stare at me as I race through the residential streets. How could I have forgotten? I only meant to stop briefly at the station, at the library. And then I got caught up in ideas. Maybe Mama is right that my dreams are dangerous things. They make me selfish. Rachel's pale, wet face flashes in my mind and I run faster, my skirts whipping about my legs.

I arrive at the Stevenses' home sweating and winded. The maid who answers the door at my knock wrinkles her nose at me, but lets me in. "Miss Alice is waiting in her studio, miss."

I thank her and scramble up the stairs. A low murmur of voices floats out from the studio. Thank heavens. Samuel is still here. I scratch at the door, not wanting to startle Alice, and at her "Come in!" I do.

Samuel is sitting rather primly in a high-backed wooden

chair, his hair slicked back from his forehead and his beard neatly trimmed. A few feet from him, Alice stands before an easel bearing a white canvas, a circular piece of wood with paints on it held easily in her left hand. She's blocked out the shape of Samuel and the chair in a watery-looking brown. A matching high-backed chair sits empty beside Samuel.

Alice is clearly upset, her lips pinched together and her eyes narrow. Samuel raises his eyebrows at me.

"I'm so sorry," I say. "I thought I had time to stop by the library and then there were all those books about the eclipse and I started reading—and then I just forgot."

Alice sighs. "When I promised to help you study astronomy, I didn't exactly mean at the expense of my own work. But as someone who has accidentally painted through dinner more times than I can count, I do understand."

I flush gratefully. "Thank you. It won't happen again."

She gestures at the open chair. "Sit down."

Samuel leans toward me. "Fashionably late, eh? City life is already rubbing off on you."

"Oh, be quiet," I say, just as Alice tells him to sit still.

For a while, there's not much sound except for the swish of Alice's brush and the rustle of clothes as Samuel or I shift. I'm not sure if we are allowed to talk, or if that would spoil the lines of the painting.

But as Alice settles back to her work, she starts to ask questions about growing up in a small town. Samuel tells her about life in Monroe, and about the time he and his brother set up a bear trap on the mountain. "We rigged up a gun to go off soon as the bear triggered the trap. We weren't halfway back to our camp, where we were watching our sheep, when the gun went off."

He pauses, drawing out the tension. "My brother wanted to go back and check the trap, but I said, 'Not on your life. Either that bear is dead and can wait till morning, or it's not, and if it's not, no way in hell am I going to face it.'"

Alice and I laugh.

"We never did find out what tripped the trap," Samuel says. "It was empty when we went back."

"I begin to see why Elizabeth likes you," Alice says. "You're funny."

"I like making people laugh," Samuel says with a shrug. "I like to see them happy."

I've spent my whole life taking care of other people, because I was supposed to, because I was told that's what God wanted. What would it be like to take care of them simply because I wanted to?

"You should meet my brother, Will," Alice says. "He's one of the funniest people I know." She tells us about a time that one of Will's friends broke his leg and was housebound for a month. "Every day, Will arranged for a different 'surprise' visitor. One time it was a grocer, who was rather put out that Will's friend didn't need one hundred pounds of turnips. One time it was a preacher, who delivered a blistering sermon on hell and damnation. Several times, it was Will himself in costume. Never at the same time of day. The next time Will showed up, his friend would cuss him out, and then laugh. I think it cheered him no end."

Samuel grins. "You're right. I like him already."

"You should stay for dinner," Alice says, and Samuel accepts.

✦

After brief introductions, and the hasty addition of another plate, we take our seats around the table, with Samuel beside me and Will and Alice across from us.

Mr. and Mrs. Stevens begin by asking Samuel questions: where he's from, what his family does.

"And you work with your father? Keeping up the family business?" Mr. Stevens asks, with a significant glance at Will, who ducks his head to study his plate intently.

Samuel catches the sideways glance and says lightly, "Only because I'm not ambitious enough to find my own work, sir. 'Ambition should be made of sterner stuff.' Truth be told, I think my father finds my efforts to introduce flourishes to our work trying."

I fiddle with my napkin in my lap. I didn't know this about Samuel, and it pricks me that Mr. Stevens has learned something of Samuel in five minutes that I didn't learn in more than five days of traveling with him. I should stop assuming that simply because Samuel does not volunteer information, he has nothing to say.

Mr. Stevens smiles at him. "Ah, Shakespeare's *Julius Caesar.* But if Brutus is to be our measure, I think it's as well not to have such ambitions. I see nothing wrong in taking the work your parents began and improving upon it."

Alice, after a swift look at Will, asks Samuel to retell the bear story that made her laugh earlier. The tension around the table eases—even Will laughs.

"I never thought I was much scared of animals," Will says, "but that encounter we had alongside the tracks has changed my mind."

Mrs. Stevens looks faintly alarmed, Samuel intrigued. Will launches into the story of the elk and her calf, building it up as a mysterious noise, then the animals erupting from the bush.

"When I finished yelling, I waved my arms at the blasted thing, trying to distract it from the girls. But it would not be distracted. Luckily, they had the sense to hide, and the only thing hurt was Alice's hat, with a big old hoofprint through the middle."

Mrs. Stevens fans herself. "Phew. I'm glad no one was hurt. But why am I only now hearing this?"

Samuel laughs and says, "You're a braver man than me. I imagine I'd have run the other way."

Will grins at him. "I very nearly did."

"I'm glad you had the sense to protect your sister," Mr. Stevens says, and Will's smile dies.

"Yes, sir," he says, and turns his attention to his dinner, though he doesn't eat anything more.

After dinner, Alice wants to continue the painting, but Mrs. Stevens insists she let us go. We make arrangements to meet up again the next afternoon, and I accompany Samuel to the front door.

"Walk with me?" Samuel asks, gesturing at the road before the house.

A clear, glittering reach of sky meets my view. With a quick word to Alice, I follow Samuel outside.

We walk for a little while in silence, but it's the kind of silence born of long familiarity. When did I start to become so comfortable around Samuel?

Finally, I say, "At dinner, you said you work with your father because you aren't ambitious enough. What would you choose if you could choose to do anything?"

Samuel scratches at his beard. "I try not to throw my heart after impossible things." He gives me a sidelong look that I can't read. "Mostly. I haven't thought about it much."

"But when you have thought about it?"

"I like the challenge of making new things. In another life, I might have studied engineering. But truth is, I like farming and carpentry just fine, so long as I can tweak things so that it is not always the same thing, time and again."

Samuel told me that he came to Denver to learn new woodworking techniques. "But your father doesn't like your additions? Why?"

Samuel sighs, shoving his hands in his pockets. "Pa doesn't

much like change. Learning new techniques when solid woodcrafting has served him well for decades seems foolish. I'm lucky he let me come. Just wish I could stay longer."

I halt, shock arrowing through me. "You won't stay for the eclipse?"

Samuel stops to face me. "I'd like to. Only I'm about out of funds. If I can find short-term work for a carpenter or some other work, I'll stay."

I resume walking. It's not like I'll never see Samuel again. He'll be back in Monroe when I get back. But I didn't expect the thought of him leaving to feel so much like loss.

Samuel keeps pace beside me. He slips his hand from his pocket and his fingers brush mine—I can't tell if it's accidental or not. But I don't move away.

"Whatever I do, I hope you see everything you want. This place suits you—you seem happier than you did before you went to your sister. Less weighed down."

"I'm doing something for me," I say, smiling. "It's nice. You should try it."

"I am doing something for me right now," he says, returning my smile. He tips his head back, points upward. "There's Vega of the Lyre. The star reminds me of you."

"You've been brushing up on your constellations," I say, following his gaze upward. Vega is high overhead, twinkling bright. The fifth-brightest star in the sky.

"Aren't you going to ask why it reminds me of you?" Samuel stops staring at Vega to look at me. His face is full of starlight.

Something inside clenches tight. I am not sure I want to hear his answer, so I try for a joke I think he would appreciate. "Because I'm not quite as bright as other stars?"

But Samuel doesn't smile. Still serious, he says, "Because Orpheus's lyre was supposed to charm everyone who heard it."

Oh.

I wish I could laugh at his line, turn it into a jest, but I can't. I rub my hands against my arms, suddenly prickling with gooseflesh. "I should go back now."

And while Samuel doesn't protest, even offers some light conversation as we walk, he doesn't say anything else about stars.

chapter twenty

Wednesday, July 24, 1878

Denver, Colorado

Five days until eclipse

As soon as my shift at the Trans-Oceana is over, I head for the Denver and Rio Grande station. I'm rather proud of myself, negotiating the streets of this new city without help. Perhaps, if I can find my way about Denver, I can find my way around cities even larger, even farther afield.

I make my way to the corner office at the station, but a newspaper discarded across a seat snags my attention. Something about Mr. Edison. I unfurl the paper and read the blaring title: "Edison's Go-By: How the Great Inventor, Who Will Not Visit Denver, Is Progressing." The wounded dignity in the author's tone makes me laugh—I didn't realize how much the citizens of Denver were counting on Edison's visit, until his determination to remain in Rawlins was absolutely confirmed.

That train robbery has turned out lucky for me, in more ways than one. I'd never have met Mr. Edison without it. Or Alice and Will. Or Miss Mitchell.

I continue to the office and ask the clerk, a thin-faced man with a long nose, if a parcel has come in for Miss Maria Mitchell. The clerk consults some sort of ledger, then disappears back into the room, nosing about among all the collected luggage. For a moment, I'm distracted, thinking of all the trunks and parcels crisscrossing the United States independent of their owners.

The clerk returns. "There is, indeed—a long, narrow sort of box."

My heart leaps. The telescope. "Oh, this is wonderful! May I have it?"

He squints at me. "Are you Miss Mitchell? Have you been deputized by her to take up the package? A note of some kind? We can't just go handing out parcels willy-nilly to anyone who asks."

I falter. In Monroe, where everyone knows one another, such a thing as a note giving one permission to take up a package would be unthinkable. "Thank you for checking. I'll inform Miss Mitchell at once."

I walk the long blocks to Dr. Avery's home and knock.

The honey-haired young astronomer, Miss Harrison, opens the door. Her eyebrows lift in surprise at my flushed face. "Yes?"

"Miss Mitchell's telescope has come," I say.

At that, her whole expression changes, delight chasing surprise across her features. "Please, come in," she says, but she leaves me standing in the hall as she races back to the parlor. "Miss Mitchell! Miss Mitchell! The telescope is here."

I hear a muffled murmur of voices from the parlor, and then Miss Mitchell herself comes out into the hall, hands outstretched. She takes my hands up in hers. "God bless you, Miss Bertelsen. Now my heart can be easy. Do you know, this is the very same telescope that I used to discover my comet? It has been with me nearly my entire career as an astronomer."

Dr. Avery and the forthright Miss Culbertson crowd into the hallway behind her. Miss Mitchell turns to Dr. Avery. "Alida, can your man go to the station and fetch the telescope for me? Have him bring it to the field near St. Joseph's home, where we mean to set up our eclipse site. I wish to ensure the site's suitability as soon as possible. If it will not work, best to know now, when we can still scout out another."

"The station clerk won't release the telescope without a note," I say. "I tried before."

"Oh yes, of course," Miss Mitchell says. "Emma, do fetch me a pen and paper."

Miss Culbertson disappears back into the parlor, and Dr. Avery heads down the hallway, presumably in search of her man.

I wait, my entire body tense with a mixture of excitement and fear. Having accomplished my errand, I should go, but

I can't bring myself to. I want to know how this plays out. I want to feel a part of it, for a little bit longer.

Miss Mitchell studies me, her eyebrows dark under her graying hair. "Would you like to come with us, Miss Bertelsen? We shall need two carriages at least, so there will be room."

Heat sparks in my chest, flaming out through my body. All at once, I'm conscious of every detail around me: the soft shushing of silk dresses that Miss Mitchell and Miss Harrison wear; the scents of roses and vanilla that fill the house, with a subtle undernote that I can't place; the trilling of a sparrow outside; the faint breeze that curls through the hallway from an open window nearby. Have I ever been so fully in my body, in my heart?

"I should like that very much."

Miss Mitchell smiles at me, just as Miss Culbertson returns with writing equipment. "Good. Then that's settled."

It's not until I watch Miss Mitchell set pen against paper that I remember: I've promised myself to Alice for this afternoon, for another sitting. I haven't got the time to go out to a field to set up a telescope and be back for my appointment. But if I refuse to go with Miss Mitchell now, I may never have another chance.

I know I promised Alice I would not be late for a sitting again, and I don't want to hurt her.

But.

This is the kind of opportunity I've wanted my entire life, since I discovered there were books about stars and people who studied them. Rebekka said there will always be babies needing care, and I can't hold myself responsible for all of them. There will always be people needing things from me—paintings, domestic chores, things I haven't begun to imagine. What is my duty to all of them? To myself? To put oneself first all the time is surely selfish and ungodly. But does it follow that one should *never* put oneself first?

I've given myself this window, here in Denver, to see if astronomy is something I can make a life of, if maybe there's another path than the one I always thought I was meant to follow. The path of a comet, flaming across the sky, can seem unpredictable—but comets orbit our world in fixed arcs. It's just a matter of determining the trajectories. Maybe this is the trajectory my life is meant to follow.

I have to take this chance.

Alice will understand—in the same kind of situation, with an opportunity to study with an artist she admired, wouldn't she do the same?

I borrow some paper from Miss Mitchell and scribble off my own note. Turning to Dr. Avery, who's come back to the hallway, I ask, "Can your man deliver this to the Trans-Oceana on his way into town?" Alice is known there and often stops by to visit her grandfather or her mother. They'll pass the word to her.

✦

Perhaps an hour later, I stand on a field somewhere east of Denver, staring up at an overcast sky. Before me, the field stretches broad and empty. To the south sits a three-story brick building topped with a cross, a hospital run by Catholic nuns.

Miss Mitchell's students carefully unload the telescope boxes from the back of the carriage and begin to open them. I wander over to observe, but don't offer to help, fearful of damaging the enormous metal and wood contraptions, gleaming even in the dull afternoon light.

Miss Culbertson stands beside me and swipes a hand across her forehead, pushing a strand of dark hair away from her eyes. "They're a fine sight, aren't they? That one's by Dollond and this one's by Alvan Clark. Are you familiar with their work?"

The way she studies me makes me uneasy, as though her hazel eyes see through me to the lie I'm trying to hide. "Not those, no. Nothing so fine. Just an old scope that my teacher happened to have. Much smaller, of course."

"I remember my first." Miss Culbertson smiles, showing her teeth. "Telescope, that is."

Miss Harrison looks up at us. "Don't let Emma rile you, Miss Bertelsen. She's not so fierce as she seems."

Miss Culbertson colors, and I remember how she looked at Miss Harrison at the station, as though there were something important between them.

I ask Miss Harrison what it's like to study astronomy at college.

"Oh, it's marvelous—and the hardest thing I've ever done. I love the girls I study with, but the work demands a lot."

The freckled Miss Abbot says, "We certainly put in many late hours at school, watching the stars at night and then rising again early to study through the day."

"There's not much leisure time," Miss Culbertson says. "That can be hard on friendships—and beaus."

Miss Harrison says, with a slight, flickering look at Miss Culbertson, "There was a young man who wished to court me but would not wait for me to finish my studies."

Miss Mitchell steps away from the telescope and turns to look at us. "It is hard to strike a balance between one's study and one's private life, and many women find they are not cut out for serious science and return home to their friends and families to build a domestic life. There is no shame in that. I myself never married, and I do not see my family so often as I might like because of my teaching duties, but I have not had to sacrifice friends and family entirely."

"Per aspera ad astra," I say.

"To the stars through hardship," Miss Mitchell says, smiling. "Precisely."

"But you mustn't think it's all hardship," Miss Harrison says. "Studying astronomy is the best thing I've done."

Miss Mitchell continues, looking at me, "But I do think that those who feel called to this work must take it seriously. The woman who does her work better than every woman did before her helps all womankind, not only now, but in the future. But a woman whose work is loosely done, ill-finished, or not finished at all does wrong by herself and all other women." Her eyes hold mine for a beat, then she turns to

Miss Culbertson. "Come, Emma, help me fit this telescope to the tripod."

The patchwork clouds overhead permit only flashes of sunlight, but the clouds break just then, as if in confirmation of her words, and the little swath of grass we stand in illuminates like an angel has reached down and brushed against us. The grass is so bright in contrast to the still-dark clouds that it hurts to look at it. I look up at the distant mountains instead.

I suspected that it might be difficult to balance the domestic life my mother wants for me with the study I want for myself. Now I know for certain. Miss Mitchell's words echo through my head: *A woman whose work is loosely done does wrong by herself and all other women.* Samuel's face flickers before me, and I hear his voice telling me he finds me charming. Something inside me wrenches.

What is it that God wants for me? What do *I* want?

Miss Mitchell's students talk and joke around me as they fit the telescopes to their mounts, and then, one after another, we take turns sighting the telescopes—first on the far hills, then up at the sky at the angle of the possible eclipse. The words swirl around me, touching me yet somehow apart. But I don't mind. I may not have earned my place among these women yet—

But I want to.

It's late when we return to Denver—past suppertime. My stomach growls at me as I climb down from the carriage, and I think of the dinner probably waiting for me at the

Stevenses'. Which then leads me to Alice, and the groveling I have ahead of me.

But oh, it was worth it. My veins still buzz with the thrill of standing in that wide stretch of field, the darkened sky vaulting overhead, surrounded by some of the best female astronomers in the world.

Miss Mitchell thanks me, again, for bringing word of her telescope.

"I'm glad I could help," I say.

"Come visit me again after Dr. Colbert's drawing class. I should like to know how you get on, and very likely we'll visit our viewing site again. I think it will do nicely, but one can never be too prepared."

"I will," I promise.

✦

The Stevenses' house is ablaze with lights when I arrive, though the summer night is still bright, the sun lingering above the horizon.

It's time to face Alice.

I let myself into the house, and pad down the lighted hallway toward the dining room, where I can hear the clinking of silverware. Peering around the corner, I see the Stevens family sitting at the table as usual, murmuring as a maid brings trays around the table. There's no space set for me.

Clearing my throat, I step through the doorway.

Mrs. Stevens sees me first. "Miss Bertelsen! Alice was not

sure if you would be joining us. Shall I have the maid bring another place?"

Alice glances up, her hand freezing on her knife. Her posture is stiff, her face tight with hurt.

"I'm so sorry I was late," I say to Alice, sliding into an empty spot beside her. "Did you get my note?"

"What note?"

"I had a note sent to the hotel for you, explaining that I had found Miss Mitchell's telescope and had gone to take them word. They invited me to see the field where they plan to set up their equipment to view the eclipse."

Alice's face softens a fraction. "I see. Was Mrs. Kendall there?"

For a moment, I do not remember who Mrs. Kendall is— ah, Miss Mitchell's sister, the artist. "No. She stayed behind with Dr. Avery."

But now Mrs. Stevens is frowning. "Do be careful, Miss Bertelsen. I've nothing to say against Dr. Avery, who is a very good woman, but you should know that there is some talk about the scientific women who are with her—it's not natural for girls their age to neglect home and family for such study."

Mrs. Stevens's advice is kindly meant, but it sends a creeping chill through me. Is she regretting letting me into her home? First the worry over my being Mormon, now this. Does she think *I* am neglecting my home and family to be here? I glance at Alice's father and see a frown mirroring his wife's.

"I appreciate your concern, Mrs. Stevens, but you needn't worry about me. It's only a hobby, you know, and it was curiosity more than anything that took me out to their eclipse site. My interest isn't serious." These reassuring half-lies come easier than the ones I told Miss Mitchell.

"Well, I'm very glad to hear it," Alice's mother says, slicing a bit of meat with a deft flick of her knife.

Alice's knife clatters onto her plate. "Only a hobby?"

"Alice," her father says. "Mind your tone."

She turns to me, her eyes blazing. "Is my art only a hobby as well? All that stuff about passions and God-given gifts—did you mean that? Or was that only a convenient lie? You seem practiced at them." She takes a long, steadying breath. "You know what? I'd rather you were a liar. Because if you're not a liar, you're a hypocrite, telling everyone what they want to hear and meaning none of it."

I flinch. It wasn't just my dream I was dismissing by trying to mollify her parents, it was Alice's as well. "No, I—you don't know what it's like, being poor," I say, my voice low, painfully conscious of her parents and Will listening in shocked silence. "You have opportunities I can only dream about. This may be my only chance to learn from Maria Mitchell. You'll have other chances to paint, even to study painting if you want."

"What do you know about my chances, my opportunities? You have no idea what it's like to be a black woman and an artist. To have even a hope of studying in Pennsylvania, let alone France, I have to be perfect." She drops her face to her hands. "And I'm so damned tired of being perfect."

She doesn't look angry anymore, just defeated, and somehow that's even worse.

Louisa Stevens says, faintly, "Don't swear, Alice."

"Alice, I'm so sorry—" I start.

"Don't," she says. "You think it's all right to dismiss me because I have money, but you have no trouble taking advantage of our wealth and connections when it suits you. I thought you were better than that, Elizabeth."

Shame creeps up my throat, burning across my face.

Will says, "Don't make such an issue of this, Alice. It's just a misunderstanding—it doesn't matter. Just plan another time to work on your picture."

"It doesn't matter?" Alice shoves her chair away from the table. "Maybe not to you. But then, nothing much matters to you, does it? Certainly not my comfort or interests. You're as bad as Elizabeth. Worse, maybe, because at least she has the guts to go after what she wants, even if she has to lie to do so. But you? You're too cowardly to confront Papa about what you really want from your life."

Mr. Stevens frowns at his son. "Will?"

But Will ignores him. He glares at his sister. "Too cowardly? It wasn't cowardice that faced that elk or took me out on the trestle—" He stops, appalled.

The anger sloughs away from Alice's face, and she casts a quick, almost frightened look at her father.

I should leave. Alice doesn't want me here, and the others can't want me to witness the unveiling of family secrets. But I cannot seem to make myself move.

Mr. Stevens looks at Will. "The trestle? Did you cross that trestle bridge between Rawlins and Laramie on foot?" His voice is low and calm, without inflection, yet somehow menacing for all that.

Will seems to shrink, his shoulders drawing up.

Mr. Stevens continues, his voice grim. "You don't deny it. I must therefore conclude you did. Have you gone mad, son? We talked about this, how your travel to California was an opportunity for you to prove to me that you've outgrown your childish antics. And where was your sister during all of this? You left her alone, open to the insults of strangers?"

"I was fine, Papa," Alice says, but he doesn't seem to hear her.

"I was with her," I say.

Mr. Stevens turns to me. "This is between me and my son. Please leave us."

I unfreeze finally, and I flee up the stairs.

A dull, sick throbbing courses through me.

If I hadn't pretended to be something I was not, if I hadn't hurt Alice, she wouldn't have lashed out at Will, and he wouldn't have struck back so incautiously. I think of the happy, friendly family that accompanied me to the ball that first night in contrast to the tense, unhappy group I left tonight.

Please leave us.

You have no trouble taking advantage of our wealth and connections when it suits you.

I can't stay here.

In the bedroom upstairs, I pile as much as I can into my carpetbag. I can't do anything about my trunk, but perhaps Samuel will fetch it for me later.

Scribbling a note to leave on the dressing table, I thank the family (especially Alice) for their kindness. I hope Alice won't burn the note before reading it. I leave a pile of coins next to it, everything I owe Alice and then some, all my earnings from the hotel. Alice's accusations sting because there's truth in them, but I did not set out to abuse her generosity.

Creeping down the back stairs, I let myself out the servants' entrance and stand for a moment in the gathering dark. Overhead, Cygnus glimmers at me like an old friend. I find the smudge of the Messier 8 nebula, and then the North Star.

Steadied, I follow the North Star into town, to the Trans-Oceana.

I ask the desk clerk for a room, and he laughs at me. "Everything here's booked solid through the eclipse. Even had a fellow offer to pay me to let him sleep on the billiard table."

I thank him and turn away, with some vague idea of finding another hotel in town. The clerk calls after me, "You won't find anything else. Everywhere is just as booked as we are." I suppose it's a good thing for the Trans-Oceana, but it's pretty rotten for me.

I hesitate, balancing the merits of sleeping in the train station against disturbing Samuel at this hour.

Samuel wins out by a hair.

chapter twenty-one

Wednesday, July 24, 1878

Denver, Colorado

Five days until eclipse

At my knock, Samuel opens the door.

"Are you all right?" His glance takes in the bag at my side.

"I'm fine." I step toward him, but he doesn't move to let me in.

"If you're not injured, then where were you for our sitting today? You hurt Alice, for no reason that I can see."

My eyes start to sting, and I blink fiercely. I will not cry right now. "I know." I explain about Miss Mitchell, how I tried to send a note, but it didn't reach Alice. I gloss over the disastrous conversation. "I made everything worse by botching my explanation of where I'd been. The whole family is in an uproar now, and I can't stay there. They must be wishing me in perdition."

"Or at least in Utah," Samuel agrees, the faintest trace of a smile tugging at his lips. "For some, that's likely the same thing."

A huge wave of relief washes over me. If Samuel can laugh, he's not irredeemably angry at me.

"Can I come in?" I ask again. "I don't have anywhere else to go, except the streets."

"I hear they're quite nice this time of year," Samuel says, and my heart drops all the way to my toes before his face cracks. "Come on. My mother wouldn't let me darken her door if she knew I'd let you sleep on the streets." He opens the door wider and steps out of the way for me to enter.

"Just don't tell *my* mother," I say. "I think she'd rather have me sleep on the streets than in a man's room, unmarried."

Samuel looks at me, amusement crinkling his eyes. "What, are you afraid your mama will drag you to the altar?"

I blush and look away. That is precisely what I fear. Though I much prefer Samuel to Brother Yergensen. And at that thought, my blush deepens. I can't let myself think this way. I remember Miss Mitchell's words earlier, about the sacrifice required to study astronomy.

If I mean to take this study seriously, I can't be thinking of marriage at all.

Samuel continues, much softer, "If you marry me, it will be of your own free will and choice, not because your mama makes you."

"Are you asking me?" I try to make it a joke, but it doesn't sound funny as I say it.

Even quieter, Samuel says, "Do you want me to?"

I don't know how to answer that, so I turn away to face the room, and that's almost worse, because the single bed seems to dominate the space. What would it be like, to sleep next to Samuel all night, to share his warmth, to feel his breath on my cheek? My whole body seems to tighten at the thought, and my face heats.

"I'll sleep on the floor," Samuel and I both say in a rush, our words tangling together. We look at each other and laugh, breaking the tension of the moment.

Samuel wins the argument, though I'll admit I do not fight too hard. The emotional whiplash of the last twenty-four hours has left me wrung out, and I'm glad enough to curl up in the comfort of the bed. It smells like Samuel, like soap and summer sunshine and wood dust and some indefinable boyishness. I like it far more than I ought to. Samuel beds down on the floor with a borrowed pillow and blanket, and while he drops off almost at once, I lie awake for a long time, listening to the gentle puff of his breath, wondering what it would be like to fall asleep to that sound every night of my life.

A line from Mary Somerville's now sold book floats back to me. *Each body is itself the centre of an attractive force extending indefinitely into space.* Though she writes of gravity, I think the same might be true of human bodies. Even now, separated by the length of the bed, I can feel the pull of Samuel's warmth.

You're a fool, Elizabeth Bertelsen. If things go as I hope, I'll spend my nights watching the stars, then falling asleep to the quiet of my own room. But even as I think this, my heart gives a traitorous pinched twist.

Why do I always seem to want more than I can have?

✦

Ironically, given that I'm already in the Trans-Oceana, the following morning is the first time I'm late for my shift.

I wake in the darkened room, blinking at the ceiling with a sudden surge of terror at the unfamiliar shape and smell of the room. But then Samuel lets out a snore, and I remember where I am.

And where I'm supposed to be.

With a renewed surge of alarm, I throw back the bedclothes. I don't have to change my dress, since I've slept in it, but I splash water from the basin onto my face and do my best to straighten my hair and clothes in the dark.

I let myself out of the room, and come face to face with Frances, who has already begun her shift.

We stare at each other. Her gaze flickers from my hair to my rumpled dress, and back to my face.

"It's not what it looks like," I say.

She only nods shortly and continues on her way. I slip downstairs for my instructions, my heart hammering madly.

All through my shift, I half wait to receive word from Alice, even while knowing that's ridiculous. At first, because the time is far too early for Alice to be up, let alone alert enough to send a message. And then later, because why should Alice forgive me?

In the end, it's not Alice that sends word, but Mrs. Segura.

＊

Mrs. Segura waits for me in her office, a small, tidy room next to Mr. Davis's. Her rounded face is grave as I enter. She indicates my trunk, filling one corner of the room. "This has come for you, Miss Bertelsen."

My breath whooshes out in mingled relief and guilt. I was afraid Frances had gotten me in trouble. But it's only the Stevenses returning my trunk.

I thank Mrs. Segura, but her expression does not change. "I've received a disturbing report that you spent the night in one of our customers' rooms."

I flush, my heart pounding again. So Frances did snitch on me. "Nothing happened. I needed a place to stay and my friend gave me one."

She glances at my trunk, her frown deepening. "I understood you were staying with the Stevens family. Was I misinformed?"

"No, I was—there was a difficulty—" I break off, aware that I'm making things worse.

"The Stevens family is highly respected at this hotel," Mrs. Segura says. "Given that you were seen coming from a guest's room and you are no longer welcome at the Stevenses' home, I'm afraid your services are no longer required."

"Please," I say. The position was nice when I had a secure place to stay—a way to maintain my self-respect. But it's no longer nice, it's necessary. I have no other resources to my name. "It was a misunderstanding."

She shakes her head and folds her hands over her desk. "Nevertheless, we cannot be too careful of appearances. I bear you no ill will, and you can continue to stay with your *friend*"—her mouth twists a little at the word—"but you cannot work for us anymore."

And just like that, I'm dismissed.

✦

After lugging my trunk up to Samuel's room, I spend the rest of the day in the library at the high school, not even stopping for lunch (which I can't afford now anyway). I try to throw myself into my research—at least I have not yet disappointed Miss Mitchell—but I cannot seem to sustain my focus. My thoughts keep breaking up, worrying about what I am to do for funds, how I will get home. I suppose I could go to Mrs. Stevens and beg her to get my job back for me, but I don't feel I have the right to ask for any more favors from Alice's family.

And anyway, I'd rather bite off my own nose at the moment than beg.

Samuel buys me dinner that night, soup and bread in the hotel restaurant (the cheapest items on the menu). I tell Samuel about the corona drawing class, and he offers to come with me. I hesitate for a long moment. A part of me wants

Samuel to come, wants the comfort of his familiar presence in a new setting, but I know I cannot do that. If I mean to follow this path, I can't bring Samuel with me. Sooner, rather than later, I need to accustom myself to relying on my own resources.

"Surely you'd find it boring," I say. "I promise I'll be all right on my own."

Samuel frowns. "Will you at least let me meet you at the end to walk you home?" He knows I mean to share his room again that night, though I haven't told him yet that I've been fired. After everything else, I can't bear his pity.

He reaches across the table and sets his hand on mine. And though I know—*I know*—I shouldn't let him, I leave my hand in his. I touch a thousand things a day—cloth and wood and iron and glass—but nothing moves me like this. All the nerves in my skin are firing, sending heat signals to my brain. Even my toes feel some of the residual electricity.

Abruptly, I pull my hand away. "I'll meet you at nine."

I make my way back to the high school, climb the steps to the double doors, and look around the long, tiled hallway with classrooms on both sides. Miss Mitchell didn't tell me what room the drawing class was to be held in, but voices echo from down the hall, so I head toward them, moving away from the library. I peer into a classroom with the door ajar, looking for anyone who looks as though they might belong to something as prestigious as the Chicago Observatory.

An older man, with graying beard, pale skin, and protruding belly, stands before a chalkboard. A collection of men and women of varying ages cluster in the desks in front of him. I take a seat near the windows. A few moments later, Miss Culbertson also enters the room and selects a chair near mine. I'm surprised: I didn't think she liked me above half.

The older gentleman is indeed Professor Colbert of the Chicago Observatory, and he begins by welcoming us all and explaining the importance of what we are to accomplish. "We know so little about the corona, the aura of light that surrounds the sun. We don't know for certain what it's made of, or how it behaves, though we believe it is solar light reflected from meteors falling into the sun. Any observations we can gather during totality will be valuable. To add to those observations, our job tonight is to train you how to make accurate sketches of the corona."

Our sketches should be made in pencil, upon a plain sheet of paper to be provided. The circle of the moon can be sketched beforehand, saving time for valuable observations, and we should position ourselves ten degrees south of the west, to face the sun at totality. He makes assignments to everyone in the room, to sketch one-quarter of the corona. I wonder if he gives some of us the same assignment for comparison purposes—or because he expects some of us to fail.

"It's best to have a partner with you, someone who can blindfold you before the eclipse so that your eyes are most sensitive to the dim light and you can best observe the corona and radiances. Be sure to have a lantern already lit: few people realize how dark it can become in the moments of totality."

I glance sidelong at Miss Culbertson, who is taking precise notes in a small journal. I wonder if she would be willing to partner with me at Miss Mitchell's observation site, or if she has other duties.

Professor Colbert continues, describing how we are to sketch the outline of the corona, including dotted lines where we can't precisely see the shape of it. He finishes the lecture and invites us all to return the following night, where we'll practice drawing the corona from photographs. A few students go to the front to ask Professor Colbert questions. I stand and head toward the door.

Miss Culbertson intercepts me and holds out her hand as if to shake mine. "Miss Bertelsen, I feel as though we've gotten off on the wrong foot. May we have a do-over? I'm Emma Culbertson, aspiring physician."

I take her hand. "Elizabeth Bertelsen, aspiring astronomer."

She falls into step beside me, asking questions about my home, my family. I find myself telling her about Monroe, about Mama and Hyrum and Rachel, and all my other siblings.

"You must miss them," she says.

"Every day," I answer. "But I'm glad to be here all the same."

"How does your mama manage with so many?"

I smile. "With help." That's one of the great things about a small community like ours—even though much of the daily work falls on me, or on Emily now, there are always hands ready to help us should we stumble. "Even Aunt Olena would help, if we needed her."

"Your father's sister? Or your mother's?"

I'm still caught up in the corona, only half attending to my answer. "Oh, she's not really my aunt. She's my father's wi—" My wits catch up with my words.

"Wife?" Miss Culbertson finishes for me. "You said your father was Mormon. Are you as well?"

I nod, weakly.

"I wondered, when Mrs. Jackson asked you about your family. I won't judge you for hiding that—I know what it's like, to hide something of who you are from the world's judgment. But I don't think you realize how much you could jeopardize the work Miss Mitchell is doing."

My jaw falls slack. "How could I harm any of you? I'm nothing, no one."

"You're Mormon. You're from the West. You don't know what it's like, just now, at schools like Vassar. Our parents, other concerned citizens, already complain to the paper that we women become unsexed in our studies."

Even Mrs. Stevens echoed the same concern.

Miss Culbertson continues, "Worse, people worry such schools become breeding grounds for unnatural affections, or what has been called the 'Vassar libel.'" Her mouth screws tightly. "As though a woman who loves another woman were the worst fear they could name."

I remember the way Miss Culbertson watches Miss Harrison. I think of Hyrum, who doesn't know if he could ever love a woman enough to marry. Perhaps I should be shocked, but all I feel is a flush of sympathy. "When people look at you and see only the 'Vassar libel,' they are looking with an outsider's eyes. When outsiders look at Mormons and our plural marriage, all they see is moral deviance, someone living a life they wouldn't choose for themselves. But who besides God and those living inside the relationship can judge it?"

Miss Culbertson's expression softens. "I knew you would understand. We have to maintain the highest possible standards to shut down such accusations, or we risk public censure stopping our work entirely. Surely you can see that the presence of a Mormon woman in our crew could taint all of us? If you admire Miss Mitchell at all, you cannot want that for her. For us."

We've reached the outer doors. Through the glass, I can see Samuel waiting for me beside the street. My insides are ice.

"But who should know? Or care? Please, this is the kind of opportunity I've dreamed of."

"And what of our dreams?" Miss Culbertson asks. "Don't those matter? Or is it enough if you achieve what you want, the rest of us be damned?"

Her words cut so closely to Alice's accusation that they knock the wind from me.

"Is it so important to you to be Mormon? If you must be a believer, there are other, more acceptable faiths." Her expression turns pleading.

Far would agree that I'd be better off outside the church. Doubts churn inside me. Is my particular faith more important than the study of astronomy? I think of how I felt at the Methodist church with the Stevens family, how I feel increasingly called to this study. Every church holds that they have the truth, but perhaps to God it is enough that we believe?

If you must be a believer. And what of faith itself? What I feel is belief, not certainty—what if my study of science reveals ultimately that such belief is empty? I might give up science for faith only to find that I've mistaken fool's gold for the real thing.

Miss Culbertson holds my gaze for a long moment. "Please do the right thing, Miss Bertelsen."

And then she's gone.

I stand at the door so long that a dozen people pass me, talking animatedly, on their way out of the high school. I stand there so long that at last Samuel climbs up the stairs himself to meet me.

"Elizabeth?" he asks, studying my face and catching my hands up in his. "What's wrong?"

"Nothing," I say.

chapter twenty-two

Friday, July 26, 1878
Denver, Colorado
Three days until eclipse

I wake to Samuel shaking my shoulder, saying urgently, "Elizabeth! Wake up!"

Morning light streams through the muslin curtains. My heart jolts: I'm late for work. I sit up, turning my head away from Samuel to hide my breath, which tastes foul on my tongue.

Then I remember: I don't have a job to rush to. I let my head fall back on the pillow with a *whump.*

Samuel studies me in some concern. "Are you ill?"

I shake my head. "Only unemployed."

"What?"

"I was let go yesterday. For sleeping in your room."

Samuel goes very still. "You didn't tell me that. I could have said something to the housekeeper. We didn't do anything." He flushes a bit as he says this last. If the subject wasn't already mortifying, I'd find his blush charming.

"It wouldn't help. It was the appearance of evil she objected to, not any evil itself."

"I wish you'd told me." Samuel walks to the window and rests his head against the pane, watching the street below. His shoulders are tight, the line of his back stiff.

"Samuel?"

He lets out a long breath, but his shoulders don't ease. "I've got to head back. Today, most like. I've been trying to stay as long as I can, but I haven't been able to find temporary work and the money's nearly gone. I'd hoped you'd be all right, with your job, but now—I think I've got enough money to get us both to your sister's place, where we can wire home for more."

He turns back to face me. "I'm sorry. I know how much this eclipse means to you. I wanted to give it to you, to give you everything you wanted. If I could, I'd pluck the stars from the sky for you." He laughs, a harsh note I've never heard from him. "But I can't even manage this one thing."

"It's not your job to give me things," I say, my heart pounding. I don't know if it's from fear, or anxiety, or something else. "And if you plucked the stars from the sky, there'd be nothing for me to study."

He doesn't smile at my weak attempt at humor. "I know it's not my job. But I'd like to make it my business. Elizabeth

Bertelsen, would you let me court you when we get home? If you think you could tolerate me, that is. I don't know how it is, but somehow you've worked your way into my heart so that I can't imagine a life without you."

A thousand different thoughts and feelings fly through me. My hand lifts to my uncombed hair, still bound in its nighttime braid. I want to laugh. Or maybe cry.

How can he ask me this now, when I'm still in bed, with morning stink in my mouth? When he's just told me he has to leave Denver, and wants me to come with him, wants me to leave the eclipse behind?

His question feels like both a promise and a trap.

I want to shake Samuel.

I want to kiss him.

"Only you, Samuel Willard, would ask a girl that when she's still in her nightclothes."

For the first time this morning, a glimmer of humor appears in his eyes. "Should I have waited for you to dress first? Make an occasion out of this?"

"Samuel," I say, and stop. He has been brave, and I owe him the same courage. But I don't know how to say what will hurt us both. Outside, clouds are lowering, as they have been all week—part of the high desert rainy season. "I can't."

"Can't what? Come home with me now or be courted?"

"Both." I can't go home. Not now. Not so close to the eclipse. I'll find some other place. Maybe Dr. Avery or Miss Mitchell knows someone, since all the hotels are full.

A very long silence hangs between us. I settle the

bedclothes around my waist, wishing I were dressed. Clothes have a dignity to them that I never appreciated before.

"I see. I know you've found me irritating, but I didn't realize I was so intolerable."

My heart twists. "You're not intolerable." *Far from it.* I like Samuel too much for my own comfort. "The fault isn't in you at all. It's me. I'm not sure I'm meant to be a wife. I want to learn. To go to high school and university and make a career out of studying the stars."

"I would wait for you," Samuel says. "I like that you want to learn—it's one of the things I like best about you. You make me think about ideas I'd never thought on."

I shake my head. How can I make him understand? "I'm not sure I will go back to Monroe, not for good. That life you want—a quiet home, a wife, children—I can't do that. I'm not good at those domestic tasks. They make me feel like a stranger in my own skin."

"Are you saying no to me, or to the life you think I want you to lead?"

I want to reach out and smooth the furrow between his brows with my finger, but I keep my hands clenched tight. "Aren't they the same? You're a farmer; you need a farmer's wife."

"I have sheep," Samuel says, "but I'm a carpenter, not a farmer. I can practice my trade anywhere. And I don't want a farmer's wife. I want you. If you don't love me and don't think you ever can, that's one thing. But don't say no because you don't see how I fit into some future you've imagined. I can fit. I can find work where you go to school. I can help you, however you need."

A surge of emotion washes through me, so powerful I can't quite tell if it's good or not. *I want you.* Samuel Willard, who has never wanted a thing for himself if it would inconvenience someone else, wants me. Yearning pricks at my throat.

I want to say yes.

Each body is itself the centre of an attractive force extending indefinitely into space.

But I can't. Saying yes to Samuel means saying no to too many other things.

No matter what he says, I don't think we want the same things. I'd rather hurt a little now than face the pain later, after our lives are twined together and we still don't fit. "And then what? When I get work in an astronomy laboratory, charting stars, who will make your clothes? Who will care for your children? If you mean to take a second wife, I don't want that life. If you intend me to do it—I'm not sure I can." I want so much that seems impossible—I'm not sure I can bear wanting Samuel too and being disappointed.

I feel as though I stand at a crossroads, with one road leading to home and family and faith, the other to science and learning and adventure. But the crossroads does not feel like a choice so much as a crucifix or some other torture device, tugging me in impossible postures—two oxen set to a plow that refuse to pull together and will leave only destruction in their wake.

"It won't work," I say.

And then Samuel loses his temper at last.

"Because you won't try to make it work! I don't want a second wife—just you. I've offered everything, even remaking my life around you, and you won't even let me try. I wish you'd just say you don't love me and be done with it." He throws a few clothes into a battered suitcase, snatches his hat off the desk, and looks at me.

"Don't choke on your pride," he says, and then he walks out.

✦

I don't know how long I sit in bed, staring at nothing, before rousing myself to pull on clothes and do my hair. I feel odd, as though someone has taken a scraper to me and scoured out my insides. My arms and hands are strangely heavy.

The door bangs open while I am still pinning up my hair. Frances lifts her nose and stares down at me.

"This room's been let. Your man paid his bill and left, and it's time for you to leave too."

Given the demand for rooms, I'm not surprised this one is already claimed. But I doubt the new owner is already waiting to take possession—I think Frances is just being spiteful. She's enjoying this, watching me with narrowed eyes.

So I take my time, finishing my hair and then gathering my things into my carpetbag. I drag my trunk into the hallway, down the stairs. In the grand entry to the hotel, I stop.

What am I to do now?

I persuade the clerk at the desk to hold my trunk for me. By nightfall, either I'll have a new place to stay, or I'll have to lug the trunk to the railway station and sleep on it there. (Safer to sleep there, with other passengers, than on the streets, I reason. I hope it won't come to that.)

Walking the long blocks to Dr. Avery's house, I try not to think about Samuel, likely waiting now in the station for a train home. Perhaps already aboard. Hating me.

It's for the best. Someday he'll thank me.

Clouds spit cold rain in my face. What if the storm carries through until Monday, and despite everything and everyone I've sacrificed to be here, I can't see the eclipse after all? The irony would almost be funny if it wasn't so personal.

I climb Dr. Avery's steps and knock.

Miss Culbertson answers the door. "I thought you might turn up," she says warily, folding her arms across her chest.

"I've thought about what you said about faith," I say, drawing a deep breath, thinking of that crossroads. I've already sacrificed Samuel on an altar of stars—what's one more sacrifice? *Per aspera ad astra.* "My faith won't be an obstacle. I'd rather be a scientist than a Mormon." I pull at a long hangnail, then press my finger against the blood, against the sharp spurt of pain.

I follow Miss Culbertson into the now familiar parlor. Dr. Avery, she tells me, is at her practice, but the other women are gathered in a close circle. Miss Harrison plays the piano softly, and Miss Abbot turns pages for her. Miss Mitchell smiles when I walk in. I pinch my hangnail again.

I settle beside Miss Mitchell, and her sister brings us both tea.

Miss Mitchell gestures with her cup at the window. "These wide-open western spaces and mountains always seem strange to me. So much space. I grew up on a small island, you know, boxed in by water and customs. Have you lived out west your whole life?"

I nod. "I was born in Salt Lake City. Though my parents are immigrants, my father from Denmark and my mother from England. They met in Utah Territory."

"They must be very proud of you."

I study my hands in my lap. After a moment, I look up at Miss Mitchell. "I hope they will be proud of me someday. But my mother would rather I stayed home to raise a family, as she has done."

Miss Mitchell nods. "Such an attitude, unfortunately, is not uncommon. Are you here on your own, or with your parents' blessing?"

I swallow. "My parents know where I am—but I would not say I have their blessing."

Despite the warm room, despite the watery sunlight just now spurting through the clouds outside, I am suddenly cold, as though all the things that make me substantial have evaporated in the sun and there's nothing of me left. I pinch my finger again, but it doesn't make me feel any more real.

Miss Mitchell asks something else—I hardly know what—

and I answer at random. This is wrong; it's all wrong. Much as I want to be here, I want to be here as *me,* not as someone I'm pretending to be. The whole mess at Alice's started because I was trying to soften myself to make other people more comfortable. Maybe it goes back even further: if I wasn't trying to hide from Mama, I'd never have left Rachel while she was napping.

"Miss Mitchell, I—" I start, stop.

"Whatever it is, you can tell me. There's nothing more critical to the work we do than the truth."

The truth.

"I'm afraid I haven't been entirely truthful with you. I told you my father was no longer Mormon. That was true. But my mother is." I take a deep breath. "I am."

Miss Culbertson looks at me from across the room, her brows drawn together.

"And yet, when you first met us, you allowed us to believe otherwise," Miss Mitchell says.

"Yes. I'm sorry. My experience suggested I wouldn't be welcome if you knew my background." I drop my eyes again, unable to meet that steady regard. "And I didn't think my faith would matter in this." I glance at Miss Culbertson, now speaking in a low voice to Miss Harrison.

"In that belief, you do both yourself and us a wrong," Miss Mitchell says. "Why would you deny who you are? If you cannot bring your whole self to your work, what do you bring instead?"

There's a tightness in my throat, and I can't bring myself to answer. I'm not sure I know the answer.

Miss Mitchell continues, "And what of your background in astronomy? Do you truly have experience handling telescopes and sighting stars?"

I release a long, low sigh. All my chickens are coming home to roost, it seems. "I've handled a telescope once, ma'am. I don't have formal schooling. But I've read as much as I possibly can about astronomy, and I'm a fast study. I'll do exactly as I'm told, and I won't need repeated instructions."

Miss Mitchell shakes her head, her graying ringlets dancing. "It grieves me to tell you this, Miss Bertelsen, as I can see you are eager, and I like you. But the eclipse is serious. We have only a few minutes to record everything we can, and we cannot afford mistakes made by amateurs. It has been nine years since I was last able to study an eclipse with my students—the next eclipse in America is not until 1889, and I might not live so long, to rectify any missteps. I encourage you to assist Dr. Colbert with the drawing of the corona on your own time—but we cannot bring you with our party."

When I do not answer immediately, she adds, "I appreciate your honesty now. In a year or two, when you've had some formal schooling and finished your studies, send me a letter, and I will see if I can help you find a place at Vassar. But I hope you can understand that you simply are not ready yet."

I nod, not trusting myself to speak. I suck at the roof of my mouth, trying to keep tears at bay. Mumbling something I hope sounds like thanks, I escape as soon as I can.

I walk at random for a while, trying to decide what to do. I've forgotten to ask if Dr. Avery knows of anyone with rooms to let, but the humiliation is still too raw for me to force myself to return to the doctor's house.

Perhaps I should just give up, go back to the train station, and beg enough money to get to Rebekka. To get home. Helping Mama, watching my siblings, those are tasks I know, tasks I'm good at. This—watching the eclipse, studying the stars—I might not be any good at. I might fail.

But everything in me resists the idea.

If I go home now, for the rest of my life, I'd wonder what would have happened if I stayed. I'll sleep on the streets if I have to. Summer evenings in July can't be that cold.

A splatter of rain lands on my nose.

All right, I will have to find a place out of the rain, but I can make do. I can even draw the corona for Dr. Colbert, if nothing else presents itself—though after the prospect of working with Miss Mitchell, it feels rather like snatching at crumbs from a table, after everyone else has been fed.

Still, crumbs are better than nothing.

Eventually, I wind up at the library again, where I flip through a few recent newspapers, searching for reports of other astronomers in town for the eclipse. I know from conversations at Dr. Avery's that Dr. Charles Young, from Princeton, has a camp somewhere south of town, but I cannot find any specifics of where.

Finally, I give up and walk to the headquarters of the *Denver Tribune,* where I pester passing journalists until one of them, at last, gives me the directions I need.

Professor Young's camp lies a couple of miles south of

downtown, in a cottonwood grove alongside Cherry Creek. The camp is bustling when I arrive, mostly sunburned young men wandering between the tents and some wooden shacks. The scent of a savory stew floats over the trees.

A tall, dark-haired young man is the first to spot me. "Well, hello there. Are you lost, miss?"

I take a deep breath and square my shoulders. I can do this. "I'm looking for Professor Young. Is he available?"

The boy squints at me. "Twinkle? What do you want him for? You a reporter?"

I shake my head, trying not to feel daunted. "I'm an astronomer. That is, I'd like to be. I can do anything you need—help with instruments, fetch things, time the eclipse. I even know how to draw the corona."

The young man stares at me for a long moment before giving a crack of laughter. "You? An astronomer? And will you bring your knitting and your darning to the eclipse? Go home, girl. You don't belong here."

I don't move, though my cheeks burn. Maybe this was a mistake. "I'd like to speak to Professor Young."

By this point, our exchange has drawn a few more boys. The first tells them, "This girl is looking to join us."

"For what?" a blond boy with a scraggly mustache asks. "Do we look like we're hosting a dance out here?"

"Says she wants to be an astronomer."

"And become one of those sexless prudes in Mitchell's group?" a third boy asks. He turns to me. "Lady, you don't want to do that. Trust me. You're better off finding yourself a nice boy."

The blond boy elbows in. "Only not him. He's a bit of a masher."

I don't know what that word means, but it hardly matters. It's clear these boys don't take me seriously. I know Princeton is supposed to be a fancy school, but I don't think much of it if this is how they encourage their students to behave.

"Is Professor Young here?" I persist.

An older man with dark, silver-threaded hair makes his way from one of the tents. "What's all this about?"

With great delight, the boys tell him about my ridiculous request. Professor Young—at least I assume it's him from the way the tall boy calls him "Twinkle"—turns to me with pursed lips.

"Your interest in science is commendable, young lady, if perhaps a bit misguided. I'm afraid we're an all-boys setup here. Hardly a suitable place for a girl, even if we had work for you. But my students have everything covered."

He smiles kindly at me, but the dismissal is clear. I thank him, then ask, "And Professor William Pickering? Do you know if he needs assistance?"

The dark-haired boy wrinkles his nose. "Pickering? That MIT crowd is even rougher than we are, miss. You'd do better to stay in town and watch the eclipse with the other locals."

"Wait," the blond boy says, with the exaggerated air of one coming to a brilliant conclusion. "I've got it! We just had a wire from Pikes Peak that one of their astronomers is down with altitude sickness. No doubt you could be of great use to them." He sniggers.

"If you can make it that far," another adds, and then they all dissolve into laughter.

I can still hear them cackling as I round a bend in the road, making my way back to Denver.

chapter twenty-three

Friday, July 26, 1878
Denver, Colorado
Three days until eclipse

It's late afternoon before I reach the Trans-Oceana to make good on my promise to retrieve my trunk. I'll sleep in the train station for the night and figure out a new plan in the morning.

It amuses me—as much as I can be amused, just now—to think how far I've come from that scared country girl on the first night of my journey east, afraid to spend the night outside the station in Salt Lake City. I don't look forward to a night on my trunk, but I'm not scared of it anymore.

There's a different clerk waiting behind the front desk now, and I rush forward, words of explanation about my trunk dying on my tongue as I see someone rise from one of the wingback chairs in the lobby.

Alice.

I shouldn't be surprised to see her in her grandpa's hotel, but shock still pricks through me. I assumed we'd tacitly agreed to avoid each other.

"This came for you," Alice says, holding out the familiar rectangular shape of a telegram. Her voice is cool, but a tiny divot between her eyebrows betrays some feeling—worry? She didn't have to wait for me. She could have left the message with the desk clerk.

"I'm sorry," I say.

"I know," Alice says. "I read your note. I'm sorry too. I shouldn't have said the things I did."

"You were right to say them. I deserved that, and more." I take the telegram from her but don't open it at once. It feels hot in my fingers, as though the contents might burn. "How's Will?"

Alice turns her elegant profile toward the window. "Will is . . . struggling. Papa has told him he can't leave the house except when he comes to the hotel to help Grandpa, and Will prowls the house like a wild thing. Papa wants him to learn responsibility, threatened to disown him if he doesn't stop acting like a young fool, but he hasn't given Will any directions on how to do that, and I'm afraid Will might do something rash in the meantime."

I widen my eyes. "More rash than walking across a train trestle?"

Alice laughs, then sobers. "Maybe more permanently rash. He needs a distraction, but I don't know what to offer him."

She turns back to me and nods at the paper in my hand. "You should read that."

My hands shake as I read the few words printed. *Mama is poorly again wants you home. Emily.* Rebekka must have sent them my address.

I read it again, trying to figure out what my sister left out in the gaps between her words. Mama is poorly, how? Is it her usual troubles, or something different? "Again" suggests her usual dark moods, but I can't be sure.

"Are you all right?" Alice asks. "Here, you should sit down."

I take the chair she was sitting in earlier and stare up at her. The tips of my fingers tingle, but I cannot figure out what I feel. I should be shocked, or alarmed, or sad, but all I feel is a heavy weight, as though everything from the past day has gathered up into a great lump in my chest.

Alice calls to the desk clerk, telling him to fetch us some tea from the kitchen, then sits in a seat facing me. "Trouble at home?"

"My mama's sick."

"I saw," Alice says, a trifle apologetically. "Hard not to see, with a telegram. It came to the house earlier and I've been looking for you all over. Mrs. Segura said you don't work here anymore. What happened?"

"Someone saw me coming out of Samuel's room. It wasn't anything, but it looked bad. I just came back to fetch my trunk."

"You're heading home, then?"

Until the last five minutes, I'd have said no. I meant to stay for the eclipse. But Mama—Mama is a responsibility I can't easily ignore. "I don't know. My family needs me."

"And the eclipse?"

I run the toe of my boot across the carpet. "I've always done what my mama needed, up until this journey. And now everything has gone to pieces. So maybe I was wrong to pursue what I wanted." Rebekka told me I should come to Denver, to the eclipse, to see if that's what God wanted for me. Maybe this is my sign that it isn't.

"Or maybe it's not what you wanted, but how you pursued it," Alice says. "You can't lie about who you are and expect everything to turn out right."

"I know," I say, my voice small. "I told Miss Mitchell the truth. She was very nice about it, but I'm not welcome back to their site. No one else in town seems to want my help either. Perhaps this is for the best."

Alice taps her fingertips together. "You gave me your sister's words when I needed them. Let me tell you something my mama taught me. You know she isn't like most society mamas. She works at the hotel almost as hard as Grandpa. She's had to give up some things to do that—time with us, charity work. But she makes sure all those things get done. She donates to charity, hires people to take care of the house and meet our needs.

"Mama says it's like a scale." She raises one hand. "On one side are the needs of our community—our family, friends, even people we don't know. On the other are our own needs.

If the scale gets out of balance, if we give too much to our community and neglect ourselves, we get sick or unhappy, and then it's hard to meet those needs." She lifts the other hand. "If we only fill our own scale, then the community suffers, and our lives are poorer."

A maid brings two cups and saucers to us. Alice takes them and sets them on the dainty round table between our two chairs. "It's not wrong to want something for yourself. It doesn't make you selfish to honor your needs, to believe your dreams matter. It only becomes selfish if the balance tips too far."

Picking up my cup, I hold my hands around the fragile curve of the warmed porcelain. I think of my parents, how Far collects papers and spends time with Aunt Olena, how he smokes behind the barn when he thinks Mama doesn't know. When Mama isn't sick, she walks into town to gossip with the sisters. She sleeps when she's tired. When she doesn't get those things, she's short and unhappy.

"How do you know," I ask, "whose needs are more important in the moment?"

"If I knew that, I could be the richest woman in America, selling that answer to folks." Alice laughs a little. "Mama always tries to approach it practically. Can anyone else do this thing for me? Or is this a small desire I can put aside until time allows?"

In all the days since I've come to Denver, I haven't prayed about my path. It's as if I've been so focused on becoming an astronomer, I've forgotten how to be Mormon too. While

Alice sips her tea, I offer a silent prayer: *Father, Mother, what should I do?*

For a moment, there's nothing but stillness. Then—

A powerful warm wave shudders through me.

Stay.

I look back at Alice to find her watching me, a smile in her eyes.

Experiencing the eclipse, deciding if I should be an astronomer—this isn't something anyone else can do for me.

"I'm going to stay," I say. "I'll go home as soon after as I can, but I need to do this for myself."

Alice grins at me. "Good."

A glimmer of an idea takes shape. "But I won't stay here in Denver. I want to see the eclipse from Pikes Peak."

The boy in Dr. Young's camp never intended me to take his words seriously, but if the scientists at Pikes Peak need an extra hand, it's worth the chance. Even if they don't need me, the extra altitude of the peak might make a difference to my experience. Miss Mitchell explained to us that the thinner air of Colorado might be the very thing astronomers need to see the planet Vulcan. And if the air in Denver is good, then wouldn't the air of Pikes Peak, some eight or nine thousand feet higher, be even better? I might have to sell everything left to my name—my spare clothes, my carpetbag, even my long, curling hair—but I'll find a way to get there.

"Why Pikes Peak?" Alice asks.

I explain my reasoning, then study Alice. "You should come with me. Just think what you could paint of the view from Pikes Peak during the eclipse. I know you said you were focusing on domestic pieces, but this eclipse is going to change the West—it'll put Colorado on the map of scientific achievement. Why not make art of that?"

After a moment's hesitation during which I wonder if I've offended Alice again, her smile blooms. "Why not? I think it's a splendid idea."

Outside, rain spatters against the windows in the growing dark, but everything inside seems suddenly flooded with light.

When Alice sets down her teacup and stands, I rise and throw my arms around her. "Thank you," I whisper, choking. "Thank you for helping me find myself."

There's a long pause while Alice stands stiff with surprise. Then she returns my hug. Her voice isn't entirely steady when she says, "We helped each other."

She steps back and surveys me, a considering light in her eyes. Before she even speaks, I suspect what she's going to say.

"We should bring Will."

✦

I spend that night in my old room at the Stevenses' house—a vast improvement over a trunk in the station. The morning finds us back at the train station, Alice having worked everything out to her satisfaction. She's loaned me some supplies and funds, which I mean to pay back, and expertly managed to talk her parents around to this last-minute scheme.

"Be sure to bring warm clothes for the mountain," Mrs. Stevens said, just before we left. "It can be cold on the peak, even in July."

"Take care of your sister," Mr. Stevens told Will. "I expect you to bring everyone home safe and sound."

"Pikes Peak or bust," Will said, drawing a cross over his heart.

A tiny smile tugged at Mr. Stevens's mouth. "No busting, if you please. Just come back." I think secretly Mr. Stevens was relieved to have a reason to let Will out of the house.

While we wait for the train, I dash to the telegraph office to send a note home saying I'll be back after the eclipse and sending my love. *I have faith in you,* I write to Emily. I want to send a note to Samuel too, but what would I say? I'm sorry we fought, but I haven't changed my mind. And anyway, he'll be another week or more on the road. I'll catch him nearly as soon as a telegram would.

By late morning, Alice, Will, and I are rattling south on the narrow-gauge lines of the Denver and Rio Grande Railroad, slicing through hilly country toward the mountains around Colorado Springs. Will looks tired, with dark circles under his eyes, but he's in good spirits, teasing Alice about her art supplies.

"What kind of young lady packs more paints and brushes than dresses and boots?" he asks.

"The kind that isn't above painting her brother's face in the middle of the night if he doesn't knock it off," Alice says calmly.

Will laughs and leans across Alice to point out some landmark in the distance.

I let the siblings' easy chatter wash across me and hope I've made the right decision—about not going home, about going to Pikes Peak. It's so easy to get decisions wrong. Like switches on a train track: a little choice, a small shift, and you can wind up hundreds of miles from where you thought to go. For all I resisted the choices Mama tried to make for me, there was comfort in not having to choose.

It's early afternoon when we reach Colorado Springs. We walk the few blocks from the depot into the heart of town. The air is close and chilly for July. I cannot see any sign of Pikes Peak: any mountains ringing the growing town are hidden behind low-hanging clouds. I hope the clouds lift by Monday, or our view of the eclipse will be a valley full of clouds.

We stop by a wooden building whose sign reads LIVERY, FEED, AND STABLE, asking for a guide up the mountain, but are told all available guides have been hired already for the eclipse.

Back on the street, Will studies the base of the mountain. "I'll bet I can get us up there."

"Mmm," Alice agrees noncommittally. "And they'll be digging our bodies out of a snowbank in another month. I'd be easier with someone who has been up the mountain before."

Will wrinkles his nose at her but doesn't argue. "Who do we know in Colorado Springs? Someone must know of a guide still in town."

While he and Alice run down a few unlikely options, I remember the writer Alice and I met. "There's Mrs. Jackson—that writer we met at Dr. Avery's. She seems pretty keen on traveling and the outdoors, so she likely knows someone."

Alice brightens. "Good idea!"

A quick inquiry at a nearby hotel turns up directions to Mrs. Jackson's. She must be something of a celebrity, because the clerk doesn't have to ask us who we mean.

A maid answers the door, and, after a searching look over our unfamiliar company, calls Mrs. Jackson instead of letting us in the house. I wonder if strangers turn up at the door often, or if the maid is just being cautious.

Mrs. Jackson, however, recognizes Alice and me almost at once. "Good afternoon! We met at Dr. Avery's, yes? But I'm afraid I've forgotten your names. Come in, come in! I was just about to sit down to some tea and sandwiches. Would you like some?"

Alice begins to demur, but Will accepts with such enthusiasm that it makes me laugh.

Mrs. Jackson sees us settled into a parlor, with shelves lined with fat volumes of books, before bustling out again. Will and Alice sit down, but I prowl along the bookshelves, marveling that a single person could own so many—almost as many as the library in Denver. But maybe that's part of the job of a writer.

At the end of one bookshelf, I find an old newspaper wedged between two books. Curious, I work it loose.

It's a copy of the *Woman's Exponent,* from last year. My

fingers tremble a little as I work over the familiar names of the writers: Emmeline Wells, Lula Greene Richards. I've come across an unexpected bit of home, in the voices of these Mormon women. My throat begins to ache from missing Mama and my sisters.

When Mrs. Jackson returns to the room, followed by her maid bearing a heavy tray, I brandish the newspaper at her. "How did you come by this?"

Mrs. Jackson looks briefly startled but comes to inspect my prize. She smiles. "Oh, yes. I met the woman who now edits that paper when I was in Utah. She sent it to me some months ago, thinking I might enjoy it."

It does not look as though it has been well enjoyed, stuffed where I found it. "May I have it?" I ask.

Her eyebrows lift again in surprise. "If you wish."

"Thank you!" I fold the paper and stick it in my pocket, then drift toward the others. Mrs. Jackson sets out plates piled with sandwiches, and my stomach growls at me. But Mrs. Jackson only laughs. "I like a girl with a good appetite. I have one myself." She hands me a plate and a sandwich, and I take a seat and begin to eat.

Alice explains that we've come to try to see the eclipse from the peak but we're looking for a guide to take us safely up the trail.

Mrs. Jackson purses her lips in thought for a moment, then says, "Try Mr. Navarro, over by the Methodist church. He's one of the best. If he's not available, his daughter knows nearly as much as he does."

We chat easily as we finish the meal—the Stevenses and Mrs. Jackson have a number of common friends in Denver, and Mrs. Jackson has lots of questions about Alice's proposed eclipse painting.

When she waves us off, I feel better for the food and the new directions, despite the still-lowering clouds.

Mr. Navarro isn't at home, his services already being spoken for by another traveling party. But his daughter, Daniela, answers the door and says she'd be ready enough to take us up, for a fee. She's a tall girl, taller than me by a good five inches and nearly as tall as Will, with black hair braided around her head and wearing men's trousers.

She inspects us carefully, her eyes lingering on the skirts Alice and I wear—particularly Alice's. It's a serviceable gray, but the flounces across the hem and sleeve don't exactly scream practicality. "Are you sure you're equipped for this? It's a hard climb at times, and mountain sickness is fairly common among townfolk."

"We're tougher than we look," Will says, grinning at her.

She only raises her eyebrows at him and shrugs. "Well, it's your funeral. My father usually takes people up the mountain on horseback, but I've only got two mounts left in the stables. We'll have to ride double, which will slow us down. But we should be able to get to the peak by Monday morning."

"Good enough," Will says. "I'll ride with you."

Again, that slow eyebrow lift. "You can ride with your sister, Mr. Stevens."

Alice laughs. Will murmurs, "I am cast down but not disconsolate, Miss Navarro."

"What you are is delusional—and you talk too damn much for a man with any sense," she says, and leads us around the house to the horses.

chapter twenty-four

Saturday, July 27, 1878
Pikes Peak, Colorado
Two days until eclipse

Our chatter comes and goes in pockets of talk interspersed by silence as we ride out of the valley and wind our way upward toward Pikes Peak. I ride in front of Daniela, my skirts hitched up to my knees.

Alice and Will tell Daniela about their grandpa and his hotel, and about their father and his family, who settled in New York and then Ohio before coming to Colorado. Daniela tells us about her own father, who was part of the original gold rush on Pikes Peak twenty years earlier, then stayed on and made a living farming in the valley and leading expeditions up the mountain. Daniela's mother, who died when she was small, was Tabeguache, one of the bands of Ute Indians living in Colorado.

Daniela nods toward the faint trail before us. "My mother's family used to live on the mountains before the prospectors came. They hold it sacred. Look." Daniela points to a ponderosa pine nearby, the bark showing an old scar. "You can see where Tabeguache have gathered the inner bark for medicine."

Her story echoes that of Sarah and Brother Timican, the Paiutes from back home who came to church the Sunday before I left. They also talked about how the coming of settlers to build cities in the Rocky Mountains changed their way of life. I don't know how to undo those actions, but I can listen. I can try to understand my own role in all of this.

Daniela tells other stories of her mother: How she knew the times and seasons for all the plants that grew in the mountains and valleys. How she knew when to burn, when to gather, how to make and use and store. "My mother's baskets were always the most prized for their tight weaves and fine patterns."

When Daniela's stories end, I tell them about my own parents coming to Utah from Europe and England. I think about all the different stories behind ours, all the lives and distances crossed for the four of us to intersect in this moment.

We pause at the base of the mountain for a meal, sometime in the late afternoon, and I stare up the slopes in dismay, wrapping the coat I borrowed from Mrs. Stevens closer around me. I cannot see the top of Pikes Peak: the clouds are too low, an impenetrable ceiling cutting off our goal. Right now it seems impossible that we are only two days from an eclipse of the sun. It feels as though we may never see the sun again.

Daniela squints up at the sky. "I was hoping to reach Tweed's homestead around dark, but I don't think we'll make it before the storm bursts."

We keep moving.

The flat gray light makes it impossible to tell the time or gauge our distance. We pass through miles of trail, interspersed by long golden meadows dotted with bright red desert paintbrush and blue larkspur. The air is fragrant with the smell of pine. Though the trail up the mountain is greener than the mountain trails back home, I find myself missing Monroe. Not just my family, but the pinyon and scrub pine too.

And yet, when I think about home, it doesn't feel as settled as it used to—as though Monroe is only a stopping place, somewhere that I'll return to but leave again.

It begins to spit rain—cold, stinging drops that turn to a sudden burst of hail. We leave the trail and take shelter under the trees to wait for the worst of the fury to spend itself. My wool coat begins to reek as it absorbs the water, and my fingers, curled inside the sleeves, are like ice.

We struggle to set up tents in the growing gloom, and only manage to get one upright before the rain begins in earnest. We all crowd in together, leaving the horses lashed outside.

The crowding I don't mind so much, as it reminds me of sharing a bed with Emily and Mary back home. But the sky outside lights up with periodic lightning, and I can't help thinking how the whole tent could go up in flames if we get hit, and the water seeps across the ground, through even the coat I'm wearing, and then I can't sleep for the cold.

In the morning, when we resume our climb, we all move stiffly.

A thin layer of snow blankets the ground. The horses inch upward as the trail becomes steeper.

The bristlecone pine trees grow shorter, clinging desperately to increasingly sheer rock walls. Some look like flags, all their branches pointing in a single direction from the assault of the wind, which howls around us.

Sometimes we skirt the edge of the peak. Alice glances across the trail, to where the sides of the mountain tumble down. "I don't like heights," she mutters, reminding me of her white-knuckled intensity when we crossed the trestle bridge.

"It's all right," Will says, for once not teasing. He eases their mount closer to the reassuring rocks, as far from the edge as he can reach. "I'm here. I've got you."

We pass by a squat cabin, from which the smell of warm bread wafts in tantalizing waves. This must be the homestead Daniela was talking about. A pair of eclipse tourists, two middle-aged men, emerge from the barn in coats and scarves and start up the trail just ahead of us. They look warm and dry, and for a moment I hate them with a very unchristian intensity.

The meadows and flowers give way to sage and then to moss and lichen, and we leave the trees behind entirely, along with the tourists. We see a pair of mountain goats, but they disappear as soon as we come within sight of them, springing nimbly across rocks in a way that seems to defy gravity.

The clouds swirl around us, peppering us with rain and hail, and then in a fit of cold, a flurry of snowflakes. I've heard you can see for miles from Pikes Peak. All we can see is the trail some sixty or seventy feet ahead of us. Everything else is swallowed in mist.

I try to pray for our safety, for Alice's, but my prayers seem swallowed by the mist too. Nothing seems to penetrate, and I feel the sudden terror of standing on the edge of a chasm— not so hard to imagine here, where not far from the trail the world falls away into nothingness.

It's Sunday morning. If I had never come to Denver, I would be at church now. Suddenly, I miss that familiar, homely crowd with a fierceness that slices through me. Instead I'm on the side of a mountain, growing more chilled by the minute. I've never really believed in a fire-and-brimstone hell. But maybe this is hell: slowly freezing to death, cut off from God and nearly everyone that I love.

Will has kept up a steady stream of good-humored conversation, but by early afternoon, even he has been wrung dry of words. The air here is thin, and though I drink deeply from my canteen, I cannot shake the beginnings of a headache.

Guiding their horse to the side of the trail, Will tumbles from the saddle and vomits into the bushes. Alice dismounts after him.

Daniela watches Will with concern. "Is your head aching?"

Will rises and wipes his mouth on his sleeve. His skin is ashy, his eyes dull. He nods, then winces.

"Mountain sickness," Daniela says. "The heights take some like this. You'll be all right when you get down—best if you wait for us back at the homestead."

Will shakes his head. "No. I'm all right. I'm here for Alice and Elizabeth, not my own comfort."

Daniela presses some water on Will, then we move on. As the last of the hardy grasses and short vegetation give way to sheer rock, she stops us.

"We're perhaps an hour from the summit, but it's getting dark and I don't trust the trail in the darkness." As she speaks, a few flakes of snow begin to fall.

We set up tents against a jutting wall of rock and boulders, where we're protected somewhat from the wind. We secure the tents with rocks, as stakes won't penetrate the ground, and crowd inside.

The snow is coming more heavily now.

It is so cold, summer feels like something I have dreamed up. Will curls in a ball inside the tent, his face wan and strained. My own head feels like drummers have taken up residence in my temple. Daniela insists that we drink water, that the liquid will help with the altitude sickness, but it doesn't seem to do much. I wish we could build a fire, but it's too wet for that.

The cloud cover swallows any light from the stars.

Alice snatches a bedroll and blanket, and Daniela and I

help her shift Will onto it. Alice bends down to set her hand against Will's forehead. "He's hot." She settles down beside him and looks up at me. "Can you take his other side?"

I unroll my bedroll and lie down beside Will, thinking that in any other circumstances our proximity might be shocking. He groans and reaches blindly for my hand. I take it, feeling a rush of concern and affection like I might feel for Hyrum.

Will drops off quickly, followed by Alice on his other side, and Daniela beyond her. I can't shut off my thoughts. I've never been so far from home, or so high in the mountains. The certainty I felt when Alice and I decided to attempt the peak is gone, swallowed up by a vast yawning gulf of doubt.

Rocks press into my spine as I shift. I try to take even breaths, to calm the spiking panic inside me, but I can't seem to get enough air.

I worry about Will, groaning a little even in his sleep. Is altitude sickness fatal? Maybe we should send him down the mountain in the morning—or go down with him ourselves.

I worry about the eclipse, that tomorrow will dawn as cloudy and miserable as the past few days, and for all my efforts, all I'll see is a misty veil shrouding the sky.

Then I worry about Mama. Was I right to delay leaving? What if she's worse off than Emily suggested?

And threaded through all the rest of it, I worry about this path I've chosen. Suppose tomorrow shows that I'm utterly unfit as an astronomer—what then? Can I bear to go back home and tuck my dreams away as though they were nothing? And suppose it shows me that I do have the makings of an astronomer. What then? I can find some way of going to school, I think, but what of *me*?

Miss Mitchell suggested that I need to bring all of myself to my work. I don't know what that means.

I know how to be Mormon, and not be an astronomer. I've done that my whole life.

I can see from Miss Mitchell and the others what it looks like to be an astronomer and not be Mormon.

But to be both?

Does being a person of faith—particularly a Mormon—disqualify me for scientific rigor? What if my training as a scientist makes me question, even abandon, my faith?

I don't know what it looks like to be both, if it is even possible. All the voices around me—Mama, Dr. Morton, Miss Culbertson—believe it is not.

In the snow-chilled dark on the side of the mountain, I am not sure of anything.

Except this: tomorrow is the eclipse.

chapter twenty-five

Monday, July 29, 1878
Pikes Peak, Colorado
Approximately seven hours to eclipse

The morning of the eclipse, I leave the tent to find that though it's still cloudy overhead, the clouds have broken on the plains and sun streams across them. It's the most curious effect, the light coming up to us instead of down, the meadows luminous yellow and green, as if the sun rises not over the horizon, but comes swimming up to us through translucent layers of grasses.

Daniela is already up, currying the horses. Will emerges from the tent. His skin is still chalky, his eyes bright with pain, but he is upright.

"How are you feeling?" I ask him.

"As though someone has placed a giant bellows in my brain and is plying it for all they're worth and I'm trapped on a ship during a storm."

My own head still aches. I force myself to draw slow, shallow breaths, but every time I think about how difficult it is to breathe, panic stirs in my gut.

Breathe, I think. I'm in no immediate danger; it's only the altitude.

Alice exits the tent, yawning and stretching, in time to hear Will's words. She frowns at him. "You're ill. You need to get down the mountain before the symptoms worsen."

Will shakes his head, but gingerly, as though afraid to trigger a deeper headache. "I promised Papa I'd be responsible for you and Elizabeth. How would it look if I abandoned you now?"

Alice puts her hands on her hips. "Papa won't be impressed if you kill yourself, William Lancelot Stevens. We can care for ourselves just fine."

"I've seen your type before, climbers wanting to summit the Peak in the worst of weather, just to prove they can," Daniela says, her lips curling. "I don't see the sense in it. You can't get through life without some risks—not if you're living—but you can be smart about those risks. What are you proving here?"

Will sways for a moment, tight-lipped. Then, "I'm proving myself a man of my word. I'll be all right. I promise if it gets any worse, I will go down the mountain."

Alice and I exchange glances. Sense has never been Will's strongest suit, but maybe this expedition is changing him too.

Once we've eaten some stale bread and cheese and dried fruit, we head up to the summit. Daniela won't bring the horses up any farther, so we crest the mountain on foot, picking a way along mossy outcroppings, around boulders.

The summit of Pikes Peak is covered in uneven rocks, some the size of small houses. A dozen or so people already cluster on the peak. A tourist party, complete with blanket spread across a large boulder and bottles of wine chilling in a nearby snowbank, sits some distance from a more scientific group. Several men work near a stubby stone building at the far edge of the plateau, adjusting a massive telescope on a wooden platform.

My mouth goes dry. We're here. The ghosts of last night's doubts return: What if the sky doesn't clear in time for the eclipse? What if I cannot do this?

After a moment, one of the men in the scientific party catches sight of us and clambers across the boulders toward us. The man is middle-aged with a curly beard and muscular frame, wearing some kind of uniform. He's rather red-faced by the time he draws close, muttering something under his breath.

"Damn it, I thought I'd made it clear that no civilians were to be allowed on the summit."

I'm nearly positive he meant for us to hear that. I glance over at the clearly civilian group, just now enjoying their breakfast.

The man follows my gaze. He haws a bit, then says, "That party is here as my guests. I'm General Albert Myer, US Signal Corps, and head of this operation."

I drop a curtsy, trying to hide my dismay. Of all the rotten luck, to make it all the way to the summit only to run into yet another obstacle. "I'm Miss Elizabeth Bertelsen, of Monroe, Utah."

Beside me, Alice and Will introduce themselves as well. Daniela doesn't say much, just watches. General Myer stares at us for a moment, then says, "Well, now you've seen the summit. You can head on back down the mountain. I don't care where you stop, so long as it's not here."

I straighten my back. "General Myer, I was told that one of your men was taken sick and that you're shorthanded just now for the eclipse viewing. I've come to help."

He squints at me. "Who told you that?"

"One of Professor Young's students."

He sighs and rubs his beard. "Well, it's true enough. Dr. Abbe came down with that blasted altitude sickness. Fool man could hardly see for pain but was determined to stay up here. I sent him down the mountain." He peers more closely at Will. "Here, now, you don't look so good either."

Will, drawn but game, says, "A good soldier doesn't desert his post, sir. I won't desert my sister either."

"Good man." General Myer nods approvingly. He turns back to me. "You know anything about telescopes and eclipses?"

"Only a little about telescopes," I say honestly, "but a fair

313

bit about astronomy and eclipses. I know how to sketch the corona anyway, and about timing the eclipse."

"Then tell me, what causes the eclipse?"

"The moon's orbit coming between us and the sun at just the right position—the moon's shadow falling on earth blocks out the light of the sun."

"And what is it we're looking for?"

I smile a little, remembering Professor Colbert's lecture. "The shape of the corona. Possibly the presence of the planet Vulcan."

General Myer grunts, which I take as approval. "And the rest of you?"

"I'm an artist," Alice says. "I mean to make sketches of the eclipse, and the view from the peak during it, and paint it later."

"I'm her assistant," Will says, pointing at Alice.

Daniela says, "I'm the guide. I think you know my father." With her head, she indicates a wiry, dark-haired man picking his way across the rocks from the tourist party.

The general brightens. "Ah, Navarro! Yes, I know him." He tugs at his beard a moment in thought, then says, "Well, I suppose you can all stay, provided you make yourselves useful. I'd like a copy of your sketches, Miss Stevens, after the eclipse. You can send them care of the US Signal Corps in Washington, DC."

Alice curtsies again. "Of course, sir."

Daniela leaves us to go talk to her father, who gives her a

tight hug. General Myer stumps off, then turns around after a few paces and asks, "Well, are you coming?"

We scramble after him. Daniela, her mission to guide us to the peak accomplished, stays with her father.

General Myer introduces us to a pair of men who work for the Signal Corps, and to Professor Samuel Langley, of the Allegheny Observatory. A middle-aged man with a dark beard beginning to gray, he's the owner of the large telescope.

The mention of Samuel makes me think of a very different Samuel, and I blush a little as I take Professor Langley's hand.

"Miss Bertelsen says she knows some astronomy," General Myer says.

"Capital!" Professor Langley says, smiling. "I'm sure we can find work for you to do, though it may not be the most exciting of work."

I tell him what I told General Myer, that I know how to sketch the corona, and add, "I'm willing to do anything you need, though I'm afraid I don't have much formal training."

"My friend Miss Mitchell claims that women make the best astronomers, because of their eye for detail. And while a good astronomer needs training, we can show you what we need. Hey, John!" he calls out, and a youngish man with glasses ambles over to us. "My brother, John," Mr. Langley says. "He's a medical doctor and professor at the University of Michigan, which has begun admitting women students and has a fine astronomy department besides."

Dr. John Langley peers at me. "Are you interested in astronomy?"

I nod, not quite trusting myself to speak. A sudden, wild hope is blooming in me.

Dr. Langley continues, "I'm a chemist, not an astronomer. But I do know Mr. Watson a bit, who's in that department— he's out in Wyoming just now, for this same eclipse. It's a good school and not terribly expensive. Twenty-five dollars to register, if you are not a resident of Michigan, and another twenty-five for incidental fees."

School has always seemed so out of reach because I could not imagine how to make it happen. But here, now, on the summit of Pikes Peak just before a total solar eclipse, so many things seem possible. I can write to the schools for admissions information, take classes at the Brigham Young Academy in Provo to learn whatever subjects I might be lacking. I can work to pay for my own schooling. Fifty dollars is a huge sum, but not an impossible one.

"Thank you," I say, and mean it.

For the rest of the morning, the Langley brothers put us to work carrying equipment, explaining what each is meant to do, positioning things just so, and then repositioning them when sudden gusts of wind scour over the peak. I do my best to ignore the headache still pounding dully at my temples and watch the cloudy sky.

Alice prowls around the summit, looking for the perfect spot to observe the valley. Will mostly lies down on a large boulder.

"I'm conserving my strength," he says, trying to smile.

"You do it quite well," I tell him, and he laughs.

Professor Samuel Langley explains the procedure for the eclipse: General Myer will observe through the telescope left behind by Mr. Abbe, looking for signs of the planet Vulcan. Dr. John Langley will attempt to measure the brightness of the corona through a photometer he's improvised. Another of the Signal Corps officers will man the second telescope, a large, bronze thing that was covered in lard to protect it on the way up the mountain. The grease has now been wiped away, and it gleams in the dim light. A third Signal Corps officer will measure temperature and radiation using Professor Langley's newly invented bolometer, and a fourth will monitor the spectroscope readings. The array of complicated instruments—most of which I have never seen before—is both exciting and daunting. It represents the height of scientific progress, but it also reminds me of the extent of my ignorance.

Will volunteers to time the eclipse, and Samuel Langley and I are to sketch the corona, the same work I would have done in Denver, for Professor Colbert. But somehow it feels more important here—perhaps because Professor Langley is doing the same, when he might have done any of the more technical work.

The scientists around us check and recheck their coordinates, adjusting the telescopes and their instruments. General Myer passes out blue-tinted glass, said to be more effective than the smoked glass sold on the streets in Denver. The sky overhead is still dark with clouds, the valley mottled in shadows and far-off sunlight. Professor Langley watches the sky and mutters something that sounds like an expletive. I whisper a prayer.

Around noon, Alice brings some fruit and sandwiches out from her bag, but I can't eat. My stomach is too knotted up and my head still aches with the altitude change. Will struggles upright and manages a few bites.

A wind picks up, screaming across the summit and requiring both Langleys to hold fast to the telescope and readjust its position. The cold air sears through me, and I pull my coat tighter about me.

The wind stirs the clouds overhead. Sluggishly, they break apart, revealing blue sky.

I've never seen such blue, like every perfect fall day rolled into one. A ragged cheer breaks from our group as the clouds sift away, torn gray banners waving defeat across the sky.

Holding up our blue glass, we study the sky and valley with renewed energy for any sign of the eclipse.

At 2:22 p.m., Dr. John Langley breaks away from a telescope to shout, "Here it comes!" He allows each of us to peer through the telescope to see the sliver of sun blocked by the advancing edge of the moon.

The eclipse is starting.

I want to laugh and cry at once, my whole body filled with a well of elation.

As the sun moves across the sky, the moon slides into position, blotting out a quarter of the sun, then half.

Alice begins sketching, blacking in the shape of the moon

on the sun, using watercolors to brush in the general shades and shadows. She draws first one angle of the valley, then another, working so quickly that sometimes her colors bleed together.

Around us, the shadows sharpen. Professor Samuel Langley explains that this is because when the sun shines normally, it's so wide in the sky that the rays of light arrive at different angles and make the edges of the shadow blurry. Now there are not so many angles, and everything appears crisper.

The shadows shift too. Where the sunlight falls through holes in the rock, the shadows adopt the appearance of an oblong, then a wide crescent, reflecting the changing shape of the sun. Everything darkens, taking on a curious orange cast.

The sun's light is thin and ghastly, and all the color seems to leach from the peak. In contrast, pigments flare along the horizon: fire-red and gold.

A hundred miles away, snow-capped peaks burn white in the sunlight. Then darkness falls over the mountains as if someone has dropped a curtain.

The scientists around me flurry in action, recording measurements, checking their instruments one final time.

I look out across the valley and gasp.

A vast wall of darkness, surrounded by colors ranging from yellow to red-orange to purple, speeds across the plains below. The moon's shadow, miles wide, sliding over valleys and ridges, devouring the light as it roars toward us.

We're nearly to totality now, an eerie grayness suffusing everything. Strange bands of light and shadow ripple across the rocks around me, like the sun filtering through clear water at the edge of a lake. Above, the sun is only the thinnest strand of brightness.

At 3:31 p.m. the sun winks out. General Myer calls out the time.

A final, brilliant string, like so many gold beads on a thread, spans out from the edge of the masked sun. Then even that disappears, and it's only the eclipse: a dark disk where the sun stood, surrounded by the narrow band of radiance that marks the corona, extraordinary streamers several times the width of the sun extending from the black circle like white wings.

Professor Samuel Langley plucks up paper and a pencil and begins sketching furiously; his brother inspects the photometer and scribbles something down. General Myer peers through the telescope and begins declaiming his observations.

As my eyes grow used to the darkness, stars emerge in the sky around the sun—stars that are always there but hidden by the sun's glow.

A thousand points of light, touched by the spreading solar streamers, each one connected somehow to the nerves in my skin, so that my whole body feels suffused with light.

Tears prick my eyes. I feel as I do when the Holy Spirit touches me, as though I stand before the altar of heaven, and only the thinnest of veils separates me from the face of God. I feel at once whole and insignificant, both found and lost before the immensity of space.

A total eclipse of the sun.

It's beautiful and terrifying and I think my heart may already be broken trying to hold all of this singular moment.

"Thirty seconds!" Will shouts.

I shake myself out of my stupor. I've already lost thirty precious seconds of work.

But my fingers don't obey my silent command to pick up my pencil.

The pounding in my head grows. Acid burns in the back of my throat.

This is my one shot at capturing the eclipse—and I'm already failing.

Rachel's white face flashes through my mind, followed by the elk charging beside the tracks. This is what I do in the face of urgency: I freeze.

No.

I can work under pressure. Think of Rebekka's labor, of Ida's birth.

I can do this.

I pick up my own pad and begin sketching, moving slowly to quell the trembling in my hand. The coronal light—a soft, glowing halo around the sun—stretches multiple times the width of the sun. The streamers extending at forty-five-degree angles are longer on one side than the other, and I skip my pencil across the paper, trying to capture everything.

Energy surges through me. I think of the scientists on the peak, of Edison and Dr. Morton and the others in Rawlins, of other scientists scattered across the length of totality. Once, I thought of science as something that happened only in distant laboratories, in faraway cities. But scientific discovery isn't limited to those spaces—it's happening right here, right now, in the very mountains of the West that are my home.

And I am part of it.

Samuel Langley looks up briefly from his sketch. "This atmosphere offers extraordinary clarity. Just look at those streamers! Easily twelve times the length of the sun. Must be ten million miles. Maybe more."

Ten million miles! And yet the streamers only occupy a small part of the sky. The scientific part of me marvels at the way distance skews our sense of proportion. The rest of me thrills at the vastness of the created universe.

"One minute," Will calls out. I glance at him. He still looks ghastly, but he's gamely propped up against a rock, a fine pocket watch in his hand.

I've caught less than half of the corona, the radiant light that surrounds the dark circle where the moon blocks the sun's light. I push my hand to move faster, my pencil racing across the page.

"Two minutes!" Will shouts.

I've captured three-quarters of the corona now. Samuel Langley abandons his finished sketch and elbows the Signal Corps man away from his telescope to catch the last of totality.

"Over!" Professor Langley says. "Will, what's our time?"

"One hundred sixty-one seconds," Will says. "Nearly three minutes."

I scramble to sketch the last bit of the corona. It doesn't

disappear at once, as the sun begins to peek out from behind the moon, but fades in degrees—first, the long outer streamers, then the brilliance nearest the sun. And then the sun emerges, the unnatural daytime darkness dissipating before the growing light.

I sag back against my perch, grinning foolishly at the world.

Everyone chatters, sharing observations and speculations. I wish Samuel was here, to share this moment. Neither General Myer nor Professor Langley spotted Vulcan, but "I'll bet James Watson has something to say about it," Professor Langley says. "He's got the most at stake in this theory."

The rush of the eclipse fades and I have the curious feeling of returning to our world from another one, of passing through some kind of veil as color returns. I set my sketch down and wander over to Alice, who has also drawn the corona, but mostly only as an idea in the sky, overlooking an eerie gray-washed valley. Even as a rough sketch, her work has a raw power.

Will drops his watch back into his pocket and sways as he tries to stand. Alice and I exchange glances, then Alice moves to support her brother and helps him back to his seat.

He tries, feebly, to push her away. "I can stand. I don't need help."

"I know you don't," she says. "But it's all right to accept help sometimes. It doesn't make you weak. You're probably stronger than anyone here—none of the rest of us had to work through such severe altitude sickness as you have."

Will grins at her, but the smile slides off his face after a moment.

"Elizabeth, help me pack up," Alice says. "Then we'll head down the mountain."

We collect Alice's gear, and I pass my drawing to Professor Langley. "You've a good eye for this," he says, inspecting it. "I hope you'll consider my brother's idea of studying at the University of Michigan."

"I will," I say.

For so long I have seen my life as a question of faith *or* science, as though choosing one meant abandoning the other.

But I've just seen the moon and the sun in the sky at once, and things I have thought impossible are beginning to seem possible. Whether Michigan or Vassar, the eclipse has confirmed for me that this is part of the life I want.

But perhaps not the whole part. Miss Mitchell's question still haunts me: If you do not bring all of yourself to your work, what do you bring instead?

In the Denver library, I found a book that described old alchemical texts, where the eclipse symbolized an alchemical marriage, the union of both sun and moon. For those alchemists, the sun and moon weren't adversarial—in their highest form, they were complementary.

I've felt lifted by religious faith and prodded by scientific questions, and I don't know if I can sift through my life and pinpoint the moment where they diverge. Maybe they don't diverge at all—maybe they're part of the same vast system, but I don't see all the connections yet.

Maybe I have been looking at everything wrong, seeing "or" where I should have seen "and."

When I watched the eclipse today, I wasn't a woman of faith or a woman of science.

I was both.

chapter twenty-six

Monday, July 29, 1878
Pikes Peak, Colorado
Six hours after eclipse

I walk alongside the rocky shore of a glittering lake, a stone's throw from a small cabin and a barn. Gold still washes the horizon behind me and glints in the folds of the lapping waves, but far above, the stars have begun to emerge for the second time that day.

Will is tucked into a bed inside the cabin, cared for by the same doctor who was summoned to see to Cleveland Abbe, the scientist sent down for altitude sickness. The rest of us will have to make do with lodgings in the barn, as the owner of the cabin was wholly unprepared for the tourist horde descending from on high after the eclipse.

Something crinkles in the pocket of my skirt, and I remember the *Exponent* pages I stashed there, ages ago, at Mrs. Jackson's home. I pull the pages out and unfold them, squinting in the fading light to read. There's news from home and from abroad, all old news. My eyes fall on an editorial by Lula Greene Richards, President Young's great-niece and the first editor of the newspaper.

I urge readers to utterly repudiate the pernicious dogma that marriage and a practical life-work are incompatible.

I stop, find a seat on a nearby boulder, and read the line again.

Then a third time.

How have I missed this? For months, I have read every issue of the *Exponent* faithfully, looking for something that might tell me how to be a woman in my church. Something to tell me how to study the natural world without losing sight of God. Something to tell me how to make my own life without devaluing my mother's. Something to reconcile the relentless pull between my heart and my mind.

This issue is older, dated from before I began my searching, but it has been here all along. I read the line again. *Marriage and a practical life-work.* Is it possible to have both? Most women with careers do not seem to have families—Miss Mitchell, Dr. Avery, Miss Culbertson. Or if they are married, like Mrs. Jackson and Mrs. Kendall, they don't have children at home. Those few women I know with an avocation and a family follow work that might reasonably be seen as an extension of women's domestic work: midwifery, millinery, baking. Even Dr. Romania Pratt and Dr. Ellis Shipp, who garnered so much attention when they went away to study medicine, are primarily healers.

But astronomy? Where is its domestic use?

I picture Samuel, smiling at me, teasing me, and my heart twists. I resigned myself to living alone, telling myself it was enough to have a shot at one dream.

Maybe I haven't been dreaming big enough.

Just because I don't know any woman living the kind of life I want doesn't mean that life is impossible. I used to think that people were like comets, living their lives in fixed trajectories. But maybe that isn't quite right. People can change their course, if they choose to.

I'm a person, not a comet—I don't have to follow the orbit laid out for me.

If no path exists for the life I want, then I can make my own path.

Joy sings all the way through me. A cold wind whistles across the lake and I shiver, but I don't go back in, not yet. I hug my arms around my torso and throw my head back, soaking in the emerging stars.

Science and faith. Work and marriage.

Not *or*.

And, I think, as though I've found a mystic talisman to unlock the universe: *and, and, and.*

By evening the next day, we are back in Denver. A night's sleep at a lower elevation has helped Will considerably. Daniela led us down the trail back to Colorado Springs much more quickly than we ascended: the skies were clear and bright, and the storms that plagued us on our ascent had vanished.

We reach the Stevenses' home just as Mr. and Mrs. Stevens are sitting down to dinner. They abandon their places and exclaim over us, particularly Will, whom Mrs. Stevens sends to bed with the promise of a hot tray as soon as it can be assembled.

Mr. Stevens claps Will on the shoulder as he passes. "I'm proud of you, Will."

Will ducks his head, but his lips stretch into a grin.

"You must be famished," Mrs. Stevens says to Alice and me. "Come along. I'll have the maid set you both places."

"How was the eclipse?" Mr. Stevens asks. "We had a marvelous view from down in the valley—everyone in the hotel turned out into the streets to see it. That lady astronomer is set to speak on it tonight at the Methodist church on Lawrence Street."

I stop walking. "Miss Mitchell?"

"That's it," he agrees.

Even after our last uncomfortable interview, even with my stomach growling at me that I haven't eaten in hours, I want to see her still. I want to know how the Vassar party fared at the eclipse, how their observations differed from ours.

Alice laughs. "Now look what you've done, Papa! We'll never get Elizabeth to eat now."

"Would you mind?" I ask, a bit tentatively. I don't want to make the same mistakes again, of putting ideas before people.

"Of course not," Alice says. "But have our driver take you there. It'll be much faster."

I have just time to change my dress into something neater and splash water on my face before the driver is ready. Alice presses a warm dinner roll into my hands and wishes me good luck.

"Do you want to come?" I ask.

"No," she says, smiling. "I mean to eat a good dinner and then disappear into my studio to paint. My fingers itch just thinking of my canvases. But I hope you enjoy yourself."

"Then good luck to us both!"

✦

The church is crowded when I arrive, but I find a spot in a pew near the front. I nod at Miss Mitchell's students, sitting together in the front row, and, to my surprise, Miss Culbertson not only returns my nod but also rises from her seat and approaches me.

"How was your view of the eclipse?" she asks.

"Breathtaking," I say. "I climbed Pikes Peak and assisted the Langley brothers."

Miss Culbertson's eyes widen a little. "I'm impressed.

With that determination, perhaps we'll make an astronomer of you yet."

"I hope so."

She smiles a little and turns away, as if to return to her seat.

"Wait," I say. When she looks back, I push out, all in a rush, "I've been thinking about what you asked me—why I choose to be Mormon, when it would be easier to adopt another faith."

"Sheer cussedness?" Miss Culbertson raises her eyebrows at me, and I'm surprised into laughing.

"Maybe. My church isn't a perfect church—is any?—but it's mine. It's where I find God. It's a little like the eclipse. I could have chosen to view it anywhere around Denver, but I chose the Peak. My view didn't perfectly match yours, but that's all right. It was still worth the journey."

"And only think how uninteresting our work would be if every journey, every view, was exactly the same," Miss Culbertson says, grinning at me before returning to her seat.

Our work. My heart lifts.

Miss Mitchell's lecture is as interesting and smart as she is, and I soak in the details—both the mundane ones, like how the sisters at the nearby Saint Joseph Hospital brought them tea as they waited for totality, and the scientific ones, how they hurried to record everything—the shape and color of the corona, the timing of the eclipse—and their fruitless sweeping of the sky for Vulcan.

She talks about Caroline Herschel, as great an astronomer

as her more famous brother William, but who has been forgotten where her brother has been lauded, because she subordinated her own needs to her brother's. "If what Miss Herschel *did* is an example, what she *did not* do is a warning."

I think of my conversation with Alice, about our responsibilities to ourselves and to others, and then of Mama. I pray that she's all right, even as I'm putting my own needs first for now.

Afterward, a large mob of people crowds around Miss Mitchell to comment, admire, and even pontificate about their own eclipse experience. She's given a huge flower arrangement, shaped like an *M* and bordered with rose and gray, the colors of Vassar College.

I wait in my seat until they disperse, then approach the great astronomer.

"Miss Bertelsen!" Miss Mitchell beams at me, the discomfort of our last meeting forgotten in her triumph tonight. "Emma tells me you've been up Pikes Peak for the eclipse, helping the Langleys. Will you tell me about it?"

And so I do, with Miss Mitchell's bright eyes fixed on me. Her attention is not that of a teacher hearing a lesson, but that of a colleague.

When I finish, she says, "When you're ready for university, will you write me? I can put in a good word at our admissions office, and perhaps scare up some scholarship money. We need more girls in the West to get as good an education as our eastern girls."

For a moment I'm afraid I might cry at her kindness. I

blink back the tears pricking my eyes and draw a deep breath. "Thank you," I say. "I was hoping to ask you a question, if you don't mind."

Miss Mitchell waits, smiling gently.

"I read that you were born to a Quaker family. And you are still religious?"

She nods. "Yes, though I do not practice the faith I was born into. I'm Unitarian these days. Maybe something else before I die! I think it is good to believe, better to ask questions."

Something tight in me breaks open. I hoped my epiphany on the mountain was right, and her words confirm this. "So it is possible," I say, "to be a scientist and a person of faith?"

She stares at me in astonishment. "Of course it is, child. Who has been telling you otherwise?"

Mama, I think. Not to mention all the newspapers that proclaim the triumph of science over religion. Mr. Draper's book, arguing that science and religion are ultimately incompatible.

"It is not always easy," Miss Mitchell says. "Sometimes we find questions that have no easy answers. Sometimes we find that we outgrow the faith we began with and need to try on a new faith. But let us have truth, even if the truth be the awful denial of the good God. Scripture tells us to try all things and hold fast to that which is good. I am hopeful that scientific investigation, pushed on and on, will reveal new ways in which God works, and bring to us deeper revelations of the wholly unknown." In truth, I'm not sure if she said "wholly" or "holy," but I'm not sure it matters.

And, I think again. Why have I believed for so long that my life had to be a series of "ors"? Why have I been afraid? If I believe in God the Father and God the Mother, they are not so small or so fragile that my questions can break them. They are not so narrow that I cannot find my own faith, my own way, within my religion. If they can encompass seeming paradoxes, like the sun and moon sharing the sky during an eclipse, they can encompass all of my contradictions and failings without being lessened.

And now I do begin to cry, because I have been afraid, because I have been small, because I thought myself trapped by the expectations of others when it has really been my own fears that have trapped me.

"Thank you," I say, and wipe my eyes with the handkerchief Miss Mitchell holds out to me. I take down her address and say a polite goodbye to her students, wondering if someday I might be counted among them.

And having come so far, I'm ready now to go home.

✦

I hug Alice tightly at the train station. "Thank you. For everything."

She presses a kiss to my cheek. "Write to me."

I promise faithfully to do so. I turn to Will and offer my

hand. He shakes it, and grins at me. "I'm afraid your life will be much less exciting without us."

"I'm afraid you're right. But it's time for me to go. I miss my family—and there are things I need to get settled. What about you? What do you plan to do, now that your father has lifted your confinement?"

Will rubs his chin. "I've been thinking about new adventures."

"*Not* more trestle bridges!" Alice says.

Will laughs. "No. Or mountains. I don't think either of those agree with me. Do you remember that fellow who came to find Mr. Edison in Rawlins, waving his pistol?"

"How could we forget?" Alice says. "Please don't tell me you're thinking of imitating that man. I don't think our parents would approve of a career that involved waving guns at people."

"No, not that. I was thinking about what the hotel manager told us, that Texas Jack used to perform in those Wild West shows and now guides people to hunt in the West. After the eclipse, I was thinking about how all these people came to Denver to see something amazing, how they climbed a mountain just for a few minutes of glory."

Alice wrinkles her nose at him. "You don't exactly look like a mountain man, if you're thinking of being the next Buffalo Bill."

"Why don't you let me tell you what I *am* thinking? You've guessed wrong twice now."

Alice subsides, with only her pressed lips showing her irritation.

"I'd like to travel, to find places in the world that make people feel that same kind of wonder as the eclipse, and then guide people to those places. They can even stay at Grandpa's hotel, if our routes pass this way. There's so much wonder in the world, and I don't want to miss any of it. You can come paint the most spectacular scenes," he says to Alice.

"I'll bet it will be brilliant," I say, watching as a porter lifts my battered trunk into the luggage car. "Maybe you can take me to Egypt for another total eclipse in four years."

"Naturally, it will be brilliant," Will agrees. "And I'd be honored."

"Mama will definitely like travel better than the trestle bridge," Alice says.

"I should hope so. I've been thinking about what she always tells you about responsibility, how we have to balance what others want from us with what we want for ourselves. I think maybe risk is like this too. Sometimes we have to take risks, for ourselves and others. But the problem with the trestle was that it was a risk I took that served no one but myself. If I take risks in the future, I want them to be for more than just me."

The conductor blows the whistle, and I check my bag one last time for my ticket—I've had to borrow money again but promised, again, to pay it back—then turn to Alice.

"Send me word of your art school," I say.

"I will. Here's to dreaming!"

"And adventure," I say, and head toward the train.

Will calls after me, "If your train gets robbed again, stay away from the elk!" His laughter follows me into the train, and I'm still smiling as we pull away from the station.

chapter twenty-seven

Wednesday, July 31, 1878
Outside of Cheyenne, Wyoming

Ammon picks me up from the train station in Cheyenne and drives me back to see Rebekka. There are dark circles under his eyes that suggest he is not sleeping enough, but he's in a cheerful mood and peppers me with questions about Denver and the eclipse.

Rebekka waits on the front doorstep when we arrive, gently bouncing Ida in her arms. As soon as Ammon helps me down from the wagon, Rebekka thrusts her daughter into Ammon's arms and folds me in an enormous hug.

She pulls back to look at me but doesn't release me. Like Ammon, she has dark smudges under her eyes, but her gaze is bright. "Well?"

"You were right," I say, hugging her again. "It was wonderful."

"I'm always right," Rebekka says, and draws me into her home.

That night, I rock Ida in the rocking chair and tell Rebekka and Ammon about the eclipse. Ida seems to have gained at least a pound and an inch in length since I saw her last, and she rubs her tiny face sleepily into my chest. I stroke a finger along her downy cheek.

As we talk, I watch Rebekka and Ammon, how they smile at each other as if no one else is in the room, how Ammon teases Rebekka and she teases him in turn and their laughter seems to light up the small sitting room. *And,* I think. I want this too.

I can't stay long at Rebekka's, since I need to get back to Mama, but I try to soak in this moment. Already my heart is tugging me onward, toward Monroe, toward home—toward Samuel.

✦

The road from Monroe up to our house has not changed in the six weeks I've been away. The sun still beats down on my head; dust still clouds around my feet. It's been a long road back from Cheyenne, first by train, and then a series of rides from Salt Lake City to home.

I reach the mill first and hesitate, but I don't like to

interrupt Far and Hyrum at their work. The door of the house is wide when I arrive, propped open by a rock to let the breeze in. Voices tangle in the air. Distant shouting and splashing echoes down the canyon—probably my brothers. There's a tickling that starts in my feet, hums up my bones, fills my heart and throat so full it prickles my eyes too.

I step inside.

Emily chops vegetables at the table and quarrels with Mary, who is sitting beside Rachel and helping her form her letters with a bit of paper and pencil. Rachel looks rosy and healthy, and her high child's voice pierces me with relief. I don't see Mama or baby Albert—maybe they're both in the bedroom.

I stand on the threshold and say nothing for a moment, just absorb the sounds and sights of *home.*

But the room feels odd, as though it has shrunk or I have grown, as though no matter how familiar, it is no longer entirely mine. I've outgrown this space, I realize, though part of me will always be drawn back to these hills, this house, these people. Finding a new place for myself does not mean I have to abandon all the places that have claim on my heart: there is room for old *and* new.

And, I think again.

A thin wail interrupts my thoughts. The fighting at the table stops, as everyone turns to the noise. Rachel sees me first, erupting from her chair to hurl her arms around my knees. Emily and Mary crowd in behind her to hug me. Mary, contrary child that she is, actually has tears in her eyes.

Henry blows in through the front door, shouting about something. He's followed by John and David Charles, who all mob me at once.

Six weeks ago, I would have felt overwhelmed by the noise and bodies. Now it feels comforting, like a blanket I can pull over myself at night to ward off the chill but set aside in the morning when I do not need it. Families are like that, though sometimes you might need them more than others.

Albert is still crying, and I disentangle myself from the others and head to the darkened back room. A shape lies, unmoving, on the bed. *Mama.*

I lift the baby from the crib. He's warm and flushed in my arms, and blinks watery eyes up at me and struggles to get away. He's bigger than I remember, and he does not seem to recognize me at all, pulling toward Mama as soon as he spies her.

"Mama?" I ask softly.

She doesn't move.

"Mama?" I say again. "It's Elizabeth. I've come home."

That seems to reach her. She rolls over and blinks up at me. "Elizabeth? You're back, are ye?" She struggles to sit upright, then begins unbuttoning the top of her nightdress. She holds out her arms for Albert, and I hand him over. "Well? And was your selfishness rewarded?"

The low hum of satisfaction that has followed me home from Denver stills. Mama might as well have slapped me. "I wasn't being selfish, Mama." Well, perhaps I was, but it was more than that.

"Ye left Rebekka to manage a small baby alone, ran off to Denver, and didn't come back though ye were told we needed ye home. What else do ye call that besides selfishness?"

Discovery, I think. "I went with Rebekka's blessing. I had to go, Mama. I needed to understand what I'd be giving up if I stayed in Monroe all my life. I needed to see the eclipse, to know if I was capable of being an astronomer."

"And what of your family's needs? My needs? They are nowt so exciting as a new city, but do they matter?"

I sit gingerly on the end of her bed. "Of course they matter, Mama. That's why I came home. I'll help as much as I can while I'm home—but I mean to go to school, Mama. In the fall."

"And will your stars save ye?"

Maybe. "Knowledge is important too, Mama. I can't say exactly how my life will look, but I believe this is what I'm supposed to do."

"Then I've failed ye." The anger in her face fades, replaced by a yawning despair. She leans her head against the headboard of the bed, her eyes sliding closed. She looks old, wrinkles gathering about her eyes, gray threading through her hair.

"No," I say. "You taught me that it was important to listen to your heart, to the whispering of the spirit. You listened to your heart and left behind everything you knew to come to Utah. What I'm doing now, it's the same thing. It doesn't mean that what you did, what you've sacrificed, to raise our family is wrong. Or that what I'm doing now is wrong. They're just two different paths."

Mama is quiet for so long I begin to think maybe she's gone back to sleep. The only noise in the room is Albert, sucking greedily. Then she opens her eyes and looks at me. "You always did love the stars, even as a small girl. Will this make you happy?"

"I don't know if I'll always be happy. But I think I'll be filled."

✦

When Far comes in for dinner, he folds me in a hug. Hyrum hovers behind him, a shy smile reserved just for me. Over bacon rashers, fried potatoes, and berry pie, I tell my family about my adventures—about the robbery on the train and meeting Mr. Edison, about Rebekka's baby, about the Stevens family and Miss Mitchell.

About the eclipse from Pikes Peak.

The younger children listen, rapt, and when I finish my story, they make me tell it over again, especially the part about the man who burst into Edison's room with a gun, and watching the eclipse shadow thunder like a train across the valley. Even Mama has emerged from the bedroom in time to hear my story. She smiles at me, both bemused and a little sad.

"You seem different," Far says. "More sure of yourself, somehow."

I take a deep breath, and tell them all of my plans, how I mean to write away to schools and discover what I need to enroll, then take any classes I might be missing at the Brigham Young Academy in Provo before going away to college.

Far blinks. "College? What of home? A girl doesn't need so much."

I try to smile at him across the tightness in my gut. I want my family to support me in this—but I will do it regardless. "God gave me a mind as well as a heart, and I mean to use it."

"We can't help you pay," Far says.

"I'll find work to support myself. I can do it, Far."

Far blows out his breath. "I don't like it," he says.

But he doesn't say no.

✦

After dinner, Hyrum and I slip outside, to walk along the creek beneath the stars. They're the same here as they were in Denver.

"So you're leaving again," Hyrum says. His voice sounds small, and I stop walking to lean over and hug him. After a surprised moment, he hugs me back.

"It won't be forever," I say. "And I'll take some of this place, some of you, with me wherever I go." I pause. "You could come with me."

Hyrum shakes his head. "I like it here in the valley. I like the slow pace, the familiarity of everything. I like working with Far, seeing Mama every night, and the children. I'm not

like you. I've never been hungry for everything in the world."
He eyes me sidelong, smiles. "Far was right. You seem different."

"I'm still me. I don't think I became someone new, exactly—I just figured out who I wanted to be, outside of all the voices telling me who I should be. I thought that because I didn't see someone like what I wanted to be in Monroe, what I wanted to be was wrong. Turns out I just wasn't thinking big enough."

I find a log and sit down. Hyrum settles beside me. I continue, "I thought maybe God wanted me to be small and narrow—but our father and mother in heaven aren't small at all. How could they want that for us?" I look up, tracing a line from Polaris to Vega of the Lyre and back again.

Hyrum leans back beside me. He doesn't look at me, but I can hear the tightness in his voice. "And for me?"

I turn to face him. "For you above all."

He doesn't quite meet my eyes. "Much as I love this valley, this church, I don't always fit neatly."

"I don't either," I say, reaching out to squeeze his hand. "But if you're asking if there's a place for you here—always. Our church community may help us worship God, but your faith is your own. Whatever you worship, however you worship, you don't do it for anyone but yourself."

It's not a perfect answer, but Hyrum seems pleased with it, humming softly to himself as I point out constellation after constellation. I like to think of us as stars: From a distance, we humans look much the same. It's only when you get close, when you observe carefully, that you mark the traits that make us individual. That you learn to really love.

✦

There's still one thing that I have to do.

I put it off until after dinner the next day, after I've helped bake bread and scoured the stove and darned the boys' socks. I find I don't mind the chores so much after taking a break from them, knowing that this won't be all of my life.

But after the last of the dishes are cleared up and the food is put away, I tell Mama I've business in town.

She lifts her gaze from her spot at the end of the table, where she's been going over a recipe book. She's been up today, but is weaker than I like, so she sits a lot. "Borrowing more books from that teacher lady? Are you tired of us so soon?"

"No," I say, though I should go see Miss Wheeler before too long. She'll have good advice for me on applying to school—and I still have to tell her about selling Mrs. Somerville's book and ruining the other. I hope she'll understand. My face heats, and I press my lips together in annoyance. "I thought I'd go see Samuel Willard. Did you know he was in Denver too?"

Her face lights. "Was he now? Nice boy, that one."

"Yes," I agree, my face burning hotter.

Mama gives me a shrewd look. "Don't ye go chasing him. Boys don't like that."

In truth, I'm not sure what boys do or don't like—I've never paid much mind to that. But I do know Samuel. At least, I think I do. *Don't choke on your pride.* If I want to fix things between us, I've got to sacrifice some of that pride.

"You should put on your blue cotton dress," Mama says. "It's prettier than that old thing you're wearing."

Samuel has seen me first thing in the morning, with mussed hair and bad breath—I don't think he'll care about my dress. Though of course I don't tell Mama that.

And I do change into the blue dress.

The Little Green Valley is full of golden light when I reach the Willard cabin. Vilate Ann opens the door at my knock.

"Elizabeth! You're back! Oh, tell me everything. Samuel says he saw you in Denver, but he won't say anything more than that."

I shift uncomfortably. "Actually, I was hoping to speak with Samuel. I'll tell you everything later, I promise."

Vilate Ann pouts. "You mean you haven't come to see me?" Her expression trembles, and she bursts out laughing, pushing a strand of blond hair from her eyes. "I knew it! I knew you liked him."

"Vilate Ann—" I reproach her.

Still hooting, she skips past me down the stairs, into the field beyond the house, calling for Samuel.

I grip my hands together. Maybe this is foolish. I should just go home—

I'm already down the steps when Samuel appears in the yard before me. He's in his shirtsleeves, brushing wood dust from his trousers, holding his hat in his hands. The sight of him dries my throat.

"Elizabeth?" He approaches slowly, as if he's not certain he's glad to see me. Or perhaps he fears I'll bite. "Have you been home long?"

"Yesterday," I say. "And you?"

"Some four, five days ago. It's good to be back. And how was the eclipse?"

"It was marvelous. Everything I'd hoped for."

"And Miss Mitchell's party?"

"Oh—" I forgot that Samuel didn't know what happened after he left. I'd gotten so used to him knowing everything about my life in Denver. "I'll tell you all about it, but that's not really why I've come. Will you walk with me?"

Samuel nods, then fits his hat onto his head and follows me into the golden street. The wide brim of his hat casts a shadow across his eyes so I can't rightly see him. I wish I could—it would make what I'm about to do easier.

But I haven't made any of this easy for Samuel, so why should it be easy for me now?

We fall into pace beside one another, heading south toward my house, toward the narrow canyon whose stream feeds the mill. I tell Samuel about Miss Mitchell and going up Pikes Peak with Alice and Will. Samuel listens, but he doesn't offer up much on his own. When I run out of my story, silence settles between us. It's not a comfortable silence, though: it prickles and nips at me.

I don't like this new distance between us.

"I owe you an apology, Samuel Willard."

He doesn't say anything. I take a deep breath. This is harder than I expected. "Before you left, you asked if you could court me. I told you no."

Is it my imagination, or have his shoulders gone stiff? "This is an odd kind of apology, Miss Bertelsen."

"I'm getting there. You were angry because I assumed I knew what you wanted, without asking you. And you were right. I'm sorry I didn't listen to you or ask you what you wanted. I'm asking now."

We've come up level with the grist mill, but I don't stop there. Without really thinking about it, I lead Samuel away from the road, up the canyon trail toward my favorite rocky perch above the valley. "I'd like to be with you. If—if you still want that."

Samuel doesn't answer for a minute, and I wonder if he's changed his mind about me, now that he's had time to think about it. I clamber up the side of the foothill and settle onto my rock, still warm from the summer sun, and curl my arms around my knees. Samuel joins me, but there's enough room between us for half my siblings.

Looking down at the valley rather than at me, Samuel says, "I still want that, if you're open to it. I think I started to love you the day I saw you, ridiculous and drenched, coming out of the hot springs and trying to hold on to your dignity."

I choke on something that might be a laugh or a cry. "I

don't know yet if I love you—but I like you an awful lot. I missed you when you left. I imagine I'll miss you again when I go away for school."

"So you are going. I thought maybe your apology meant you'd decided to stay." Samuel sighs and takes his hat off. There's a line across his forehead from where it sat. "I guess I don't understand what we're talking about, then. You already told me you can't be an astronomer and have a family. If that hasn't changed, why are we here?"

"Because I was wrong," I tell Samuel, scooting closer to him. "I don't have to make that choice, unless I want to. And I don't want to. I still want to be an astronomer, but I'd like you to be part of that future too."

"Would you now?" Samuel's eyes light up, even more luminous than the miles spread out below us. He closes the gap between us, and slips a hand around my waist, another hand coming up to cup the back of my neck.

I rest my hands on his shoulders and lean in, bridging the remaining distance between us.

Fire spreads from our joined mouths, sparking through my veins, igniting deep in my stomach, threatening to undo my joints and melt my bones. Why did no one tell me kissing could be like this?

By the time we break apart, the light has mostly bled from the valley. The moon is waxing gibbous. Samuel says he is willing to wait for me, while I study. Or we can marry, and he will find work while I go to school. For now, I choose to wait, because the idea of saying yes to both school and Samuel is still new to me.

That voice inside me is singing again: *and, and, and.*

The valley looks different in the moonlight from how it did in the fading glow of the sun. I think of the eclipse, how the shifting light and shadows made the familiar world utterly strange and new. I think of how a kiss can utterly unmake everything I thought I knew, can change the shape of my future.

I think of trying to be a scientist and a wife, an astronomer and a mother. I don't know what that world will look like.

There's so much I don't know. But for once that ignorance doesn't seem like a trap—it seems like an opportunity.

I don't know what I'll find. Maybe what we see and understand now is like the mountain during an eclipse, and all we can see around us are shadows. Where we can only guess at what's real because we see it not by direct light, but by the indirect glow of the corona. Maybe someday we'll emerge from the moon's shadow and see things as they really are. Meantime, both faith and science try to provide answers, and we try to live by whatever light we have.

Overhead, the constellations dance across the sky. We follow their movements as best we can, forever reaching beyond the mapped stars.

AUTHOR'S NOTE

✦

This has been the hardest novel I have written to date—largely because it is also the most personal. Elizabeth Bertelsen was inspired by a real-life Elizabeth Bertelsen: my great-great-grandmother, who was eighteen in the summer of 1878 when the eclipse swept across the West. The first seeds of this story were planted listening to an NPR broadcast about the 1878 eclipse, focusing on those who came west to witness it. I started wondering what the eclipse might have looked like to those already living in the West, particularly to Mormons, like my ancestors.

To my knowledge, the real Elizabeth never left Utah, but the circumstances of my character's life are drawn from historical accounts of Elizabeth's: her father owned a grist mill in

Monroe, Utah; her mother was a second wife; her father left the LDS Church because of his experience with the United Order. Samuel Willard is similarly inspired by my great-great-grandfather (Samuel Willard Collings). However, the plot of the story and the personalities of the characters are largely invented (I did give Samuel my grandfather's—his grandson's—sense of humor). As my great-great-grandmother only lived to twenty-four, I like to think this book grants her adventures she was never able to have.

I don't know if Elizabeth's mother, Hannah, had depression (such things were not often recorded), but it was not uncommon among frontier women, and depression has been widespread in more recent generations of that branch of my family.

Mormons and the American West

As a story that touches primarily on one character's journey, it's impossible to do justice to the historical context of the time in this one novel. I hope to expand on some of that here.

The formal name of the Mormon Church is the Church of Jesus Christ of Latter-day Saints. However, I use the term "Mormon" in this book deliberately, both because it is the term that nineteenth-century members would have used to describe themselves and because it encompasses a cultural identity that is broader than strict membership in the LDS Church. I should note here that I personally identify as Mormon. It's not always an easy identity, as it is not for Elizabeth. There are things I value about my faith community, but there are also, as the following history makes clear, things that I and other members must wrestle with, both in our past and in our present.

Mormons have historically had a somewhat contentious relationship with the rest of the United States. In 1838, Mormons were driven out of Missouri by mob violence, fueled by neighbors who didn't trust their political influence or their strange new religion. The persistent rumors of polygamy, already practiced but not openly acknowledged by the Church until 1852, didn't help either. Not only did it offend mainstream sensibilities, but it also fanned fears of racial mixing (see W. Paul Reeve, *Religion of a Different Color*). The governor of Missouri issued an executive order authorizing the expulsion, even extermination, of Mormons—an order that wasn't formally rescinded until 1976. After being forced from Illinois in 1846, members of the LDS Church made their way across the plains to Utah, the vanguard company arriving in the summer of 1847.

While the Mormons were sometimes victims of violence, they also perpetrated instances of frontier violence. The idea of the frontier is itself problematic: while Mormons and other white settlers saw themselves expanding the "frontier" of America as part of Manifest Destiny, the lands that they chose were already homelands to Indigenous peoples. While most LDS settlers were initially kindly disposed toward the Indigenous people already in Utah, primarily as potential converts, that interest waned as local tribes rejected conversion and competition over land and other resources began to intensify.

Mormons clashed with their Paiute and Ute neighbors, particularly during the Black Hawk War (1865–1872), which included the tragic Circleville massacre of Paiute men, women, and children in 1866. Some Mormons participated in the enslavement of Indigenous people, justifying their involvement in the slave trade by rationalizing that they were purchasing (mostly Paiute) slaves from Ute and Mexican traders to save them from being sold to Mexico or from being killed by slavers. But the up-to-twenty-year indentured servitude that followed probably didn't look much different, and many adoptees were not treated as equals (see *Nuwuvi: A Southern Paiute History;* also Martha C. Knack, *Boundaries Between: The Southern Paiutes, 1775–1995;* and Brian Q. Cannon, " 'To Buy Up the Lamanite Children as Fast as They Could' "). In 1857, not far from where I live now, Mormons planned and executed the Mountain Meadows massacre of approximately 120 Southern emigrants who were traveling by wagon to California, sparing only seventeen children. Though LDS Church leaders denounced the crime, arresting and excommunicating the organizers of the massacre, many Mormons laid much of the blame on local Paiutes (see Richard E. Turley, Jr., *Mountain Meadows Massacre*).

These practices, along with the perceived theocracy (both religious and civic life were governed by Mormons) of Utah Territory, led many Americans to see Mormons as a threat to the authority of the United States. In the 1856 presidential election, the Republicans ran on a platform that promised to eliminate the dual barbarisms of their day—slavery and polygamy—the latter targeted particularly at the Mormons. In 1878, a Salt Lake City journalist, John Coyer, wrote: "If something is not done soon to stop the development of this law-breaking, law-defying fanaticism, either our free institutions must go down beneath its power, or, as with slavery, it must be wiped out in blood."

The plight of Mormons was never as serious as those faced by people of color, particularly Black and Indigenous people. However, they were clearly outsiders. Like many Roman Catholics (especially the Irish and Italians), Mormons were seen as a subclass of whites (not white enough to mix with the top tiers of society, but not quite people of color) until the twentieth century. Protestant Americans could find no explanation for the adoption of polygamy by whites unless their racial identity was somehow corrupted (see W. Paul Reeve, *Religion of a Different Color;* and Max Perry Mueller, *Race and the Making of the Mormon People*); this racial difference was used in part to justify mistreatment of Mormons.

In response to the othering by Protestant America, Mormons began to distance themselves from their Black members. While the founder, Joseph Smith, had sanctioned ordination of Black men to the church's priesthood, in the 1850s, Brigham Young and other leaders initiated a ban on Black men holding the priesthood and a temple ban on both Black men and women, which persisted until 1978.

Despite those injustices, there were Black Americans who joined the LDS Church. Quincy D. Newell's recent biography of Jane Manning James offers a detailed and nuanced look at the life of this Black convert, who had little official power in the Church but nonetheless claimed a rich spiritual life for herself. As Newell argues, James is an important figure in the history of Mormonism, and her cameo in this book is a deliberate nod to that history. (For more history of Black converts to the LDS Church, check out the University of Utah's digital archive "A Century of Black Mormons.")

In the mid-twentieth century, the Church of Jesus Christ of Latter-day Saints made a bid for mainstream acceptance. They succeeded so well—the pinnacle of that acceptance perhaps coming in Mitt Romney's bid for president—that most people have forgotten that there was ever a time when Mormons were considered Other. The contemporary LDS Church continues to be, as scholar Terryl Givens describes it, defined by paradox—both American-born but seeking a global place; hierarchical but open to individual inspiration; struggling to be a safe place for some members of color and LGBTQ+ members but committed to worldwide humanitarian work. Still, the real heart of the Church is its members, who derive meaning from their faith in different ways: in theological exploration, in private devotion, in community service, and more. Like all religious believers, Mormons are not monolithic, and my perspective may not align with someone else's.

Race in the American West

Many American readers learn the history of the American West through the stories of white pioneers and their encounters with the Indigenous peoples already living in the West. As a result, we tend to forget how diverse the nineteenth-century West truly was. Historians Elizabeth Jameson and Susan M. Armitage note that between 1860 and 1900, approximately one-quarter to one-third of people living in the West were immigrants from other countries. While many of these were European immigrants (Elizabeth's town of Monroe was settled by Danish, Swedish, and other Scandinavian immigrants), Chinese immigrants recruited to work on the rail lines often stayed in western towns when the railroads were completed. Japanese immigrants gathered in Hawaii and western states at the end of the nineteenth century. Spanish colonial settlements shaped the culture of the Southwest.

Black Americans also contributed to settling the West (see Quintard Taylor, *In Search of the Racial Frontier*). Many followed the railroad: Ogden, Utah, had a large Black population in the 1870s because it was a hub of the Union Pacific railroad line, and the Pullman Palace Car Company employed significant numbers of Black porters (by 1900, they were perhaps the largest employer of Black Americans).

In some cases, the contact zones of the West ushered in relatively peaceful coexistence between cultural groups. In many cases, however, that contact proved uneasy or violent. Many white settlers of the American West brought with them the biases cultivated in the American East. While interracial marriages existed in all states and territories, as non-white populations increased (and therefore the perceived risk of interracial marriages), most western states passed anti-miscegenation laws, prohibiting such marriages (see Aaron Gullickson, "Black/White Interracial Marriage Trends, 1850–2000"). Colorado passed such a law in 1864, after Mr. and Mrs. Stevens would have married, though such a law would have undoubtedly affected some public perceptions of their marriage.

Some may argue that this book is not accurate because Elizabeth and her friends adopt more progressive attitudes toward race than were likely for the era. To this I would say, first, attitudes in the West toward race were as varied as the individuals living there. Second, this is a work of fiction, not a historical study, and some liberties are allowed for the sake of the story. Historical fiction is always a balancing act between the mores of the past and present values.

Some Notes on Historical Characters

Most of the main characters in this book are figments of my imagination, but a number of the secondary characters are drawn from historical records of the West in 1878. Where possible, viewpoints and dialogue are adapted from those records.

Monroe, Utah

Phoebe Wheeler is listed in local records as the first teacher at the Presbyterian school, built in 1877.

Sister Aditi Tait: Caroline Crosby recorded in her journal that an Indian woman married a Mormon missionary in India and followed him to Utah (though she lived in Cedar City, rather than Monroe).

While **Brother Timican** was invented, there were historically Paiute converts to the LDS Church (local ecclesiastical records in Sevier County show a handful of ordained elders), though at this historical distance it's hard to know if such conversions were genuine or a means of survival and resistance (a way to accommodate their more powerful neighbors in order to create space for their own cultural beliefs).

Salt Lake City, Utah

Jane Manning James: As mentioned above, James is a significant figure in the history of Mormonism. The recent movie *Jane and Emma* offers a fascinating look at the relationship James formed with Emma Smith, the prophet Joseph Smith's wife.

Rawlins, Wyoming

Thomas Edison, George Barker, Henry and Anna Draper, and **Henry Morton** were all historically present in Rawlins for the eclipse. Thomas Edison likely needs no introduction. Though not an astronomer, Edison went west to test out a new invention, the tasimeter, a device intended to measure heat from distant stars. Unfortunately, he could not get the sensitive device to work as he had hoped during the eclipse. George Barker, a professor of physics at the University of Pennsylvania, extended the invitation to Edison to join the Rawlins party.

Henry Draper was a chemistry professor at New York University with a passion for astronomy that he shared with his wife, Anna. Dr. Henry Morton was president of the Stevens Institute of Technology. I owe an apology to Dr. Morton, as I don't know if his views were as sexist as depicted here, though such feelings were common, perhaps most notoriously embodied in Dr. Edward H. Clark's 1873 *Sex in Education, or a Fair Chance for the Girls.* In his book, Clark decried higher education for women. He believed women who studied in a "boy's way" (that is, vigorous mental activity) were at risk for atrophy of the uterus and ovaries, sterilization, masculinization—even insanity or death.

Texas Jack, born **John Omohundro,** a frontier actor and guide, did indeed confront Edison at the hotel in Rawlins and shoot at a weathervane. The account of the incident and much of his dialogue are adapted from Edison's record of the event. He was also the inspiration for a series of dime novels, much like the one Elizabeth reads in the opening scene.

The child **Lillian Heath,** who follows Elizabeth to see the telescope in Rawlins, later became the first female physician in Wyoming.

Denver, Colorado

Will and Alice's grandpa, Barney Lancelot Davis, is inspired by **Barney Lancelot Ford,** who was a prominent Black businessman in 1870s Denver. A former escaped slave, Ford, by 1870, was one of the wealthiest men in Denver and an important member of the community. **Henry O. Wagoner,** whom Elizabeth meets at a dance at the Trans-Oceana, was another prominent African American in Denver. In 1876, Wagoner was appointed a clerk in the first Colorado State Legislature, and he later became the first Black deputy sheriff of Arapahoe County, in 1880.

Maria Mitchell was the preeminent female astronomer in the nineteenth century, famed for her discovery of a comet in 1847. She went on to become the first female astronomy professor at Vassar College and was a firm advocate for women's education. Bits of her speech here come from Renée Bergland's *Maria Mitchell and the Sexing of Science;* others come from *Maria Mitchell: Life, Letters, and Journals,* assembled by her sister Phebe Mitchell Kendall, an artist who accompanied Miss Mitchell to Colorado for the eclipse.

Miss Mitchell's students are based on the few extant records I could find, though their characters have been fictionalized for this story. **Emma Culbertson** became a well-respected physician and leader. Although she never married, she was one of many women who popularized "Boston marriages," where two women lived together for economic and emotional support. **Cora Harrison** went from Vassar to study mathematics at Harvard, but she later contracted consumption and died in Denver in 1889. **Elizabeth Owen Abbot** later became a registrar at Barnard College.

Dr. Alida Avery was a former Vassar colleague of Miss Mitchell, living and working in Denver at the time of the eclipse. She was one of the few prominent women included in W. B. Vickers's *History of the City of Denver.*

Helen Hunt Jackson (Mrs. Jackson), a friend of Dr. Avery's, was a prominent writer about the American West living in Colorado Springs. In the 1880s, she became a vocal advocate for Native Americans (writing both *A Century of Dishonor* and *Ramona*). The opinions she espouses here about Mormons come largely from her book *Bits of Travel at Home.*

Pikes Peak, Colorado

General Albert J. Myer founded the US Army Signal Corps in 1860, just prior to the Civil War, and later adapted the use of the corps for the National Weather Service.

Samuel Pierpont Langley was a well-known astronomer, physicist, and aviation pioneer. There is some dispute as to whether Langley could have brought a bolometer to Pikes Peak for the eclipse. Anthony Aveni writes that he did, while other sources claim the bolometer was not invented until 1880. Langley's biographer Charles Doolittle Walcott says he began work on the bolometer in 1878, but Langley's own published work on the bolometer suggests he began systematically working on it in 1879, and his account of the eclipse says his job was to sketch the eclipse—he makes no mention of the bolometer. But Cleveland Abbe mentions that a Signal Corps member measured temperature and radiation, which is what the bolometer does.

Samuel Langley's brother, **John Langley,** was a chemistry and physics professor at the University of Michigan. The brothers were invited by General Myer to observe the eclipse from the summit of Pikes Peak, but when they arrived on the mountain, they found that the local Signal Corps officers had not been informed.

Cleveland Abbe was the first chief scientist of the National Weather Service. His published record of the 1878 eclipse is invaluable for its thoroughness: most of my description of the eclipse borrows from his account. He did contract nearly fatal altitude sickness and was sent down from the peak by General Myer after the general's arrival on Sunday, July 28.

Changes to the Historical Timeline

I've tried to be as accurate as possible in terms of recorded history, but I did make a few tweaks to the timeline to allow for my story. I sent most of the scientists west earlier than the historical record shows. Thomas Edison left New York on July 13, where in this story he's already arrived in Rawlins by that point. (I did not feel it too much of a stretch, as Edison took an extended vacation after the trip to hunt and tour the West, and, in fact, George Barker recorded that the ten days they had to set up proved only just enough time.) Miss Mitchell arrives a couple of days early in my account, as does her telescope, which made it to Denver on Friday, July 26, rather than Wednesday. I've also moved Cleveland Abbe's illness forward by two days so that Elizabeth could hear about the Signal Corps' wiring for a doctor. Occasionally, distances have been fudged in the name of narrative pacing.

I hope readers enjoy reading this book as much as I enjoyed researching and writing it.

Sources for Further Reading

Aveni, Anthony. *In the Shadow of the Moon: The Science, Magic, and Mystery of Solar Eclipses.* New Haven, CT: Yale University Press, 2017.

Baron, David. *American Eclipse: A Nation's Epic Race to Catch the Shadow of the Moon and Win the Glory of the World.* New York: Liveright, 2017.

Bergland, Renée. *Maria Mitchell and the Sexing of Science: An Astronomer Among the American Romantics.* Boston: Beacon Press, 2008.

Cannon, Brian Q. " 'To Buy Up the Lamanite Children as Fast as They Could': Indentured Servitude and Its Legacy in Mormon Society," *Journal of Mormon History,* vol. 44, no. 2, 2018: pp. 1–35.

Givens, Terryl L. *People of Paradox: A History of Mormon Culture.* New York: Oxford University Press, 2012.

Gordon, Sarah Barringer. *The Mormon Question: Polygamy and Constitutional Conflict in Nineteenth-Century America.* Chapel Hill: University of North Carolina Press, 2002.

Hafen, P. Jane, and Brendan W. Rensink, eds. *Essays on American Indian and Mormon History,* Salt Lake City: University of Utah Press, 2019.

Jameson, Elizabeth, and Susan M. Armitage, eds. *Writing the Range: Race, Class, and Culture in the Women's West.* Norman: University of Oklahoma Press, 1997.

Knack, Martha C. *Boundaries Between: The Southern Paiutes, 1775–1995.* Lincoln: University of Nebraska Press, 2001.

Maria Mitchell: Life, Letters, and Journals. Compiled by Phebe Mitchell Kendall. Boston: Lee and Shepard, 1896.

Mueller, Max Perry. *Race and the Making of the Mormon People.* Chapel Hill: University of North Carolina Press, 2017.

Newell, Quincy D. *Your Sister in the Gospel: The Life of Jane Manning James, a Nineteenth-Century Black Mormon.* New York: Oxford University Press, 2019.

Nuwuvi: A Southern Paiute History. Published by the Inter-Tribal Council of Nevada and the University of Utah, 1976.

Reeve, W. Paul. *Religion of a Different Color: Race and the Mormon Struggle for Whiteness.* New York: Oxford University Press, 2015.

Richter, Daniel K. *Facing East from Indian Country: A Native History of Early America.* Cambridge, MA: Harvard University Press, 2001.

Taylor, Quintard. *In Search of the Racial Frontier: African Americans in the American West, 1528–1990.* New York: W. W. Norton, 1998.

Ulrich, Laurel Thatcher. *A House Full of Females: Plural Marriage and Women's Rights in Early Mormonism, 1835–1870.* New York: Vintage, 2018.

ACKNOWLEDGMENTS

✦

If an author is lucky, as I have been, each new book pushes them beyond the mapped confines of their comfort zone. This book has been both a challenge and a joy to write, and the joy comes largely from the smart and generous people who have served as guides along this writing path.

First, I owe a huge debt to the brilliant guidance of my editor, Michelle Frey—particularly for her early question: What would happen if we got rid of the villain and changed the inciting incident? Her question changed the trajectory of this book for the better. My thanks also to the talented team at Knopf: Arely Guzmán, copy editors Jenica Nasworthy, Janet Renard, Artie Bennett, and Alison Kolani. The cover designer, Angela Carlino, and Whitney Manger created a stunning cover that made me cry the first time I saw it. And, of course, thanks are due to my agent, Josh Adams, who made this trail possible in the first place.

This book would have lost its way without the help of many experts: Dr. Jeanette Lawler and Dr. Cameron Pace for answering questions about physics and eclipse science; Dr. Lisa Tait, Dr. Paul Reeve, and Margaret Blair Young for vetting my details of nineteenth-century Mormonism; Dr. Gia Miller for patiently answering any medical question that came up; and several authenticity readers who helped me create a vibrant nineteenth-century world. Dr. Roni Jo Draper, Dr. Farina King, and Larry Cesspooch all helped me better understand the complex relationship between Indigenous peoples and Mormons. My thanks also to Jascin Leonardo Finger, who runs the archives at the Maria Mitchell House, for answering my questions about telescopes. If mistakes survived their scrutiny, it is doubtless my fault.

My writing is infinitely better because of my readers, particularly my writing group and sister friends: Erin Shakespear Bishop, Helen Chuang Boswell-Taylor, Tasha Seegmiller, and Elaine Vickers. I'm also indebted to many thoughtful readers who read various drafts of this book: Cindy Baldwin, Christy Belt (who also served as my guide on the ground to Monroe), Heather Harris Bergevin, Sheena Boekweg, Mette Ivie Harrison, Katie Henry, Amanda Rawson Hill, Carey Hord, Melanie Jacobson, Sandra Clark Jergensen, Brittany Larsen, Erin Olds, Jolene Perry, Stephanie Huang Porter, Lori Widdison, and Amy Wilson.

I'm part of too many writing communities to name here, but to all of my fellow writers who have talked shop with me, to the readers and book bloggers and librarians who have written encouragement and shared my books: thank you.

My endless gratitude to my family, who serve as my lodestars: my husband, Dan, who finally gets his own dedication, and my children; my siblings, Jared, Jenilyn, and Justin, who helped inspire Elizabeth's large family; my in-laws, Robert and Trisha, whose help makes it possible to write; and my parents, Bruce and Patti, who read this book and didn't hate it, and who have supported my writing since my very first scribbles started decorating our house (sometimes quite literally).

Last of all, to readers and friends who are still finding their path: thank you for joining me on this one, and may you find joy in your journey, and wholeness in its realization.